The Hanging Girl

JUSSI ADLER OLSEN

The Hanging Girl

A DEPARTMENT Q THRILLER

Quercus

First published in Great Britain in 2015 by

Quercus Publishing Ltd
Carmelite House
50 Victoria Embankment
London EC4Y 0DZ

An Hachette UK company

A CIP catalogue record for this book is available
from the British Library

HB ISBN 978 1 78429 588 2
TPB ISBN 978 1 78429 583 7
EBOOK ISBN 978 1 78429 589 9

10 9 8 7 6 5 4 3 2 1

Typeset by CC Book Production

Printed and bound in Great Britain by Clays Ltd, St Ives plc

Dedicated to Vibsen and Elisabeth, two strong women

Prologue

November 20th, 1997

She saw grey hues everywhere. Flickering shadows and gentle darkness covered her like a blanket and kept her warm.

In a dream, she had left her body, hovering in the air like a bird. No, even better, like a butterfly. Like a multicoloured fluttering piece of art, put in the world only to spread happiness and wonder. Like a hovering being high up between heaven and earth whose magic dust could awaken the world to endless love and happiness.

She smiled at the thought. It was so beautiful and pure.

Now the ceaseless darkness above her fought with dim glints like distant stars. It felt good, almost like a pulse conducting the sound of wind and rustling leaves.

She couldn't move at all but she didn't want to anyway or she'd wake from the dream, and reality would suddenly kick in, and then the pain would come and who would want that?

Now a myriad of images appeared from life-giving times. Small glimpses of her and her brother hopping out over the sand dunes, parents shouting that they should stop. *Stop!*

Why was it always *stop*? Wasn't it there in the dunes that she'd felt free for the first time?

She smiled as beautiful beams of light slid under her like streams of *mareel*. Not that she had ever seen the milky sea effect before, but it must be like that. *Mareel* or liquid gold in deep valleys.

Where was it she'd come to?

Wasn't it a thought of freedom? Yes, that must be it because she'd never felt as free as she did just now. A butterfly that was simply its own master. Light and inquisitive with beautiful people around who didn't tell her off. Creative hands in all directions, pushing her forward and only wishing the best for her. Songs that lifted her and which had never been sung before.

She sighed momentarily and smiled. Allowed her thoughts to take her everywhere and nowhere all at once.

Then she remembered school and the bike, the icy cold morning and not least her chattering teeth.

And just in that moment, when reality rushed in, and her heart finally gave up, she also remembered the crack when the car hit her, the sound of bones breaking, the branches of the tree that caught her, the meeting that . . .

1

Tuesday, April 29th, 2014

'Hey, Carl. Wake up. The telephone is ringing again.'

Carl looked up sleepily at Assad, who was camouflaged like a yellow parade. When he'd started in the morning, the overalls had been white and his curly hair black, so if there was even a splash of paint on the walls it would be a miracle.

'You interrupted me right in the middle of a complicated train of thought,' said Carl, reluctantly taking his legs off the table.

'OK! Sorry!' The wrinkles of a smile appeared under the jungle of Assad's nine o'clock stubble. What the heck was it his happy round eyes expressed? A hint of irony, perhaps?

'Yeah, I know it was a late one for you yesterday, Carl,' continued Assad. 'But Rose goes nuts when you let the telephone ring all the time. So could you please just get it next time?'

Carl turned towards a glaring light from the basement window. A little cigarette smoke should put an end to *that* problem, he thought, reaching out for the pack and slamming his feet back up on the table as the telephone started ringing again.

Assad pointed at it insistently and slid out of the door. It was turning into a hell of a situation with those two loudmouths jabbering at him incessantly.

'Carl,' he said, yawning, with the receiver resting on the table.

'Hello!' came from below.

He took the receiver up to his mouth with his arm limp. 'Who am I talking with?'

'Is that Carl Mørck?' said a voice in the lilting dialect of Bornholm.

Definitely not one of the dialects that did it for Carl. It was like bad Swedish with some grammatical errors, and no use anywhere except on the small island in the Baltic.

'Yes, I'm Carl Mørck. Isn't that what I just said?'

The sound of a sigh came from the other end. It almost sounded like relief.

'This is Christian Habersaat. We met each other a lifetime ago but you probably don't remember me.'

Habersaat? Carl thought. From Bornholm?

Carl hesitated. 'Yeeah, I—'

'I served at the police station in Nexø when you and a superior were over here some years ago to escort a prisoner to Copenhagen.'

Carl racked his brain. He remembered the prison escort well enough, but Habersaat?

'Oh, right,' he said, reaching over for the cigarettes.

'Yes, sorry for disturbing you but maybe you've got time to hear me out? I've read that you've just solved the complicated case in the circus at Bellahøj. My compliments, although it must feel frustrating when the culprit commits suicide before the trial.'

Carl shrugged. Rose had been frustrated about it but Carl couldn't give a damn. It was just one less asshole in the world to worry about.

'OK, but you aren't calling because of that case, are you?' He lit the cigarette and tilted his neck back. It was only one thirty. Far too early to have used up his daily ration of cigarettes, which meant he should probably increase it.

'Yes and no. I'm calling about that case and everything else that you've so impressively solved in the last couple of years. As I said, I serve with the Bornholm Police and am currently sitting in Rønne, but I'm retiring tomorrow, thank God.' He tried to laugh. It sounded forced. 'Times have changed so it's not very exciting to be me any more. No doubt we all feel the same but only ten years ago I was the guy who knew everything about what was happening on most of the mid- and east-coast island districts. Yeah, you could say that's why I'm calling.'

Carl let his head fall. If this guy wanted to convince them to take on a case, he needed to nip this in the bud immediately. He certainly didn't want to get involved with anything connected to an island where the specialty was smoked herring and which was closer to Poland, Sweden and Germany than Denmark.

'Are you calling because you want us to look into something for you? Because if that's the case, then I'm afraid I'll need to direct you to our colleagues on one of the floors above us. We've got far too much to do down here in Department Q.'

It went quiet on the other end of the line. Then the caller hung up.

Carl stared in bewilderment at the receiver before slamming it down. If the guy was so touchy, then he damn well didn't deserve any better.

Shaking his head, he'd hardly managed to close his eyes before the stupid thing rang again.

Carl took a deep breath. Some people really needed it hammered home for them.

'*Yes!*' he shouted into the receiver. Maybe that would scare the idiot into hanging up again.

'Err, Carl? Is that you?' It wasn't the voice he'd expected to hear. He frowned. 'Mom, is that you?' he asked tentatively.

'I get really frightened when you holler like that! Do you have a sore throat, sweetie?'

Carl sighed. It had been more than thirty years since he'd left home. Since then he'd dealt with violent criminals, pimps, arsonists, murderers and rows of bodies in all manner of degrees of decomposition. He'd been shot at. His jaw had been broken along with his wrist, and he'd lost his private life and all the respectable ambitions inherent to anyone from Northern Jutland. It had been thirty years since he flew the nest and finally told himself that he was in charge of his own life. Parents were people you could choose to deal with or ignore as you pleased. So how the hell was it possible that she could make him feel like a baby with just a single sentence?

Carl rubbed his eye and sat up a little in his chair. This was going to be a long, long day.

'No, Mum, I'm OK. We've got workmen in, so you can't hear yourself think.'

'Right, well, I'm calling you with some very sad news.'

Carl pressed his lips together and tried to gauge her tone. Did she sound sad? Was she about to tell him in a second that his dad was dead? After he hadn't been home to visit them in more than a year?

'Is Dad dead?' he asked.

'Goodness gracious me! Certainly not. He's sitting here beside me drinking a coffee. He's just been out to the stable to dock the piglets. No, it's your cousin Ronny.'

At that Carl took his legs down from the table.

'Ronny? Dead? How?'

'He collapsed suddenly out in Thailand while having a massage. Isn't it terrible news on such a beautiful spring day?'

In Thailand, she said, and during a massage. Well, what else could you expect?

Carl searched for an appropriate answer. It wasn't really something that came naturally to him.

'Terrible, yes,' he managed to say while trying to repress a horrible image of the presumably very comfortable end of his cousin's bulk.

'Sammy is flying out in the morning to collect him and his things. Best to get everything home before it's spread to the four winds,' she said. 'Sammy is always so practical.'

Carl nodded. There would probably be a thorough appraisal when Ronny's brother stepped in. The crap in one pile and anything of any worth in the suitcase.

He imagined Ronny's faithful wife. A stalwart little Thai woman, in fact, who deserved better. But by the time Ronny's brother had searched through the drawers, there wouldn't be much left for her other than the boxers with Chinese dragons. That was the way of the world.

'Ronny was married, Mom. I don't think Sammy can count on just coming and taking what he wants without so much as asking.'

She laughed. 'Oh, you know Sammy. It'll be fine. And he's going to stay out there for ten to twelve days. You might as well get a bit of colour in your cheeks when you're travelling so far anyway, he says. And he isn't wrong there. He's a smart man, Cousin Sammy.'

Carl nodded. The only significant difference between Ronny and his little brother Sammy was a single vowel and three consonants. Nobody living north of the Limfjord could miss that they were related because they were like peas in a pod. If there was a film producer in need of a bragging, self-obsessed, absolutely untrustworthy show-off in a garish shirt, at least Sammy was still available.

'They've set the date of the funeral for Saturday, May 10th, here in Brønderslev. It'll be wonderful to see you up here again, son,' continued his mum. While the predictable update of the day-to-day life of a country family from Vendsyssel was rattled off, with particular stress on pig farming mixed with his dad's dodgy hip, the usual censure of politicians in Parliament and some other similarly depressing talk, Carl was thinking about the unpleasant tone of Ronny's last email to him.

That email had undoubtedly been meant as a threat, something that had unsettled and frustrated Carl. After a while he came to the conclusion that Ronny intended to blackmail him with the nonsense. Wasn't his cousin exactly the type who would do that? And wasn't he always short of cash?

Carl didn't like it. Would he now have to deal with that ridiculous claim again? It was utter drivel. But when you lived in the land of Hans Christian Andersen you knew only too well how quickly a little feather could turn into five hens. And five hens of this sort, in his position of trust and with a boss like Lars Bjørn, was really something he could do without.

Damn it, what had Ronny been up to? On numerous occasions the idiot had blurted out that he'd murdered his dad, which was bad enough in itself. But worse was that he'd dragged Carl into the dirt by publicly declaring that Carl had been an accomplice to murdering Ronny's dad during a fishing trip, and in the ominous last email had informed Carl that he'd put it in writing as a book and would be attempting to get it published.

Carl hadn't heard anything since then, but it was a terrible situation that needed to be laid to rest now that the man was dead.

Carl fumbled again for the cigarettes. Without doubt he should go to the funeral. It would be the place to find out if Sammy had been successful in getting Ronny's wife to surrender some of the inheritance. Similar inheritance cases out east had ended violently, and of course one could hope that might happen again. But Ronny's wife, little what's-her-face, seemed to be made from another and better mould. She'd probably keep anything of financial value that belonged to her and give up the rest. And that might include Ronny's alleged attempt at a literary career.

No, it wouldn't surprise him at all if Sammy succeeded in getting the notes home with him. And if so, then he'd better get his hands on them first before they made the family rounds.

'Did you know that Ronny was really rich in the end, Carl?' chirped his mother somewhere in the background.

Carl raised his eyebrows. 'Really, was he now? We'll have to assume he was dealing in drugs, then. And you're sure he didn't end up with his head in a noose behind the thick prison walls of the Thai justice system?'

She laughed. 'Oh, Carl. You've always been such a funny child.'

Twenty minutes after the conversation with the Bornholm policeman, Rose stood in the doorway waving away Carl's tobacco smoke with obvious disgust.

'Have you just spoken with a Sergeant Habersaat, Carl?'

He shrugged. It wasn't exactly the conversation he was thinking about most just now. God only knew what Ronny had written about him.

'Take a look at this.' She threw a piece of paper on the table in front of him.

'I got this email two minutes ago. You might just want to call the man?'

There were two sentences on the printout that brought the mood in the office down even further for the rest of the day.

Department Q was my final hope. I can't take any more.
  C. Habersaat

Carl looked at Rose, who stood shaking her head like a harpy who'd given up on her marriage. He didn't like the attitude at all but it was best that way with Rose. Better to receive a couple of slaps around the face in silence than two minutes of complaining and hassle. That's how it worked between them, and Rose was good enough when it came down to it. Even if you did sometimes have to go very far down to get to it.

'Well, whattaya know! But seeing as it was you who got the email, Rose, you deal with the mess. Then afterwards you can tell me what you managed to get out of it.'

She screwed up her nose, causing her warpaint to crack. 'Like I didn't know you'd say that. That's why I called him right away, of course, but I got an answering machine.'

'Hmmm. Well, then I assume that you left a message saying you'd call back, right?'

As she confirmed that she'd done just that, a black cloud formed over her head and stayed there.

She'd apparently called five times, but the man just didn't answer.

2

Wednesday, April 30th, 2014

Staff retirement receptions were normally held at the police station in Rønne. But that was precisely what Habersaat had not wanted. Since the new police reforms had come into force, his good close contact with the local citizens and what happened over on the east coast of the island had been transformed to a constant transport back and forth from east to west, and suddenly endless decision-making processes sneaked in from the moment a criminal act occurred until something serious was done about it. Time was wasted, leads were lost, criminals got away.

'It's a golden age for crooks,' he always said, as if someone cared to listen.

Habersaat hated the direction society was moving in, both generally and more locally. And colleagues who supported the system, and didn't even know him and the extent of his forty years of loyal service, shouldn't be at his retirement reception like bleating sheep, acting like they were honouring him.

As a result, he decided to hold the main reception in the local setting of Listed Community Hall, just six hundred metres from his house.

With what he had planned for the occasion, it would be more decent in every way.

He stood in front of the mirror a moment, inspecting his parade uniform, noticing the folds that had formed in the material as a result of not being used for so many years. And while he meticulously and clumsily ironed the trousers on an ironing board that had never been put up before, he let his eyes wander around the room that had once been the family's warm and lively living room.

Almost twenty years had gone by since then and now the past stalked about like a purposeless, stray animal among heaps of rubbish and junk that no one wanted.

Habersaat shook his head. When he looked back, he didn't understand himself. Why had he allowed all the coloured ring binders to take over the shelves instead of the good books? Why was it swimming with photocopies and clippings on every available surface? Why had he put all his life into work rather than those people who once cared about him?

And yet he understood.

He bowed his head, trying to give free rein to the emotions that momentarily came over him, but the tears didn't come. Maybe because he was all cried out a long time ago. Yes, of course he knew why things had gone the way they had. It was the way it had to be.

He took a deep breath, straightened out his uniform on the dining table, picked up a worn photo frame and caressed the picture in it as he'd done hundreds of times before. If only he could have the wasted days back. If only he could just change his nature and decisions and one last time feel the closeness of his wife and boy.

He sighed. Here in this room, he'd made love with his beautiful wife on the sofa. Here on the rug, he'd crawled about with his son when he was very small. Here the arguments had begun, and here his gloom had established itself and multiplied.

It was in this living room that his wife finally spat in his face and once and for all left him alone in life with the knowledge that a trivial case had ripped the happiness out from under his feet.

Back when it all started, it had knocked him for six and left him in an almost permanent state of dejection, yet he just hadn't been able to let the case go. That was the way it was, unfortunately, and with good reason.

He stood up, tapped one of the piles of notes and clippings, emptied his ashtray and took out the bin with the week's ration of empty, rattling cans. Finally, he gave his inside pockets a last check in case he'd forgotten something and looked to see that his parade uniform was just as it should be.

Then he shut the door.

Despite everything, Habersaat had probably expected that more people would've turned up for the reception. If nothing else, then at least those he'd helped out during hard times over the years, but maybe also those for whom he'd smoothed out injustices and put a stop to unfairness. At any rate, he'd expected to see a few of the old retired colleagues from the uniformed police in Nexø and maybe also some of the citizens he'd provided authority with over the years in the small community. But when he saw that it was only the chair and substitute accountant of the civic association, the police commissioner and his immediate subordinate, together with the police union representative, who had dutifully turned up, over and above the five to six people he had invited personally, he dropped his long speech and let things come as they came.

'Thanks for coming out on this wonderful sunny morning,' he said, nodding to his old near neighbour Sam that he could start filming now. He poured white wine into the empty plastic glasses and emptied peanuts and crisps onto foil trays. There was certainly no one else offering to help.

He took a step forward and invited everyone to take a glass. And while they assembled around in front of him, he discreetly put a hand in his pocket and took the safety off his pistol.

'Cheers, ladies and gentlemen,' he said, nodding to each person individually. 'Fine faces for judgement day,' he continued smilingly. 'Thanks for turning up under the circumstances. You all know what I've been through, that I was once like most men, especially policemen. I'm sure that those of you who haven't gone to seed can still remember me as a quiet and calm guy who could talk around a psyched-up fisherman with a broken beer bottle in his fist and a little too much adrenaline coursing round his veins. Isn't that right?'

Sam gave a thumbs-up in front of the camera but only one other person nodded. Even so, with downcast eyes there was an expression of agreement here and there.

'Of course, I'm sorry that after all this time I'm remembered as the man who burned the wick at both ends on a hopeless case, which finally tore apart my family, friendships and happiness. I'd like to apologize for that, as I'd like to apologize for the years of bitterness from my side. I should've stopped when I could. Sorry once again for that.'

He turned toward his superiors, his smile fading and his hand now clutching the pistol in his pocket. 'Colleagues, to you I want to say that because you're so new in office you can't be personally blamed for my problems. You carry out your work without fault in the way the foolish politicians tell you to. But many of your older colleagues, and those who came before you, let down not only me with their insufficient backing, but also a young woman through their indifference and thoughtlessness. For this betrayal I want to reciprocate with my contempt for the system that you've come to protect. A system that isn't capable of carrying out the police work we're employed to do. Nowadays, it's all about the statistics and not whether you really get to the bottom of things. So I say to you: I'll be damned if I ever got used to that!'

A few quiet protests came from the police union representative, as he was required to make, and another reproached Habersaat for what he judged as an unsuitable tone for such an occasion.

Habersaat nodded. They were right. It was unsuitable, just like most of what he'd boxed their ears with over the years. But now it had to end. He needed to put a stop to it all and make an example that would never be forgotten among his colleagues. And as unwilling as he was, the time had come.

He yanked the pistol out of his pocket so violently that those closest to him disappeared from his field of vision.

For a brief moment, he noticed the fear and horror that spread over his superiors, as he pointed the pistol at them.

And then he let it happen.

3

It had been a typical night so Carl made a start on the paperwork by putting his legs up on the table to catch up on some sleep. After clearing up the cases from the last few months, the time since had been a diffuse hotchpotch of conflicting emotions. It had been a real winter of discontent on a personal level, just as his almost three-year-long and growing resistance to bowing to Lars Bjørn's boorish authority on the work front hadn't been anything to smile about either. And then there was the business with Ronny and the uncertainty about his damn writing. To be exact, it was affecting both his sleep and his waking day. There were going to have to be some serious changes or he was going to go to ground.

He took a random folder from the pile, dropped it in his lap and grabbed a pen. After some practice with different positions, he knew how to avoid dropping things when he took a nap. Still, the pen fell on the floor anyway when Rose woke him with her cutting tone.

He looked drowsily at the clock and realized that, despite everything, he'd managed to sleep for the best part of an hour.

With a certain satisfaction he stretched, ignoring Rose's harsh look.

'I've just been in contact with the police in Rønne,' she said, 'and you certainly won't be glad to hear why.'

'I see.' He moved the folder from his lap to the table and picked up the pen.

'An hour ago Police Sergeant Christian Habersaat turned up to his own farewell reception at the community hall in Listed. And fifty minutes ago he released the safety on his pistol and shot himself in the head in front of ten shocked witnesses.'

She nodded tellingly as Carl's eyebrows shot up. 'Yeah, well, that's what I'd call really bad. Wouldn't you say, Carl?' she said sharply. 'I'll know more when the police commissioner in Rønne gets back to the station. Turns out he witnessed the whole thing. But until then, I'll book tickets for the next flight.'

'OK, it's really all very unfortunate. But what are you talking about? Next flight? Are you flying somewhere, Rose?' Carl attempted to look confused but he knew where all this was leading. It had better be a damn joke.

'Look, I'm sorry to hear about Haber-what's-his-name, but if you think I'm getting on a flying sardine can to Bornholm just because of that, you've got another thing coming. And besides—'

'If you're too scared to fly, Carl,' Rose butted in, 'you'd better get a move on and book tickets for the ferry from Ystad to Rønne leaving at twelve thirty, while I talk with the police commissioner. It's your fault that we need to respond, after all, so you'd better do it yourself. Isn't that what you're always saying to me? I'll go and tell Assad that he can stop splashing around with paint in the other room and get himself ready.'

Carl rubbed his eyes.

Was he really awake?

*

Neither the drive from the police station to Ystad through the southern spring landscape of Skåne nor the hour-and-a-half boat trip to Bornholm could subdue Rose's indignation.

Carl had been looking at his face in the rearview mirror. If he didn't watch out, he'd soon look like his granddad, with vacant eyes and lifeless skin.

He adjusted the mirror only to replace the view with a clear look at Rose's angry face. 'Why didn't you talk with him, Carl?' came the constant refrain from the back in the worst imaginable tone of reproach. If there had been a taxi driver's compartment window between them, he'd have slammed it shut.

And now, in the restaurant onboard the large catamaran ferry, the cold from the Siberian winds that sailed in over the foam-topped waves, at which Assad stared worryingly, was nothing compared to the cold emanating from Rose. She'd definitely got herself stuck in a mood of which there was no getting out.

'I don't know what they call it, Carl. But in less tolerant societies what you did to Habersaat could easily be called neglect of duty . . .'

Carl tried to ignore her. Rose was Rose, after all. But with her final trump, '. . . or even worse, manslaughter,' the bomb exploded anyway.

'That's enough now, goddamnit, Rose!' he shouted, slamming his fist on the table, causing all the glasses and bottles to bang together.

It wasn't the angry look she flashed at him that stopped him in his tracks, but Assad's nod over towards the guests in the cafeteria, who were staring at them, openmouthed, with their pastries wobbling on their cake forks.

'They're actors!' Assad apologized to the other customers with a cheeky smile. 'Just practising a play at the moment but they won't spoil the ending, I promise.'

Some of the guests were obviously speculating where the hell it was they'd seen those actors before.

Carl leaned in over to Rose and tried to lower his tone. She was all right when it came down to it. I mean, hadn't she been there for him and Assad on numerous occasions over the years? He certainly wouldn't forget all she'd done for him when he was close to burning himself out in the Marco case three years ago. No, you just had to avoid picking at her quirks too much, because that was how she worked best. When it came down to it, she could be a little unstable from time to time, but if you wanted to help her calm down the best thing to do was take the knocks or things would only get worse.

He took a deep breath. 'Listen here, Rose. Don't think I'm not sorry about what's happened. But might I remind you that what happened to Habersaat was his own choice and doing. He could've just called back or, alternatively, answered the phone when you called him. If he'd warned us in an email or letter about what he was going to do, then things would've looked different today. Wouldn't you agree, little Miss Holier-than-thou?'

He smiled conciliatorily, but something about the way Rose looked told him he should have dropped the last sentence.

Thank God, Assad managed to avert anything developing further.

'Rose, I get your point. But Habersaat committed suicide and we can't do anything about that now.' He froze suddenly, gagging a couple of times, looking drearily out over the top of the waves. 'So shouldn't we just try to find out why he did it?' he continued a little feebly. 'Isn't that why we're heading to Bornholm on this weird boat?'

Rose nodded with the faintest of smiles. It was acting at its best.

Carl leaned back in his seat again and nodded gratefully to Assad, whose colour had changed in a split second from his usual Middle

Eastern glow to green. Poor guy! But what could you expect from someone who could develop seasickness on an inflatable raft in a swimming pool?

'I'm really not so keen on sailing,' he said in a worryingly quiet voice.

'There are sick bags in the restroom,' Rose said drily, pulling her travel guide to Bornholm from her pocket.

Assad shook his head. 'No, no, I'm fine. I'll be OK. I've made up my mind.'

Never a dull moment with that pair.

The Bornholm Police represented Denmark's undisputedly smallest police district with its own police commissioner and a force of around sixty. On the entire island, there was only one police station left, which in addition to being manned round the clock was also responsible for those police matters concerning not only the forty-five thousand islanders, but also the six hundred thousand tourists who visited every year. A micro-universe of almost six hundred square kilometres of arable farmland, cliffs and rocks and an endless number of large and especially small attractions, which the local tourist organizations each attempted to publicize as the most unique. The biggest round church, the smallest, the best preserved, the oldest, the tallest. Every community with any self-respect had exactly what it was that made the island worth visiting.

The broad-shouldered policeman down in reception asked them to wait a moment. Apparently there had been a vehicle with an excessive load on the ferry they'd travelled on, so there were a few things that needed to be attended to.

Well, of course such an atrocious crime should take precedence over everything else, thought Carl with a mocking smile when one of them got up to point to the door they should use.

The police commissioner received them in his best clothes in the assembly room on the first floor, with a spread of pastries and a mass of coffee cups. There was no doubt here about rank or authority, or that their presence, despite the seriousness of the situation, puzzled the local boss.

'You've come a long way from home,' he said, presumably meaning *too* far.

'Yes, our colleague Christian Habersaat unfortunately committed suicide. An unusually gruesome parting,' he continued, still seeming somewhat in shock. Carl had seen it before. Police who'd taken the academic route, just like all the other Danish police commissioners, and who as a result hadn't got their hands too dirty, were exactly the sort of people in the force who were least likely to feel comfortable witnessing a colleague's brains being splattered all over the wall.

Carl nodded. 'I spoke briefly with Christian Habersaat yesterday afternoon. All I know is he wanted to initiate and involve me in a case, and that I probably wasn't receptive enough, so here we are. I've got a hunch that it won't disturb your work if we take a closer look at things. I hope you'll agree.'

If a scowl and a downturned mouth meant yes on Bornholm, then that was one thing sorted on the case.

'Maybe you can tell me what he was referring to in his email to us? He wrote that Department Q was his last hope.'

The police commissioner shook his head. He probably could but wouldn't. He had people for that sort of thing.

He beckoned an officer wearing dress uniform over to him. 'This is Police Superintendent John Birkedal. He was born on the island and has known Habersaat since long before I was appointed. John and myself, and our representative from the police union, were the only people from the station who attended Habersaat's reception.'

Assad was the first to hold out his hand. 'My condolences,' he said.

Birkedal shook his hand awkwardly, turning toward Carl with a look that seemed familiar.

'Hiya, Carl, long time no see,' he said as Carl attempted to suppress an instinctive frown.

The man in front of him was in his early fifties, so almost the same age as Carl, and in spite of the moustache and heavy eyes he seemed like someone he ought to know. But where in the world had he seen him before?

Birkedal laughed. 'Of course you can't remember me, but I was in the year below you at the police academy out on Amager. We played tennis together and I won three times in a row, I might add. Then you suddenly didn't want to play any more.'

Was that Rose grinning behind him? He hoped not, for her sake.

'Yeah . . .' Carl tried to smile. 'Actually, I wanted to all right, but wasn't there something about a dodgy ankle?' he said without the least recollection of the episode. If he'd ever played tennis then the error had been well and truly buried.

'Well, that was quite a shock with Christian,' continued the superintendent, thankfully of his own accord. 'But he'd been depressed for some years, even though those of us at the station didn't notice it so much day to day. I don't think we can criticize his work as a uniformed policeman, can we, Peter?'

The police commissioner shook his head in the appropriate manner.

'But at home in Listed, it seems things were different for Habersaat. He was divorced and lived alone, extremely bitter about an old case that he'd turned into his life's work to solve, despite not working in criminal investigation. It was a very trivial case concerning a hit-and-run driver, some would say, but as the accident cost a young girl her life, it wasn't quite so trivial after all.'

'OK, a hit-and-run driver.' Carl looked out of the window. He knew this sort of case. Either they were solved in a flash or else they were archived. It was going to be a short stay on the island.

'And the driver of the vehicle was never found, is that correct?' asked Rose as she held out her hand.

'Correct, yes. If we had, well, then Christian probably would be alive today. But I'm afraid I have to run. I'm sure you can imagine that we have a certain amount of internal formalities to take care of in connection with what happened today, not to mention dealing with the press, whom we need to try and send on their way first. Couldn't I come over to your hotel a little later, and answer your questions then?'

'You must be the police over from Copenhagen,' assumed the receptionist at Sverres Hotel without further niceties, selecting the keys to those rooms that were without doubt the least appealing she could offer. Rose, as usual, had haggled on the price.

A little later they found Police Superintendent John Birkedal in one of the imitation leather chairs in the lounge above the dining room. Up here on the first floor there was a good view out over both the industrial harbour and the back of a Brugsen supermarket. It wasn't pretty. If only the view had included a couple of freeways then the overall impression would have been perfect. Probably not the best place to write a travel guide on this otherwise fairy-tale-like island.

'I'll be honest with you. I couldn't stand Habersaat,' began Birkedal. 'But to see a colleague shoot himself in the head because he felt insufficient in his work is something that really hurt. I've experienced a lot in my police career but I fear this will stay with me. It's quite horrible.'

'Definitely,' Assad interrupted. 'Excuse me, but I just want to understand correctly. He shot himself in the head with a pistol, you say. It wasn't his service weapon, was it?'

Birkedal shook his head. 'No, that was done by the book. He left it down in the weapons depot just before handing in his ID badge and keys to the station. We aren't exactly sure where he got the pistol from but it was definitely a 9mm Beretta 92. A real nasty piece of work to be carrying about. But you'll know it, of course, from the *Lethal Weapon* films with Mel Gibson?'

Nobody answered.

'Right, well, it's a relatively big and solid fella, which I thought was a fake at first when he pulled it out and aimed at the police commissioner and myself. It isn't a weapon he had permission for, but we know that a similar Beretta disappeared from the estate of a deceased person near Aakirkeby five or six years ago. Whether or not it's the same weapon, we've got no way of checking because the former owner didn't have any papers.'

'A deceased estate? In 2009?' asked Rose, smiling with pouting lips. Was John Birkedal really her type?

'Yes. One of the teachers at the folk high school died midsemester. According to the autopsy, it was death by natural causes as the result of a weak heart, but nevertheless, Habersaat was especially interested in the death when the property was checked. The deceased, Jakob Swiatek, according to some former students and teachers, had been tremendously interested in small arms, and on several occasions had shown some of the students a pistol which, according to their descriptions, could be a match with the pistol Habersaat used this morning.'

'Yeah, you don't see a semiautomatic like that every day, so I just have one question,' Assad interjected. 'Was the Beretta the basic model or was it a 92S, 92SB or 92F, FG or FS? Because it can't have been a 92A1, seeing as that series is from 2010.'

Carl slowly turned towards Assad. What on earth was the guy talking about? Was he also an expert on Berettas now?

Birkedal shook his head slowly. So he didn't know damn all about that either. But no doubt he'd dig up an answer before the sun went down over Rønne harbour.

'Hmm, maybe I should sum up briefly what Habersaat stood for and what he'd been through,' continued Birkedal. 'Then later on you can have the keys to his house and take things from there. They'll be left in reception later tonight. I've conferred with the police commissioner and he's giving you a relatively free hand. I also think our colleagues are about ready with the house now so you can get started. We just needed to check the property first. There could've been letters or something similar that indicated why he took the drastic action he did. But you know all that. It is you, after all, who have the most experience with this sort of thing.'

Assad was nodding, holding up his index finger ready to speak but Carl checked him with a look. Whether it was one pistol or another the idiot had blown his brains out with was totally irrelevant. As far as Carl was concerned, they hadn't travelled to this godforsaken place specifically to uncover why Habersaat had committed suicide, but more importantly to make Rose understand that the case she thought Carl should have done everything in his power to take on for Habersaat didn't actually have anything to do with them.

For the approximately fifty students from eighteen upward enrolled at Bornholm Folk High School for the winter half-year, taking courses in music, glasswork, painting or pottery, November 20th, 1997, had been another typical day, with good humour and certainly no sense of danger, explained Birkedal. A totally normal group of mostly happy young students who got along well.

They didn't know yet that Alberte, the gentlest, prettiest, and probably also the most popular girl at the school, had been killed in a car accident that morning.

A little more than a day went by before she was found hurled so far up in a tree by the roadside that it was almost impossible to see her. And the man who happened to look up at precisely the moment his car passed the tree, to his own misfortune, was a uniformed police officer from Nexø by the name of Christian Habersaat.

The sight of the fragile, limp body hanging from a branch burned itself into him, exactly like the inscrutable look that had forever attached itself to the girl's face.

Despite only the slightest of leads, it was determined that she hung in the tree as a result of a serious car accident. A rather unpleasant episode that didn't resemble any other hit-and-run cases in the more recent history of Bornholm.

Skid marks were searched for but never uncovered. There had been hope that paint flakes would be found in her clothes but the vehicle had slid past without leaving any trace. Those who lived by the road were questioned but no one and nothing pointed towards anything or anyone specifically. Only that one person on the stretch of road had heard a car at a terrible speed disappear off in the direction of the main road.

After that, perhaps due to the death being suspicious or because there were no other cases, a systematic hunt was instigated for vehicles with dents to the front carriage that weren't immediately explainable. It was probably a day too late but, regardless, all cars on ferry departures to both Sweden and Copenhagen were closely monitored for the whole week, and all twenty thousand vehicles on the entire island were called in for inspection by motor vehicle diagnostics in Rønne and Nexø.

Despite the obvious disruption, the locals were surprisingly understanding and actively helpful, to the extent that no tourist could move on four wheels without the bonnet being scrutinized by hawkeyed locals.

Birkedal shrugged his shoulders. 'And in spite of all the efforts, the result was zero.'

The Department Q staff looked tiredly at the police superintendent. Who wanted to tamper with an equation where the end result, regardless of what you did, was always zero.

'And you know with certainty that it was a traffic-related death?' asked Carl. 'Couldn't it have been something else? What did you learn from the injuries at the post-mortem? And what did you find at the collision scene?'

'That she was probably alive for a time after she was hurled up there. Otherwise: fractures, internal and external bleeding, all the usual. And then we found the bike Alberte had cycled on quite a distance in the thicket and mangled almost beyond recognition.'

'So she'd cycled there,' Rose said. 'Do you still have the bike?'

Police Superintendent Birkedal shrugged. 'It was seventeen years ago and before my time, so I'm not sure. Probably not.'

'It would be wonderful if you could do me the favour of finding out,' said Rose in a sweet voice and with bashful eyes.

Birkedal pulled his head back. A handsome and married man tends to know when he's on thin ice.

'Why are you so certain that she was thrown up into the tree?' Assad quietly asked. 'Couldn't she have been hauled up there? Was there a search for any sign of cordage on the branches above the body? Could a hoist have been used?'

Did Assad say cordage? A very specific word coming from him.

Birkedal nodded, as there was certainly nothing wrong with the questions. 'No, the technicians found nothing to indicate that.'

'You can refill from the thermos in the dining hall,' came the message from the hotel proprietor standing in the doorway.

It took no more than a split second before the coffee flowed dark in Assad's cup while he poured sugar directly from the bowl. How could his poor hardworking taste buds survive all his strange challenges?

The others shook their heads when he offered to pour the coffee for them.

'How can it be that there weren't any leads from the collision?' he asked, turning around. 'You'd expect some skid marks or at the very least tyre marks. Had it been raining?'

'No, nothing to speak of, as far as I know,' answered Birkedal. 'The report mentions that the state of the roads had been reasonably dry.'

'Then what about the direction the body was thrown up in?' Carl continued. 'Was that properly investigated? Were there visibly broken branches from where the body had been hurled up? Or was it possible to infer anything from the position of the body on the branches or the position of the bike in the thicket?'

'Based on a witness statement from an elderly married couple who lived on a farm on the bend a little further down, it was concluded that during the morning a vehicle came speeding from the west outside their house. The old couple didn't see the vehicle but they could hear the car revving up beyond all reason just outside the property and driving at full speed toward the last bend before the place where the tree stood.

'We're quite convinced that it was the hit-and-run driver that the old couple heard and that the girl was hit head-on near the trees, and that the vehicle then drove off in the direction of the highway intersection without slowing down.'

'What's that based on?'

'On the witness testimony and the experience of the technicians from previous hit-and-runs.'

'Aha.' Carl shook his head. All these known and unknown factors. He was already tired just thinking about it. Suddenly the desk back home in the cellar of the police station seemed far away.

'Who was the girl, then?' The unavoidable question was asked from which there was no turning back once an answer had been given.

'Alberte Goldschmid. Despite her rather flamboyant surname she was an ordinary girl. One of those who suddenly felt freedom far away from Mum and Dad and reacted accordingly. You couldn't call her directly promiscuous but she was into a bit of this and that now that she had the freedom to do so. Everything certainly indicates that she took advantage of the couple of weeks she was over here, quite intensely.'

'Intensely? What do you mean?' asked Rose.

'A couple of partners here and there.'

'OK, did the girl become pregnant?'

'The autopsy said no.'

'And it would be superfluous to enquire after foreign DNA on the body,' she continued.

'The year was 1997, need I say more? Three years before the central DNA register was set up. I don't think there was an intensive search. But no, there were no traces of semen in her or foreign skin under her nails. She was as clean as someone who'd just stepped out of the shower, which she probably had seeing as she took her bike before the other students had even assembled for breakfast.'

'Let me get this right,' said Carl. 'You know nothing, is that correct? This is the story of a locked-room murder and Habersaat was the local Sherlock Holmes, who for once fell short.'

Birkedal shrugged his shoulders again. He couldn't answer that either.

'Right then,' said Assad, draining the remainder of the hot coffee in one gulp. 'Let's call that a wrap, then.'

Did he really just say that?

Rose turned unfazed toward Birkedal, again with her sugar-sweet eyes. 'All three of us will sit down together now, quietly and calmly, and read all this material you've brought for us, and that's probably going to take an hour or two. And when we're done with that we'll probably want to ask a bit more about this and that in Habersaat's investigation, and life and death.'

A hint of a smile creased Birkedal's stoical mask. It was clear that as far as he was concerned they could do just as they pleased, so long as he wasn't involved.

'Do you think we'll find something that you should have found long ago? Something that might shed some light on the mystery of the girl in the tree?' Carl said stubbornly.

'I don't know but I certainly hope so. The essence, I suppose, is that as far as Habersaat was concerned, Alberte's death wasn't just negligent manslaughter and a case of hit-and-run. It was murder,' he said. 'And Habersaat tried with all his might not only to substantiate that theory but to find the perpetrator. I don't know what he had to go on but there are no doubt other officers that can tell you more, not to mention Habersaat's ex-wife.'

A plastic case was slid across the table. 'I have to get back to the station now but take a look at this DVD. Then you'll know roughly what you need to know about his death,' he said. 'It was filmed by one of Habersaat's friends invited to the reception. His name is Villy, but over here we call him Uncle Sam. I assume you have your own PCs with you so you can play it on one of them. Enjoy, if that's the right word.' And then he stood up suddenly.

Carl noticed how Rose's eyes were glued to his well-trained backside as he left. Hardly a look his wife would have appreciated.

So radically had Habersaat's wife put the past behind her that not only had she discarded the man's name but also everything else imaginable that could bring forth memories of him, a fact she didn't try to hide when Carl attempted to get a telephone conversation going with her.

'And if you think that just because the man is dead now that I have the least desire to dredge up his and our mutual problems for anyone, you're mistaken. Christian didn't choose his family during some difficult years when I – and especially his son – really needed his attention, and now all his bad choices have ended with a cowardly suicide. You'll have to go elsewhere if you want to hear about his life's biggest passion; you won't hear it from me.'

Carl looked at Rose and Assad, who both gesticulated to him to stay firm. Yeah, what else?

'Do you mean that he was in love with the Alberte case or perhaps even the victim?'

'You cops never let up, do you? I've told you to leave me in peace, so goodbye.' There was the sound of the receiver being put down and that was that.

'She knew the speakerphone was on, Carl,' said Assad. 'We should have gone out to her, like I suggested.'

Carl shrugged. Maybe he was right, but it was late, and the way he saw it there were two types of witnesses to be avoided unless absolutely necessary: those who said too much and those who kept their mouths shut.

Rose looked in her notebook. 'Here's the address for Habersaat's son, Bjarke. He's renting a room at the northern end of Rønne so we can be there in ten minutes. Shall we get going, then?'

The decision was made. Rose was already standing.

4

The house on Sandflugtsvej was situated back from the road with a French balcony and the feeling of the good life emanating from it. Everything had been arranged down to the last detail, from the door knocker, brass nameplate and well-mown lawns. This was a place where you drove in newly washed VW Polos, French cars or, for lack of something better, SUVs. All status symbols of the first degree in provincial Denmark.

There was only one name on the door: Nelly Rasmussen.

'Yes, Bjarke Habersaat certainly does live here,' she said with a friendly stress on Bjarke, as she stood there like a cougar in the half-open front door with a duster tucked in her cleavage and a cigarette burning between her outstretched fingers. 'But you shouldn't expect Bjarke to be in the mood to talk with you,' she said with the look of a professional landlady, glancing unimpressed at Carl's ID card. He estimated that she was fifty-five. Blue housecoat, home-coloured permed hair with highlighted split ends and a crazily lopsided tattoo on her wrist that was probably, albeit in vain, supposed to make her more exotic.

'I think you should show a bit of sympathy and let him get over the shock. After all, it's only a few hours since his dad, God bless him, took his own life.'

Assad took a step forward. 'It's really sweet that you're so good to your lodger and look out for him. But what if we had a final letter with us for him from his dad? Wouldn't it be a shame if he didn't get it? Or what if his mum had also committed suicide? Do you really think we'd be allowed to tell you if that was the case? And what if we're actually here to arrest Bjarke for arson? Would it still be all right then, that you're standing here in your heels and mocking the course of justice?'

She looked a little perplexed as she took in all the information and his smiling face. Maybe she became even more confused when Assad took her arm, patted it and reassured her that he understood how much it must also affect her to have a lodger in so much distress. At any rate, she let go of the door handle and allowed Carl to nudge the door open with his shoe.

'Bjarke!' she shouted reluctantly up the stairs. 'You've got visitors.' She turned towards them. 'Wait here in the hallway a minute before you go up. And knock on the door and wait until he opens it himself, OK? Bjarke can sometimes be a little indisposed, but I hope you'll overlook that under the circumstances. I certainly do. And double standards or not, that's just the way it is.'

You could already smell the indisposition halfway up the stairs. In fact, it smelled like a hash cafe from the outskirts of Copenhagen's Nørrebro district on unemployment benefit payment day.

'Skunk,' said Assad. 'A very fine, strong smell. Not as sneaky and sour as hash.'

Carl scowled. That damned professor he was dragging along. Skunk or hash, the smell of decay was just as pathetic.

'Remember to knock,' came the reminder from the bottom of the stairs.

The message didn't reach Assad's hearing range because without further ado he grabbed the handle and opened the door.

Assad stopped immediately in the doorway and Carl understood why when he came up behind him.

'Hang on a minute, Rose,' he said, attempting to hold her back.

There, leaning back in a large worn armchair, sat Bjarke without a stitch on him, his legs pulled up under him and a bottle of cellulose thinner in his hand.

And apart from being naked, Bjarke was also stone-cold dead, as anyone could see from this distance despite the sun barely being able to penetrate the thick hash fog. Slitting his wrists, Bjarke had ended his life with half-closed eyes in a dreamlike gaze. It hadn't been a difficult death.

'That wasn't skunk you smelled, Assad. It was the combination of hash and cellulose thinner,' said Carl.

'Don't stand there blocking my way,' snapped Rose from behind as she tried to push past them.

'You shouldn't come in here, Rose, it isn't pretty. Bjarke's dead. There's blood all over the floor because he's slit his wrists. I've never seen so much blood from one person.'

Assad nodded quietly. 'But then I've seen a bit more of this sort of thing than you, Carl.'

It was a long time before the technicians and the doctor who would carry out the post-mortem arrived. As a result, Bjarke's landlady had the entire staff of Department Q to cling to while she lamented over something so horrid invading her life. How in the world was she going to get compensation for the rug and chair when she didn't have the receipts for them any longer?

When it finally sunk in for her that the young man upstairs had actually died while she was downstairs dusting, she needed to sit down to try to avoid hyperventilating.

'Imagine, what if someone has killed him,' she whispered over and over.

'I don't think that is something you need worry about, unless, of course, you've heard something unusual. Has there been anyone on the stairs over the last few hours, or can you enter the bedroom from the back of the house?'

She shook her head.

'And you didn't do it yourself, I assume?' continued Carl.

Her eyes rolled as she began to hyperventilate again.

'Right,' said Carl. 'Then he must have cut his own wrists. He was certainly in a state where he could've done anything to himself.'

She pursed her lips and pulled herself together, mumbling about all sorts. She'd reached the point where she realized that she might have been an accomplice to crime by renting to someone who grew magic mushrooms on the windowsill and who, on top of that, breathed mostly through a chillum.

It was at this point Carl left her to the other two, went outside in the gleaming sunshine and lit a smoke.

The search of Bjarke's room, seizure of his computer and the knife he'd slit his wrists with, the collection of the technical data, and the post-mortem and removal of the body down to the ambulance, all happened so quickly that Carl was only on his fifth smoke when Birkedal stood with his investigator and a technician waving a scrap of paper in a plastic bag.

Carl read the scrap containing just the words: *Sorry, Dad.* 'Strange,' said Assad.

Carl nodded. The message was so short and direct that it was moving in its own way. But why didn't the note read *Sorry, Mum*? In contrast to her late ex-husband, she at least had the chance of getting the message.

Carl looked at Rose. 'How old was Bjarke?'

'Thirty-five.'

'So he was eighteen in 1997, at the time his dad became pre-occupied with the case.'

'Did you talk with June Habersaat?' interrupted Birkedal.

'Well, it went so-so. She wasn't exactly cooperative if you ask me,' said Carl. 'Right, well then, I'll give you the chance to try again.'

'Really, how so?'

'You could be the ones to drive down to her in Aakirkeby and inform her of her son's death, couldn't you? That would also give you the opportunity to ask her the questions you're burning to ask and, in the meantime, it'll give the rest of us more time to seal the room and prepare the body to be sent to forensics in Copenhagen.'

Carl shook his head. Seal the apartment and send the body to the mortuary? How long would that take precisely?

Ten minutes?

5

Wanda Phinn had married an English cricket player who'd come to Jamaica to teach black people what he was best at: playing and winning innings. This Chris McCullum was steadier on his feet than most of the guys in whites, and armed with these skills had been tasked for six months with one mission: to get the Jamaican national team to score ten per cent better on their runs.

For that reason, McCullum stood on parched grass in the baking sun from March to September, sweating buckets more than ever before.

During a training match he saw Wanda out of the corner of his eye running around the cinder track with long muscular legs, skin glistening, and thought he was seeing things.

Wanda was very aware of what people thought they were witnessing. She'd had it banged into her since her figure had developed and she'd learned to move around the track like a leaping gazelle.

'Are you Merlene Ottey?' McCullum asked her outright after the match.

Wanda bared her white teeth and dark gums in a smile. It wasn't the first time she'd been asked and it was flattering, even though

Merlene Ottey was at least twenty years her senior, because Merlene Ottey, Jamaica's top track sprinter for many years, was as beautiful as a goddess.

She flirted a little and nudged McCullum cheekily on the shoulder for the compliment. And then he took her with him to England.

Wanda loved white men. Not because they were particularly sensual. A man from Jamaica had the fire of many races in him, which the white just couldn't live up to, but on the other hand, white men knew who they were and, more important still, what they wanted to do with their lives. You could find security and a future with them, which was far from certain in Tivoli Gardens, the poor slum quarter in West Kingston where Wanda had grown up. For someone whose daily life consisted of shootings and cocaine in backyards, Chris McCullum's proposal was a fairy tale that required no more than a millisecond to think over.

He installed them in Romford on the outskirts of London in a tiny terraced house where she was about to die of boredom until the day when McCullum broke his ankle and was forced not only to sell the house but also to get a divorce from her. If he was going to continue living in the style in which he felt he was entitled, he was going to have to find a woman who was in a position to provide for him.

And so after two years of security, Wanda was back to square one and in a situation where she had only her own limited resources to keep her head above water.

Wanda was uneducated, without hope of obtaining any kind of support, no special talents to speak of other than being a fast runner, and that wouldn't take you far, as her father always used to tease. So the job as a security guard at the rear entrance of a large company on the Strand in London was not only her salvation but also the only viable alternative to Jamaica's tin huts and bodily degradation before one hit forty that would otherwise have been her destiny.

And like a lion in a cage she stood and facilitated those more important than her to come in and out of the glass doors of the large building, nodding to them as they went over to a better dressed woman who had the privilege to take their ID and press the button that enabled them to continue in the system.

Here she was, alone in an empty room between freedom and riches, watching like a custodian over the secrets of the building without knowing what they were about.

And while time went by, she had nothing else to think about other than that it was there – outside – that life ruled. It all happened out there while she stood here.

Day in, day out, she stared through the glass doors looking out over Savoy Place directly to the wall that surrounded Victoria Embankment Gardens.

There, behind that wall, is adventure, she thought. And the laughter from people who soaked up the rays of the sun in striped deckchairs or licked ice cream bought with money they'd never miss tortured her in silence and, what's more, without anyone worrying about it.

And so her new identity was born.

She was just the woman who looked at walls.

In those hours stolen from her by routine, the clouds of the past gathered over her. Wanda knew that all the serendipities and meetings of fate that had taken place before she came into the world must have had higher expectations than to simply create a person with an utterly subordinate security-guard job on the Strand. As her Rastafarian father said with pride, through Wanda's veins flowed equal measures of Dominican Arawak Indians, Nigerians and Christians, washed down with a dash of Rastafarian gunpowder. And Wanda's mother had laughed and said that she should just forget all about it and keep a cool head, then everything would be all right.

Keep a cool head! That was what seemed so especially hard in her grey and inconsequential existence. Was it really meant to be that all the advantages and history should end with an unflattering grey uniform and hair hidden under a cap?

But despite the hopelessness of the situation and the bad prospects, Wanda stood up straight when the better-off guests of the park and building sauntered by, and tried to rediscover that part of her that could get her away from the wall.

As fate would have it, Shirley – the only friend she had and who lived in the room two doors down – invited her to come along to something she called Nature Absorption Intro.

Shirley was into the occult and as such very open on her views and expectations of life. She listened to heavenly inspired music, had an interest in Polynesian kahuna fortune-telling and used playing cards or the tarot before making decisions. Through all these changeable guides she'd encountered in her life, she'd gained insight, as she called it. Wanda never knew exactly into what, but Shirley could make her smile like no one else.

And now she wanted to introduce Wanda to Atu Abanshamash, who, according to the website, was the beautiful radiant spirit who'd come from the Scandinavian dream world to London with his new teaching that could sweep everything else to one side and create a complete understanding of the energy and connections of all humanity.

Shirley was ecstatic and the price was reasonable, so if Wanda wanted to come along she would pay. It could be so much fun if they had something to share together.

Atu Abanshamash Dumuzi was not like the gurus Wanda had seen in Shirley's myriad of brochures and on the TV. He didn't sit in the lotus position or in a carved chair in elevated serenity. He wasn't preachy, and he was neither fat nor ascetic. Atu Abanshamash was a real man of flesh and blood, who with a smile and a twinkle in his eye showed them the path to how the study of nature absorption could renew a person to such a miraculous degree that you finally felt as if each and every cell in your body could suddenly resist any sort of attack, and that your body in its entirety melted together with the universe that surrounded it.

The universe and the energy of the sun were Atu Abanshamash's mantra. And there, in that simple light Bayswater apartment, where the Nature Absorption Academy London branch was housed, he walked around those sitting on the floor and regarded them with magical eyes, making their throats blush and shoulders sink while they in rhythm to his words inhaled well-being deep down in their lungs.

'Abanshamash, Abanshamash, Abanshamash,' he chanted slowly in a deep voice, and asked them to follow him in chorus.

When they'd sat for a while with their eyes shut repeating the mantra, Wanda noticed her sense of orientation and desire to return to reality disappear.

'Open your eyes now and look at me,' Atu said to his followers. 'Abanshamash, Abanshamash,' he whispered, stretching his arms, causing his light yellow coat sleeves to fan like angel wings. 'I see you,' he whispered. 'I see you now for the first time, and you are beautiful. Your souls are beckoning to me. You are ready.'

'You are as beautiful as the sun itself,' he said afterwards to each man and woman as he walked in between them.

When he came to Wanda he stood very still for a moment and let his eyes disappear into the abyss of her own. 'You are as beautiful as the sun itself. You are as beautiful as the sun itself,' he said twice this time. 'But do not listen to anyone! Do not even listen to me! Listen only to your own Atman, your own soul, and surrender yourself.'

As if under the influence of hallucinogenic drugs, these words penetrated Wanda like a long-awaited recognition and clarity. Of their own accord, her eyes opened, her skin burned and her hands twitched with the sort of cramp she only knew from her orgasms.

With lowered head, he caressed her cheek, returning ten minutes later to stretch out his palms towards her a few centimetres from her forehead.

'Let yourself relax, my flower. You have been through the first journey toward the rapture and rebirth of the empty moments, and now you are ready,' he finished.

Then she fainted.

6

Wednesday, April 30th, 2014

They stood for a moment or two and took in the whitewashed ramshackle of a house, very probably one of the most unkempt on the centrally located Jernbanegade in Aakirkeby.

Just as in many Danish market towns, streets like this were good examples of how one hundred years ago the workers had clawed their way up to own their own brick houses and small plots of land. A street like this was the daily bread in the past for stonemasons and carpenters, but it was apparent that it was a long time since they'd had much to do here. In a place otherwise called Flower Town in summer and Christmas Town in winter, there was neither much of a flower paradise nor a Christmas atmosphere to be found here on the worn-down backdrop of Jernbanegade.

Through the crack in the door, Habersaat's ex-wife could smell, much like a sniffer dog, the police badge in Carl's pocket the very second she nudged it open.

'Move your foot,' she snarled at Assad, when he tried to push the door open. 'You've got no business here.'

'Mrs Habersaat, we . . .' attempted Carl.

'Can't you read? It says "Kofoed" on the door.' She pointed demonstratively down to the nameplate and pushed the door once again. 'There is no Habersaat here anymore.'

'Mrs . . . Kofoed,' said Rose quietly. 'We're here with bad news about Bjarke.'

The subsequent five seconds were intolerably long. First her wavering look from one of the three petrified faces and on to the others. Then the second that reality kicked in to all the nerve systems and blocked them, followed by the realization that what was left unsaid was already too much, until finally a spark died in her eyes and her legs gave way from under her.

Her unconsciousness didn't last long but long enough that she had lost all sense of time and didn't know why she lay stretched out on her sofa in the utmost of spartanly decorated living rooms. She was obviously still in the state of shock that had caused her to collapse.

They looked around the living room. There wasn't much to write home about. Unopened bills in the fruit bowl, piles of dusty Danish easy listening CDs, furniture from discount stores, ugly ashtrays and vases in peeling ceramic. They let her lie there for a short while to come around, her stony eyes directed at the ceiling, while they went out to the kitchen where abnormally ugly tiles from the seventies sucked the light out of the room many Danes called the heart of the home. Even Carl could see that that description by no stretch of the imagination matched the owner's ramshackle chaos of a room.

'We can't be hard on her, not in her state,' Rose whispered. 'If we go gently, we can always come back tomorrow.'

They both noticed that Assad didn't seem to agree. 'Come in here,' June shouted with a weak voice.

'You started this, Carl, so I think it should be you who says it to her. And tell it like it is, OK?' said Rose.

He was just about to point his finger at her but felt Assad's hand on his arm. Then he walked in to the woman and looked her straight in the eye.

'We're here to inform you that your son is dead, June. But that's not all, unfortunately. I'm sorry to have to tell you that he took his own life. At approximately four o'clock, according to the medical officer.'

She sucked in her cheeks and sat a moment as though looking at herself in a mirror and trying to pull back the years from its merciless image of reality.

'Four o'clock?' she whispered, stroking her arm up and down. 'Oh God, that was just after I called and told him about his dad.' She tried to swallow a couple of times, held her throat and then said no more.

When they'd sat with her for half an hour, Carl nodded to Rose. She could let go of the woman's hand now so that they could get going.

They had only just made it through the living room before Assad started.

'Would you mind if I asked you something just before we go?' he said. 'Why didn't you go up to your son yourself and tell him about his dad, June? Did you really hate your husband so much that you never asked yourself if your son felt the same way? Did you think he wouldn't care if his dad was dead or alive? I'd like to know.'

Rose beat Carl to it in firmly grabbing Assad's arm. What on earth did he think he was up to?

Empathy wasn't normally one of his weaker points.

Trembling, June looked down at the floor, as if everything in her wanted to grab Assad's throat and squeeze.

'Why do you want to know that, you ugly ape?' she said with a muffled voice. 'What's that got to do with you? Was it your life that bastard Christian took from you? Take a look around, would you? Do you think this was what I said yes to when that once handsome man knelt in front of me on the grass out in Almindingen forest?'

Assad held his chin in his hand. Maybe to keep his mouth shut after her degrading tirade, maybe to show her that he was prepared to take the next round if it could help the case.

'Are you going to answer or what?' spat out from her hate-filled face.

Assad pulled free of Rose's grip and stepped forward. Unusually for him, his voice was slightly shaky.

'I've seen worse houses than this, June. And I've seen people who'd sacrifice their arm or leg for your ugly dilapidated roof over their head and your bloody awful junk food in the fridge. I have, and I've known people who'd kill for your dress and the half-pack of smokes lying there. But no, now that you ask: I don't think it was what you dreamed of. But aren't dreams something you have to fight for? As I see it, it isn't only Christian Habersaat's fault that you're sitting here and your son is lying in the morgue. Something doesn't add up in this story. For example, why did your son write *Sorry, Dad* in his little suicide note? Why doesn't he say sorry to you instead?'

This time it was Carl who grabbed Assad's sleeve. 'What the hell's got into you, Assad? Come on, we're going.'

June raised her arm towards them as she hoisted herself up from where she was lying. It wasn't just that the information about the suicide note shocked her, but they could see that she also refused to believe it. That it was absurd. That it belonged to another world than hers.

'It isn't true what you're saying, you evil liar,' she said with clenched fists. 'It isn't true.'

Rose nodded affirmatively that it was, as Carl pulled Assad out with him.

When the group had reached the van on the other side of the road, Carl and Rose turned quizzically towards Assad.

'Is there something going on inside you that you ought to tell us about, Assad?' Carl asked. 'This must be striking a chord or why on earth would you pull a stunt like that in there? What good did it do?'

'Clown!' was Rose's only comment. Surprisingly concise.

A thud came from behind as June banged the gate wide open.

'Now I'll answer you, you little shit!' she shouted as she crossed the road.

'Bjarke had nothing to say sorry to me for, just so you know,' she spat out at Assad.

She turned to Carl and Rose. The tears streamed from her but the face was stone cold. 'We had a good life without Christian. How should I know why Bjarke would write that? He's just a bit complicated.' She stopped, realizing her slip of the tongue. 'Was complicated,' she corrected herself, her lips beginning to tremble.

Then she grabbed Rose's arm. 'Do you know the story about Alberte?'

Rose nodded.

She looked surprised and let go of her grip. 'Well, good. Then there's no more to say.' She dried her eyes on the back of her sleeve. 'My husband was obsessed with her. Ever since the day he found her body, he no longer existed in our world. He became loathsome, spiteful and creepy. He disgusted me. Have you heard what you came for now?'

She turned to Assad. 'And to you I'll say that, despite what you think, you know nothing of my dreams or about how I've fought to make them come true, do you?'

Something happened to her in that moment. As if she didn't know the answer herself. As if standing on the road in the twilight knocked her down a gear.

It was at this moment Carl saw her properly for the first time. Not just a scorned woman over sixty, but a woman who in her mind had missed out on a huge chunk of life, while her body deteriorated. Just now, she seemed to find herself in that state of limbo that from time to time Carl wished he could bury himself in.

And then she pointed to Assad, collecting herself before opening her mouth again.

'I wish I had a river I could skate away on,' she almost sang. 'But it don't snow here, it stays pretty green . . .' She looked like she'd continue in her own train of thought, but gave up, her expression changing as she got back on track and remembered her aversion to the dark curly-haired man standing in front of her.

'So just keep your mouth shut about my dreams,' she said, and let her hand fall. 'And you took the liberty of asking me why I didn't go to my son and tell him about his dad instead of just calling. Do you really want to know?'

Assad nodded.

'You see, that's exactly why I won't tell you.'

She moved step by step backwards over the road, observing them individually with contempt. 'And now get out of here. I won't open the door for you a second time, if you hadn't already worked that out!'

They sat down in the hotel dining room with Rose's laptop in front of them. It was dark outside now so they agreed to wait until the day after to meet with the substitute accountant representing Listed Community Hall. There were a few questions and impressions that needed to be processed first. The woman who'd heard about the death of her son and ex-husband on the same day without totally losing it still haunted them.

'Why did she say that about the river she wanted to skate on?' said Assad. 'Do we know if she's had a stay in the laundry bin?'

'Loony bin, Assad – the other is for sorting out your clothes!' Rose chipped in. 'And you appear to be the loony after the scene you made today.'

'Well, it worked, didn't it? What does it say about her?'

'That she worked for many years in Brændegårdshaven Amusement Park, now known as Joboland. Make sense of that if you can. In the winter she works as a waitress in various places, so I don't see any obvious gaps in her life that point to any sort of nuthouse.'

'When we go to Listed tomorrow to see Christian Habersaat's house and the community hall, we might meet someone or other who can help us try to understand the Habersaat family better, so leave it for now. Shall we get going with the DVD?' Carl turned to Rose. 'Are you sure you want to stay and watch, Rose?'

She looked puzzled. 'Why shouldn't I? I've gone to police academy, too, you know, and seen pictures of corpses before.'

'Fair enough, but these aren't photos. As far as I know, it's a very clear recording of a man who shoots himself in the temple. It isn't quite the same.'

'I'm with Carl, Rose,' said Assad. 'Be careful. It can make you quite noxious when you see it the first time.'

Carl shook his head. Some words were obviously harder than others. 'This time it's actually *nauseous*, Assad. And yes, Rose, it can be really unpleasant.'

If he imagined that she was finished protesting, then the following minute-long tirade about how absolutely ridiculous they both were convinced him that any further shielding of Rose's mental well-being was useless.

He pressed PLAY.

'According to the meagre report we have to date about the event, the recording was filmed by one of Habersaat's acquaintances, who lived on the same road,' Carl said. 'A guy known by everyone on the island as Uncle Sam. As far as I know, it was Habersaat's own camera, so Sam wasn't too hot at handling it in the first few minutes.'

The last part was certainly true. There were some panning shots around the room, filmed with the speed of an Afghan hound and as shaky as a Lars von Trier Dogme film. It didn't make for pleasant viewing if you were prone to motion sickness.

The room wasn't exactly full. According to the list there was the chair of the civic association and her substitute accountant who had seen to the formalities. Then there was the police commissioner, the local representative from the police union, Police Superintendent Birkedal, the neighbour from one door down, Uncle Sam, a retired sexton from Nexø, a former cooperative manager, the village handyman, and one further individual who felt sick and left early.

'A poor turnout to honour someone,' Assad grunted. 'Maybe that's why he blew his brains out.'

'He shot himself because Carl couldn't be bothered to listen to him,' came the dry response behind him.

'Thanks, Rose. It's impossible for us to know that. Now, can we continue?'

It was only after a few minutes, and after Habersaat had poured the white wine, that Uncle Sam worked out how to use the video camera. Now the camera panned slowly around in the lofty run-down hall with a couple of doors leading out to smaller rooms, then to a single hatch in the wall, probably opening out to the kitchen for serving on more festive occasions, and over the walls where a series of paintings hung of differing merit and size.

Habersaat stood in his finest clothes at the end of the hall in front of the windows overlooking a road that Carl took to be Hans Thygesens Vej, with the sea somewhere in the background. OK, the dress uniform wasn't exactly modern, but then neither was Carl's. In their line of work there was seldom cause for dusting down formal wear.

'Thanks for coming,' began Habersaat. He seemed surprisingly calm, as if he had not given a thought to what he was about to do.

Carl observed the timer on the recording. In less than four minutes it would happen, because that was when the recording ended. If it had been one of Carl's acquaintances who killed himself as Carl was filming, he'd also have had enough after a couple of minutes. A damn hellish thought.

He glanced over at Rose. No doubt she was noting the timer, too, her eyes already half closed. There was certainly no protest from him if they were.

Habersaat toasted his guests and talked calmly to them, while the cameraman panned past the expressionless faces of the assembled group. He mentioned his time as a country copper in the good old days and apologized that he couldn't have stayed as he once had been. At this point the cameraman zoomed in on his pain-filled eyes, and publicly and without any sentimentality Habersaat apologized for allowing himself to be consumed by the infamous Alberte case that had robbed him of his former life. Then he directed his attention to his colleagues in the force and gave vent to his frustration and shame about the work that had been carried out.

'I wouldn't mind if he'd zoom out now so we could see what's happening,' Assad said.

Rose said nothing. She simply sat shaking her head.

Protests could be heard from the man the report stated was the police union representative at the reception, but that didn't seem to faze Habersaat in the slightest. However, it did inspire Uncle Sam to zoom out so that Habersaat and the wall behind him were in full view.

Rose gave a start when he pulled the pistol out and pointed it at the two superior officers standing right in front of the cameraman. You'd be forgiven for thinking they both had a very dark belt in judo or a similar sport with advanced falling technique because both men flew instantaneously to the side in a roll worthy of the best circus performer. Birkedal's assertion that he'd checked first to see if it was a dummy was revealed for what it was now.

'This is it,' mumbled Assad as Habersaat without the least hesitation put the pistol up to his temple and fired.

The recording just caught the head being hurled to one side together with the undefined white and red mass that lashed to the left of the room. Then the man collapsed as the camera also fell to the floor.

Carl turned to Rose but she was no longer there.

'Where did she go?' asked Carl.

Assad pointed over his shoulder to the staircase. It was too much for her after all.

'There you have it, then,' said Assad without the least sign of emotion. 'Turns out Habersaat was left-handed.'

How could someone get through something that terrible so casually and analytically?

7

September 2013

By the way the man's voice was trembling on the phone, he revealed himself to be not only nervous but totally shaken and unsure of himself. Pirjo noticed it immediately.

He could be worth his weight in gold.

'Your name is Lionel, you say. That's a nice name,' she said. 'What can I do for you?'

'Yes, as I said, my name is Lionel and I'd like to be a singer.'

Pirjo smiled. Another one of those. Great.

'I know my voice is good, but the minute I have to prove it to someone else I clam up. That's why I'm calling.'

There was a short pause. He just needed to collect himself.

She thought it best then not to ask him if he even had the voice to fulfil the dream.

'Have you tried to shut the world out, Lionel? To find nature inside you and let your primeval force direct calm, concentration and happiness through singing?'

'I don't really know . . .'

'I've heard this so many times before, you see. When you want something so badly, as I understand you do, it's easy to be thrown off-balance. You swing, so to speak, against your own energy. I think that's what's happening to you when your voice clams up. But do you experience the same sort of insecurity when you do other things, Lionel? Because if that isn't the case, then I have to advise you to seek out one of the bio-acoustic treatment methods or maybe even grounding body fission, which I can refer you to once we've ascertained what would be best and safest for you.'

'That sounds complicated, but if it works, then—'

'Listen to me, Lionel. Spiritual growth is difficult but there are methods to achieve it and develop a more specific, collective karma. It demands a lot of work, of course, but it's good to remember the bodhisattva vow "We will not rest until each and every being has been saved from suffering", and that's how it will be for you in your case. To put it briefly, I'm sure we can find a passable way for you, too.'

There was a deep sigh. Lionel was caught in the net. Yes, it would be expensive.

Sitting there, stoic as a vestal before the eternal fire, keeping guard over the lives and lifestyles of weak people, was where Pirjo was at her best. Her insufficient upbringing may have emphasized that you should never take someone for a ride, but why have scruples about that when from time to time you could lift a person's life up toward higher levels by choosing to have your thumb on the scale?

When people called her asking for a little insight into the road to a better future, why shouldn't they have it? When they fed her with information about their trivial day-to-day lives, banal dreams, and sad hopes, and she subsequently interpreted it so that they had something to look forward to, what could be wrong with that, if they only made the right effort? Hadn't she seen several times what it could mean when her clients received something to prop them up? And wasn't it true that a few people on earth were better skilled to predict things and organize the fates than others? It was certainly a skill she had. Atu had convinced her of that long ago.

Pirjo smiled. These phone advice sessions were, in all their simplicity, ingenious, lucrative and, what was better, it was her idea and all her own income. On Mondays she was the psychologist on one number and on Wednesdays she took on the role of the therapist on the other line, which she'd suggested they should call when the results of the first conversation needed further attention. A voice generator meant that on Mondays she sounded light and ethereal and on Wednesdays professionally dark and authoritative. You'd really have to know better to figure out what she was up to. It certainly wasn't possible to recognize the voice.

These two telephone lines with a call rate of thirty Danish kroner per minute to respectively the Light of the Oracle and the Holistic Chain were Pirjo's pension savings, and for that reason she was the only person from the nature absorption assembly whom Atu allowed to run their own business while being associated with the Nature Absorption Academy.

But altogether Pirjo had secured many privileges for herself, all of which she'd earned because Atu had lots of things to be thankful to her for.

'And one last thing, Lionel: what do you really want to get out of your singing talent?'

He hesitated for a moment, and hesitation always made Pirjo frown.

'You want to make music because it's an important part of you, isn't that right?'

'Yeah, that too.'

So, that's the way it was. It was just the usual. 'You want to be famous, perhaps?'

'Yes, I think so. Who doesn't?'

She shook her head. There were thirteen to the dozen of this type of idiot these days.

'And what will you do with this fame? Is it because you want to earn lots of money?'

'Yes, please, that would be great. But it's more the girl thing, I think. You often hear that it's easier for singers in that area.'

OK, it was even one of those as well. He would truly be worth his weight in gold.

'So you don't find it so easy with the opposite sex,' she attempted to say with some empathy. 'You live alone then, I assume.'

Did he giggle?

'Hell no, I'm married.'

It gave Pirjo a start, as if he'd pressed a button directly linked to the nerve endings in her spine. Equal measures of distaste and chemical reaction hit her brain. She'd spent years trying to fight that vulnerable side of herself, and at the moment not a day went by without it rebounding.

'You're married, you say?'

'Yes. We've been married for ten years.'

'And your wife is totally aware of the scope of your plans, is she?'

'Scope? No, hell no. She just likes it when I sing.'

Pirjo looked at her arms for a moment. Sometimes there were goose pimples and other times her forearms went bright red as if from an allergic reaction. Just now it was both.

This idiot should just get out of her life here and now.

'Lionel, I've become aware that I won't be able to help you.'

'What! I've just spent thirty kroner a minute talking with you, so you'll have to. It's on your website.'

'OK, Lionel, fair enough, you'll get your money's worth. Do you know the Beatles song "Yesterday"?'

She could almost hear him nod.

'Sing the first verse for me.'

A minute went by and then it was over. She hadn't listened. Judgement had already fallen.

'Lionel, it's a shame for your wife that you're such a pig but you're lucky that she encourages you to sing because your talent is completely and utterly insignificant. I have pets that can hit a tone better than you and I know deaf-dumb people who can talk better English. So be glad that I'm sparing you the biggest failure of your life, because no matter what happens, you can only ever manage to scare women off with that pathetic bleating.'

Then she replaced the receiver, calmly and gently, as she breathed openmouthedly. She'd overstepped the mark but it wasn't anything the idiot would shout about. Pirjo turned around with a start.

The sound of a click behind her made her immediately purse her lips. She closed her eyes and felt the sweat oozing from her armpits and the pulse in her neck begin to thump.

And even though she didn't want to, that was the way she reacted when Atu locked the door between her office and the atrium so he wasn't disturbed with his latest conquest.

Always the way. Several times she'd considered moving her office. She had even tried to encourage him to move his quarters to another part of the academy, but things remained as they always had been.

It's more practical this way, dear Pirjo, he'd say. Key decisions and actions, key supply lines, all in one building. A few steps from administration to you or to me. Everything just around the corner. Let's not change that, he'd continue.

She looked again at the door to the atrium, rubbing her arms, and ignored the telephone when it rang again. She ignored the disciples who waved to her through the window from the square in front. And finally she tried to ignore the image of the man who'd obsessed her for years and who right now was fondling another woman in the room next door.

But Pirjo couldn't ignore the clicking sound from the door because she detested it. It made her short-circuit. The warning that he'd shortly be lying beside another woman than her in full swing, or almost worse, that he was finished with her now and had unlocked the door. From an inner peace she exploded to wild revolt in one second and the discomfort was enormous.

But why couldn't she just accept it? Through the years the sound had always been there, Atu had never tried to conceal it from her. But did he know what it did to her, that ultimate sound of distance and exclusion and ridicule. The bitter sound of degradation. And if he did know, would he try to spare her it? She doubted it.

That was why she always ended up covering her ears, chanting to find the balance in her body.

'Horus, born of a virgin,' she began. 'Guide for the twelve disciples, raised from the dead on the third day, free me from my despondency, let jealousy fade, let the rain of new temptations stop, and I will offer a crystal that refracts the sun in all colours in your honour.'

After that, she stood for a while breathing deeply. And when the stomach cramps let up, she thrust her hand in her pocket and grabbed one of the small stones, went over to the window at the back of the room, opened it, looked out over the Baltic Sea towards the Swedish island of Gotland in the distance and threw the glistening crystal as far out to sea as she possibly could.

As the years went by, there must have been many crystals washed up on the white sand.

For almost four years, Atu Abanshamash Dumuzi's school for the study of nature absorption had had its headquarters on Öland, the elongated island off the south-east coast of Sweden, and that suited Pirjo just fine. Here, in this peaceful landscape, most things were under control, and here nothing happened other than that which Providence and the universe desired. Here, Atu's soul was undisturbed and that meant everything to Pirjo.

It was different when he recruited new customers from the centres in Barcelona, Venice, and London, meeting all the women who found themselves out there in no-man's-land. When they gaspingly accepted him as an oracle, a soul healer from the ocean of the northern lights and cosmic energy. When he penetrated their shattered dreams, frustrations and lack of grounding influences in their lives, and like a cloud as light as a feather lifted them up to the sun.

In contrast to the island, out there in the world Pirjo couldn't really do anything other than feel alone, trapped by a deep jealousy and isolated in the feeling of insignificance.

Granted, Atu treated her in a way she'd rightly fought her way to as his extra hand and think tank, diary writer, organizer, and coordinator. But Atu didn't look at her in the way she wanted him to.

He didn't look at her as he did the other women.

As the years had passed, Pirjo became the last remaining disciple who'd followed Atu Abanshamash Dumuzi from the beginning when he'd been in a completely different place in life and was called Frank. But despite their long history together, and their cooperation and intimacy, and despite it having always been her innermost desire, he'd never made love to her, body to body.

'We two make love with our souls, my friend,' he always said. 'You give me my most important orgasms, sweetest Pirjo. I obtain my most significant energy from your gentleness and the great insight of your soul.'

She hated Atu when he said things like that because she was neither gentle nor chaste. Nevertheless, she understood him. Over time they'd become more like brother and sister in spirit than anything else, but it was infinitely far from what she needed. She wanted to feel him like his other women felt him. To feel soft, moist and penetrated by his lust and passion. If he'd lain with her just once in all these years and lusted after her as a wild and sexy woman, it would've been different. Just one single time and she wouldn't have to obsess any more that it was never going to happen.

But for Atu she was nothing more than the vestal, the untouchable. The virgin symbol who guarded over him, his business, and everything. It was the way *he* had decided it should be, not Pirjo.

And virgin she still was in some ways, now, at the age of thirty-nine. At least in her relationship with Atu. If she was going to make love to him, and if there was going to be a baby as a result, for which she had a burning desire, it would have to happen very, very soon.

She clenched her teeth and imagined the woman in the atrium. She'd been picked up by Atu a couple of months ago in Paris. This Malena Michel had stood before him in towering heels and a tight, yet innocent, white dress and explained that her parents were Italian but that she had emigrated to France when she was six, and that she felt that her entire past and origin at that very moment melted together with the words he so generously ladled out. That she could feel that she had come into this world solely for Atu's sake, and that she would serve him in everything he desired.

Nobody understood how much it hurt when he fell for such a saccharine speech, or how undeserved it not only felt but in reality also was.

The consequence of all this was that Malena was now here with them, never more than a few metres away, and totally caught in the net of his charisma. And it wasn't the first time either that he had a woman like her among his disciples. On the contrary, it happened more and more often as the years went by, and Pirjo had just about had her fill.

Only a few weeks ago they'd been in London, recruiting disciples and participants for their fall course, when a beautiful young black woman had fainted.

In an unusually insistent manner, which Atu normally didn't exhibit, he asked Pirjo to ensure that the woman was taken to his private quarters to rest. What subsequently happened behind the closed door she couldn't say, but Atu had had a new look in his eyes that neither his Parisian floozy nor Pirjo felt comfortable with as they took the plane back.

Now a letter lay in front of Pirjo from the very same woman, stating that she wished to participate in Atu's next nature absorption course on Öland, which according to the website started in a week.

It was definitely bad news. The only thing that might momentarily console Pirjo was the thought that the French slave girl would, as a result, slip out of Atu's intimate sphere.

Apart from that, Pirjo knew instinctively that this time it could all go very badly. She'd noticed how the black woman had made an impression on Atu, and it was a very long time since that had happened to such a degree, Pirjo had seen to that.

No, there was no doubt that this woman could have significantly more power over Atu than was good, if she was given the opportunity.

So Pirjo was on guard.

On guard and much more.

8

Thursday, May 1st, 2014

The breakfast table had been set for three people by the window overlooking the harbour area. Rose was already sitting with her eyes lost somewhere out over the sea where the eye could never quite reach.

'Good morning,' Assad tried bravely. 'Well, you're looking pale in a bit more of a babylike way today, Rose. So at least we're making progress, as the camel said to the Arabian camel when it grumbled about being whipped.'

Rose shook her head and pushed the plate away.

'Shall I grab you something from the pharmacy?' Assad suggested.

The same shaking of the head.

'We know it was stupid that you saw that DVD with Habersaat, right, Carl?' Assad grunted.

Carl gave a feeble nod, thinking it would be better if the guy would put a sock in it or at least wait until after the first coffee of the day. Couldn't he see that she wasn't feeling any better than when she'd gone to bed?

'It hasn't got anything to do with the film,' she said. 'I didn't have a problem watching it even though it was sickening.'

'What, then?' asked Assad as he piled crispbread on his plate.

Her eyes disappeared into the distance once again.

'Leave Rose in peace and pass me the butter, Assad.' Carl looked despondently at the already almost empty dish. 'Just a little bit of what's left that you aren't planning to use yourself.'

He apparently didn't hear the comment. 'Do you know what, Rose? Maybe it would be good if you said what's going on in that head of yours,' he said, crunching, crumbs flying left and right. It was a good thing they didn't share breakfast every day.

Assad momentarily fixed his eyes on the small group of demonstrators with banners in preparation for the day's May 1st celebrations in the square in front of the Brugsen supermarket. *Stronger Together*, declared one of the banners.

'Do you also think Bjarke Habersaat was gay?' he said, without moving his eyes.

Carl frowned. 'Why are you saying that? Do you have some information on it?'

'Not directly, no. But his landlady was definitely pettable and really not bad-looking, in my opinion.'

Pettable, what the hell sort of expression was that? Speak for yourself, he thought.

'What of it?'

'He was only thirty-five, a relatively young man, whom she obviously didn't have any objections to. No doubting she was ripe for the picking.' He looked at Carl like someone who'd stuck his well-formed nose in a hornet's nest and got away with it. Pretty smug.

'I don't have the slightest damn idea where you're going with this, Assad.'

'If she and Bjarke had something going on, his room wouldn't have looked like it did. She'd have fussed over him, you saw yourself how she was. She'd have fussed and flapped, aired his bed, emptied his ashtrays and whipped his laundry away to have some love and affection in her life!'

'Really, you don't say? Interesting! But in that case, I don't see why they couldn't have had sex in other parts of the house. It doesn't prove anything, Assad. Your imagination is running wild.'

Assad tilted his head slightly. 'Yes, you could say that. You mean, then, that they could've had sex among the family photos and lace doilies with ping-pongs?'

'Pom-poms, Assad. Yes, why not? But why is the question even of any importance?'

'I also think he was gay because he only had magazines under his bed with images of men with tight trousers and leather caps on the front cover. That, and all the posters of David Beckham on the wall.'

'OK, you could've said that in the first place. But what about it? Isn't it totally irrelevant?'

'Yes, it is. But I don't think his mum liked it, and for the same reason didn't like to visit where he lived. He wasn't a pretty boy with cookies in a crystal bowl, worshipping his mummy like a goddess or who loved to go shopping with her. He was more of the tough sort.'

Carl pushed his bottom lip forward, nodding. A possibility, certainly, whatever use it might be. As far as he was concerned, Bjarke Habersaat's sexual preferences could involve sex with identical Andalusian twins over sixty-five, if it did it for him. Nothing could interest him less, so long as the rolls lying there invitingly in front of him were still warm.

Assad turned to Rose. 'Who zipped your mouth up? You normally have an opinion about everything under the sun. Whatever's wrong, just spit it out, Rose. I can feel it. If it wasn't the suicide on the DVD that shook you up, then what? Something did.'

She turned her head towards them slowly with the same suffering and open look as June Habersaat the night before. But Rose didn't cry. On the contrary, she looked strangely dry-eyed and composed. It was a look that expressed that this was something she wanted to be left alone with but wasn't being given the chance to.

'I don't want to talk about it even if I do tell you, OK? I couldn't handle watching it because Habersaat was the spitting image of my dad.' Then she pushed her chair away and left them.

Carl sat for a while staring down at the table. 'I don't think you should dig deeper there, Assad.'

'OK. Was there something special about her dad?'

'Nothing other than that he was ground to a pulp up at the workplace in Frederiksværk where Rose also worked. That's all.'

The community hall was expectedly accessible and welcoming, situated in the middle of the main street of Listed, cutting the town in two halves, with the fishermen's cottages out towards the sea and the newer additions in towards the land.

Listed Community Hall written short and sweet on the yellow facade. That sort of summed it up.

As announced in an unattractive and misplaced glass-fronted noticeboard, the elderly residents of Listed were offered line dancing, Nordic walking, and *pétanque*, while the children were offered the chance of a bonfire and baking bread over the fire, softball and carving Halloween pumpkins. There was also a short account from the civic association about the present problems and hopes of the town. Should there be a residency criteria for the homeowners of the town? Should the bench by Mor Markers Gænge Road be replaced? Was there enough money to build a pontoon bridge by the bathing area?

Exclusively local questions, nothing at all about a May 1st meeting here or anywhere else on their way across the island other than Metal Bornholm having erected a bouncy castle on something that, God help us, they'd called Chicken Mother, somewhere or other in Almindingen forest.

Here in the community hall on this remote little spot in the summer paradise people gathered for events big and small, and it was here that less than twenty-four hours ago one of the better citizens had faced the fatal consequences of his poor judgements in life.

Carl recognized the women who greeted them from Habersaat's film.

'Bolette Elleboe,' one of them introduced herself in an almost understandable Bornholm dialect. 'I'm the substitute accountant and live just at the back so I'm the keyholder.' She seemed self-assured but not comfortable with the situation. The other woman introduced herself as Maren, chair of the civic association, her sad eyes revealing that she could do without this just now.

'Did you know Habersaat privately?' he asked as they greeted Rose and Assad.

'Yes, very well,' answered Bolette Elleboe. 'Maybe too well for our own good.'

'What do you mean by that?'

She shrugged her shoulders, leading them into the meeting hall, a light room with certificates and paintings in glorious disarray on the white walls, and from where at one end of the room, through a pair of panoramic windows, there was a view out to her back garden. They sat here at a laminate table, the coffee ready and waiting.

'We probably should've been aware that this could happen one day,' the chairwoman said quietly. 'That it finally happened yesterday is just too gruesome to think about. I'm really still rather shaken by it. Christian probably did it because so few came, I think. It could be a punishment for all of us in the community.'

'Nonsense, Maren,' interjected Bolette Elleboe, turning towards Carl. 'That's typical Maren, such a gentle and impressionable soul. Habersaat did it because he was tired of the man he'd become, and that's the way it was, if you want my opinion!'

'You don't seem especially shocked, but why not exactly? It must've been a very violent event to witness, wasn't it?' asked Rose.

'Listen, darling,' said Bolette Elleboe. 'I've worked as a social worker in the back of beyond in the settlements in Greenland for five years, so it takes more than that to shock me. I don't doubt that I've seen more shotguns used for the wrong reason than most. But of course it affected me. You just have to move on though, right?'

Rose sat silently for a moment and observed her, stood up and walked over to the window overlooking the street, turned around to face the small gathering, raised her index finger on her left hand up to her temple, pretended to shoot, and fell a step to the side.

Rose looked at Bolette Elleboe. 'Was it here and like that that it happened?'

'Yes, I guess. You can just look at the floor and see the remains of the stain. They won't get me cleaning it any more. I'll be calling a cleaning company.'

'You seem irritated, Bolette. Is it because he did it here?' asked Assad, heaping sugar in his cup along with a few drops of coffee from the thermos.

'Irritated? You know what, it's just bad karma that he shot himself in this room. He could at least have done it at home or gone down to the cliffs. I don't think it was very considerate of our little hall that he did it here.'

'Bad karma?' Assad shook his head of curls uncomprehendingly.

'Would you perhaps find it especially cheerful to have to sit in this room at association meetings and eat while still envisioning what happened here in front of you?'

'That can only be the case for you two. There weren't so many of you after all from the association at the reception, right?' Rose said pointedly.

'No. But there is still a hole in the painting and a wreck of a wall at the back, isn't there?'

Bolette Elleboe certainly wasn't thrown off-balance easily. 'Right! But at least we'll finally get that wall plastered after the huge hole the technicians left when they scraped the bullet out. I've actually been agitating for that for years, so that's something at least. Look how ugly the wall is. It's made of aerated concrete, how shabby could it be! So thanks for that, Habersaat, you did something useful.'

Cynicism was apparently thriving out here in the wild east.

'Don't take any notice of Bolette,' the chairwoman almost whispered. 'She is just as shaken up by this as I am. We've just all got our own way of dealing with it.'

'Try and stand like you did before, Rose,' said Assad as he got up and stood in front of her. 'Now I'm a witness and you're Habersaat. I want to . . .'

But Rose didn't hear anything. She just stood, staring at the painting that the bullet had hit. Not because it was a piece of art that would go down in history. Just a sun, branches and birds in flight.

'Yes, he hit the bird flying there, right in the bull's-eye. Strange, it didn't fall down.' Bolette laughed. 'But at least we're free from that eyesore.'

'You don't like the painting either, then?' asked Assad as he approached. 'It's really good, but not as good as the painting of the beach next to it, is it?'

'I think you need to clean the sleep from your eyes, my friend,' she answered. 'The man is a fake. He could paint ten of those in a day.'

Rose looked away from the wall. 'I'm just going out to get some fresh air.'

Around the bullet hole in the middle of the bird there were remains of cranial splinters and brains from the man who reminded her of her father, so it was understandable enough.

'That's a very young woman for this sort of work,' the chairwoman said empathetically.

'I guess,' nodded Carl. 'But don't be fooled by her age or the liquid steel that flows through her veins. But tell me, what do you know about Habersaat? We've just arrived from Copenhagen, you understand, so our information about him as a private person is still thin.'

'I think Christian was a good sort,' the chairwoman said. 'He just wanted to do so much more than he could, and that impacted the family. He was a uniformed policeman, not in the crime unit, so why did he do all that? That's what I don't understand.' She stared ahead thoughtfully. 'It has affected Bjarke most of all, the poor boy. I don't think it's been easy for him with that mother.'

The two women don't know he's dead, thought Carl, sending Assad a warning look to keep quiet so they could keep on the trail. As Carl saw things, they could still manage to catch the evening ferry home. Bjarke's death was a case for the Bornholm Police and the rest was useless to dig up further anyway. They had done what they could, Rose had been heard and now she'd quit. All in all, it was going to be the evening ferry home.

'So it's maybe the mother's fault that Bjarke has committed suicide,' Assad said anyway.

A second passed and both women sat there with their eyebrows raised halfway up their foreheads.

'God no,' exclaimed the chairwoman, horrified.

They sat very quietly while Carl updated them. Damn Assad's outspokenness.

'They weren't really on speaking terms, as far as I've heard. Bjarke was homosexual and his mother hated it. As if she was a novice under the sheets herself,' said Bolette Elleboe.

'What did I tell you?' Assad's face lit up.

'You said she wasn't a novice. But she was single, so there's no harm in that, is there?' asked Carl.

The two women exchanged glances. Obviously there were widely known and juicy stories circulating about Habersaat's wife.

'She swarmed around like a little bee while they were together,' came the poisonous response from the chairwoman. Her angelic mask had finally slipped.

'How do you know that? Wasn't she discreet?'

'Probably,' answered Bolette Elleboe. 'You never saw her actually going with anyone, but she was suddenly so sweet-tempered. Then you knew why.'

'Did she seem in love?'

She gave out a couple of grunts, the question obviously amusing her. 'In love? No, more that she seemed satisfied. Orgasms, you know. And that was something she wasn't getting at home, if you ask me. Those she worked with were certainly not in any doubt that she was up to something with all the long, long lunch breaks she suddenly took. Her car was also seen parked outside her sister's house in Aakirkeby when her sister wasn't at home. One person I know, who lives on the street, says that she met a man outside the front door there and that it definitely wasn't Habersaat. He looked too young.' Bolette Elleboe laughed quietly for a moment, but then toned her face down and changed character. 'She never helped her husband get back on course at home, if you ask me. So they were both to blame for it all. Alberte case or not, I'm sure she'd have left him anyway.'

'It was really a blow to hear about Bjarke,' said the chairwoman. She hadn't moved on.

'No, it wasn't good news. But the girl killed in the hit-and-run, Alberte, what about her?' asked Assad. 'Do you know something about her, too? Something not in our papers, do you think?'

They both shrugged.

'Well, we can't know what it says in your papers, but we know something. It is a small island after all, and word gets about when something like that happens.'

'So, what . . . ?' Assad gave his coffee cup yet another spadeful of sugar. Was there really room for more?

'She was apparently a sweet girl, who'd probably been given a little too much freedom. Nothing out of the ordinary, but sometimes things could get a bit steamy up there at the folk high school when no one was keeping an eye on the youngsters, that's the way they are,' said Bolette. 'The girl had a couple of different guys within a short time at any rate, or so people say.'

'People?' resounded Assad's voice from within his cup.

'My nephew, he's the groundskeeper at the school, said that she flirted with a couple of guys, as girls in the first throes of love are prone to do. Walks hand in hand down in Ekkodalen valley behind the school and that sort of thing.'

'I think that sounds rather innocent. Is there anything about that in the report, Assad?' asked Carl.

Assad nodded. 'Yeah, a little. One of the boys was a student at the school. It was just a bit of fun, but she was also seeing someone else outside the school for a little longer.'

Carl turned to the women. 'Someone you know about?'

They shook their heads.

'What does the report say about him, Assad?'

'Nothing other than that they tried to clear up his identity without any luck. A few of the girls from the folk high school spoke about the guy not being from the school, but that because of him Alberte would sit and stare into thin air for hours on end as if she couldn't care less about anything else.'

'Did Habersaat's investigation come any closer to identifying the man, do you know?'

Now both women and Assad shook their heads.

'Hmm, that'll have to rest for a while. As I understand it, Habersaat is obsessed with a hopeless case that wasn't even his. The wife leaves him, taking the son with her, and the people here in the town offer him no support. A hit-and-run driver and the death of a young woman change everything for him, which is a little hard for me to understand as a policeman. We've tried to speak with June Habersaat, who isn't very keen to talk about the whole situation and also rather uncompromising concerning her husband. It seems like you know her pretty well, Bolette. Are you in contact with her?'

'Heavens, no. We were good friends once when she lived a few hundred metres down the road, where Habersaat has lived since all this happened. But when she left him it sort of phased out. Of course, I've met her at her work selling tickets, ice cream and whatnot up in Brændegårdshaven Amusement Park, but otherwise I haven't spoken to her in years. She became strange after all that with her husband and the Alberte case. But perhaps her sister, Karin, can tell you more. She lived for a while with June and the son in the house on Jernbanegade in Aakirkeby. It was originally their parents' but it obviously all got too much for the sister. Karin lives in Rønne now, I think. Try visiting Uncle Sam down at number 21 as well. He was probably the one who had most contact with Habersaat in the later years.'

Carl looked over at Assad, who was frantically taking down notes. Notes that they could hopefully lock away in the archive. 'Just one more thing,' he said. 'In the film that was made here yesterday we have one person registered who disappeared from the hall just after Habersaat committed suicide. Do you know who he was?'

'Oh, that's Hans,' answered Bolette. 'He's just a local simpleton who runs errands for people in the town. He comes up here whenever there are free drinks and snacks. You won't get anything sensible out of him.'

'Where can we find him, do you know?'

'At this time of day? Try the bench behind the smokehouse. Just across the road and to the right of Strandstien road. There's a flat grey building with a couple of smoke ovens at the end. The bench is in the garden at the back. He'll probably be sitting there, whittling or drinking beer; he normally is.'

They caught sight of Rose some way out on the horizon as they swung down Strandstien road. She was standing on the edge of some flat cliffs that only just stood above the water, and appeared strangely lost, as if the world had suddenly become too much for her.

They stood for a moment watching her. It wasn't the strong and quarrelsome Rose they were used to.

'How long has it been since Rose's dad died?' asked Assad.

'It'll be a good few years now. But obviously not something she's finished with.'

'Shall we send her back to Copenhagen?'

'Why? I assume we'll all be sailing back tonight. We can deal with those we need to talk with on the telephone from home. Just the sister and maybe some of those at the school.'

'Tonight? You don't think we should carry on here on the island, then?'

'What for, Assad? The technicians have searched Habersaat's house, so from that angle I don't expect anything groundbreaking, and there hasn't been anything concrete to cling to yesterday or today. Not to mention that Habersaat made this case his life's mission, despite which he was still unable to solve it. How should we be able to do it in a couple of days, more or less? We're talking about something that happened almost twenty years ago, Assad.'

'Hey, there's the man they were talking about.' Assad pointed toward a scrunched-up figure with a collection of beers on a white garden bench behind the smokehouse chimneys. There wasn't much you could hide from each other in such a small community.

'Howdy,' Assad said jauntily as he sauntered through the garden gate. 'So, you're sitting here, Hans. Just like Bolette said you would be.'

Good try, Assad, but the man didn't deign to acknowledge him with a single glance.

'You're sitting here relaxing, I suppose. It's a nice view.'

Still no reaction.

'OK, you don't want to talk to me, but then you brought it on yourself. It suits me fine.' He nodded to Carl as he turned on a hose and rinsed his hands. Carl looked at his watch. It was prayer time.

'Just go after Rose. This'll only take ten minutes,' Assad smiled.

Carl shook his head. 'I think she needs to be left to herself just now. I'll toddle on down the road and think things through while you do that. But, seriously, Assad – do you think this is a good place to pray? Everyone can see you. Do you even know if there's anyone home in the house there?'

'If they haven't seen a Muslim pray before, then it's maybe about time, Carl. The grass is soft and the man here doesn't want to talk with me. How hard can it be?'

'OK, suit yourself, Assad. Want me to get your rug?'

'Thanks, but I'll use my jacket. That'll have to be good enough in the open air,' he said, taking his socks off.

Carl hadn't even managed twenty metres down the road before Assad stood in the qiyam position, reciting. It looked very harmonious and natural against the blue sky. Carl would unfortunately probably never come that close to God.

He turned his head towards the figure on the cliffs standing motionless like a sphinx with clouds dancing over it. Why is she just standing there? he wondered. What's going through her head? Is it grief or are there so many secrets that there's hardly room for them? Or is it the case with Alberte and Habersaat?

Carl stopped with an odd feeling in his body. A few days ago he'd been on home turf and had no knowledge of Habersaat or Alberte. To put it bluntly, he didn't give a damn about towns like Svaneke and Listed and Rønne, and now suddenly here he was feeling so strangely alone and abandoned. Here of all places, on the extreme edge of Denmark, he was struck by the realization that people couldn't run from themselves, regardless of where they were. The feeling that you always carried the past with you, and that it was only yourself that could be held responsible for who you were.

He shook his head. How miserable it felt. Had he really thought that he'd ever be able to forget himself and what had made him who he was?

Wasn't this the way it was for most people? The time they lived in was an open invitation to a cocktail of self-denial and self-glorification. And if you didn't like the situation you were stuck in, there was always the option of running away from yourself: running away from opinions, from your marriage, from your country, from old values, from trends that had otherwise meant so much yesterday. The problem was just that out there, among all the new, you found nothing of what you were looking for deep down inside, because tomorrow it would all be meaningless again. It had become an eternal and fruitless hunt for your own shadow, and that was pitiful.

Bloody pitiful. Was he really no different?

Damn, you're such an idiot, thought Carl, inhaling the smell of half-rotten seaweed and salt as the thoughts were still whirring about. Why did he feel like this and why couldn't he have a serious relationship with anyone? Hadn't Lisbeth been both sweet and understanding with him after the breakup with Mona? She'd actually been a really wonderful woman, hadn't she? But had he been good enough to her? Strictly speaking he'd let her down and turned his back on her the very moment he met her. A fact she could have cast up and reproached him for, but she hadn't. So who had let whom down?

And what now? In the meantime there had been others like Lisbeth. But was there even enough room in his life for a real relationship? Was there anyone who could keep hold of someone like him?

He thought that at least he had Morten and Hardy. But still that seed of doubt. And then there was Jesper and maybe even Assad and the girl out there on the cliffs.

But would they still be there in the morning? Was he worth keeping hold of?

Carl looked out over the pulse of the waves for a moment before he made the decision, pulled his phone out and scrolled through the numbers.

Mona's number was still there. Almost three years without her and she was still just a little touch away.

A moment of hesitation as his index finger rested on the screen, and then he pressed.

It only took ten seconds before her voice said his name. So his number was still on her phone. Was that a good sign?

'Are you there? Hello, Carl, say something,' she said so naturally that it almost paralysed him. 'Come on, I can see that it's you who's calling. Did you dial a wrong number?'

His answer came quietly. 'No, no, I didn't. I just wanted to hear your voice.'

'OK.'

'Yes, you probably think it a bit strange but I'm standing over in Listed by Svaneke just now, looking out to sea, and just wish that you were here with me.'

'Svaneke! Funny, because just now I'm at the opposite end of Denmark, in Esbjerg actually, so for that reason alone it would be a bit difficult.'

For that reason alone, thought Carl. Not exactly welcoming.

'Obviously. I just wanted to say it. Maybe we can meet up when I get home.'

'You could try and drop me a line, right? Well, take care, Carl. Don't fall in the Baltic. I hear it's really cold.'

That was that, and it didn't feel particularly good.

When he came back, Assad was sitting on the bench chatting with the man.

'He's crazy, this one,' said the man, chuckling in the voice of a child. 'Lying on the floor with his arse in the air talking gobbledy-gook.'

Assad laughed. 'This guy thought that I was trying to bum a beer. Now he knows that that's not something someone like me would do.'

'No, he doesn't drink. Not even on May 1st. Are you heading to the demonstration in Rønne? I've been once before but now I vote for the Danish Party, just like someone I know. It is Denmark we live in, after all. So does he, the one who doesn't drink, right?' he said, laughing.

'Hans has told me that he knows everyone in town. He didn't like what Habersaat did to himself yesterday, so he ran. But nonetheless he didn't like him.'

'Yes, Habersaat! He'd lost his marbles! I'm twice as intelligent as he was. At least.'

'Why do you say that?' asked Carl.

'So beautiful, his wife. Yes, she really was. I've never seen anyone more beautiful. And still he let her get away, the stupid idiot. Yes, I saw her round and about in town with some of the fishermen, and also once up on Knarhøj with someone else. Habersaat was an idiot. Everyone was kissing her.'

He stretched his neck. 'Hey! That woman you're waiting for is coming over. Watch out, here she comes.'

He necked back a huge gulp from his beer and pointed over to Rose, who nodded back. Ruddy-cheeked and with windswept hair, and obviously about to interrupt them in what they were doing.

'Just a second, Rose. Assad is on to something here,' Carl said, turning back to the man on the bench.

'Hello, Hans, I'm Assad's friend. I'm actually a nice guy but I'm also inquisitive. These fishermen you say she kissed, do you know some of them? I'd like to chat with them.'

'There aren't any fishermen left in town. Not them at any rate.'

'But you also mentioned that June Habersaat met a guy up at . . . what was it called, was it Knarhøj? Right, do you happen to know his name at least, because if so then I'd like to have a word with him?'

A spray of beer shot out of the man's mouth as he laughed. 'You won't be doing that because I don't know what his name was. It wasn't someone here from town. But you can just ask Bjarke, the boy I taught to whittle. He looked ridiculous in his scout get-up and shorts that time up on Knarhøj, where he was digging or something with that guy.'

'Ridiculous? How?'

'Well, he was almost an adult.'

'Was he maybe a scout leader or something?'

The guy lit up, as if someone had turned on his brain functions. 'That was it, yes!'

'OK, Hans. So what you're saying is that Bjarke was talking with the guy his mother was meeting?'

'Yes. She came up there one day when her son and the guy were there. Where there's a maze now. They do call it a maze, don't they? It says that somewhere. I can read, you know. I bet you didn't know that.'

They left him with twenty kroner. Enough for the rest of the day, he said. Maybe even more than three beers.

He wasn't the kind of person who expected the impossible of life.

'Listen, you two,' Rose blurted out on the way up to the car. There were sparks in her eyes and piles of electric cables in her mind. She'd worked out something or other.

'I've stood out there thinking over and over: who was Habersaat really, and why did he do what he did? Why was he so hell-bent when it came to that case?'

'Maybe it was a counterbalance to things not going so well on the home front. You heard the two women and the guy just now. But Habersaat's professional honour might also have been bruised,' Carl said.

'Maybe. He must have been a good policeman, there can't be any doubt about that,' she said. 'He pursued his goal, but he couldn't move on, so he shot himself. But do you think he did it because he couldn't take any more?'

Carl shrugged. 'Probably.'

'Tell us what you're thinking, Rose,' Assad said, smiling.

'Well, I don't think so – not any more. I think he shot himself to prove how seriously he took the case. And do you know how seriously I think he took it? Do you, Assad?'

'I think it's serious enough that he blew his brains out.'

'Very funny, Assad. But Habersaat shot himself because he wanted to use all his power to ensure we carried on. I'm convinced of it. And he wanted that because he was no longer completely out on a limb.'

'Don't you mean the opposite?' Carl suggested.

'No. That would be the most logical, but I think he probably knew who'd killed Alberte in the end but just couldn't prove it.' She shook her head. 'Or else he couldn't find him. Or both. Yes, that's what I think, and that's what drove him crazy. I also think that if we look carefully enough in his house we'll find one answer or another.'

'Just hang on a minute, Rose. I can see you're very involved now, but wouldn't it have been much easier and more logical if he'd just put his suspicion down on paper, making it all a lot more obvious for us? If his suicide really was premeditated and calculated, why are we left with nothing to go on? Maybe the answer is that there *isn't* anything to go on.'

'No, that's not how I see it. Maybe he *has* written something down but we just haven't seen it yet. I don't know. Or maybe he hasn't.' She shook her head again. She was apparently standing at a crossroads of opportunities and couldn't make a decision. 'Or maybe he didn't even know himself but realized that the solution was right under his nose without being able to see it. So he had to have help from fresh new eyes.' She nodded knowingly. 'Yes, that's how I think it was.'

She looked at Carl with a spark in her eyes. It was something else, the way her stare could be intense and seductive.

'You know what, Carl? He chose us to take a closer look at it all, and we should be proud of that. I'm sure he knew that we'd have to come over here when he did what he did. He knew that it was the sacrifice that was needed before those around him would reopen the case. I feel totally sure about it.'

Carl nodded, glancing at his curly-haired partner.

Assad's expression indicated that he thought she'd gone crazy.

It was very difficult to disagree.

9

September 2013

Wanda Phinn didn't hand in her notice, she just left. Threw the cap on the floor, said goodbye to the woman over at the control and slipped out the door.

It was a total relief, and the wall into Victoria Embankment Gardens slid away without regret, the worries of wasted days disappeared and the sound of the park faded away. The world lay before her, her whole life and everything it held for her as one of the few chosen ones.

Because Wanda had a plan. Ever since Atu Abanshamash Dumuzi caressed her cheek, calling her his flower, ever since the blood had rushed from her head, leaving her powerless and senseless, since she had come to again and stared enthralled into his mesmerizing eyes and felt his lips on the back of her hand, ever since then she'd known that Atu Abanshamash was the future she'd dreamed of.

Informing Shirley of this realization, she faced an uninvited and endless barrage of ineffective warnings.

'I can see that it all seems enchanting on the screen. Beautiful buildings, interesting rituals, the sea just at your doorstep. But when you arrive over there you'll find out that it was just flirting, Wanda, and that your journey was wasted,' she warned. 'Atu Abanshamash can get all the women he wants. Just think about what he can do and what he looks like.' Her eyes looked like they might pop out of her head. His charisma had left a lasting impression on her, too.

'I know it's been a while since you had a man, but if you're feeling sexually frustrated, then there's loads of men here in London you can go to bed with, and who won't hurt you more than you let them.'

Wanda shook her head. Shirley made it all sound so simple.

'I don't think you understand, Shirley. I want to be Atu Abanshamash's chosen one. I want to live like he tells us to and have his children. I can feel that this is what I've been called to all my life.'

'His chosen one?' Shirley was about to laugh but managed not to when she saw the seriousness in Wanda's face. 'But, Wanda – didn't you notice the daggers the woman helping him sent you? You won't be able to knock her off her perch, I'll bet you.'

'She was old, Shirley.'

'Thanks for that,' Shirley said, taking offence. 'I think she looked to be about my age.'

Wanda looked away. Outside the window of her apartment the world was just another wall, towering above her and blocking out all light and all dreams. And behind that wall lived other people with the same unfulfilled hopes. A wall that grew greyer with every day. In this area, the future was carried by dreams. The boys wanted to be soccer players and rock stars and the girls wanted to be their trophy wives. In this area people watched reality shows and awful quiz shows, gorging themselves on junk food and moving further and further away from the opportunities that a good education or realistic ambitions could provide. In this area, the statisticians could argue with ease that only the fewest of the few would reach the promised land, refined and enriched by success, wealth and eternal happiness. As if she hadn't lived with that knowledge day in and day out.

'Sorry, Shirley,' she said when she noticed her friend frowning. 'I didn't mean it like that. I only meant that I'm still young and haven't had any children yet, and my body and soul are ready for all that now. And I can assure you that Atu doesn't sleep with that woman who was helping him. I can feel these things.'

'You'll be disappointed, Wanda, and it'll definitely end in tears, and you'll have used all your savings on this hopeless project. What will you live off then when you come back? Where will you live? There isn't room for two people in my room, you know that.'

'I'll come back and visit you, Shirley, and I'll stay at a hotel. But I'll come back as a different woman, you can count on that.'

Shirley pursed her lips. 'Who will I hang out with? Who'll I share all the gossip with when I get home from my mind-numbing job?' She began to cry. 'You can't just leave me sitting alone in this rotten place, can you?'

Wanda didn't say anything but put her arm on Shirley's shoulder, pulled her in close and held her tight.

'So the least you can do is write some emails about how you're doing. You will do that, won't you, Wanda?' she sniffed.

'Of course. I'll write every single day if I can.'

'You're just saying that.'

'No, Shirley, I promise. And I always keep my word.'

*

She wrote to the Nature Absorption Academy on the island of Öland in Sweden, informing them that she'd now decided on her date of departure and that she'd be very grateful if someone could pick her up at the station in Kalmar on the day in question. She also wrote that she expected to follow more courses at the academy than she had first signed up for and that, if possible, she'd like to stay on afterwards and work as a volunteer to help spread Atu Abanshamash Dumuzi's thoughts and ideals.

Wanda was dead certain that she'd get what she wanted. Atu Abanshamash had shown his desire for her and he could've had her that day in London if he hadn't been busy with the course. That was something they'd both realized. Now she was making up for the bad timing so they could continue where they'd left off.

The time had come.

A few days went by before an email informed her that the courses were oversubscribed. They'd let her know when there were free places again but she shouldn't expect that to be this year.

Wanda refused to believe it. When Atu Abanshamash saw her, things would be different. As long as she was fully prepared. Then she noticed the sender's name: Pirjo Abanshamash Dumuzi.

Shirley was right. It would end up as a fight between them, no doubt about that. A bloody scratch-your-eyes-out fight.

In the days and nights that followed, she absorbed herself in the alternative energy of the universe, reciting over and over Atu's utterances about the Nature Absorption Academy. She would be irreproachable in her knowledge and engagement, but that wasn't hard because everything around Atu Abanshamash Dumuzi seemed so right and logical. In fact, it felt as if through his thoughts Atu embraced all forms of belief and goodness in humanity in one pure and refined set of rules, and it took her by storm. The more she read, the more she tried to understand, the stronger she felt how these guiding principles and decrees for a purer life pulled everything ugly and foolishly mundane out of her.

Finally, she sat up straight and felt the peace of mind growing in her. No cola on the table, no flashing television screen with soap operas in the background, no noise in her head. The last doubt in her project petered away, leaving her determined and peaceful.

When she stood in front of Atu Abanshamash she'd be completely clear. Her sensuality and insight into the teachings of Atu Abanshamash would blow him away, convincing him that in her he'd finally met a woman who was worthy of him in every way.

And the other woman, who thought herself untouchable and was trying to thwart her plans, would just need to go.

10

Thursday, May 1st, 2014

Villy Kure, the skipper everyone called Uncle Sam, lived in a yellow half-timbered house with its own smokehouse on Mosedalvej, two houses north of Habersaat's home. Here along the highway between Sandvig and Snogebæk there was a mishmash of all types of property all in a row elevated a few metres above the level of the road and with the most beautiful view out over the fishing huts, harbour and sea. Perfectly idyllic, if it wasn't for the fact that someone from the town's inner circle had just blown their brains out.

They knocked on the door at the front of the house, and when no one answered they pulled into the driveway, past a smoke oven and into the yard where a four-wheel drive was parked.

Carl felt the bonnet. It was ice cold.

The back door gave no result either, which a cyclist out on the road was able to explain as they traipsed back to the car.

'Uncle Sam is out at sea. He's the captain of a fishing boat that's acting as a patrol boat just now. So you shouldn't expect to see him any time soon.'

'A patrol boat?'

'Yes. When those damn Russian captains can't raise their anchors properly, they scrape the seabed and take the cables with them. And now it's gone wrong again. Last Christmas we were without power from Sweden for a month and a half because of it, but it isn't quite so bad this time.

'So every time something like this happens, Sam's sitting out there on his boat, turning away all the boats on course with the cable ship that's busy repairing the damaged cable.'

'I see. I would've liked to talk to him about Habersaat. They were friends, weren't they?'

'Habersaat, good heavens!' he snorted. 'Yeah, maybe they were friends, but Habersaat wasn't exactly easy to be friends with. He could play cards with Uncle Sam. That was about all they had in common in the last few years.'

'So you don't think Habersaat could have confided in Sam about the case he was so obsessed with?'

'I'm a hundred per cent sure he did the first ten years. But, you know what? Even a man like Uncle Sam can get tired, OK. Sam's a nice guy, but not *that* nice. No, no. They played cards once in a while. That's all, if you ask me.'

'You don't think Sam knew just *how* bad things had become with Christian Habersaat?'

'How would he know that? He's out at sea most of the time and Habersaat wasn't exactly the sort of man to show his feelings, now, was he? But why don't you call Uncle Sam? Or maybe you don't think we Bornholm folk have access to the telephone network?'

He laughed, giving them the number. But the line was busy.

A strange feeling of loss hung over Habersaat's otherwise totally normal red brick house. It wasn't a haunted feeling, more the impression of something that would never awaken. It was like the enchanted castle in *Sleeping Beauty* that had been lying in slumber, like something forlorn and stale, waiting in vain for the redeeming and liberating kiss.

'The life never returned to this house after the family was split up, can you feel it?' Rose said as she put the key in.

The acrid sour smell that hit them confirmed it.

'Eugh, couldn't the technicians at least have aired the place out?' she continued.

In other cases, smells of this sort were usually due to waste and rubbish that had never been thrown out. Vegetables rotting in forgotten drawers. The fermenting contents of half-empty tins. Months' worth of washing up. But Habersaat's house wasn't at all like that. Overwhelming, chaotic amounts of paper in every direction dominated the first impression, but if you looked at it through different eyes, everything seemed well organized, meticulously and thoughtfully arranged and laid out. The kitchen was spotless, almost shining, and the living room neatly vacuumed, just as the dusting had also been done to the extent it could with all the hundreds of piles of paper.

'It stinks of nicotine and frustration here,' Assad said from a corner where a metre-high pile of journal papers threatened to collapse.

'More like years of withdrawal and cellulose,' countered Carl.

'Do you really believe that the technicians have been through all this?' asked Assad, his arms outstretched over the landscape of paper heaps.

Carl took a deep breath. 'Hardly,' he said.

'Where on earth should we start?' sighed Rose.

'Good question. Now maybe you know the explanation behind why he gave up, and why the police in Rønne were so willing to give us the key and let us take possession of Habersaat's material. So thanks for that, Rose,' said Carl. 'Maybe it would be an idea if Assad and I went home tonight and you stay here. With your talent for systematizing, you could have this lot in alphabetical and chronological order according to subject in . . . well, a month or two, I reckon.'

Carl laughed but she didn't react.

'There is something or other buried here that could take this case forward. I have a strong feeling about it. I'm certain we can get further than Habersaat if we really want to,' answered Rose a little harshly.

She was probably right, but it would take weeks for a whole workforce of people to plough through all this material and it went absolutely against his will. With just a preliminary view, it looked as if Habersaat had mapped the entirety of Bornholm in the days after the fatal traffic accident, not to mention the hundreds of leads he'd followed in the years since. Each lead in its pile.

But where was the pile that meant more than all the others?

'We pack it all up and take it back to Police Headquarters,' said Rose.

Carl frowned. 'Over my dead body, and anyway we don't have room. Where the hell do you think this mausoleum of paper should end up?'

'We'll make a special area in the room where Assad is painting.'

'Then I'm not finishing the painting job,' came the reply from the corner.

'Wow, wait a minute, you two. Wasn't that room earmarked for Gordon, ready for when he's finished with his training? What do you suppose our dear boss Lars Bjørn will say when his favourite doesn't get the place in Department Q he's insisted on?'

'I didn't think you cared about what Lars Bjørn thought or said, Carl,' Rose replied.

Carl smiled drolly. He damn well didn't care. *He* was the head of Department Q, not Lars Bjørn, even though he thought he was. And it was funds earmarked for Department Q that he was pinching, so if he had something to complain about, Carl knew whose ear to whisper in. No, Bjørn just had to keep his mouth shut, but that wasn't what was at the heart of the matter. Carl simply didn't want more paper and junk in the communal area of the cellar, and that was that.

'Gordon is welcome to sit in with me while the case is running,' Assad said. 'I like a bit of life around me.'

Carl was shocked. They really meant it.

'By the way, shouldn't you be calling Uncle Sam?'

'You can do it, Assad,' Carl grunted. There had to be some sort of quid pro quo. 'My battery is about to run out,' he explained.

'You can just use the landline there,' said Curly, pointing to something that looked like it came from the ark over on the dining table on top of yet another pile of cuttings.

Carl sighed. Who was in charge of Department Q these days? Damn it, they hadn't even taken the case on yet.

For a second he considered manning up but then gave in for the sake of convenience and began to dial the number.

From the other end came the sound of whistling and a shaken voice.

'Damn creepy calling from Christian's phone,' shouted Uncle Sam after Carl had stated his business and explained who he was.

There was interference on the line and the sound of a motor in the background, so Carl had to put his finger in his other ear.

'I got a hell of a shock when I saw where the call was coming from. But yes, Christian and I played cards together now and then, actually also the night before he shot himself. But listen, I can't talk just now because there's an idiot of an Estonian container ship from MSC wanting to sail through where we're working, so this old man needs to get out on the open sea and snarl a bit.'

'I'll be brief. You were together the night before, you said. That's news to me. Why don't the police know that?'

'Probably because they haven't asked. I was over at his to get some training. I had to learn how to use that bloody camera, right?'

'How was Habersaat at that point, was he OK? Could you sense anything?'

'He was a bit tipsy, you know. Linie Aquavit and a couple of porters can moisten the eyes, isn't that right? To be honest, he was a little sentimental, but then he often was so I didn't think anything of it.'

'Sentimental? How?'

'He cried a little. Sat and fumbled with some of Bjarke's old things. A blue scarf and a wooden figure that the boy had carved.'

'Would you say that he seemed unstable?'

'No, not in the least. He thrashed me at cards, I can tell you. No, he was just a bit down, he often was.'

'Did he often cry in situations like that?'

'It might have happened a few times before, I can't quite re-member. But it wasn't normal, no. Maybe he was just a bit drunker and maudlin than usual. He asked me if I could remember this and that several times, telling me about things he'd done with the family over the years. It didn't seem so strange that night. He was really lonely, after all. But, looking back, I can better understand what was going through his head. A very odd evening, it makes me sad to think about it, but there's no use in that now. Anyway, that Estonian idiot is portside now and he damn well shouldn't be. I'll have to cut you off there because that old hulk needs to move before things go wrong. Call if there is anything, but I probably know damn all unfortunately.'

Carl put the receiver down slowly. He didn't like this. The case was getting too close and there would be no turning back.

'What did he say?' asked Rose, sitting by the coffee table and flicking through one of the piles.

Carl stood up. The glasses from Habersaat's last round of schnapps at the coffee table were gone but the scarf and the little wooden figure were still there.

He picked up the figure and looked at it. It depicted a male, awkwardly carved as if by a child, and yet touching and expressive.

'Sam said that Habersaat was very down and cried the night before. That perhaps it wasn't quite normal for him, now that he thought about it.'

'So Habersaat didn't act on the spur of the moment. I told you so. He knew he was going to shoot himself. It might even have been planned for some time.'

'Maybe, but then it certainly isn't my fault, is it?' Carl said, looking around as he put the wooden figure in his pocket. There was no doubt that there was a system to the mess. The piles to the right and over the sideboard were old with yellowed paper, while those lying in a row to the adjacent room were still white. Ring binders were assembled in alphabetical order according to theme, and on the windowsills all manner of video tapes and diverse catalogs were assembled.

He stepped into the adjoining room, where Assad was looking at a noticeboard covered in photos of differing sizes.

'What the heck is that?' he asked.

'Photographs of old vans.'

As if Carl couldn't see that.

He stepped closer.

'Yes, an old Volkswagen Kombi. They're all photos of old VW Kombis.'

'Comfy? They don't look too comfy, Carl.'

'That's what people called that type of Volkswagen because they could be used for different things – a combination – Assad.'

'Really! But isn't it strange that they're all taken from the front?'

'Yes, and so different. I don't think there are two that are quite the same.'

Assad nodded. 'I didn't know there were so many types. Red, orange, blue, green, white, all sorts of colors.'

'Yes, and lots of different models, too. That one there with the spare tyre on the front is really old, and some have windows on the side, some don't. Have you counted them?'

'Yes, there's a hundred and thirty-two.'

Of course he had.

'So what's been Habersaat's hypothesis?' asked Carl.

'That Alberte was killed by a Kombo.'

'Kombi! Yes, exactly. I think so, too!'

'Most likely one of those with a cross.'

'What cross?'

Assad pointed out four to five photos. And right enough, each had a small cross in the corner.

'Look! The cars in these photos are all light blue.'

'Yes, but the light blue ones were the most common,' Carl said. 'In the sixties and seventies you could see them on the road everywhere.'

'But it isn't *all* the light blue ones he's marked, Carl. Only those with a mullion in the front-view mirror and without windows in the back.'

'That was still the most usual model, as far as I recall. A totally normal, ordinary van, even though it changed form slightly as time went on.'

'There's a finger mark on this one,' Assad said. 'Look! It's as if he's tapped that fender a lot. As if he wanted to say: there you are.'

Carl leaned in for a closer look. So there was. And it was one of the more special versions of that model, with heavy fenders consisting of vertical wings welded to the parallel steel pipes.

'Out of those with crosses, this is the only one with a reinforced fender, Assad. Well spotted.'

'Then look over there, Carl. The same model again.'

He pointed over towards the wall that formed a partition to yet another room.

It was an oversized photocopy stuck to the wall with masking tape in between two paintings that, strangely enough, had the same initials as the seaside painting down in the community hall. The painter was a local, then.

As they stepped closer, it became apparent that the photocopy of the Volkswagen Kombi with the reinforced fender was very grainy and blurred, making it impossible to see the details of the licence plate or the face of the man caught by the camera getting out of the driver's seat. Perhaps the picture had been blown up too much for what was a run-of-the-mill amateur photo. Maybe it just hadn't been done right.

'Look at what's written underneath, Carl. *BCCR/BCCEC CI B14G27, July 5th, 1997.* That's exactly four and a half months before the accident, right?' Assad said.

Carl didn't answer.

From a blurred mass of grey branches at the top of the photo, an almost unnoticeable arrow drawn with a marker pen pointed directly at the man in the van. An arrow that was ten centimetres long and accompanied by a few almost illegible words.

It startled Carl when he read the words written in pencil: *Here's your man, Carl Mørck.*

'What are you looking at?' asked Assad.

Then he gasped quietly. He'd located what Carl stood frozen to the spot staring at.

'God almighty, he's pressuring me,' sighed Carl. 'And of course it doesn't say what the man's name is.'

'Do you think we can make the man's face clearer if the technicians back home help us?'

'Not from this example.' He turned to face the door looking into the living room. 'Rose, come in here.'

From appearing in the doorway to seeing what they'd discovered took less than five seconds.

'Hell yes,' she said, nodding.

Carl pursed his lips.

'There's no way back now,' Assad said.

Carl stood for a long time looking at the enlarged picture, and then sighed. No way back? No, he supposed not. He turned to Rose.

'I have to admit that there is a certain amount that indicates you were right about Habersaat. He might have had a specific suspicion about this guy for years without being able to find him, and then he grew weary. Now he wanted others to take over, wanted it out of his head, in full knowledge that he couldn't solve the case himself. So suicide wasn't just a way to get the case out of his head, it was a way to ensure it carried on. That means that I, like you, am now more willing to believe that he certainly expected that we'd sail over here and take over. His suicide was the ticket.'

'And there is no return ticket,' concluded Assad. 'But what about the meaning of BCCR/BCCEC CI B14G27?'

'Maybe they've got something to do with the man's name who took the picture, or maybe a journal number. Have you looked in the folders in there, Rose?'

She nodded.

'And nothing rings a bell when you see these initials and numbers?'

'No. The system is quite straightforward and there isn't much in the folders actually. They're almost empty.'

'What now, Carl?' asked Assad.

'Yes, what now?' He looked at his assistants. They'd worked together for almost seven years, solved lots of cases, and yet their eyes could still light up with enthusiasm. Sometimes looks like theirs could rejuvenate his batteries, and sometimes not. Just now they couldn't quite get through so he needed to dig down to find some reserves.

He drummed his fingers on the wall beside the photocopy. No way back, Assad had said.

'OK! Rose, book two extra nights at the hotel. And you, Assad, follow me around the house. We need to have an overview of how much needs to be packed up, and roughly in what order it should be placed.'

11

September 2013

It was now the tenth time that Pirjo read Wanda Phinn's latest message about her imminent arrival, and Pirjo didn't like it. Gut instinct wasn't an applicable element in the teachings of nature absorption, but with Pirjo's background it was a tool that couldn't just be ignored.

This time the gut instinct wasn't good. With each new reading, she imagined new scenarios and probable consequences arising from Wanda Phinn's arrival on the scene, and yet the end result was always the same. Regardless of how you looked at it, what was indicated between the lines in the woman's email was catastrophic. She'd disregarded Pirjo's rejection of being accepted into a course, and now she would come to conquer Pirjo's and Atu's world, and that was something Pirjo simply couldn't tolerate. Not now when her biological clock was ticking so quickly.

Pirjo thought it was a good thing that she was the one in charge of these requests. If Atu had seen it, his curiosity and libido would've been awoken. She knew his weaknesses better than anyone. So, no, she simply couldn't allow this woman to come to the Nature Absorption Academy or the consequences would be impossible to control.

She looked at her watch and thought the whole thing through. In an hour the woman would be standing with all her talents and firm flesh at Kalmar Central Station expecting Pirjo to simply bow out.

But that was where she was mistaken.

Pirjo decided to improvise; that's what she was good at.

Everything would be fine.

She took her scooter from the area in front of the wooden pier.

She stood for a moment and watched the weathered planks out in the water with the seaweed dancing around the bottom of the poles. What could be more peaceful than that, and yet it had uncomfortable associations for her. It wasn't the first time Pirjo had had serious threats to her existence hanging over her head, and last time it had ended here.

She'd quarrelled with one of the female disciples who she realized had become a dangerous rival. It had resulted in shouting, pushing, and slapping that had become gradually harder. For some weeks the woman had become a permanent fixture in Atu's quarters, and ever so slowly had begun to agitate to take over some of Pirjo's responsibilities, she'd felt it.

So right there she overstepped a boundary from which there was no turning back.

Strictly speaking, the upshot of that confrontation was an accident, but ending as it had, it was nevertheless the best thing that could have happened.

That was all a good few years ago, and now it was the turn of this Wanda Phinn.

Pirjo looked up at the academy and chose the gravel path that went around the buildings through the plantation. It was a longer route than the more direct road up to the highway, but this path was secluded so no one from the academy would know which road she'd taken or when.

If somebody asked her later where she'd been, she would say that she'd taken a drive north to clear her head and give herself space to think. That she was in the process of developing some new ideas for her telephone line and just needed to get them in order.

It was important that her absence was understandable and be-lievable, and as long as she could avoid mentioning Wanda Phinn to anyone, then she wouldn't exist in anyone's consciousness but her own.

When today was behind her, and she'd neutralized and elimi-nated this woman, then the time would be right for Malena's turn.

She hadn't yet worked out how she would even the score with that woman without Atu needing to know about it, but if it didn't happen relatively quickly it could develop into a nasty affair.

*　　*　　*

The journey had first really begun for Wanda when she boarded the train in Copenhagen. The flight had been as flights are prone to be, but this final leg of the journey by train through landscapes unlike any she had ever seen before felt like a fairy tale. The language alone was like that in the world of the sagas: magical, exciting, and from a vanished past.

She saw extensive flat areas of farmland, broken by bedrock and mile-long dry stone walls that had seemingly been built and repaired since the dawn of time. And then suddenly red wooden houses and endless pine forests. Here, in this strange and wondrous Swedish peasant country, she'd find her kingdom and her throne. Here she'd be able to escape herself and her past and live with Atu for the rest of her life. She was more certain of this than anything else in the world.

And Wanda was well prepared. Since she hadn't been invited, she had to anticipate resistance and reluctance that could drag things out. But if that was the case, she had no intention of backing out, even if she met with point-blank refusal. She had announced the time of her arrival in yet another email and if there was someone to meet her at the station, then good. If there wasn't, she'd booked a hotel and had enough money to last several weeks. She was certain to get her audience then, she was sure of it.

'Is this your first time here?' asked the man opposite her when she began turning around in her seat. They'd passed Karlskrona now, so there was only half an hour to go until they reached Kalmar.

She confirmed that yes, it was her first time.

He smiled. 'And where are you headed?'

'I'm heading out to Öland. I'm meeting my husband-to-be out there,' she heard herself say.

A look of disappointment came across his face. 'A lucky guy. Dare I ask who he is?'

She noticed that strangely enough she was blushing. 'His name is Atu Abanshamash Dumuzi.'

The lines on his forehead were visible as he nodded, turning his face out towards the blurred light that had cast itself over yet another country town.

When they reached the station he helped her off with her suitcase.

'Do you know what you're getting yourself into?' he asked, setting the suitcase down on the platform.

'Why do you say that?' she asked. He was probably one of those bigots who could only see the world through the lens he'd inherited at his mother's breast.

'I'm a journalist working here in Kalmar. I've been out to the centre on Öland to interview the guru over there and it was a mixed experience. I'm sorry, and this is just my opinion, but I didn't see anything other than fraud and manipulation. The leader, Dumuzi, wanted to captivate me but I have to say that it was far from a successful attempt. But you're sure about what you're doing?'

She nodded. She was, and more than ever before.

'Thanks for your help,' she said without further comment and headed for the square in front of the station.

She stood for a while, leaning up against a flagpole, squinting at the sun. It was just as she'd imagined. There was no one to meet her.

She thought she might as well go down to the hotel and drop off her luggage where no doubt they'd also order a taxi for her.

Then she'd be out there in three-quarters of an hour.

She was just about to bend down for her suitcase when a woman came around the corner at full speed on a scooter. Covered in white from head to toe, clenching her teeth.

It was because of that expression she was able to recognize her. And it was for the same reason that she instinctively clenched her fists.

12

Thursday, May 1st, 2014

Habersaat's house had initially appeared to be an extremely chaotic place. The guiding rule here seemed to be that if there was space, and this included the floor, then piles would be put there. If there was any free wall space, then clippings or printouts were put up, all of which meant that there wasn't any semblance left of normal homeliness or personal objects apart from a couple of photos of a family in a glass frame. It was clear that only the initiated were allowed access to this part of Habersaat's life, which was more important than the daily grind of police work in Rønne.

But if you took the time to go carefully through the apocalypse that marked the end of a normal existence, there was rhyme and reason in each little measured area.

A painstakingly built-up collection spanning almost two decades of research into the one thing in life that Habersaat seriously seemed to care about: Alberte's tragic end.

If you were to observe this hotchpotch of material through the experienced eyes of a police officer, then there was a clear sense that the living room was Habersaat's distribution centre for all incoming material, before it was allocated according to subject to the other rooms in the house. In this room the physical papers were organized in chronological piles, while the folders on the shelves contained a register of the collective contents of the house. The dining room seemingly functioned as a sort of final station for all leads and hints that couldn't be outright dismissed, and the remainder of the house was divided into subtopics. The utility room, for example, housed the inquiries that the police had conducted parallel with Habersaat, and that material didn't take up much room. The room behind it was propped full of interview transcriptions from different local residents in the weeks following the collision. The boy's bedroom upstairs contained piles requisitioned from National Police Headquarters with connections to other hit-and-run cases, and then there was an entire bookcase that had the short and sweet heading *Alberte*, and which in turn was divided into different statements about her background. Folders and piles even for those friends pre-dating her time at the folk high school.

Habersaat's own bedroom on the first floor was more tightly packed than all the other rooms. The window had long since been covered, the air persistently stale and close.

'Have you ever stood downwind from a camel with colic, Carl?' Assad asked after sniffing the air a few times.

Carl shook his head but understood what he meant. A place where an older man had lived with himself and his pent-up gases for decades.

He looked around. Apart from the neatly made bed and a small area of floor in front of the bed and wardrobe, the entire room was crammed full of material. In front of the window there were two bookcases with more piles of general information about the folk high school, and of course folders on the students and teachers who'd been at the school at the same time as Alberte.

But it was also in this room that Assad and Carl came across the material that seemed to fit in least with the bigger picture.

'Why do you think you'd have this lying about?' Assad pointed to the floor.

Carl scanned the rows of beautifully arranged brochures and leaflets about occult phenomena and groups that lay closest to the bed. There was almost no form of mysticism that wasn't included: contacting the dead, aromatherapy, astrology, aura paintings, aura transformation, Bach therapy, clairvoyance, dream interpretation, freedom techniques, energy balancing, healing in all its forms, house cleansing, and so forth. Dozens of different areas, sorted alphabetically, and all with alternative thinking, lifestyle, or treatment in common.

'Do you think he tried to find comfort in some of this stuff here, Carl?'

Carl shook his head. 'I don't know. But no, it doesn't seem to make sense. Have you seen any sort of indication apart from this stuff here? Tarot cards, for example, or pendulums, astrological divinations? Bottles with aromas?'

'Maybe down in the bathroom on the ground floor. We skipped that.'

They went down the corridor, typically decorated with coat hooks holding jackets on the one side and opposite, a row of worn-out shoes, together with a shoehorn with a bamboo shaft on a hook. From this room, one door opened out onto a vestibule with the obligatory umbrella stand in the corner. Apart from that, there were four other doors: one door to the living room, a door to the kitchen, and then two narrow doors, behind which, Carl reasoned, must be the toilet and the bathroom.

He glanced out into the kitchen where Rose was at the sink washing her hands with a rare thoughtful look about her. She simply wasn't herself just now.

With a sixth sense she felt his eyes on her and turned around in one move. 'We can't have all this in Gordon's room in the cellar, Carl,' she said. 'But if we incorporate the wall in the hallway, we might manage. A few bookcases here and there, and it'll be fine. If you book a removal firm, maybe they can take some of Habersaat's bookcases with them, if that's all right with June Habersaat.' She dried her hands on her sides. 'Because she'll inherit it all, right? Technically, Bjarke inherited from his dad for a few hours, but seeing as he's also dead now, it must be his mom who'll take over. What do you think?'

'I say that you've got it all worked out, Rose. So you just get on with it. But if I were you, I wouldn't ask anyone about those shelves.'

She looked at him, surprised. 'Wow, was it *that* easy? I hadn't reckoned on that.'

'No, but there's quite a lot about the things in this house that you – and I for that matter – hadn't bargained on.'

'Me neither,' Assad said from behind. He'd thrown wide open the two narrow doors but there was light coming from only one of them.

'The toilet and bathroom are in the same room, and there's nothing strange in there. The other door here leads out to a narrow corridor that goes to both the garage and down to the cellar. There's a staircase.'

Sod the garage and the cellar with all their rubbish, thought Carl.

They opened the door from the house to the garage. The smell of tar and the stench of gasoline, and just a glimpse of light from two dusty windows, left little doubt as to what the main use was of this annex. There were still tyre tracks in the sand but the car was gone. It hadn't been parked at the community hall, but the police had probably collected it and parked it in the police car park.

'Garages are eerie, Carl,' said Assad, emphasizing this with clenched fists at the end of his otherwise loosely hanging arms.

'Why? Are you worried about spiderwebs?' Carl turned around; there really were a lot of spiderwebs in every direction. No doubt whatsoever that his red-haired cousin would go into a coma if she was ever forced to stay in here. He couldn't keep count of the number of summer holidays where she stormed through the farmhouse to squash spiders or scream hysterically because they were too big. But here everything looked homely. A few shelf units with bits and bobs from a bygone era. Roller skates and deflated beach animals, tins of paint with bulging lids, and all sorts of sprays that had clearly been banned for years. Up on the rafters a sail from a surfboard, skis and ski poles. Nothing eerie as far as he was concerned.

'It says something about all the hours that have passed by, and all the hours that have been used incorrectly,' philosophized Assad.

'Used incorrectly?'

'All the hours where the things in here should have been used but weren't.'

'We don't know anything about that, Assad. And why eerie? More pitiable, I think.'

He nodded. 'And garages are separate from the house and its life. When I'm in a place like this, it's like feeling death.'

'I don't get it.'

'You don't need to, Carl. We can't all feel the same way.'

'Suicide and that sort of thing, is that what you mean?'

'Yes, that too.'

'Hmm. Well, there isn't much in here at any rate. No boxes containing hidden secrets, no notes on the walls. No mystical pyramid constructions and crystals or occult paraphernalia like the stuff in the bedroom. Agreed?'

Assad's eyes circled the room a couple of times. He appeared to agree.

The cellar didn't seem to contain any noteworthy surprises either, appearing both tidy and orderly. It consisted of a laundry room without laundry, a pantry without any food and a workshop without any tools. However, right in the middle there was a newish photocopier and a collection of ancient developing equipment that only few in Denmark today would remember how to use.

'He's made a dark room down here,' said Carl. 'I just don't see any developer liquid or that sort of thing.'

'Maybe it was a hobby from his past, Carl. In fact, I think he used this most,' he said, banging the top of the photocopier. 'He probably used it to make the enlargement of the Volks Kombi.'

'Probably.'

Carl picked up the wastepaper bin at the side of the photocopier and emptied out the scrunched-up contents, smoothing them out on the desk. It wasn't hard to see how Habersaat had worked with that photo. First, he'd increased the size of the the photo up to a quarter of an A4. From there he'd doubled it, continuing up to A4 size and finally up to A3. Not exactly an ideal route for a good-quality end result.

'Have a look at the first enlargement here, Assad. You're looking across the bonnet of another car, and it's a very old car if you ask me, with all that chrome on the bonnet. Far, far behind, you can see the man and the van. I think it's a car park. What do you think?'

'But there's also grass. So it could be something else.'

'It could be, you're right. But look how this enlargement actually shows a bit of another photo on the side. What does that tell us?'

'That there were several photos on the same page.'

'Precisely. Our photo has presumably been in a photo album. It tallies with the structure of the paper the photos are pasted onto. It's often something a bit coarse and cardboard-like. Judging by its square shape, I think it's taken with a Kodak Instamatic camera.'

'I bet the original is still lying in the photocopier,' said Assad, lifting the lid. Unfortunately, he was wrong.

Assad rubbed his stubble. It sounded almost like the rhythm section of a salsa band. 'If only we could see more of that photo album so we could find out where it was taken. Or maybe even identify who took it.'

'Habersaat wasn't a detective, so that sort of logic and systematic way of thinking isn't something we should assume he understood. And anyway, he must've noted where he got it from somewhere or other, for goodness sake. There's probably something up there in one of the folders.'

'Look, Carl. There's another pile of photocopies here.' Assad pulled them out of a wooden box that Habersaat had screwed into the wall, passing them down to Carl with a smile. 'Maybe some of the last stuff he worked with on the case.'

'Very funny, Assad.' Carl threw the photocopy of a naked woman in rather precarious positions away from him across the table. The paper was completely yellowed. It was definitely many years since Habersaat had had any pleasure in that area.

'I managed to access his computer, Carl,' said Rose when they came back up. 'The password was *Alberte*, of course. How hard can it be?' Rose smiled mockingly. 'All the summaries of his research material, which you can also find in the folders, are on the computer. The difference being that inside the plastic wallets in the folders there's sometimes been added a small clipping or something else in support of the entry. I've had a bit of a look in them, but they're really nothing special. It seems to me that Habersaat gave up on the folder system and just stuck with the piles. But I could be wrong.'

Be wrong! Did she really say that?

'Is there any data that might explain something about the photo of the Volkswagen, Rose?' Carl put the smallest enlargement in front of her.

'Maybe,' she answered. 'It's very unclear. A photocopy, right?'

Assad nodded.

'Of course. I haven't seen any evidence of a scanner anywhere. He apparently only had that little printer there.' She pointed to an inkjet printer under a pile of papers. 'But don't worry, Mr Mørck. I'll trawl through the computer and maybe we'll find something about the origin of the photo. There's only a 60-megabyte memory on the old box after all, so it won't be an insurmountable task.'

OK, finally the irony was rearing its head.

She turned back to the screen with a sigh, already in her own world. That was their Rose.

'Come here, Carl,' shouted Assad.

He was staring at the enlargement, his face tense with concentration.

'What's up, Assad?'

'Try to feel here.' He pulled Carl's hand up to a spot in the middle of the copy.

'And?'

'Press harder, then you'll feel it, right?'

Now he could feel it clearly.

'Yes. Something is stuck to the back of the photocopy.' Assad nodded to himself. 'Of course Habersaat assumed that we'd take the enlargement with us, Carl, of course he did. Now I think we've found the needle in the strawstack that we were looking for.'

'Needle in the haystack, Assad.' Carl peeled the tape on the corner of the photocopy.

'Bongo,' said Assad, and he was right. On the back of the copy was the page from the photo album with the four photos.

'Maybe there's something about when they're from,' said Assad, pulling the page free from the photocopy.

But of course there wasn't.

Carl took the page with the photographs and turned it over. All four photos on the page were obviously part of a larger series with a classic car theme, probably taken at a festival of some sort or another.

Carl felt his heart skip a beat. This happened from time to time when an investigation suddenly entered a new stage. He smiled to himself. This is what he lived and breathed for.

'Here's our man,' he said calmly, pointing at a section of less than a square inch on one of the photographs. 'There, right at the back of the area, can you see him? And he's looking over towards the car with the impressive bonnet. A beautiful old model.'

'Carl, we'll never manage to get that little section clearer than Habersaat did. Never. Not even if we tried for a hundred years.'

He was right. Everything taken into consideration, Habersaat had done what he could.

'CI B14G27 it's got here under the photo. And BCCR/BCCEC down in the corner. And look what's written above the black car on the photo next to it: THA 20. And the other two underneath: WIKN 27, WIKN 28. Don't you think they refer some way or other to the cars, Carl? Do you know anything about classic cars apart from that old sardine tin you drive us around in?'

Carl shook his head. 'The only make of car I know with Ci is Citroën. But the others, THA and WIKN, I don't recognize.'

'We'll look them up,' said Assad.

Rose didn't manage to protest before Curly jumped in and pushed the computer chair, with her in it, away from the screen.

'We'll explain in a second,' Carl said, while Assad typed *Citroën B14G27* in the search box.

No match. What now?

'You two aren't the brightest bunch, are you?' said Rose, somewhat peeved as she glanced quickly over at the photo page. 'They're old cars, right? Very old in fact. From the twenties even, I'd guess. More specifically 1920, 1927, and 1928, as I read it.'

Carl raised his eyebrows. How embarrassing that it hadn't occurred to him.

'OK. Try to write *Citroën B14G 1927* instead, Assad.'

Rose was right. A second after Assad had typed it, a whole series popped up on the screen of polished examples of what the motor industry and the art of the conveyor belt could produce in the inter-war years. Beautiful, beautiful cars in all colours.

'Fantastic. What car makes do we know, then, with TH or WIKN or WI KN? Check it out, Assad.'

'Just let me,' said Rose, pushing the computer chair into Assad's hip with a thud.

After a minute of typing, she produced pictures of a Thulin A 1920 and two Willys-Knights from 1927 and 1928.

Assad looked like someone who was about to open his presents. 'Here we go then, Carl, now we'll find out,' he said when Rose typed all the car models in one and the same Google search.

'Hi-de-hi,' shouted Assad with a huge smile.

A meagre three hits came up with this complicated search, and the top hit was definitely the right one: a link to a photo series from the Bornholm Classic Car Rally 1997 and a website for the Bornholm Classic Car Enthusiasts' Club.

And with that, any doubt about what BCCR/BCCEC stood for was laid to rest.

Assad was jumping up and down with excitement. An odd sight when you took his general condition and age into account.

'Yeah, yeah, Assad. Now there's just the job of finding out where the photo was taken, who gave the photo page to Habersaat, who the man in the photo is – if anyone even knows – and then finding out if he's actually guilty, and where he is, and how Habersaat . . .'

All of which put a stop to Assad's jumping.

'Give it a rest, Carl,' said Rose. 'I'll check if Habersaat's printer works and, if it does, print out everything I can find on that club, OK? Then we'll take it from there.'

Carl pulled out his mobile, noticing again that the battery was almost dead. He typed Police Superintendent Birkedal's number.

'Carl Mørck here. I just have two things to say,' he said briefly when the call was answered. 'We're taking all Habersaat's research with us over to Police Headquarters, is that OK?'

'Well, I think those inheriting his estate will be glad. But why?'

'We've become curious, someone has to be. And the other thing is—'

'If there's something more specific in relation to the case, Carl,' interrupted Birkedal, 'you'll need to talk directly with the man responsible from that time. He's a good guy, so go easy on him, all right? He's actually one of the good guys, works hard, does a good job. I'll transfer you. His name's Jonas Ravnå.'

'Just one more thing. Did you find anything at Bjarke Habersaat's place that we should know about? Motives for the suicide or anything like that?'

'No, nothing. His computer was just chockablock with pornographic photos of a homosexual nature and old games.'

'You'll send it over to us when you're finished, right?'

'You've got it. I'll transfer you to Ravnå.'

A worn voice came from the receiver, and it didn't sound any less tired when Carl told him what he was calling about.

'Believe it or not, I really did want to help Christian Habersaat,' he said. 'The problem was that we just didn't get anywhere, and at the same time there were all the other cases since then. It's almost twenty years ago after all, don't forget that.'

Carl nodded. He knew the game better than anyone. If there was just one thing in life you could be sure of, it was that criminals didn't suddenly stop committing crime.

'Habersaat harboured a suspicion about a man in a VW Kombi whom he traced in a photo album from 1997. Do you have any idea who might've given it to him, and has he ever told you about his suspicion?'

'Christian and I didn't discuss the case over the last five to six years. Actually, I banned him from bringing it up unless he had groundbreaking new evidence, otherwise he should just get on with his work in the uniform division. So I suppose it points to it not being something groundbreaking, and that it's something he discovered more recently.'

'What about you? Did you ever come across anything conclusive in the case? How do you view it today?'

'I have my theories.'

'And they are?'

'If it was an accident, the driver of the vehicle could've been under the influence of alcohol or drugs, as there were no skid marks. If it wasn't an accident, but premeditated murder, we're totally lacking a motive. She wasn't pregnant and she was well liked, so why murder her? It could've been spontaneous. Maybe even carried out by a random sick person who had a sudden impulse to kill another human being. But again, there must have been a reason for Alberte to cycle out there so early in the morning, and we don't know the answer to that with any certainty. Was she supposed to meet someone, and if so, why there exactly? I assume it *was* there that she had a meeting and had got off the bike to wait. She'd left it a little way from where she was standing, otherwise she would've been cut up by the parts of the bike. And we found absolutely no tissue residue on it. So I think she arrived a bit too early and walked around a little while waiting. Maybe for the person who killed her.'

'Any theory about who she was waiting for? Was it the man in the van?'

'Yes, that's just it. We know she had a boyfriend, as detailed in my report. We know that he was staying on the island, but whether he disappeared before or after the accident, I don't know.'

'Do you have his name and a place of residence on the island?'

'He probably lived in an interim camp located on a farm by Ølene, but we don't have a name. The farmer who was renting out his land didn't write a contract, he just got his five thousand kroner in cash for the rental period. Yes, he even declared the income to the taxman.'

'Probably, you said. How did you find out about him? This isn't mentioned in the report.'

'I honestly don't remember. I expect it was something Habersaat had discovered. He was sniffing about twenty-four hours a day.'

'Hmm. What period did the rental payment cover?'

'Six months in 1997. June to November.'

'Do we have a description of the tenant?'

'Yes. He was in his twenties, maybe even a bit older than midtwenties. Handsome, long dark hair, hippy clothes. Military jacket with sewn-on labels. *Nuclear Power No Thanks* and that sort of thing.'

'And?'

'Yes, that was it.'

'Not bloody much. And you're sure that the landlord told you everything he had?'

'I sincerely hope so because the man died three years ago.'

Carl shook his head and ended the conversation. No case should ever be allowed to drag on so long.

'I have a little detail to tell you, Carl, but there's no guarantee it'll please you,' said Rose. Then why on earth did she flash him that demonic smile?

'I've booked two more nights at the hotel.'

'That's fine. And what's the problem?'

'Oh, there's no problem apart from the fact that both your bedroom and Assad's have been allocated to other people.'

'OK, then we'll just change hotels, right?' Assad said cautiously, beating Carl to it.

Rose looked at them as if they were a couple of spoiled teenagers. There wouldn't be any other hotel.

'Then we'll just be transferring over to a couple of other rooms?' Assad continued.

'Exactly. There weren't any single rooms left, but I managed to book a double room for you both instead. With double bed and double duvet, the whole caboodle. That'll be cosy, won't it?'

13

September 2013

The woman with the suitcase and a far too waspish waist stood in the square in front of the large yellow building, leaning up against one of the flagpoles like a gracious sculpture. Lording over it with her glistening brown skin, she appeared to mock all the genes that had survived the fight with the darkness up here in the far north. Mocking the twenty years during which Pirjo had dedicated her life to Atu and his world, believing she'd win his heart in the end. This woman was far too beautiful and graceful, far too athletic, intimidatingly different and exotic.

Pirjo sat for a moment astride her scooter wondering if she should turn around. But rationally it just wouldn't do. Now that the girl had come so far, wild horses couldn't stop her from finding the way herself, so Pirjo trembled inside.

But before she went to extremes, which she now realized might be necessary, she simply had to try other methods first.

'Hello,' she said as naturally and perkily as possible, crossing the square. 'I'm Pirjo, the one you've been writing with. I see you've come over here anyway. It's actually a real shame because as I already warned you, you've come in vain.'

Pirjo gave her a sympathetic smile. That tended to work.

'But as you're here, and probably due to a misunderstanding and bad communication on our part, we've decided that we'd like to pay for your return journey to London. Then you can possibly come another . . .'

'Hello, Pirjo, nice to see you,' the woman interrupted her, unaffected. 'Yes, I'm Wanda Phinn.' She offered her hand with an innocent smile, as if she hadn't heard a word of what Pirjo had said, but Pirjo knew better. She could see it in the woman's eyes and from her smile. This woman with the seductive cheekbones wouldn't be satisfied until she stood before Atu.

'Fair enough, Wanda, but we've actually arranged a return ticket for you, didn't you hear?'

'Yes, and thanks a lot for the sentiment. But I've come to meet Atu Abanshamash Dumuzi and I can't go back before I've done that. I understand that there aren't any course places available, but I have to see him.'

Pirjo nodded. 'I understand, but I'm sorry. Atu isn't at the course centre just now.'

For a brief moment the woman looked disappointed, but then seemingly managed to compose herself. 'OK! Then I'll just wait. I know there's a hotel called Frimurare Hotellet only two minutes from here. I checked from home that there were rooms available, so it's no problem if I have to wait a couple of days. I can just go down to the hotel now and you can call when he's back. You've got my number in the email.'

When a predator attacks, it's normally after a prolonged state of deep concentration and patient waiting. The snake that lies quietly as if dead, the predator that waits flat on the ground, the falcon before it suddenly dives. In the same way, this woman appeared incredibly determined, with eyes that seemed too relaxed and focused. The awareness that her arrival would meet with resistance literally radiated from her. That she was well aware of what she was up against and that she knew the weaknesses in the system. Like she knew the full extent of Atu's susceptibility, knew what a weak position Pirjo had in the game, and when she should strike.

But that's where she was mistaken because while Pirjo might not be feeling on top just now, she was a long way from feeling weak or vulnerable. She'd just been in doubt about what measures to take, but not any more. She'd resorted to drastic decisions in similar situations in the past, successfully and without regret.

After all, this woman had thrown the dice herself, not her, and she'd soon regret it.

'Frimurare Hotellet?' she said. 'OK, but it would be a shame if you had to use your hard-earned cash on a hotel, so we'll just have to see if we can't arrange a short audience before you go back. Atu is probably down on the south end of the island or out on the moor in the middle of the island, what we call Stora Alvaret. He often goes there to meditate and get into his soul. He isn't keen on being disturbed but seeing as you're so insistent we'll just have to try.'

Pirjo smiled the best that she could. Apparently the woman bought it.

'But, Wanda, I'll say it now so you aren't disappointed, that will have to be all, and then I'll drive you back to the station afterwards. Your return flight from Copenhagen doesn't take off until tomorrow afternoon so we've got plenty of time.'

The woman nodded towards the scooter with its flimsy luggage rack, helmets and foldable spade. 'What about my suitcase?' she asked. 'There isn't room for that, too.'

'No, you're right. We'll put it in a locker. We're going to be back in an hour or two anyway.'

The young woman nodded. It was very obvious that when it came to it she thought they'd both be involved in that decision. No doubt she thought that the suitcase would be brought to where she wanted it to be when the time came.

'Have you ridden on a scooter before, Wanda?'

'We don't do anything else where I come from,' she answered.

'Good. You'll need to hitch your skirt up and then just hold tight onto my jacket. I don't really like people holding me around my waist.'

Pirjo collected herself and turned up the charm. The most important thing was that Wanda Phinn didn't suspect anything untoward but enjoyed the journey, surroundings and beautiful landscape, secure in the knowledge that the first stage of her conquest of Atu Abanshamash's undivided attention was going smoothly.

'Öland is a fantastic place, you know. When you come over here another time, I'll give you a better tour, but I can show you some of the attractions on the island while we drive,' shouted Pirjo.

Behind her, Wanda sat with a light grip on Pirjo's jacket, staring out across the sea and over toward the promised island. On both sides of the Öland Bridge the waves whipped the sea up into foam. The breeze from the mainland had changed direction, with the wind now coming from due east and somewhat cooler than might have been desired.

Pirjo thought to herself that when they reached the windmills up on the ridge, she'd find somewhere to shake her off, resulting in a hard and unexpected fall that would likely kill her outright. If not, she'd just have to help the process along.

'There are loads of windmills out here on the island,' she shouted. 'No families wanted to share them so they split the parcels of land up and each built their own. The only problem was that they also split the parcels up within families, and at one point the parcels became too small to be able to live off. In the end people had to leave the island if they didn't want to starve to death.' She felt that Wanda was nodding behind her but that she was probably totally uninterested in Öland's past, which suited Pirjo. It meant she could concentrate on getting this done right and using the side wind to her advantage.

Despite the time of day and year there were a good number of cars on the road. It was probably due to a group of artists on the highway down toward Vickleby and Kastlösa coordinating their openings, exhibitions, and receptions, which meant a large group of art enthusiasts from the mainland were currently on a sort of Öland tour of the world of glass and painting. It was only a little south of these towns that the traffic petered out, but so did the opportunities.

Pirjo was unsure what to do about Wanda's questions. They'd passed a couple of signs pointing toward Alvaret and Wanda asked again and again why they weren't turning.

'Not yet,' she shouted back. 'Atu sometimes prefers the areas a little further south. There are more ancient monuments to excavate there.'

'So that's what you use the spade for,' she shouted back.

Pirjo nodded and looked ahead. Perhaps Gettlinge was the answer. The cliff was definitely steep there. And even though she couldn't drive right up to it and push Wanda down into the deep directly from the seat of the scooter, it was the best place to do it given the options.

Pirjo felt the excitement intensify, but she wasn't really nervous. If it had been the first time she'd had to do away with a rival it would probably have been different, but it wasn't.

'We'll stop at Gettlinge because that's one of Atu's favourite places. It's not dead certain that he's here today but at least you'll have seen it.'

Wanda smiled when she stood down and made some flattering comments about how thoughtful Pirjo was and that it looked wonderful.

'No, I'm afraid I can't see him anywhere. What a shame,' Pirjo said, gazing out around the landscape. 'But look around before we drive on. This is a very special place,' she continued, spreading her arms out over a strange and protected landscape of stone that formed the outline of a ship.

'Impressive,' Wanda said, nodding. 'Like a sort of Stonehenge, but much smaller, right? And there's one of those old mills, too. Is this a place where Vikings are buried?' she asked.

Pirjo nodded and looked about. The landscape was barren and flat and more importantly, deserted. The bleak moorland of Stora Alvaret was behind her on the other side of the highway, and was just as desolate.

Over on this side and behind the graveyard was the cliff. There were more trees and bushes on the slope than she remembered but that could be advantageous. She wouldn't need to move the body straightaway since it would be lost in the wilderness. And if the body was found at some point, who would connect the find with a woman called Wanda Phinn? Not to mention connect the discovery to Pirjo.

She came to the conviction that all in all it was the perfect place, while she checked that there were no cars driving on the highway between the moorland and the graveyard.

'Come over here a minute, Wanda,' she shouted, trying to control her voice so it didn't sound false. 'You can see how the island was formed from here, and why the inhabitants disappeared.'

She pointed out over the cultivated fields far below them in the lowlands, and further westward towards the settlements along the shores of the Kalmar Strait on both sides of the glistening waves.

'Over there on the other side of the sound you can see Kalmar, where you've just come from,' she babbled. 'The farmers lived up here in the highlands for a few decades in the last century, dividing and portioning off their land endlessly, like I told you before.'

She pulled Wanda forward toward the edge and turned her around, her pulse racing. 'Look at the landscape on the other side of the highway. That's Stora Alvaret, where Atu might be just now. It was fertile pasture less than a hundred years ago, but the peasants were too brutal in their use of it and the cows grazed it all away.'

She grabbed Wanda's arm.

'Is it understandable that a people couldn't find a way to help one another to feed themselves in such a fertile place?'

Wanda shook her head. She appeared to be totally calm and relaxed, so it had to be now while the highway was still deserted.

'In my opinion, you could rightly call Öland the island of egotism, considering a significant number of the inhabitants had to leave in the end to avoid dying of hunger, all because they couldn't work together,' she ended, pulling Wanda's arm vigorously while knocking her hip at full force toward her lower back.

The result was initially just as planned. Wanda's upper body dipped backwards while she flailed about with her free arm. Then she took a step backwards without being able to find her footing, the idea being that she would fall the second after. Fall and fall and tumble among the vegetation, stumps and large rocks. A bad fall that could easily mean death. And if it didn't result in that, there was always the spade to finish things off with.

And Wanda did fall, but against all calculations not alone. In the exact second where she lost her balance she instinctively grabbed Pirjo's waist with her free arm.

The result was unavoidable. They both fell down the slope, intertwined like a ball. Suddenly there were two pairs of legs hitting the tree trunks.

As the limbs of two bodies take up more space than just one, the fall was stopped before the cliff slope became really steep, leaving them suddenly lying entangled together on the slope among twigs and rotting leaves, staring into each other's wide-open eyes.

'Are you trying to kill me?' hissed Wanda Phinn, throwing an arm up, securing her hand in between low-hanging branches and exposed roots.

Pirjo was in shock. Not only from being knocked about after the failed murder attempt, but over the whole situation. Wanda must be aware now that something really wasn't as it should be and so would be on guard.

How would she be able to stop her from seeing Atu? How to prevent the woman from voicing her misgivings to the one person who really mustn't know anything about this?

'I have epilepsy,' improvised Pirjo, falteringly and with her face turned to the ground, while she tried to induce shaking all over her body. 'I'm terribly sorry. It was a small attack. I normally feel them coming in advance, but not this time. I'm so terribly sorry, Wanda. It could have ended so badly.'

She tried to bring forth tears but couldn't. Instead, she managed to force a bit of spit, letting it drool out of the side of her mouth.

'Come on,' said Wanda without any sign of compassion.

She hauled them both up to their feet, while Pirjo thought so hard it hurt.

At the far end of the square there was a shed with old-fashioned toilets. A seat and a hole in the ground, just like their ancestors had done. Pirjo had been there several times before and could recite by heart the rhyme that some idiot had written on the wall in faltering handwriting.

If you're sat there coiling one
leave some paper when you're done
other people after you
need to wipe their asses too

More than once she'd thought that the worst fate for someone must be to be blocked down a toilet hole to end your days choking on other people's excrement.

Was that a possibility? Could she get Wanda over there and knock her out?

Pirjo felt only too clearly that her thoughts were going in circles. The situation had become crazy and her defences were falling.

She just wasn't herself right now.

All Pirjo could think was that Wanda was going to steal her position and give birth to Atu's children, making her nothing more than a simple housekeeper.

It was enough to drive her crazy. Why hadn't she been able to prevent this? Why hadn't she just discredited the girl to Atu? Why had she even answered her emails? Why, why?

'If you aren't feeling too good I'd better drive the rest of the way,' came Wanda's voice from behind her.

Pirjo turned to face the woman who was standing there in her tattered clothes and with her hand outstretched towards her.

'The keys, thank you!' she said with a look that couldn't be misunderstood. She was really on guard and knew that she had good reason to be.

'Which way are we going?' she asked, putting the scooter in gear.

Pirjo pointed. 'Back on the highway up toward Resmo, then to the right and into Alvaret. It's about a ten-minute drive to get there.'

It would have to happen on the moor. She didn't know how, but it would have to be there.

14

Friday, May 2nd, 2014

The night in a double bed with Assad was a somewhat motley affair.

How a relatively small person could produce such a varied range of noises was a mystery to Carl. He'd certainly never before heard anything of a similar human origin vary between subsonic snoring and squeaky whistling sounds reminiscent of an overworked church organ. And just as never-ending as Assad's one-man orchestra was, it was equally impossible to bring him back to the surface again. In short, Assad not only slept like a log, he slept like a tree. Actually, more like an agitated rookery, thought Carl as he lay discouraged between three and five in the morning.

When the snoring finally subsided, Carl heaved a sigh of relief in the few seconds before these inarticulate sounds were replaced by an equally incomprehensible mumble from Assad's gaping mouth.

The sounds were definitely words, which Carl in his daze interpreted as gibberish or just Arabic, until a few seemingly random

Danish words appeared among the gibberish, causing Carl to lie wide awake once again.

Had Assad said *kill*? And had he said *I don't forget?* as he'd begun to writhe about. The words were unclear but it was obvious that Assad wasn't OK inside. Just as obvious as Carl not being able to get any shut-eye after that.

As a result, he was dead tired, and no matter how much he might want to, he was in no fit state to return Assad's beaming smile when he finally opened his eyes.

'I'll say this for you, Assad, you can certainly talk while you're sleeping,' he managed to say before a woman's voice down on the street began to yell.

Carl jumped out of bed. She must have been standing right in the hotel entrance because he certainly couldn't see her.

'Was I talking?' came the question from behind in a very, very subdued voice. 'What was I saying then?'

Carl turned around to face Assad, intending to direct a disarming smile at him, but the guy was sitting with a deadly serious expression, pale, with his back crouched up against the headboard resembling a soldier who'd stabbed his comrade.

'Nothing special, Assad. It was almost unintelligible. But you spoke Danish and didn't sound happy. Did you have a nightmare?'

Assad wrinkled his heavy eyebrows and was about to answer when the woman on the street shouted up again.

'I know you're in there, John,' she yelled. 'You've been seen. Do you hear me? You've been seen together with her.'

Carl jumped out of bed and over to the window, from where he could see an attractive middle-aged woman snarling on the steps of the hotel like a fighting dog that had caught the scent of blood. Her eyes were wild and her fists clenched.

Damn it. So Rose had caught John Birkedal in her net after all. Poor, poor man.

'I suggest we split up today,' Carl said at the breakfast table, struggling to keep his eyes open. When the other two were off on their way, he'd creep back to the room and try to claw back some of the sleep the night had robbed him of.

'I was thinking the same,' said Rose, already in full black regalia as the evil queen in *Snow White*. Not a word on the morning's clash and no apology for what it had caused. The incident between man and wife in front of the hotel was apparently already ancient history in Rose's eyes. She seemed both satisfied and recharged. God only knew how Birkedal must be feeling.

'I'll head over to Habersaat's house and get the packing started,' she continued. 'I struck a deal with a local removal company yesterday and they're coming to pick me up here in twenty minutes.'

Carl nodded approvingly. That was her taken care of.

'And I've found out that June Habersaat's sister lives in a nursing home not far from here. No doubt a job for you, Assad?' she added. 'Seeing as *you* made sure that June probably won't tell us anything about what her husband might have told her about his enquiries, it seems fitting that you're the one who should pump her for information. June might have complained to her.'

Assad took the blame on the chin. Rose was Rose after all, and just now he was more concerned with pouring sugar in his coffee without it overflowing.

She turned towards Carl, cold and indifferent to his chalky-white complexion and suppressed protest that she was now taking control. 'I've also arranged a tour of Bornholm Folk High School for you at nine thirty, Carl. Afterwards, it's been arranged for you to visit the former rector couple who ran the school, if you want to, which I'll assume you do. They don't live far from there.'

How in the world had she managed to do all that on top of everything else?

Carl took a deep breath and looked at his watch. It was five past nine. That would give him just under ten minutes to try to summon up an appetite, eat something, drink his coffee, shave and catch the nap that he so desperately needed.

'I think you'll have to ring the folk high school again and post-pone, Rose. I've got a few things I need to sort out first.'

She smiled, so she'd obviously been expecting that answer. 'That's OK, but then it'll have to wait until the day after tomorrow because the school is closed tomorrow for a trip. But if you really want to sleep here at the hotel for another few days, that's fine by me. It's not as if there's anyone else waiting for us.'

Carl nodded, realizing the pointlessness of suggesting a later time in the day to the battleaxe who currently represented the execu-tioner at Nuremberg, the nail in his coffin and the stone in his shoe.

'And when you two are done, I think you should meet me in Listed to give a hand. You'll probably be finished first, Assad, but you can take a taxi. What do you say?'

'I say that I've never tasted such great coffee before,' he replied, swinging his cup in front of them as Carl accepted defeat.

'I think it might be easier if you and I go together, Assad,' he said. 'June Habersaat's sister can wait until later today.'

Carl's phone rang. He looked at the display with equal measure of resentment and awe.

'Yes, Mum. What's up?'

She particularly hated that expression. It sometimes had the ad-vantage of paralysing her completely so the conversation was over before it began. Unfortunately, it apparently didn't annoy her one bit today. She cut straight to the chase.

'We've heard from Sammy in Thailand now. He reversed the charges, but that's fine because it was quite rough what he had to say, if you ask me. He's gone out there now to sort everything out, and do you know what?'

Carl threw back his head. The memory of both Sammy and why he was bumbling around in that quintessential exotic playground of the Danes had luckily been hidden somewhere deep in Carl's brain, somewhere he didn't often visit.

'Sammy is so angry, and I can understand why, because Ronny's already sent his will to someone else. It's almost as if he couldn't trust his own brother, isn't it?'

Ronny's will. Hopefully Ronny had limited himself solely to sharing his usurped goods, but Carl wasn't certain. Why did he get such a bad taste in his mouth whenever Ronny's affairs were brought up?

'If Sammy was my brother, I'd have myself adopted,' he replied.

'Goodness, Carl, you rascal. You're always coming out with such funny stuff. Your dad and I would never let you do that.'

The folk high school was located in exactly the kind of place you'd expect, surrounded by fields and forests, directly up to the spectacular Ekkodalen valley, probably the biggest attraction on Bornholm, and on which masses of schoolchildren from all over Denmark descended as part of their compulsory school camp. Carl had often heard about it but never seen it before because where he came from you didn't go to Bornholm but to Copenhagen, where the highlight was a ride on the roller coaster in Tivoli Gardens and subsequent throwing up.

A flagpole with a pennant gently dancing in the sun, and a mas-

sive engraved boulder greeted them in true style with the words
Folk High School, behind which there was a series of red and white
buildings from all periods, spread out in the landscape, framed by
bushes and windbreakers, home-made totem poles, and a coffee
pavilion in miniature.

A presentable red-haired woman was waiting in front of the entrance to the administration building, whose presence immediately
prompted Assad to straighten up the few centimetres that were
possible.

'Welcome,' she said, starting out by saying that she wasn't
employed at the school when Alberte was there but that their
groundskeeper had been. 'We've got publications from that year,
and our former female rector has also written a diary throughout
the extensive period when she and the rector were at the helm
here. I don't really think she'll have made many comments on the
Alberte case, though.'

Assad nodded like one of those bobbing-head dogs kept by some
strange people in the back of their cars. 'We'd really like to talk to
the groundskeeper,' he said with half-closed eyes and an almost
certainly flirtatious look, 'but maybe you could show us around so
we know a bit more about what Alberte's life was like here.'

Carl couldn't help but wonder what he was doing there, thinking
that Assad would do fine on his own, and noticing how keen he
was. Maybe he could sneak onboard the ferry later this afternoon
and leave the rest to them. Another night with Assad's outbursts
would kill him.

'Some of the buildings are later additions, including the two
facing the road, where we house the glass workshop, for example,'
she continued. 'But you can see where Alberte ate, painted and
slept at night.'

It turned out to be an extensive tour, and Assad was thrilled. 'What did they eat for breakfast? Was there a morning assembly? When did they sit in the lounge with the fireplace?'

It was only when the groundskeeper, Jørgen, a well-preserved man with slightly greying temples and a lean workman's figure, turned up that the tour really had any substance. The man appeared to have a good memory, so Carl became more interested. He'd been employed here since 1992 but the events surrounding Alberte's disappearance and the questions about how she'd come to end her days had naturally caused the year 1997 and the young girl Alberte to be imprinted more in his memory than so much else.

'She disappeared on the same day we held the topping-out ceremony for our workshop building, and I was busy that day. You remember things like that.' He led them over towards a cluster of low bungalows in yellow brick. 'She slept over here in the house we call Stammershalle. They all have funny names like Helligdommen, Døndalen and Randkløv, but don't ask me why. That would be a longer explanation.'

'OK, so they're single rooms,' surmised Carl. 'And with a window directly out to the lawn. So she could easily have had late-night visits from outside, couldn't she?'

The groundskeeper smiled. 'Nothing is impossible when young people dance in the night, is it?'

Carl thought about Rose for a moment and shook his head. He didn't dare think about how she would have reacted in the same situation.

'But the police questioned the other girls who lived in the house and none thought she'd had a male visitor in her room. And they would've heard, as thin as the walls are.'

'How do you remember her? Was she special in any way?'

'Hmm, how? She was probably one of the prettiest girls to attend the school in my time. Not only because of her fantastic features and eyes, but because she moved about like she was a princess. She had a special way of walking, almost gliding across the floor like Greta Garbo used to. She wasn't very tall, but all the same I think you always noticed her most in a crowd, if you get what I mean?'

Carl nodded. He'd seen pictures of Alberte.

'Who's Greta Garbo?' asked Assad.

The groundskeeper looked at him as if he'd fallen from the moon, and maybe he had. Who knew anything about Assad? And what did Assad know? Two unknowns of the same sort.

'And then she sang so beautifully. You could clearly hear her voice rise above the others during the singing at morning assembly.'

'So what you're saying is that she was unusually attractive and something a bit special. Do you remember anything about who she flirted with at the school?' asked Carl.

'No, I don't know anything about that, unfortunately. The police asked me the same thing, but no doubt some of the other students had something to say about that. I just know that once in a while she took the bus or a taxi into Rønne with some of the others to have a good time. Had a beer and that sort of thing. I saw some of the other girls and boys smooching over in the greenhouse behind the solar collector, but never Alberte. She cycled a bit, too. She was really taken with the nature here, she said, but I don't know how much she ever managed to see. She was often only gone for half an hour, I noticed, maybe even less than that.'

'We didn't get much out of that,' said Carl half an hour later as they sat in the car on the way to Aakirkeby and the home of the former rector couple.

'It's nice here on Bornholm,' Assad said with his legs up on the dashboard, taking in every detail of the landscape. 'And that secretary, I could've eaten her up.'

'I did notice your amour, Assad.'

'My what?'

'Maybe you could find a job over here if you're so taken with it.'

He nodded. 'Yes, maybe. People seem nice here.'

Carl turned toward him. Was he serious? It certainly looked like it.

'You like redheads, then?'

'Nah, not especially. It's just a feeling I have at the moment, Carl.' He pointed to the dashboard display. 'Your phone's ringing, Carl.'

Carl pressed. 'Yes, Rose, what's new?'

'I'm sitting in the middle of a load of boxes and paper on the first floor in Habersaat's house. Have you two noticed that there are several folders full of transcripts of interviews with the students from back then?'

'We haven't really looked yet, but yes, we've noticed.'

'I've had a little look. Several of her friends report that Alberte flirted with most of the guys and that it was really annoying for the others because the guys only had eyes for her.'

'So it might be one of the girls who hurled her up in the tree?' Carl grunted.

'Very funny, Mr Mørck. But one of the boys at the school got a little further than the others, it seems. They kissed and were together for a while before she found the other one.'

'The other one?'

'Yes, the one who didn't go to the school. But we can talk about this later, right?'

'Yes, of course, but then why are you calling?'

'I called to tell you about the folders and to ask if either of you have come across anything to do with the guy she was with at the school? His name was Kristoffer Dalby.'

'We didn't get much from the trip to the school, no. Kristoffer Dalby, you said? We're on our way now to the former rector couple, so we can ask them if they can tell us anything about it.'

A tall and thin elderly man, who beyond his corduroy trousers, tweed jacket and well-groomed beard needed only a pipe hanging in the corner of his mouth to give him the look of a professor of literature from Oxford, led them to the kitchen, where the windowsill had more pots filled with herbs than in a garden centre.

'Allow me to introduce my wife, Karina.'

Principal Karlo Odinsbo's complete opposite took to the stage with smiles and embraces. She was dressed in multiple layers of clothing in such an array of colour that she looked like she'd stepped out of the musical *Hair*. All she needed was a turban fashioned from three gaudy scarves and she and Carl's turbo-tuned ex-wife Vigga could have been hatched from the same nest.

'Kristoffer Dalby, you say?' The principal mulled over the name once he had them seated at the Formica table. 'Hmm, we will have to bring forth the annals to help. But let's have some coffee first.'

Assad looked quizzically at the former principal. 'Annals?'

Carl gave him a nudge to stop him. 'Annals are old records and books, Assad, not what you're thinking about,' he whispered.

Assad's eyebrows skyrocketed. 'Oh,' he said in recognition. A new word had found its way into his vocabulary.

'What do you say, Karina?' the principal asked while pouring.

'Do you remember a student by the name of Kristoffer Dalby from Alberte's group?'

She thrust her bottom lip forward. Apparently not.

'Just a second, I might have something to jog your memory,' said Carl and dialled Rose's number.

'Do you have a picture of Kristoffer Dalby, Rose? If you do, could you take a photo of it with your phone and send it to me?'

'No, not of just him. But I have a photocopy of the entire group. Habersaat marked off everyone in the photo that he spoke with, and wrote out their names.'

'All right, so snap a photo and send it to me.'

He turned toward the couple and the cookie jars.

'Good cookies,' said Assad, his hand rotating between the tins.

Carl nodded. 'Yes, and thank you for being so accommodating. It feels very welcoming here, just like at the school. It's been said that it's down to your efforts that the school has become a sort of home away from home for the students during their stay. Everything is there: art on the walls, newly tuned piano, comfortable common room, and rooms that give a special atmosphere. But is there always such a pleasant mood? Aren't there also fights between students and teachers as well as among the students themselves?'

'Yes, of course,' answered the principal. 'But it has always been reserved to petty affairs, I would venture.'

'How was it to lose one of your students in the way you did Alberte?'

'Frightful,' answered the wife. 'Frightful.'

'The school is very old,' continued Carl. 'We saw some pictures that were over a hundred years old.'

'Yes, we celebrated our centenary in November 1993, so you're quite right.'

'Wonderful,' Assad threw in, brushing crumbs from his stubble. 'Have there been any other stories like this in your time?' he continued.

'Stories like this? Erm, we did have a couple of silly incidents of theft a few years back, where a couple of guitars, amplifiers and cameras disappeared. That wasn't at all amusing, but it gave our country policeman, Leif, something to sink his teeth into back at the square in Aakirkeby instead of the usual vandalism in the graveyard and such,' said the lady rector.

'Yes, and then there was the unfortunate business with one of our teachers who died here at the school, of natural causes, but he had an illegal weapon in his room.'

Assad shook his head. 'No, I'm not thinking of that sort of thing. Like the Alberte case, I meant.'

'Fatalities, rapes, serious assault,' elaborated Carl, and nodded to Assad. Excellent turnabout over the cookie crumbs.

'Goodness no, nothing like that. That's to say, there was a girl who tried to commit suicide a few years ago but without success, thank heavens.'

'Troubles of the heart?' Carl scrutinized their faces as they looked questioningly at each other. These two didn't seem to have any reason to hide anything.

'No, I think it had something to do with family back home. Some of our younger students come over here just to escape home. However, they don't always manage to create the desired distance.'

'What about with Alberte? Did she also come here to distance herself from her family?' asked Carl.

'Yes, I suppose she did. Her family was what one might term some-what orthodox. Yes, Alberte was Jewish.' For a moment, he looked almost apologetically at Assad, but he just shrugged his shoulders.

He looked indifferent, however that should be interpreted.

'Yes, she was Jewish and arguably kept on too short a leash. She only ate kosher, so she must've had some orthodox morals and ethics from home.'

'But as far as her emotional life was concerned, she distanced herself from her family?' asked Carl.

The lady rector smiled. 'I think she was as most young girls that age tend to be.'

There was a noise from Carl's pocket. He took out his phone. It was a text from Rose.

'Here he is,' he said, pointing to someone in the group photo. *Fall Semester 1997* was written under a series of handwritten names and arrows pointing to the respective faces. 'He's the one called Kristoffer Dalby. Sitting in the front on the floor.'

The elderly couple squinted. 'It's certainly very small and unclear,' said the man.

'We have the yearbooks in the sitting room. I'm sure Karlo will bring it. Would you, darling?'

Carl nodded as the amenable husband stood up. There was an enlarged photo from the yearbook of decent quality in the folder back in the hotel room. It would've been a good idea to have brought it.

'Shouldn't we look at this one here? It's much bigger,' said Assad, pulling the folder out of his bag.

Why on earth hadn't he done that ages ago? Had he managed to stick home-baked goods in his ears while he'd sat here tucking away?

He winked at Carl, putting his version of the photo on the kitchen table at the same time as the principal came back with his worn example of the yearbook in hand.

'It's him here,' Assad said, putting his finger on a youthful guy wearing an Icelandic sweater and sporting a downy beard.

Two pairs of experienced eyes were furnished with reading glasses and came closer.

'Yes, I remember him, but not very well,' said the rector.

'You don't mean that, Karlo,' the wife shot in, squinting her eyes as her breast began to heave up and down. Was it repressed laughter?

'He was the one who played the trumpet at our hat party. It was so out of tune that the rest of the musicians stopped. Don't you remember?'

Her husband shrugged. Fun and games seemed to be more her department.

She turned to Carl and Assad. 'Kristoffer was sweet. Very shy, but also very sweet in his own way. He lives here on the island. There were a few locals in every group, otherwise they come mostly from Jutland and Zealand, and of course we always have a few foreigners. The Baltic countries are usually overrepresented, as far as I can tell. There were eight to ten from Estonia, Lithuania and Latvia, and then a few Russians that year, too.'

She pointed to a couple of the girls in the photo and then rested her finger on her cheek pensively.

'Was Kristoffer's surname really Dalby? I don't recognize that name in any connection with him. Check the names in the year-book, Karlo.'

His finger ran down the list of names under the photo.

'You're right. His name wasn't Dalby but Studsgaard, of which there are many over here. So I don't know why it says Dalby on the police copy,' said the man.

'Kristoffer Studsgaard, yes, yes, yes!' the wife shouted clearly. '*That* was the name.'

'Well, it seems that while he went to the school he had a short affair with Alberte, if you can call it that. Can you tell us anything about it?' asked Carl.

They couldn't. It was many years ago, and they probably couldn't have commented back then either. They had never really known much about the students' movements outside of school hours.

On the way back to Rønne, Carl called Rose to inform her that she'd have to deal with the packing up herself, which she didn't take especially well. Had it been possible to transmit all the facets of her quivering dissatisfaction over the telephone, they would've been cooked alive.

'We're going to check out this Kristoffer Dalby now, if he's home,' added Carl to change the direction of the conversation. 'There's only one on the island, living just outside Rønne, so that should be easy enough. Afterwards, we'll drive over to June Habersaat's sister in Rønne. You'll manage, Rose,' said Carl.

But she *wasn't* happy.

15

September 2013

Funny sort of epilepsy, thought Wanda. She'd seen epilepsy and then some. From a family of seven children, and among them an ailing and beloved little sister, who suffered almost weekly torments of small focal seizures as well as monthly unconsciousness-inducing seizures, Wanda knew all the signals and aspects of epilepsy. The illness had frightening, paralysing, and grotesque faces, but none of them resembled the one Pirjo had feigned just before.

When Wanda lifted her foot and shifted gears, the woman immediately put her arms around her tightly, so why couldn't Wanda do the same when it had been Pirjo driving? Weird!

Wanda looked down at the hands wrapped around her waist. Small, white hands that radiated a certain age but also innocence and vulnerability, and which were seemingly trembling.

Why were they trembling? Was she scared that they'd swerve and crash? Was she freezing? Or was it her own little personal aftershock from an epileptic attack?

If that was the case, then Wanda had been unfair and the episode just before had been the accidental result of a seizure, even though it didn't seem like it was based on Wanda's experience.

But was she a doctor? And, at the end of the day, had she been there for her little sister when things went wrong? Did she know all the characteristics of these attacks?

She probably didn't, when it came down to it.

'You need to turn right here,' shouted Pirjo.

Wanda put her foot down when they came round the bend and onto the road through the well-grazed moorland. From now on, the woman behind her shouldn't be in any doubt about who was in charge of the speed, so she could just as well get used to it. There couldn't be any shadow of a doubt that her arrival wasn't welcomed by this Pirjo, just as Shirley had predicted. Wanda could feel the instinctive impulse to hit back, but she'd decided to control herself. There were other ways to win this fight.

Wanda had once been the woman who only had the wall to look at, and she wasn't going to be that again. And no one should get in her way.

Wanda decided to take a careful approach when Atu saw her again, going over in her head what she'd say when she found him. How she'd thank him for taking such good care of her in London to remind him of the looks they'd exchanged. That she had come to serve him, and without hope of payment, and that she was trained in sports and could help to get his course participants in shape. Who knew, maybe she could secure a permanent place here for herself straightaway.

'A bit further down and we'll come to the nature reserve, Wanda. To the right the area is called Mysinge Alvar, and to the left Gynge Alvar. That's where Atu probably is.'

She sounded more believable now than before.

Wanda turned her head toward her and saw her smiling face.

Actually, too smiling.

Whenever one of his children had come to him with ulterior motives, Wanda's father had always said, *Your smile is crystal clear but the reason behind it is unclear.* His life experience had long ago taught him that certain special smiles cost more than others. Sometimes a few coins, sometimes substantial concessions or indulgences.

And it was one such special crystal clear smile that Wanda saw on Pirjo's face. The question was why. She didn't like it.

She sped up and tilted her head back, so the wind tickled her scalp. Like all Jamaican women with an ounce of respect for themselves or their religion, her dreadlocks were carefully and tightly braided so that her hair shone and appeared sculptural. For Wanda, hair was an invitation to be touched, and she could still feel Atu's hands from that day in London when they gently and sensually brushed over it. She wanted to experience that feeling again, and right now it was her driving force.

'Park over by the sign on the wall,' said Pirjo, pointing over Wanda's shoulder, and pulling the keys from the exhaust before Wanda could react. It seemed like a reflex because she was apparently more concerned just now with one of her feet.

'I twisted my foot when we fell so I don't think I can go out there with you,' she continued, pointing toward a stone-covered path that disappeared off in the flat landscape. 'You aren't allowed to drive motorized vehicles in Alvaret, but you just need to follow the path a kilometre or two before you'll find Atu, if he's there, which he probably is. There are so many legends about this area, and Atu collects energy out here as he melts together with the weatherworn landscape. It tends to be beautiful and colourful, but at this time of year you won't find so many orchids, even though that's what defines the area. Really fascinating, isn't it?'

Pirjo turned toward the scooter, but evidently thought of something and turned around again.

'In order to catch the train back to Copenhagen you need to be back here in an hour and a half. The walk out to where Atu will be doesn't take more than a good fifteen minutes, so you'll be fine for time.'

Pirjo sounded totally trustworthy now. Maybe she was adjusting herself to the new state of things. In that case, Wanda would also be able to show magnanimity. After all, she understood the woman and her situation perfectly. Everything would sort itself out when she became Atu's chosen one. Even the situation with Pirjo.

Wanda felt a rush in her stomach. Fifteen minutes the woman had said, and then she would meet him.

For Wanda, who had lived for most of her life in an exotic and lush climate with both rainforests and savannah, this barren landscape was the most colourless she'd ever witnessed. In the outermost part of the moor there was admittedly a hint of green, but after a while both the grass and cobbles disappeared from the path, replaced by an indefinable whitish layer reminiscent of salt or chalk. Along the side of the path, the colours of the dead plains in arid tones changed from withered green to brown and white, and neither birds nor insects were to be seen. It was a lonely place, which reminded her of the time she stood, day in and day out, as a door guard. There wasn't any human contact here either.

She smiled. It was at least different here, not the marble-covered back entrance of 80 Strand, but earth and sky and life-giving air.

She thought that if Atu could find peace out here, then she could, too. But she also wondered if she would find him and puzzled over where someone could hide in this flat nothingness.

She scanned back and forth and considered her options. A few hundred metres further ahead low bushes and reedlike grasses swayed in the wind. A way off to the side, rainwater lakes had accumulated between scattered areas of grass on the stone-hard ground, and if you looked closer, it looked as if footprints led over there.

Wanda wasn't sure; she wasn't exactly a specialist. As far as she knew, the prints could just as well be from animals as from humans, and they could be from yesterday or from months ago for that matter. Nevertheless, she went in that direction.

'Atu, are you out here?' she shouted a few times in the direction of the vegetation without any answer.

A misgiving about what was going on came rushing to her again.

Shit! So the stupid bitch had won the first hand anyway. The woman had lured her out here and no doubt left by now.

'I shouldn't have left her with the keys to the scooter,' she whispered. 'That was stupid, Wanda.'

She shook her head at herself, turned around, and went a few hundred metres, cursing her naivete.

Then she heard a sound like distant thunder rolling over the landscape.

Wanda looked up. The sky was a bit grey but the drifting clouds didn't appear threatening or heavy with rain. Was the sound coming down from the highway? It would be strange if you could hear it all the way up here.

She shook her head and shouted Atu's name again a few times, now sure that she'd been tricked and that the road back to some random person who could help her to Kalmar and the hotel would be tiring and long.

'But just you wait, Pirjo! Tomorrow I'll take a taxi to the Nature Absorption Academy, and then we'll see what your next move will be,' she mumbled. 'No matter what you do, it'll only end up hurting yourself.'

Even though she was now behind in the game, the game was still hers, she reasoned to herself when suddenly the indefinable noise sounded much closer.

Wanda squinted her eyes and stood on tiptoe. Now she heard what it was.

A ticking noise from a scooter coming towards her.

Wanda wondered if Pirjo had had second thoughts and ignored the ban on motor vehicles in order to drive out and meet her. No doubt arriving with some story that she'd had contact with Atu and that he wasn't in a position to meet Wanda where he was. Yes, that's what she'd be up to. But this time she wouldn't pull the wool over her eyes.

Wanda decided that she'd just come straight out and tell her that she didn't believe her. When you did that, the person's face tended to give away the truth.

She stopped, standing completely still, watching the yellow blob moving ever closer to her, getting bigger and bigger, stirring up dust in its wake. Now she could see Pirjo sitting up on the scooter with both hands on the handlebars. There couldn't be any doubt that she'd already seen Wanda out in the open and would soon pick her up.

Wanda waved to her but Pirjo didn't wave back.

Poor woman, thought Wanda, feeling a momentary tinge of compassion for her as she realized Pirjo just didn't know what to do to get rid of her.

It was only when there were twenty metres between them and

she could clearly see Pirjo's face that Wanda realized she was mistaken. Pirjo knew exactly what to do.

Wanda's pulse raced as the thought ran through her head that the woman was crazy and wanted to kill her.

And then she ran.

The ground underneath her quickly became swampy. Wanda wondered if she should keep going in this wet earth and hope Pirjo became stuck. She could only hope that the surface would stop the scooter, but nothing indicated that. Just now the sound from the scooter was so loud that she could only be a few metres behind her.

With a jerk she jumped to the side, landing in the split second where the heat from the scooter hit her, and the would-be yellow death-trap roared past. Pirjo's expression was one of frustration, but also cold and hard. Nothing would get in her way. That was clear enough.

Then she thrust her feet hard in the ground and spun the scooter round on itself, throwing up mud and earth from the rear wheel.

Pirjo thought she could catch her without any effort but she was about to realize that this was the fastest woman she had ever met in her life, thought Wanda as she stepped out of her shoes and accelerated in her bare feet.

But the speed wasn't enough.

Wanda's specialty on the ash track of the national stadium had been the four hundred and eight hundred metres, and at those distances she felt she was totally in symbiosis with the ground, her breathing and the flailing arms of her competitors. In front of her here, the ground was uneven, unpredictable, and full of pebbles that made her forward leaps painful and so uncertain that she was in danger of twisting her ankle at any moment.

Wanda knew that she couldn't keep this up for long, her pulse racing faster and faster as she decided that if Pirjo saw this as a hunt to the death, then she'd just have to turn the tables so she was the matador and Pirjo the bull.

She sensed the scooter right behind her again. The screeching of a motor in low gear enveloped her, signalling danger, but she wasn't afraid.

Wanda thought about how she would jump to the side just like before and then, when Pirjo passed, swing her arm out towards her head and knock her off. But she knew she had to be careful that the scooter didn't hit her, especially as the ground was becoming softer underfoot.

It was only in the second before the scooter reached her that she turned her head.

Realizing it was now or never, she jumped to the side for the second time and stopped.

As she lifted her arm to take a swipe, she saw Pirjo's crazy expression and a small, compact spade in her hand being swung right at her face.

That was the last she saw.

16

Friday, May 2nd, 2014

'Let's check the tree on Skørrebrovejen, Assad, it should be here near the highway.' He pointed at a cross on the map. It wasn't far from Aakirkeby.

'OK, but shouldn't we take the backside, so we can follow the same route as the guy who drove into her?'

'The back road, Assad, not backside. Yeah, but can *you* work out the route?' He looked down at the map and watched as Assad's finger moved over it as he described the way. It looked right enough.

'First, we drive out of Vesterbro in Aakirkeby. Then we take Rønnevej, then right at Vestermarievej. From there he could have driven down Kærgårdsvej, but I don't think he did do that. I think he drove right down to Skørrebrovejen and then right along it at full speed, because it was down there at the end where the old couple lived who heard the car.'

'Yes, but strictly speaking he could've come from the north and *then* turned down onto Skørrebrovejen, Assad, but that's irrelevant if he came from Vestermarievej, like you said.'

'He almost can't have driven any other way.'

Carl nodded.

When they turned up the road from the south, Carl stepped on it. Looking toward the first bend at the farm, where the old couple lived, there was a good six hundred metres, and further up to the tree along the fields another one and a half kilometres. It was a godforsaken place that made you want to hit the gas.

The tyres screeched as they ploughed round the bend. There couldn't be any doubt that a noise like that could be heard in the house where the old couple had lived.

'This spot right here is as flat as a pancake, Carl. So if Alberte was waiting with her bike up there at the end of the road, she would've been able to see the car very clearly for the last five to six hundred metres.'

'Yes, and what does that tell you?'

'I don't know. Maybe that she'd been waiting for that car and maybe she also recognized it, and that the last thing she would've expected was that it would drive directly into her.'

Carl looked at him. Not far off what he thought.

'Do you mind slowing down a bit?' said Assad with an apprehensive eye on the speedometer. Carl nodded, but increased speed to a hundred kilometres an hour. If it was going to have an impact, there needed to be some force behind it.

Just before they reached the cluster of trees further up, the car swerved. He heard Assad shout something or other in Arabic but Carl had enough to think about. The entire car shook as it grazed the edge of the ditch and swerved from side to side over the verge. He slammed on the brakes. Thirty metres, and the car came to a halt leaving a trail of skid marks as black as coal in its wake.

'I almost swallowed my tongue there, Carl. You'd better not do that again.'

Carl bit his top lip. There were only two options left.

'There were no visible skid marks after the accident, were there?'

'There was nothing even resembling them found anywhere.'

'Then the vehicle couldn't have driven as fast on the bend as I did, could it?'

'Thank God for the person driving,' replied his passenger.

'Then it must've been murder, right?'

'Looks like it.'

'Yes, because the car only sped up after the bend, it's the only possibility. And as Alberte stood on this side of the trees – otherwise she would have been thrown in the other direction, away from the tree – the driver can't claim not to have seen her. He certainly had enough time.'

'It could've been an idiot who wasn't watching the road, Carl, couldn't it?'

'Then Alberte would just have moved into the kerb and nothing would have happened. No, she didn't harbour any misgivings about the person approaching her. Something or other led her to think about anything other than danger.'

A rasping sound came from Assad's stubble.

'Are you thinking that he didn't drive so fast?'

'Fast, yes. But only in relation to the circumstances and the characteristics of the road. Maybe somewhere between seventy and eighty kilometres an hour, I reckon.'

They both looked up at the trees. It was as if Alberte was hanging up there, nodding down at them.

Carl looked away. Why was he trying to keep his guard up in this case? Why fight it?

He observed Assad's strange eyes. They seemed sad, and yet his face shone with determination. All three of them from Department Q were in agreement. This case had to be solved.

'Yes, that's it,' Carl said quietly. 'We're going to have to get that bastard.'

They stepped out of the car and could see why the girl hadn't initially been spotted hanging up there during the investigation, despite the fact that the leaves of the three trees, the tops of which supported each other, would already have fallen at the time.

'What's that greenery covering the top, Carl?'

'Some sort of parasitic plant, I think. Ivy perhaps.'

Assad nodded, impressed at the comment. Botany definitely wasn't one of his strong points.

'It almost looks as if the trees have already got leaves on them, Carl.'

They walked around the cluster of trees, looking up. From each of the roots, several strong trunks sprung up, dividing further into numerous forked branches. Plenty of opportunity for Alberte's body to be wedged there.

'She hung up there in one of the lower forks, approximately four metres up. She must've rotated in the air, seeing as she came to hang with her head facing down, wouldn't you agree, Assad?'

He nodded and tried to put himself in the situation.

'Habersaat was driving from the direction of the main road when he found her,' he said. 'So he was coming from the wrong side, where it was most difficult to see her through all the ivy or whatnot. It was lucky that he saw her at all.'

'Lucky? Well, maybe. Just not for him.'

Assad waved Carl over to him. On the other side of the trees, a dirt track in the field led down to a farm a few hundred metres away. On the opposite side, close to the highway in the direction of the main road, there was a yellow building, the main part of yet another farm. Other than that, there was no sign of civilization nearby.

'It was in there they found the bike, Carl,' he said, pointing across the track towards a tight green carpet of undergrowth below yet another group of trees. Strange that the bike had been flung so far.

'Are we thinking the same thing, Assad?'

'I don't know but I'm certainly thinking that it must've been a strange car that could throw her up in that way.'

'And the bike?'

'I think she'd left it supported on its pop stand and went to meet the car. That the vehicle hit the bike just after it hit the girl, and that it was thrown up in the air just like her, but only more askew.'

'Prop stand, Assad, not pop stand. And yes, I think so, too.'

They stood for a moment, each trying to imagine the scene. The vehicle that had come thundering past the farm a kilometre and a half from here. How the driver had become more and more determined that this was just something they needed to get out of the way. And then the bend further up and the decrease in speed.

'I think the driver and Alberte make eye contact at the bend,' said Carl. 'She's put the bike on the prop stand behind her and steps forward. Maybe she waves. She's happy and smiling, a smile she takes with her to the death. I don't think she's scared because she's happy and expectant. Then, only at the last minute, the vehicle speeds up and rams her, causing her to be hurled from the road and up into the branches. The driver straightens up the vehicle immediately, but clips the bike anyway a bit further up the road, maybe with the side of the vehicle. That's why the bike ends up a good bit over to the right.'

Carl looked again up at the road from the direction the vehicle had come in. 'It's very possible that the driver's foot hasn't been on the brake at all most of the way, only easing up on the gas after the event. Cruising past the yellow farm on his left at a more normal speed before finally sliding up towards the transverse Almindingensvej and away. Do you agree, Assad?'

'Damn bastard,' he mumbled. So he did agree, then. 'What sort of car could hurl her all the way up there when going so slowly?' he continued, looking up.

'I don't know, Assad. A snowplough could manage, but it wasn't winter yet, and even if such a big boy had driven past, she would've moved out of the way of it. But the vehicle that hit her was definitely specially adapted, you're right about that.'

'Then why didn't they find it? They looked all over the island. And even though they only had video surveillance for ferry departures on the first two days after the incident, a vehicle like that would've been noticed driving on deck, wouldn't it?'

'Yes, unless what shovelled Alberte up into the tree was something that could be removed and got rid of, Assad.'

'Yes, but what? Are you also thinking about the VW Kombi?'

'Of course I am.'

'There must have been something on the front, resting on that weird fender, because it couldn't have been up to it on its own.'

'No, it probably couldn't. We'll have to ask the technicians.'

Carl looked up again at the treetops, imagining the outline of that young dead girl. He momentarily felt melancholy but also a sense of reverence, as if standing on holy ground. Had he been Catholic, he'd probably have crossed himself, but he was far from being that, which in its own way felt both empty and sad.

He looked at Assad, who was standing with his back to him. 'Tell me, Assad, do Muslims have something they can honour the dead with, a prayer or something?'

Assad slowly turned around to face him.

'It's done, Carl. It's already done.'

And while the fields and shady groves were left behind them, Carl imagined the beautiful young Alberte cycling over there on the other side of the road with her hair flowing and expectant face en route to her death.

'Kristoffer Dalby lives over in Vestermarie. So we need to go the same way back and then a bit further on,' said Assad, moving his phone away from his ear. 'That was Detective Jonas Ravnå I was just talking with and he says that Dalby is a schoolteacher now. And then he told me something else, which I'm not sure is so good.'

'Oh, what's that?'

'They've found the bike.'

'OK. Isn't that good?'

'Yes, but it turns out that they'd kept it for ten years before just throwing it out. On February 25th, 2008, to be exact.'

'Isn't it irrelevant that they did that? They've found it again.'

'Yes, but it was more than likely a coincidence. One of the locals, back in 2008, knew that it was Alberte's bike lying in the pile of junk. He recognized it from the newspaper and that's why he took it.'

'I don't understand where you're going with this.'

'He took it because it was special and had a special history to it. So he welded it into a scrap sculpture, which he called . . .' He looked down at his paper. '. . . Fateopia.'

'God almighty! And where is this so-called artwork now?'

'We were lucky there because he's just had it in an exhibition in Verona, but now it's back home again.'

'And where is *home*?'

'In Lyngby. Strange, right? You race through there every day when you drive home from the station.'

They found the way down to the smallholding where Kristoffer Dalby lived, north-west of the small cluster of houses known as Vestermarie. The plot where the house was situated was probably the smallest for miles around, but still there were swings, slides and sandpits enough for an entire army.

'Do you think we've taken a wrong turn?' asked Assad.

Carl looked at the GPS and shook his head. He pointed out of the window at the postbox on the side of the road. *Kristoffer and Inge Dalby* and a small sticker underneath adding *Mathias and Camilla*.

They rang the doorbell, noticing at least fifty cigarette butts in a small bucket by the side of the doorstep. Someone's kept under the thumb here, thought Carl, as they heard movement from behind the door.

'We'll cut straight to the chase, Assad,' he managed to say before a man opened up.

There was no doubt that it was Kristoffer Dalby standing there, supposed master of the house, despite a bit more meat on his bones, wispy beard with grey touches to it and worn-out shoes. Probably not someone Alberte would fall for if she'd been alive today.

His good-natured expression collapsed when they told him why they were there, and all Carl's warning lights flashed. He observed from Assad's expression that he'd also noticed it.

A typical reaction from those with more to hide than was good for them.

'You've been expecting us?' said Carl.

'I don't know what you mean.'

'I can see that it's shocked you that we've come here on this business, so we assume it's something you've been dreading. Is it something you've been thinking about for almost twenty years, Kristoffer?'

All his features suddenly shrunk. Pinched lips and squinting eyes, cheeks sucked in. A very peculiar reaction.

'Come inside,' he said unwelcomingly.

He pointed to a chair between a sea of wooden toys on a play mat decorated with roads, crossroads, and houses. It was a real hotchpotch in every possible colour, and over on the windowsill lay the trumpet he'd once tried to charm the crowds with.

It was covered in dust now.

'Do you have a lot of children?' asked Assad.

He tried to smile but without success. 'We have two, but they've left home for now. My wife's a childminder,' he answered.

'Oh, right! Yes, well, we don't want to waste anyone's time so we'll get straight to the point, Kristoffer,' said Assad. 'Why aren't you called Studsgaard any more? Did you think that something as simple as a change of name would make it difficult for us to find you? Then you shouldn't have found a house so close to the school, should you?'

It was a bit of a gamble, but why waste time.

Carl looked around. Two older teenagers in a photo frame on top of a monstrosity of an analogue TV. Masses of VHS cartoons on the shelf. Strange to think that you could still find them.

'I don't know what you mean. I changed names because my wife didn't want to be called Studsgaard, so I took hers.'

'Listen here, Kristoffer. We know that you once had a thing with Alberte, so you won't deny it now, will you?' said Carl.

He looked across the floor with his head at an angle. 'No. It's true that Alberte and I had something together, but it was honestly perfectly innocent and didn't last for more than a couple of weeks.'

'But you were really in love with her, right, Kristoffer?' asked Assad.

He nodded. 'Yes, I suppose I was. Alberte was amazingly sweet and beautiful, so—'

'So you killed her when she decided she'd rather be with someone else, right?' Assad threw in.

He looked confused now. 'No, not at all.'

'So you weren't particularly sorry when she didn't want to be with you any more?' he pressed.

'Yes, of course I was. But it's a little complicated, you see.'

'Complicated how?' asked Carl. 'Can you tell us why you think that?'

'My wife'll be home in a minute and we're going through a bit of a rough patch at the moment, so I'd appreciate it if we could hurry this along.'

'Why, Kristoffer? Haven't you told your wife everything? Or does she know something that she maybe shouldn't. Have you confided in her, is that it? Are you scared about her reaction?'

'No, no, we're just going through a bit of a rough patch where . . . Listen, OK, we have two kids who are away at a residential school just now and, to put it bluntly, they're not damn well coping too good. So things aren't so happy on the home front, can you understand that?'

'What's that got to do with you and Alberte? Why can't your wife hear it?'

He sighed. 'Inge and I had already started dating back in spring 1997, so we'd been together for almost half a year when we went to the folk high school, and then Alberte came on the scene, so that's why! I don't want to dig all this up. Not just now anyway.'

'I see. So that means that Alberte bagged Inge's guy from right under her nose?'

He nodded almost imperceptibly. 'It made her feel completely miserable, and still can. I betrayed Inge back then and she'll never forget it.'

'She didn't just hate you then, but Alberte, too?' concluded Carl. He turned to Assad. 'What does the report say? Has Inge Dalby been questioned in connection with the murder of Alberte?'

'Murder?' Kristoffer Dalby moved forward to the edge of his seat. 'It was an accident. It said so everywhere.'

'Yes, but we have a slightly different theory. What about it then, Assad, has she been questioned?' he repeated.

Assad shook his head. 'There wasn't anyone called Inge Dalby in that group.'

The schoolteacher shook his head. 'Nonsense, she was there . . .' He stopped midsentence and nodded briefly. 'No, that's right. She was called Inge Kure back then, but she preferred her mother's maiden name. There are so many called Kure, Studsgaard, Pihl and Kofoed over here on the island, but you'll know all about that. So we agreed that we'd rather have a less common surname when we got married, that's all.'

Assad took out the folder, laid the yearbook with the group picture on the coffee table in front of him and went through the names underneath. 'Inge Kure, hmm. Yes, there she is. She's up here behind Alberte.'

Carl leaned closer. A slightly plump girl with dark curly hair. Very plain, not particularly pretty. An absolute contrast to the angel sitting in the front row lighting up the whole scene.

Assad flicked through the pages. 'Regardless, we'll have to talk to your wife,' he said.

Dalby sighed and bit his cheek, offering reassurances that neither of them had anything to do with Alberte's death. Alberte was just the girl in the group whom all the boys were crazy about, and for that reason she annoyed most of the girls. Alberte was popular enough, but all the same her presence disturbed the harmony that exists if everyone has roughly the same chances, romantically speaking. That's how he expressed it. It seemed rehearsed.

'Were you bitter that Alberte left you?' asked Carl.

'Bitter? No, I probably would've been if she'd found another guy at the school, but that's not how it was.'

'Did Inge just take you back, then?' asked Assad.

He nodded and sighed. Could it be a decision that he'd since come to regret?

'So Alberte found a new guy outside the school? Who was he?' asked Carl.

'I don't know, really, but Alberte mentioned that it was someone who lived in a commune at Ølene. I wasn't really told anything else. I don't think anyone at the school was.' So that was how Habersaat had found the lead about the commune. 'He was apparently a bit of a Don Juan,' continued Kristoffer.

'How do you mean? Was he involved with someone else at the school?'

'Err, no. Not as far as I know anyway.'

'So how do you know that he was a bit of a Don Juan?'

'I don't know. It's probably just how I pictured him, given that he could just run off with Alberte.'

'You never saw him?'

He shook his head.

'You're sure? Check here!' Assad put the photo of the man getting out of the VW Kombi in front of him. 'You didn't see this guy? Maybe you saw him waiting for Alberte outside the school?'

Kristoffer picked the photo up and fumbled about for a pair of reading glasses in his breast pocket. Carl looked at Assad, who shrugged his shoulders. Yes, he'd seen correctly. Kristoffer Dalby's reactions just now seemed both logical and understandable. His subdued manner and fear about digging up a past betrayal could explain his reaction when they rang the doorbell.

'The photo is really unclear, but no, I don't think I've seen him before. But I can tell you that I often saw a VW like that parked a little way down on the highway by the folk high school. I never saw it from the front, but the one that used to be there was definitely light blue like this one, and as far as I can remember, it also had dark-tinted side windows.'

Insanely well remembered after so many years. Suspicion began to gnaw away at them again.

They heard rustling out in the corridor and Dalby's expression changed.

'Who's visiting?' shouted a woman's voice from out in the corridor. 'I don't recognize the six-oh-seven out there. Has Ove been fobbed off with another old heap of junk?'

A hefty woman appeared in the doorway. Very difficult to recognize from the group picture on the table.

She frowned and let her eyes move from Kristoffer's bowed head to the two strange men and down to the coffee table with the case folder and yearbook from the folk high school.

'Is this that old case coming up again?' She looked hostilely at her husband. 'What is it *now*, Kristoffer? Will we never have peace from that bitch?'

Carl introduced both himself and Assad and explained the reason why they were on the case.

'Habersaat, you're kidding me! The man who blew his brains out, how pathetic can you be? Even when he's dead he's irritating,' she snorted. 'I was certain that now he was gone, Alberte would be, too.'

'You hated her, didn't you, Inge?'

'Not like you think. And not like Habersaat thought, either. But ever since Alberte turned up at the school things were never the same again, and if you should get the strange idea that I was happy about that then you're definitely very much mistaken.'

'We'd like to have your version of the story. Is that OK with you?'

She looked away, so it obviously wasn't.

But she told it anyway.

17

In the beginning, everyone liked Alberte. She'd doled out generous hugs, and she was the one who waltzed from house to house larking about, and who could make the girls scream with laughter. To begin with, that is, but then things changed. Her inconsideration for the other girls who had their own dreams about the boys at the school was ruinous. Not because anyone ever suspected her of wanting to hurt someone; she was just thoughtless.

She could say things like, *Niels is so hot, don't you think?* while one of the girls in the back of the class sighed. It was her guy's turn.

And Alberte's eyes could sparkle when she talked about the kisses she'd received. She could talk about the boys' hot breath and scent without giving a thought to the fact that it might hurt other people.

She was called spoiled and accused of being used to getting whatever she pointed at. But that wasn't true, or at least Inge knew it wasn't.

The truth was that Alberte didn't need to point at something to get it. It came of its own accord.

And that was the cause of Inge's bitterness. She wasn't going to deny that. Not because Alberte took her boyfriend from her, but because he offered himself, and that fact stayed with her, eating away at her even now, seventeen years later.

Carl glanced over at Inge's husband, sitting passively, huddled on the sofa opposite them with his eyes lowered. Obviously Alberte had had a magical form of sensuality that no one could match, and a dangerous form at that.

'Inge, I asked your husband if he knew the name of a guy that Alberte was seeing up until her death. Are you familiar with that name?'

'I was asked that at least ten times by Christian Habersaat back when he did his rounds at the school. We'd already told the police in Rønne, but Habersaat wanted to hear it again. He always did. I said that Alberte had mentioned it once because she thought it sounded so exotic. But I couldn't really remember it then, and not at all now.'

'Not at all?'

'No. Nothing other than that there were several names, and that it sounded weird together. The first was shorter than the others. Something biblical about it.'

'Short, how? Like Adam?'

'No, maybe only three letters, but to be quite honest I don't want to think about it.'

'Lot, Sem, Job, Eli, Koa, Gad, Set, Asa,' fired off Assad.

How the heck could he, a Muslim nonetheless, sit there and recite that litany?

'No, I don't think it was any of those. As I said, I don't really want to think about it.'

'And the other names?' insisted Carl.

'No idea. Something crazy, like I said before. Like Simsalabimkruttelutski.' She smiled. She had reason to.

'So you know absolutely nothing more about him? Are you sure?'

'Yes, nothing else other than that he apparently came from Copenhagen. He definitely wasn't from Bornholm, or Jutland for that matter, as far as I knew. Then there was the VW of course, which Kristoffer and I have spoken about together.'

'This one?' Assad pushed the photo from the parking area over to her.

She looked at it for a moment. 'The same colour and shape at least. But you can't really see it clearly.'

'Can you remember any details about it?'

'Details? I did only see it from behind and from a distance up on the road.'

'Maybe some larger dents or scratches, colour of the licence plate, curtains in the windows? Anything significant?'

She smiled. 'The windows were matt, and I think the licence plate was one of the old-fashioned types, black with white numbering, and then a sort of black curved line that looked like it came up from the roof, and I think it had white on the tyres, a sort of broad streak round the hubcap, but I can't be sure. It could also be another car I saw up on the road.'

'A curved line, you said?'

'I don't know if it was dirt or . . .' She turned to her husband. 'Can you remember anything about it, Kristoffer?'

He shook his head.

OK, black licence plates. At least they knew that the vehicle was registered before 1976, whatever help that might be.

'What do you say, Carl? Are the Dalbys off the hook?'

Carl changed gears a couple of times before answering.

'The question for me is who on earth Alberte was, Assad. That's what I'm thinking about just now. I'll have an answer to your question when we know a bit more about Alberte. Inge Dalby is definitely a very tough and angry woman, but she seems otherwise down-to-earth, so I don't suspect her of anything particular just now. And then there's Kristoffer. He's a slowpoke, standing and smoking on the doorstep, and he'll never dare to stand up to his wife. Could he be fiery enough to commit a crime of passion? I don't really think so.'

'Don't you think it strange that he could remember that a VW had dark-tinted windows so many years later? And that she remembered that it had white tyres, a line on the side and black licence plates? Would you have been able to remember that?'

Carl shrugged. He allowed himself to believe he would.

'Just a minute, aren't we going in the wrong direction? Aren't we going to the nursing home in Rønne to visit June's sister?' asked Assad.

'Yes, but I'm thinking we should find that place called Ølene first. There might be someone who lived there at the time and who can remember the hippies.'

'Don't you think Habersaat did what he could in that area?'

'Yes, but the question is whether or not he did it well enough. He's sort of given us several hints that we should concentrate our efforts on the man in the enlarged version of the photo back at his house, right? So I'm trying to picture it all and work out what kind of man we're dealing with, because I sure as hell can't just now, Assad.'

The distance was greater than Carl had reckoned, and the sun was already fading. Even though there was at least an hour and a half until it set, the shadows were long and the colours had been sucked out of the landscape.

'There are a lot of trees here, Carl. Do you have any idea where we're heading?'

He shook his head. 'Call Jonas Ravnå. He'll know where to find it.'

'It's almost six. He won't be on call any more.'

'Try. You've got his number, and put the speakerphone on.'

People obviously ate early in these parts, so Ravnå didn't exactly sound happy about being disturbed. Didn't they have a GPS – couldn't they use it?

Despite himself, he took pity on them and explained to Carl that they needed to find the path to Øle Brook, which went from Ølenevej just across from the signpost for the national park. You couldn't miss it. An image of a bird with the less-than-welcoming message *Zutritt Verboten* written underneath.

Ølenevej meandered up and down, but they found the sign opposite another and somewhat smaller sign pointing toward Øle brook path, a cul-de-sac with what appeared to be an abandoned house with a barn and accompanying lawn.

'Strange place. What do you make of it, Carl?' asked Assad when they'd crawled out of the car.

Carl shook his head. It was hard to imagine a hippy camp in this anaemic-looking place.

'Maybe that man there can tell us something.' Carl pointed towards a blot on the path that was toiling closer.

They waited for a minute before a male figure in shorts and a good seventy-five years behind him trudged towards them at what the man himself would no doubt have described as a jog.

He didn't look like stopping, maybe because he knew it would be difficult to get going again, but decided to stop all the same, arms at his side and gasping, before he finally composed himself enough to reciprocate their acknowledgment.

'Well done, my man,' said Carl, referring both to the man's age and sporting efforts.

'Yes, you have to get fit before you hit sixty,' he answered, out of breath and with a thick accent.

Only sixty? Bloody hell. They'd better send him off on his way again immediately.

'Do you live nearby?' asked Carl.

'No, no, I live in Hamburg. I've just strayed a bit too far from home. I shouldn't have turned right so late.'

Assad laughed. So there were two present who understood that sort of humour.

'I assume you know a bit about the history of this area?'

'What do you want to know?'

Carl pointed to the abandoned building and let him in on their story.

'We've been asked about that hundreds of times before by that meddlesome policeman from Svaneke,' he answered. 'But yes, some young people lived here for about half a year. The former owner didn't look too closely at how he earned his money.'

'Why do you say that?'

'Because there were a load of hippies who didn't belong here. Gaudy clothes and big hair. And they went about doing a lot of strange things.'

'Like what, for example?'

'Running about waving their arms at the sun. Lighting fires in the evening and running around it, sometimes completely naked and in that mystical way. Not something the rest of us would do,' he said with a twisted smile.

'Mystical?'

'Yes, they painted their bodies with symbols and chanted as if they were Catholics. Some said they were Asa followers, believers in the Norse gods, but those of us here just thought they were crazy like so many other tourists.'

'Interesting. What sort of symbols?'

'No idea. Just some sort of gibberish.' His face lit up. 'Almost like Indians.'

'Strange.'

'Yes, they also had a large sign hanging above the main door. *The Celestial Sphere*, I think it said.'

'But they didn't proselytize or cause trouble in the area?'

'No, no, they were very nice and peaceful in their own way. Just a bit cuckoo, as they say.'

Carl pointed to Assad's bag, and the photo of the man with the VW Kombi was produced.

'And this man here? Do you recognize him?' asked Assad.

'Oh yes, the policeman had this photo with him every time as well. I *have* said that they had an identical van, but that I have no idea who the man is. I didn't see those sorts of people now, did I?'

'So you didn't gasp about jogging in those days, then?'

'God, no. Why do you think I need to do it now?'

They got a few additional details. Yes, the licence plates were black, and yes, there was a curved line on the top of each side of the van, but otherwise nothing noticeable in terms of markings, dents or scratches. And yes, there had been about nine to ten young people on the site, four to five of each sex. Then one day they were just gone. That's the way it was, and since then the owner had only taken Germans. They brought more coins in to the coffers.

'Could you or others confirm the date of their departure from here? Was it around the time of the search for Alberte Goldschmid?'

'No idea, but in my case, no. I'm away a lot, and was at that time.

I'm a biochemist specializing in enzymes, and was in Groningen on a research trip. It was about the manufacture of potato flour, if you must know,' he said, laughing.

Assad's eyes popped. 'Potato flour! Really, that *is* good. When you have a camel with saddle sore, you . . .'

'Thank you. I don't think the camels are something for this gentleman right now.' He turned to face the man. 'And your former neighbour who rented the house out? Surely he must know exactly when they split from the place?'

'Him! He knew damn all. He lived in a completely different part of the island. As long as he got his rent, he left people to their own devices.'

He told them his name, got himself together and trudged on with his bellows working overtime.

'I think we need to make a start on familiarizing ourselves with the investigation team's files and not least Habersaat's private records. There seem to be many things we could've read about instead of knocking about here in the sticks.'

'What's that about sticks?'

'Forget it. It's just a saying.'

The nursing home where June Habersaat's sister lived, Snorrebakken, was a nightmare of sparkling glass and grey plastered walls. A shiny newbuild in every conceivable way. Seen from the outside, it would've been a perfect location to house an extortionately expensive accountancy firm or a private plastic-surgery clinic. Not exactly what you'd imagine to be a municipal setting for the last stop in life.

'Karin Kofoed has become a little slow on the uptake,' informed the nursing assistant, ushering them in. 'Unfortunately, the dementia and Alzheimer's have combined, but if you stick to one subject at a time, she sometimes has her better moments.'

June Habersaat's sister sat huddled up with dancing arm movements in her armchair. The smile seemed frozen in time, but the hands were lively enough, as if directing a symphony orchestra in a fictional concert.

'I'll leave you alone awhile, otherwise I'll take all her attention,' the nursing assistant said with a smile.

They sat opposite her on a narrow sofa and waited until her eyes met them of their own accord.

'Karin, we'd like to talk to you a little about Christian Habersaat and his investigation,' Carl said finally.

She nodded and was gone again. Sat for a moment staring at her outstretched fingers and turned towards them, perhaps a little more present.

'Because . . . Bjarke!' she stated.

Carl and Assad looked at each other. This wasn't going to be easy.

'Yes, Bjarke isn't here any more, that's right. But it isn't because of him we want to talk about Christian.'

'Bjarke's my nephew, he plays football.' She paused. 'No, he doesn't actually. What's it called?'

'Bjarke and your sister June and you used to live together, we've been told.' Assad shifted himself to the edge of the sofa so they were closer. 'It was back when June and Christian got divorced and she was seeing another man. Back when you lived together many years ago. Do you remember?'

A worried fold cut across her smooth forehead. 'June. She's angry with me.'

'With you, Karin? Wasn't it with Christian?' Now Carl moved closer, too.

For a moment they lost her again. She looked out of the window, tilted her head up and down a little, as if answering herself in an inner monologue. Her hands shook slightly. Then the wrinkle in her brow disappeared, and her body relaxed. It didn't seem to lead anywhere.

'Did June complain about Christian's investigation, Karin, can you remember that?'

There was no doubt that the question had reached her as she turned towards him with expressive eyes. But there was no answer.

'Bjarke's dead. He's dead,' she repeated a few times, her hands rotating in front of her again.

Assad and Carl looked at each other. It would be totally coincidental if they got any relevant answer from her, so they might as well shoot from the hip. Carl gave Assad the nod, and with that he pulled out the photo of the man with the VW Kombi.

'Have you heard Christian or June talk about the man in this picture?' asked Carl. It was a gamble.

'The handsome one with long hair,' added Assad.

She looked at them, confused. 'Bjarke had long hair. Always long hair,' she said. 'Like the man.'

'Yes, the man. Did anyone mention anything about him?' Carl attempted to keep on track.

She seemingly tried to focus on what his finger pointed at, but nothing happened.

'Can you remember his name, Karin? Was it Lot?'

She tilted her head back and laughed openmouthedly. 'Lot! His wife was turned to a pillar of salt. Can you remember that?'

Carl looked at Assad. 'I think we'll take a break. What do you think?'

He shook his head in resignation. There didn't seem to be a suitable camel joke for the occasion.

'We'll call June Habersaat and cut right to the chase about the guy in the picture. She can't do anything other than put the phone down.'

Assad nodded thoughtfully, putting his foot up on the dashboard.

'She will, and that's a guarantee. Maybe we should drive back instead and confront her with the photo in a surprise attack.'

Carl frowned. Drive back to Aakirkeby? Over his dead body. He dialed June Habersaat's number and got a voice at the other end that could shatter glass.

'Sorry to trouble you again, June. I don't mean to bother you. We've just come from the nursing home where your sister is. She said to say hello. We've spoken a little with her about the old days, you know, and in connection with that we'd like to ask you some questions regarding your knowledge of a young long-haired man that used to drive around the island in a light blue VW Kombi.'

'Who's led you to believe I knew him?' she snapped. 'My sister? She's demented. Haven't you noticed that, you stupid idiot?'

Carl squinted. This form of directness favoured by June Habersaat was just something he'd have to get used to.

'Yes, you couldn't really help but notice. But perhaps I didn't make myself clear. It isn't whether you knew another man back then that interests us, but rather that you have *known* a man who lived up at Ølene in a sort of hippy commune, with a short name reminiscent of something from the Bible, and he was from Copenhagen, too. Ring any bells?'

'Is that what you've questioned Karin about? You can't just go asking people about me or who I've known, you shit. I've just lost my son, so you can just damn well stop calling me. Got it?'

Carl opened his eyes wide. She didn't hold back. 'Yes, June, I get it. But isn't a telephone call preferable to being taken down to the station for questioning? We need information about that man and you're one of the people who *may* have heard about him. We have a photo . . .'

'I have no idea what man you're talking about. It's just a pile of shit you've found in Christian's papers,' with which she hung up.

'What?' asked Assad.

Carl swallowed. 'Nothing. She misunderstood and mixed things up, and I couldn't get through. She's got all her defences up with us.'

Assad looked wearily at him. 'Shall we drive out there and stick the photo in her face?'

Carl shook his head. Why should they do that? June had displayed her unwillingness to cooperate. Karin was beyond helping, and Bjarke was somewhat indisposed as far as contributing anything went. They might as well give up on any form of help from the pitiful remnants of Christian Habersaat's immediate family.

'What then?'

'You drive to Listed and help Rose,' Carl said, smiling. 'I'm afraid I'll have to stay here in Rønne and read the files tonight.' Then he reached over for Assad's folder and in a moment of rashness passed him the car keys in return. 'In honour of the occasion, I'll let you drive me to the hotel first.'

It was a gesture Carl regretted only moments later, as he should have realized.

Unbelievable how often and how dangerously someone could overtake other cars on the short drive through Rønne.

There were several noteworthy things in the papers Superintendent Birkedal had handed over to them. First, that the information in them hadn't been updated since 2002, and, second, that the theory of a premeditated murder had never even been considered in the investigation. Maybe it was on the grounds of police politics, because if it was murder, the case could never be shelved. Another possibility was that the scene of the impact had never been sufficiently analysed.

But Carl knew that the reason could really be something as monstrously banal as the pressure exerted by Habersaat stopping everyone in their tracks. Wasn't it true that he'd pushed people away when he became too officious with his theories?

Carl nodded to himself. Murder wasn't your normal run-of-the-mill case on an island like Bornholm, and the mobile task force had never been given the case, so who should have sown the seed of doubt about the cause of death in the minds of the less experienced local investigators? Habersaat?

Hardly.

As he was now able to read in the files, the police in Rønne had unified around the hit-and-run theory, but had never managed to pinpoint the vehicle involved and definitely not who the driver might have been. Only Habersaat's stubbornness and enormous input of time and energy had led the case in a more specific direction, but who was to say he was right?

A few hours went by before Carl heard Assad and Rose letting themselves in the front door of the hotel.

Assad looked dead beat and collapsed on his half of the bed straightaway. Two minutes later he lay there with his mouth wide open, snoring so loudly that anything not nailed down in the room shook.

Rose wasn't particularly informative about her assessment and packing-up of Habersaat's estate either. Obviously, it would have to wait until they had it all at headquarters, because right now all she wanted to do was sleep.

Lucky woman, thought Carl as he lay again beside the curly combination of a pneumatic drill and a herd of stampeding gnus. Despite being tempted, he resisted the urge to put a pillow over Assad's gaping mouth and press down.

He looked around in despair until he spotted the minibar.

Probably better than earplugs, he thought, as he opened the fridge door.

Two lagers and at least ten miniature spirits of various sorts later, his eardrums finally cut out.

18

October 2013

Pirjo tried to calm down, washed her boots and hosed down her trouser legs, the spade and the scooter in the rose-coloured building they called the Stable of Senses. It was in this part of the centre that the new disciples in particular – weighed down by depressive tendencies and bad karma – went to unburden themselves by stroking the ponies' muzzles and inhaling the scent of newly strewn straw and fresh horse droppings. It was normally quite busy here with grooming and mucking out the boxes, but at this time of day, when everyone was in deep meditation in their rooms, she was free from any disturbance, thank heavens.

Pirjo matter-of-factly told herself to stop and think, shake all this away, and remember that it was insignificant in the grand scheme of things.

Only an hour ago she'd murdered someone for the third time in her life, and that sort of thing left its mark. Her forearms were bright red and her heart thumping.

'It couldn't have been any different,' she whispered to herself.

That woman Wanda Phinn had forced her way into her world despite all the warnings, simple as that. Now the consequence was that the high priestess of the Nature Absorption Academy had rightly put a stop to her, thereby preserving her position at Atu's side once again. The fact that it took its toll each time was another story. Inner peace was put under attack, the soul unbalanced, but what else could you expect?

There was just the problem of Atu finding out about it if things weren't handled properly.

Pirjo told herself to get her pulse down, crawling up the ladder to the highest loft in the stable.

'Horus, born of a virgin,' she chanted on the way up, 'guide for the twelve disciples, raised from the dead on the third day, free me from my despondency.' And when that didn't help, she repeated it a few times, still without effect, which shocked Pirjo because it hadn't been like this the other times. How could she move on if the demons took over and if the spirit wasn't with her? Hadn't she, as always, taken action for a righteous cause? Hadn't this Wanda arrived to overthrow what she and Atu had built up? So why were her fingers still trembling?

She closed her eyes, put her palms together in front of her face and breathed slowly and deeply. Now she'd unequivocally spared everyone at the academy from Wanda Phinn's evil energy. She knew it. So it couldn't be wrong.

She chanted one more time and noted to her relief that her pulse had fallen.

She nodded in thanks toward the bundle of rays coming in through the skylight windows, thanked Providence and went over the course of events with renewed energy and power.

The last few hours had been incredibly intense, and so mistakes were easily made. Something could be forgotten or overlooked, and if that was the case, then the only thing to do was to rectify it, and quickly.

Pirjo closed her eyes and rewound the film in her head to the scene of the crime. As far as she knew, she hadn't made any mistakes or overlooked anything.

The body of the naked woman wouldn't be found anytime soon, if ever. She was sure of that. It had been left in a remote place. That was one thing ticked off her list.

The ground under the deepest of the puddles out in Alvaret had been soft, so it had been easy to dig deep enough that the grave wouldn't be exposed in the event of a downpour. That was sorted, too. Check!

She'd meticulously erased any tracks that might lead a stray botanist or tourist off the beaten path and over towards the grave. Check!

And, finally, she'd ensured that nobody had seen her out there, or when she drove out of the area. Check!

Pirjo nodded with satisfaction and pushed a couple of cardboard boxes to the side over the loft planks. She needed to get going. The communal assembly at the academy would begin soon, now that the disciples' meditation and self-examination in their rooms was over. Just now the courtyard was empty. So only the treacherous security cameras, which she'd convinced Atu to install both inside and outside the area, could document that she'd been gone and what she'd done since she'd arrived back.

She would make sure to delete the video recordings when she got to the office, so that wouldn't be a problem either.

Now all that was left was the woman's belongings.

She looked over at the pile of clothes that she'd taken from the body: skirt, blouse, underwear, a two-tone belt, scarf, stilettos, coat, and stockings. Everything needed to be destroyed and burned, of course. But until a better opportunity presented itself, it would have to stay here in one of the removal boxes in the storage loft among the clothing left by individual members of the academy, rejected in their future aesthetical lives.

The rest, consisting of the woman's handbag and its contents: a pack of condoms, various items of make-up, phone, keys – including the key to the luggage box at the station – a few hundred euro in notes, travel documents and passport, would have to be dealt with immediately.

What else did she need to think about?

Wanda Phinn had written in her application that she alone in her family had emigrated from Jamaica some years ago and that she'd quit her job. She rented a room on the outskirts of London, a life that she wanted to leave behind her. There was nothing for her to stay for in London, it was a finished chapter in her life. She'd cancelled all her subscriptions, including the Internet. She'd sold all her worldly goods: computer, radio, TV, furniture and a few clothes. And after that, and hopefully a successfully completed introductory course at the academy, her only wish was to be inducted as a permanent resident.

There was nothing else, so the situation seemed safe. The woman had left no noticeable trace of this, her final journey in life. And even if she had, when the occasion arose Pirjo would just deny any knowledge of her existence and proposed plans. How in the world would anyone ever be able to prove anything different? Wanda Phinn's computer had been sold. She had no next of kin in England. She had nothing to stay for in London and as such probably hadn't had any friends or colleagues she confided in.

On top of this, that morning Pirjo had already deleted from her hard drive any information that could connect her to the woman, so what else was there? Could there be someone who'd seen them on their journey from Kalmar out to Alvaret? Yes, there was sure to be, but nobody Pirjo knew. And even if she had accidentally been seen together with the woman, would strangers really remember something so insignificant in a couple of weeks?

Impossible, she thought, reasoning that there had been a lot of new faces on the west side of the island today.

Right enough, the last big wave of tourists had gone, but at least a hundred visitors had been trawling the roads on the west coast all day in connection with the collaborative event organized by the art association.

It was definitely not a day where a single event or a few people on the road would be remembered more than any other. No, she needn't think about that any more. Wanda Phinn would, with all probability, not be reported missing for a very long time, and who would remember a day like today by then?

Pirjo shook her head and placed a couple of large pieces of sandstone in the woman's bag. After she'd thrown it as far as she could out into the Baltic Sea, she just needed to make it back to the assembly hall before the communal assembly got under way.

Thank God things were still such that if Pirjo wasn't there to do everything, nothing worked.

She dressed in white and calmly entered the hall. She'd show all the disciples their rightful places according to rank and association before Atu came in. Since it was October, the light from the skylights in the hall was still crystal clear, and the glass-tiled section in the floor, on which Atu would shortly stand, seemed almost as golden, warm and captivating as if looking at the master himself.

When he entered, the assembled disciples were sitting silently on the floor as usual, faces full of expectation. Everyone lived and breathed for these sessions because Atu's words were the high point of the day, regardless of whether it took place here or on the beach at dawn. In the presence of Atu Abanshamash Dumuzi, you found the answer to all quests and questions, and disciples flooded here.

It still felt so profound to be a part of, thought Pirjo.

When Atu stepped forward in his yellow robe with the beautiful detailing on the arms, it was as if a light in the darkness – an aura of energy – was suddenly lit. It was like beholding the truth of life itself when he opened his embrace towards the assembly and took them into his world.

Some of the people said that they considered these assemblies the end of a pilgrimage, wherein they achieved the ultimate cleansing of both body and soul, and where unexpected and de-finitive new life paths were stretched out before them. Others were less concrete and objective, letting themselves go without reservation, allowing what they called the wonder in the soul to occur.

But regardless of how they were affected, they all had two things in common. They'd paid a fortune to be sitting there on the floor with crossed legs, and that it was Pirjo who was in charge of who was invited in and where they should sit. And while Pirjo, like every-one else at the academy, idolized Atu, it was at least in a different and more complete way than it was for the others.

For Pirjo, Atu symbolized man and provider, incarnate sexuality, spearhead, security and, finally, spirituality, all in one and the same person. That's how she'd felt ever since she first met him. Maybe she'd become a little thick-skinned over the years in terms of the status Atu had fought his way up to as prophet and spiritual guide. But it definitely hadn't always been this way.

It had, after all, been a long road.

The town of Kangasala, apart from being well-to-do and situated at a suitable distance from Tampere, Finland's second biggest city, was also very close to the small rural town where Pirjo's parents settled down and decided to raise their children. Here, in close proximity to that fabled and poetically famed place where affluent tourists and stunningly picturesque nature melted together, her parents had placed their enormous aspirations for the future. It should have been so good, but it wasn't, as neither Pirjo's father nor mother possessed the qualities necessary to realize these aspirations.

A small and abysmally stocked kiosk was all that came of their dreams. A kiosk with a poor customer base and out-of-the-way location, just a simple shed built during the First World War from timber and other material that couldn't be used elsewhere. Ice-cold winters and lukewarm summers where mosquitoes from the small lakes nearby plagued them to death. That was about the sum of it.

Their entire lives emanated from this wretched starting point. Here, the parents and their three children were supposed to secure both their livelihood and status, and get their hands on the raw materials that in times of hardship could serve as both a cultural upbringing and general education.

So it was only through the glitzy magazines in the kiosk that the spectacular events and attractive perspectives to be found in the world could creep into Pirjo's uneventful life. Through them, future possibilities were opened, but only with the understanding that you had to leave. And Pirjo dreamt of having possibilities in her life, which little by little became limited to absolutely nothing when her dad pulled her out of school so she could serve in the shop when he couldn't be bothered himself.

But that's not how things shaped up for Pirjo's two younger sisters, who were both loved more by their parents. Nothing was too good for them. They could go to dance classes in town, and they had to learn how to play musical instruments and look respectable. All of which cost money, which Pirjo had to scrape together. A reality that both rankled and frustrated her every single day, or to put it bluntly, pissed her off, made her green with envy and gave her a real thirst for revenge.

It was only when her younger sister came home with a kitten and was allowed to keep it that it really hit her.

'Whenever I've asked for a pet you've always said *no*,' she shouted. 'I hate all of you. You can all go to hell.'

The price of her honesty was being boxed around the ears. The kitten stayed where it was.

When she turned sixteen the following week, the expected shower of gifts never materialized. It was that day that she finally realized that everything was completely meaningless, because no matter what she dreamed of or aspired to, it was her lot that life's great experiences would be few and far between.

As a result of boredom and a hatred for her sisters and her own life in equal measure, that same evening she began hanging out with some troublemakers from Kangasala, and the result was probably a little more exciting than was good.

When her dad found her sitting behind the kiosk with these scum smoking hash, the beating he gave her was so brutal that she couldn't lie down to sleep for several days.

And while her bodily wounds and soul healed, she overheard her mother warn her sisters never ever to end up like their big sister.

'But that won't happen. There's only one rotten apple in the cart. Your big sister is a vile girl, not like you, my angels,' she ended with a final twist of the knife.

'So maybe we should just throw the apple out?' said the youngest, laughing.

Throw the apple out? That was her they were talking about.

If Pirjo could have cried, she would have, but she'd realized long ago that her vulnerable side couldn't be used for anything. But there had to be some sort of reaction, otherwise she'd go mad.

In an act of defiance, she crept out of bed that night and killed her sister's kitten and then placed it right in the middle of the shop counter.

She then took everything from the cash register that she thought she'd been cheated out of, and left the rest of the contents out for whoever might walk by. With her bag over her shoulder and the door left open behind her, she ran away from home with the intention of never coming back.

She hooked up for a while with some Brits and a group of crazy bohemians from Helsinki in a rented cabin on the other side of town. And as these friends, who were older than her, lived somewhat more unconventionally than the local residents could deal with, they became the talk of the town, and the young Pirjo along with them.

From these very alternative characters in the commune, she learned for the first time to appreciate the surreal blaze with which the northern lights lit up the sky. The stillness of the lakes. The ecstasy of home-brewed schnapps mixed with casual sex. And even though, in its own way, it seemed like a happy time, she noticed with sadness how the last few innocent moments of youth were slipping away.

In the end, child welfare had received so many venomous complaints from neighbours about the commune and from the parents themselves that they felt compelled to intervene.

By the time they arrived at the commune it was already too late because Pirjo had split, having emptied the piggy bank of every last coin.

With this small fortune in her pocket and with the belief that happiness was just around the corner, she reached Denmark and Scandinavia's least prejudiced city, Copenhagen.

She passed her life here in a youth house in Nørrebro, where all kinds of people imaginable – and especially unimaginable – hung out, and before long she'd tried every form of stimulant that could be smoked or drunk.

Following a few heated disagreements with a couple of the leading girls about which of the guys you could have sex with, she was thrown out and saw no other alternative than to live on the streets. After having knocked about destitute for a month, doing nothing other than begging for small change for the next high or buzz, she met a slightly older guy who had his own apartment. He was nice, with a gentle smile, and was called Frank. He told her that the strongest driving force in life was neither sex nor alcohol but the cultivation of the soul and its journey from one level to another. It sounded strange but maybe it was a way out of the crappy situation she was in, so she listened.

What he said sounded simple enough. As long as you made an effort to understand that the body and flesh could only be freed of their needs if you worked with spirituality and meditation, you'd be free and happy.

So why not? She didn't get beaten and she didn't wake up with her head full of bugs and self-loathing.

Pirjo became stronger and slowly felt better about herself, while the experiments researching the soul and its energy grew in number and range. During the day, they both worked in the Burger King at Rådhuspladsen in little fancy hats and uniforms perfumed with cooking fat and the aroma of fast food and sweet drinks. They had to live off something. The rest of the time was given to the expansion of consciousness: from clairvoyance, yoga courses and meetings with clairvoyants to horoscopes and tarot cards. There weren't very many branches of the world of mysticism that they didn't try in that period.

In spite of Pirjo's lust for Frank, they lived in celibacy for the first few years to allow the soul unhindered space to feed into all available energy. And yet the time came when Frank felt that the planets, psychological forces and future pointed toward other goals, and he abandoned that path.

'I'm ready to feel my body against others,' he said. A transformation that was reserved only for him and which she reluctantly accepted. But then why should she have sex with other people when it was only Frank she wanted?

It was with that change of realization that Frank laid the roots of his alter ego Atu Abanshamash Dumuzi and the vestal Pirjo Abanshamash Dumuzi.

From that moment, Pirjo's role in their relationship was primarily to be both knight and servant to Frank's alias, Atu. And while it was a desirable position in relation to that of so many others, in reality it was also very restrictive.

A disparity she would do everything possible to change.

Because Pirjo had ambitions.

19

Waking up in the morning was abrupt and disagreeable, made worse by a pounding head and an all-too-clear conviction that minibars should only be frequented with a certain reservation.

When they drove onto the car deck of the ferry, Rose's cargo of goods had already arrived. And it was clear that the axle load definitely wasn't to the benefit of the undersized removal van. Damn it, all this rubbish had to go down in their basement area. Carl could hardly believe it, not to mention that Rose had reserved seats for them in the cafeteria at a table between her two well-built removal men.

Carl nodded to them extremely cautiously. Better to keep his thumping head as still and calm as possible.

'Weather's getting up,' said one of the drivers by way of introduction to what could easily become an endless round of nonsense and mindless chatter.

Carl tried to smile.

'He's got an overhang,' said Assad.

Carl couldn't be bothered to react.

'Ha! An overhang,' burst out the removal men, shovelling fast food consisting in equal measure of fat and white flour into their mouths. 'I think you mean hangover, mate,' one of them said, laughing, and gave Assad a friendly thump on the back that could have split a boulder in half.

'Eew,' uttered Assad as his otherwise enviable southern colouring took on a less than charming hue. He stared out at the waves, already prepared to give up.

'Do you get easily seasick?' one of them asked. 'Well, I've got a miracle cure for that.'

He produced a small bottle and poured the contents in an empty glass.

'You've got to down it or it won't work. It does something with your stomach that makes you feel better.'

Assad nodded. He was ready to give anything a try that might save him from the walk of shame out to the toilets to get some sick bags.

'Down she goes!' shouted the removal men when Assad tilted his head back and poured the contents down as directed.

It was less than a second before the poor guy grabbed his throat and his eyes became even rounder than usual. Then the colour of his face changed to crimson as if he couldn't breathe.

'What on earth was in that bottle?' asked Rose without any noticeable worry as she folded out the morning paper. 'Nitroglycerin?'

The removal men laughed so much that everything rattled, and Assad tried in vain to laugh along.

'No, just eighty per cent Slivovitz,' answered the man with the bottle.

'Are you crazy?' Carl was seriously indignant on someone else's behalf for once. What a pair of idiots. 'Assad's Muslim, he can't drink alcohol.'

The man with the bottle put his hand on Assad's arm. 'Hell, I'm really sorry. I didn't mean it, mate. It's not the sort of thing I normally go around thinking about.'

Assad raised his hand. It was already forgotten.

'Relax, Carl,' said Assad, when he got his voice back. He seemed surprisingly perky despite the fact that the wind was up and the crockery was dancing the fandango on the table. 'I didn't know what it was.'

Carl directed a dejected look out over the waves and suddenly felt the contents of his stomach go in the opposite direction. A few more hours of this and he'd know about it.

'But you're OK?' Carl asked cautiously.

Assad nodded, probably with misplaced relief.

Rose looked up over the paper. 'But the colour on *your* face isn't good, if you weren't aware of it yourself, Carl,' she said unsympathetically.

Assad patted his hand with a hazy look. 'It'll be all right, just look at me. I think I've just about got the hang of sailing. Maybe you just need one of those sli . . . itsjers.'

Carl swallowed again. Just the thought.

'I'll get a bit of fresh air,' he said, getting up with Assad at his heels.

Carl gagged a couple of times, only just making it to the deck before the sluice gates opened, and boy did they open.

'Thank you very much,' groaned Assad, assessing the extent of the consequences. 'Maybe you don't know the saying, Carl: a wise man doesn't puke into the wind.'

The weekend came and went before Carl dared think of anything other than dry crispbread and small glasses of water. If it hadn't been for Morten's daily visit to Hardy down in the living room, he'd definitely have abandoned all hope. Since he and Mika had moved a few years ago, cheerfulness wasn't something you could take for granted in this house. He even missed his stepson, Jesper, occasionally, but that always faded quickly, thank goodness.

Around midnight on Sunday he went to bed, tired of his own company and the meaningless things he'd been occupying himself with. A good sleep would do wonders for body and soul: no one in the house to disturb him, no upset stomach, just peace and calm.

The telephone rang at five in the morning, causing Carl to jump up as if simultaneously hearing fire alarms and sirens.

'What the hell!' he shouted in confusion as the digital clock revealed the time. Unless it was news of death or at the very least a military emergency, someone was going to get it.

'*Carl Mørck!*' he shouted, a warning of his frame of mind.

'Oh, shut up, you idiot. Do you have to shout?'

He recognized the voice. Not one he wanted to hear. 'Sammy, you fool, do you know what time it is?'

A moment passed. 'What's the clock, honey?' he asked someone in the background.

'It's ten!' he exclaimed, slurring his words.

Carl was fuming. The man was completely brain-dead.

'It's five here, just so you know.'

'Carl, damn it, it's you . . .' He burped, so the party was obviously neither just begun nor finished.

'I said . . . it's you Ronny's sent the goddamn fucking will to. Don't you think I've worked it out?' A rattling sound came from the receiver. 'No, honey, not now, take your hands away. I'm on the phone.'

Carl counted to ten. 'If I had that goddamn fucking will, I'd shove it down your throat so that once and for all we'd be free of your shit. Good night, Sammy!'

He ended the call. Damn Sammy, damn Ronny, and damn that will. It made him feel ill just thinking about it.

Then the telephone rang again.

'You'd better not hang up on me, I'll tell you that for nothing, Carl. Now admit it, you stupid pig. What's Ronny written in his will? Are you pilfering everything?'

'Just stop there. Did you call me a pig? That's five days at least, Sammy. It's not the first time, is it?'

There was a deep sigh and giggling at the other end. 'Yeah, Diamond, but wait a couple of minutes, OK? Yes, sorry, Carl, the girl here's . . .' He chuckled. 'Shut the hell up. You know how it is. I just want to say, Carl, that you're a great guy. And that stuff with the will, we'll work it out together, right? My God, Diamond . . .' And with that, the connection died.

So now he had that to think about.

For the rest of the night, actually.

When he arrived in the basement at Police Headquarters just before eleven, he was neither in the mood for reading journals nor ready to face the fear-inducing sight that waited for him in the basement.

Not so much as an inch was left so the colour of the wall could peep through. On both sides of the large noticeboard with all the cases and bits of string, the shelves were lined up like a pumped-up North Korean military parade, and Assad and Rose had long ago started filling them up.

'The fire inspectors will get a shock,' was the first thing he said.

'Then it's good they've just been here and won't be coming back for the foreseeable,' came the reply from deep inside the removal box in which Rose's upper body had disappeared.

Carl staggered to his seat and flung his legs up on the table.

'I'm reading,' he shouted for good measure, in case they badgered him to help with the unpacking.

He sat for a moment to consider what would serve him best: a couple of cigarettes or a doze?

'Might as well put it in here straightaway,' Rose was saying even before she entered Carl's office.

God only knew how she'd managed to get that huge pile in her arms. At any rate, it ended up between Carl's legs, threatening to break the table.

'They're photocopies, and they *are* in order. Just start from the top. Enjoy!'

Regardless of whether or not Carl would admit it, the material Rose had picked out of the boxes made for interesting reading. Too interesting, you might think. If you wanted to gain a reasonable overview of all these examples of information that Habersaat had collected, you'd need to have either a photographic memory or a huge amount of free wall space to hang the rubbish up so you could form an idea of what was really rubbish and what was gold.

Carl looked around the chaos that he called his office. Actually, an unlikely amount of stuff had piled up that didn't need to be there. All that mess and dirt that Rose, in a rare moment, described as Carl's 'spice of life,' and which she more usually referred to as the only colourful and interesting thing in the office, himself included.

'Gordon!' he shouted. 'Come here a minute, you lanky whiner.' He could have the job of getting rid of the stuff.

'Gordon's busy being depressed,' Assad said from out in the hallway.

Depressed? As if that was anything special; who wasn't in this workplace? It would've been worse if they'd placed his desk among the removal boxes.

He got up and took an empty removal box from the hallway, filling it with all the superfluous rubbish and junk from the office. Rose would probably have a heart attack when she saw the hotch-potch of documents from completed cases mixed together with dirty dishes, pieces of paper with undated conclusions, folders, journals, broken pencils and worn-out pens.

He took a step back and nodded with satisfaction. Now you could glimpse a bit of the tabletop and a little more of the wall above the small bookcase on the opposite side.

If he started right at the top of the wall, he could probably find room for most of the photocopies Rose had handed him.

True to his word, within an hour the wall was plastered with everything imaginable under the sun, and with a system of sorts. Nevertheless, it was still hard to make head or tail of the material, he thought, as he took a few steps back to admire his work. Of course Rose had made sure to include the most important papers, like the photo of the VW man, the crime-scene report, the autopsy and the group photo from autumn 1997. But there were also papers that, to put it mildly, seemed out of place. For example, copies of brochures for alternative therapists and movements, shop receipts and inter-views with various and sundry locals, to mention just some of them.

And in the middle of it all hung a relatively large colour copy of a photo of Alberte. Like an angel, pure with red cheeks and healthy, strong features and teeth, she reigned in the middle of all these loose threads, staring directly at Carl as if he were the only one in the world who possessed the philosopher's stone. And regardless of where he sat in the room, those beautiful crystal-green eyes rested on him as if pleading with him to get to the bottom of it all.

No doubt Rose had chosen the photo carefully.

'Rose, Assad! Come in here and see!' he shouted with something approaching pride in his voice.

'OK,' said Rose with her hands at her side while she stared at the accomplishment. 'Suddenly I can see dust that's been hidden for months. Nice, Carl.' She wiped a demonstrative finger on one of the shelves and held it up.

'Good going, Carl,' Assad said, more to his liking, while nodding at the wall.

'Won't you come with me then, Carl?' Rose grabbed his sleeve without further warning and pulled him down towards the room where Assad had stood spreading paint around a few days before.

'Have a look.' She let her index finger point around the series of shelves in the corridor. 'Luckily we've been able to find room for all our basic material out here in the hallway. That's what we're in the middle of sorting, following the same categorization as in Habersaat's house, but with a few splashes of professional logic,' she continued, pulling him into a basement room further down the corridor. 'Down here, on the other hand, we've found space for what Assad calls the situation room. Everyone thought the room should be Gordon's, but Assad offered to let him share with him, so go ahead, Carl!' She spread her arms out to the bright yellow walls that they'd plastered not only with the originals of the papers Carl had been given a copy of, but also with a series of appendixes.

Carl was shaking his head when Assad joined them. Why the hell hadn't they told him? It would've saved him from working his butt off in his office.

'We – that's to say, Assad and yours truly, but also to some degree, Gordon – have worked on it all weekend. Here are the most important notes and hints in Habersaat's material. Are you satisfied, Carl? Can you use it?'

He nodded slowly but really just felt like going home.

'We thought we might put a couple of office chairs in here so we can swivel around while trying to get an overview,' said Assad.

'Yes, and for every category of file, we now have the extra option of going to the shelves not just for Habersaat's material, but hopefully also to get an overview of the strategy and goal with his investigation and subsequent conclusions,' elaborated Rose.

'Thanks,' said Carl. 'That's really great. And where's Gordon now? You shouted that he was depressed.'

This time it was Assad who dragged him off.

There was a clattering noise coming from Assad's office, so it turned out the towering beanpole was in the process of moving in.

'Good afternoon, Carl,' Gordon said timidly from the other side of Assad's desk. To be honest, he did look depressed. The beanpole had so little space that his knees protruded above the top of the desk, while the remaining parts of his gangly legs were presumably curled up underneath. In fact, there was so little space between him and the shelves behind, with all the pictures of Assad's old aunts, that just in order to be able to stand up he had to push himself upright from the tabletop.

Some would call it claustrophobic. Carl would sooner call it pure torture. But the man's body was put together in such a way that he must be used to it.

'Nice place you've got in here with Assad, Gordon,' he said with a barely comforting smile. 'You're lucky you've got such a good roommate. What do you think?'

Maybe it was because of the pressure from the table, maybe exhaustion, but didn't his voice shoot up half an octave when he tried to confirm?

'We've decided to call Gordon the case manager,' said Rose. 'The idea is that he'll develop an overview of all Habersaat's documents so we can use him like an encyclopedia. Leaving the three of us to concentrate on following up on the leads. Gordon can then subsequently try to find a system to show how they're all connected.'

'Great. And where do I fit in, if I might ask?' said Carl.

'You're the boss, of course, as always, Carl,' Assad said, smiling.

The boss! Had that word just been given a new definition?

It quickly became apparent in the situation room that they needed to sort out some of Habersaat's numerous and sometimes unhelpful leads before the team could seriously get going.

'You could ask yourself why all these papers about occult phenomena take up so much space? Is it anything to do with us?' asked Carl.

'Habersaat might have tried a bit of everything to try and feel better,' suggested Assad. 'When people aren't feeling good, they attempt all sorts of crazy things.'

Rose frowned. 'How do you know it's crazy? Maybe *you've* had personal experience with the prophets? No, I didn't think so. And yet you have a strong belief in them, which is fine by me. Because there's nothing wrong with that specifically, is there?'

'No, but . . .'

'Good. So Indian mystics, clairvoyants, healing, visions and so on can't just be totally dismissed either then, can they?'

'No, but . . .'

'But what?'

'It's just, all these strange words are so silly. A bit hard to take seriously, I think.'

Carl scanned the papers on the wall displaying a bit of everything: DNA-activation with archangels, Vedic sound therapy, transformation lecture, psychic maps, and much more.

You had to hand it to Assad; most of it sounded curious, to put it mildly.

'I think I've said it before,' he began, 'but if you ask me, I don't think a down-to-earth man like Habersaat resorted to things like this. I'm more inclined to think that it's part of his investigation.' He swivelled in the chair and stared at the photo of the man with the VW Kombi. 'What we do know is that this man lived in a sort of hippy commune that had some special rituals, midnight séances with dancing, painted naked bodies and so on. And then there was the sign over their door, the one the old jogger mentioned. What did it say, Assad?'

He flicked through his notebook, going back at least twenty pages, so it took some time.

'The Celestial Sphere,' he said drily.

'Listen, Rose. I think this material is important in some way or other, so I want you to take charge of it. Call all the associations, or whatever they're called, that you can find on Bornholm involved in this sort of thing. Try to see if anyone had contact with even one person from that commune back in 1997. Meanwhile, Assad can try to absorb some of the material in the room and maybe also arrange a meeting with the artist who swiped Alberte's bike.'

Assad gave him a thumbs-up. 'Shouldn't we also have a little table in there to put our tea on?'

Carl shuddered. Would they ever escape from that nauseating stench?

'I'm heading up to talk with Tomas Laursen about how we can get the technicians in Rødovre to reevaluate the case and take another look at a couple of things.'

'You'll need this, then,' said Rose, taking one of the pages down from the wall.

'OK, what is it?' Carl took the piece of paper with loosely scribbled sentences and some tape securing a thin splint of wood no more than two centimetres long.

Splint found in a straight line between the recovered bike in the thicket and where by all accounts it was hit – written in Habersaat's handwriting.

Rose removed some notes that had been hanging under the piece of paper with the splint. 'Here's the progress on the splint,' she said.

It was a note referring to a date four days after Alberte's disappearance and three days after Habersaat had found her. Carl read it aloud:

Report for own use.

Monday, November 24th, 1997, 10.32.

Subsequent to the technicians all clear for the area, the undersigned found a splint from some processed wood lying on the ground six metres in a northerly direction from Alberte Goldschmid's bike. The location of the discovery is therefore deemed to form almost a straight line from the place where the bike was hit and where it came to land.

The splint was examined by a local team of technicians. The material is apparently birch. And the remnants of glue suggest that it's a splint originating from plywood.

As no similar fragments have been found in the collision area, the technicians conclude that the splint doesn't stem from the collision.

However, the undersigned believes this to be incorrect, and reports it to the leader of the investigation, Detective Jonas Ravnå, requesting a closer analysis by the police technical department in Copenhagen. Following the summons of all the vehicles on the island, no material has been found to date that can be connected to this find, and the request is denied.

During a subsequent interview with me on local TV, looking for any finds of plywood with defects, twenty mostly local people report back with finds of wooden building boards. All the finds are of pine.

Hereafter, no leads.

Christian Habersaat, Listed.

Carl nodded. Eighty per cent sweat, two hundred and fifty per cent dead ends. That's what it meant to be an investigator.

'But look at this, Carl,' said Rose, taking down a third piece of paper. It was another of Habersaat's home-made journals.

Wednesday, August 2nd, 2000.

Find of wooden board wedged in the rocks at Hammerknuden.

Ten-year-old boy, Peter Svendsen, of Hasle, pulls free a wedged board while playing at Camel Head Cliffs.

The board is heavy and he leaves it on land. His father, local community officer Gorm Svendsen – who worked with the undersigned on the find of a washed-up body from the wreck of the boat Havskummet – contacts the undersigned. Gorm Svendsen recollects an interview with me on local TV, where I was looking for a plywood board that the splint might originate from.

The board fragment discovered at the cliffs is part of a larger board, but had probably been a metre in height and two metres in width. It is extremely battered but evidently originally watertight, as several of the layers of glue remain intact.

A couple of boreholes are visible on the board, and faint shadows on one side. Undoubtedly remnants of print or similar.

I request a thorough analysis of the wood type and am given authorization after some back and forth with the department superiors.

The material is also birch, but a closer analysis is unable to determine with certainty if the splint originates from the same board.

My theory, due to the plywood being glued together in several layers, is that the splint originates from one of the outer layers, which over the course of time has peeled away from the board due to its time in the water.

I estimate, with the technicians, that it was probably a board between 20 and 24mm thick, of which the middle 18mm remain intact.

I request a comparative analysis of the glue from the splint and the plywood, as this had been neglected previously, but authorization is not granted.

It is finally my absolute theory that this board is involved in the collision, while at the same time recognizing that flotsam and jetsam are of such common occurrence here on the island that I must resign myself to the fact that the finding of the same wood types can be put down to coincidence.

Christian Habersaat

And added underneath in red ballpoint:

Plywood board, found 8/2/2000, has gone missing. Possibly destroyed.

'What did he say the cliffs were called?' asked Assad.

'Camel Head Cliffs.'

He nodded enthusiastically. It didn't take much.

Carl turned to Rose. 'I'm not sure, but I feel as if it's almost impossible to get anywhere here. If the splint has been so thoroughly analysed, and the board is missing, what do *you* think that the technicians should work on, Rose?'

'Finding something to make it plausible that the splint might originate from that board, Carl.'

'Do we have something as simple as a photo of it?'

'I'll check,' shouted Assad, disappearing out into the corridor.

'But if they can't find the connection you want, what'll you talk to the technicians about, Carl?'

He sat for a moment, staring at the splint. 'Habersaat hints at a suspicion that the board was used in the collision. So that's the starting point. Do you know if a diagram has ever been drawn of the presumed trajectory of the body following the collision and up into the canopy? And of the bike for that matter?'

She shrugged. 'There's a few hours' work before we'll have been through everything out there, Carl. But I hope I find a drawing like that. What are you thinking about?'

'The same as you and Habersaat. That this board has been attached to the front of the VW Kombi. That's why I need to see a photo of that board and the position of the boreholes. To see if it seems logical that the board could've been attached to that custom fender.'

He passed Assad in front of the shelves with a nod. If that photo was to be found among this colossal chaos, then Assad was the right person for the job.

In the cafeteria on the fourth floor, he found an astonishingly pale and scrawny version of the portly figure that Tomas Laursen had been only a few weeks ago.

'Are you sick, mate?' he asked, concerned.

Laursen, formerly the best technician in the force and now manager of the cafeteria at Police Headquarters, shook his head. 'The wife's on the 5:2 diet, and she's forced me on it, too.'

'Five: two diet – what's that?'

'Well, it's actually five days of not much food and two days of fasting, but I feel more like it's the opposite, five days fasting and two days with little food. It's damn well not easy for a man with a waist like Santa Claus to keep up with this.'

'What about this up here?' Carl pointed to a couple of tempting lunch plates in the glass counter. 'You can't eat your own creations?'

'Are you crazy? She has me on the scales every time I come home.'

Carl slapped his friend on the shoulder. Sorry fate.

'Can you get some of your old pals at the lab in Rødovre to pull some old analyses out of the drawer and have another look at them? If they have photos of the material, it would be great. Things always go more smoothly when you're involved.'

Laursen nodded. The former technician in him had never totally disappeared.

'And if such a photo is still to be found, you might try and ask them to consider what the markings on one side of the board might have been? And then I'd also like to know if there's been any sort of idea about how long that board had been in the water.'

Laursen looked quizzically at Carl. 'I can't see why the result wouldn't still be there. Murder cases are never shelved in Denmark, are they?'

'No, but that's exactly the problem, Tomas. This case has never been treated as a murder.'

20

'Did you find a photo of the board, Assad?' asked Carl on the way over to the garages.

'No.' He shook his head. Too many shelves. Too many papers.

'Did you arrange with the junk artist that we could drive out there?'

'Yes, he'll be at his studio in an hour and a half.' He looked at his watch. 'So we've got time to stop at Alberte's parents' first. They live on Dyssebakken, out in Hellerup.'

Carl frowned. 'Right. How did they react when you told them the case was reopened?'

'The mom cried.'

Just as he'd expected, so this was going to be a cheerful visit.

After five minutes they turned down a road of villas, where Assad pointed to a well-kept red-painted bungalow. Everything needed to create a good and desirable framework for a healthy Danish family life was there: a wooden garden gate, weeping birch tree and privet hedges in the front garden, a moss-grown path you could play hopscotch on and, in the middle of the garden, a flagpole flying the Danish flag.

At least there was someone who remembered Denmark's Liberation Day in 1945. He hadn't seen so many flags out in Allerød that morning. But would *he* have remembered it, if he'd had a flagpole, that is?

'Come inside,' said the woman, her eyes lifeless. 'My husband's a bit reluctant, so you'll be talking with me,' she said a moment later.

They greeted a plump man with trousers pulled halfway up his stomach. It obviously wasn't him Alberte took after most. When he sat down and turned his head, his kippah slipped to the side a little. Didn't they secure them with clips?

Carl looked around. If it hadn't been for the kippah and the seven-armed candlestick, he never would've imagined this to be an orthodox Jewish home. Mostly because he didn't have a clue what an orthodox Jewish home tended to look like.

'Have you found something new in the case?' asked Mrs Goldschmid in a faint voice.

They brought her quickly up to speed, from Habersaat's suicide to the establishment of a situation room in the basement of Police Headquarters.

'Christian Habersaat brought us more sorrow than joy,' came the resounding voice from the man in the armchair. 'Is that what you're also intending?'

Carl said no, but that he'd like to try to build on the picture they had so far of Alberte, though he knew that it might be hard for them to talk about her.

'Know more about Alberte?' Mrs Goldschmid shook her head, as if she couldn't contribute anything decisively new, and that was what pained her. 'That's what Habersaat was after, too. First the criminal investigation team from Bornholm and then Habersaat.'

'He insinuated that our little girl was a whore,' the man took over, his tone hateful rather than angry.

'That's not what he said, Eli, to be fair. The man's dead. He possibly committed suicide for the sake of our little girl.' She stopped and tried to compose herself. The hands in her lap became agitated. The scarf around her neck seemed suddenly to choke.

The man nodded. 'That's right, he didn't use those words. But all the same, he implied that she'd been in relationships, and we don't believe that could be true.'

Carl looked at Assad. The body hadn't been subjected to sexual assault, but was she a virgin? He grabbed Assad's notebook out of his hands and wrote *virgin?* before passing it back.

Assad shook his head.

'It *might* be the case that she'd had an affair,' suggested Carl. 'That wouldn't exactly be unusual for a girl of nineteen, not even then. We know for certain that she was seeing someone, as they say, which you'll no doubt have been aware of.'

'Of course Alberte had suitors. She was a beautiful young girl, as if I didn't know that.' Now it was the man's voice that faltered.

'We are a totally normal Jewish family,' the woman continued, 'and Alberte was a good daughter in our faith, so we don't think anything bad of her. We can't and we won't. But Habersaat always went further than that. He maintained that Alberte wasn't a virgin, but I told him that no one could know that because she had done a lot of gymnastics, and it's possible that . . . well, that . . .'

She couldn't get the word 'hymen' past her lips.

'That's why we wouldn't talk with Habersaat any more. He said so many horrible things, in our opinion,' she continued. 'I know it was his job as a policeman to look at things in that way, but it became so vulgar. He also went behind our backs and asked friends and family about Alberte, but he didn't get anywhere with that.'

'So there was nothing back then that might have given you cause for concern about Alberte's behaviour during her stay at the folk high school?'

They looked at each other. They weren't old, possibly early sixties, but they seemed it. The dust didn't seem to have been shaken from their habits or ideas in years, and it showed most when they looked at each other. Their look seemed to say that things would never be different, and it didn't have anything to do with the limitations or restrictions of their orthodox view of life, but rather the bitterness that follows when your life takes a knock.

'I can see that this is hard for you, but Assad and I would like nothing more than to bring the person responsible for Alberte's death to justice. So we can't rule out any theories, and we can't allow ourselves to take sides about either your or Habersaat's understanding of your daughter's comings and goings. We hope you can understand that.'

It was only the wife who nodded.

'Was Alberte your oldest?'

'We had Alberte, David and Sara, but now we only have Sara left. Sara is a wonderful girl.' She tried to smile. 'She gave us a darling little grandchild on Rosh Hashanah. It couldn't be better.'

'Rosh Ha . . . ?'

'The Jewish new year, Carl,' mumbled Assad.

The man of the house nodded. 'Are you Jewish?' he asked Assad with increased interest.

Assad smiled. 'No. But I try to be a cultivated person.'

A knowing look of recognition spread across both their faces. A cultivated person, would you look at that.

'You mentioned David. Was he an older brother?' asked Carl.

'He was Alberte's twin. But yes, he was the oldest, but only by seven minutes.' Mrs Goldschmid tried to smile, but it wasn't easy for her.

'And David's not with us any more?'

'No. He couldn't bear what happened with Alberte. He simply faded away.'

'Nonsense, Rachel, David died of AIDS,' her husband responded harshly. 'Excuse my wife, but it's still hard for us both to accept what David stood for.'

'I understand. But he and Alberte were close?'

Mrs Goldschmid raised two crossed fingers. 'Like peas in a pod, yes.' She turned to her husband. 'And he *was* crushed, Eli. You can't say otherwise.'

'Can I ask about something totally different, Mr and Mrs Goldschmid?' interrupted Assad.

They nodded, relieved at the change of topic. You don't just say no to a cultivated person, and especially not when you consider yourself to be equally so.

'Didn't you receive postcards from Alberte? Letters or something? After all, she'd been away from home for over four weeks and maybe for the first time in her life, wasn't she?'

Mrs Goldschmid smiled. 'We received a few, yes. With scenes of the local attractions, of course. We still have them. Would you like to see them?' She looked at her husband as if looking for his approval. It didn't come.

'She didn't write much. Just about the school and what they were doing. She was a good singer, and she could also draw. I can show you some of her earlier work?'

Her husband was about to protest but he regained his composure and stared at the floor instead. Carl sensed that in spite of his brusque manner, he'd moved on more than his wife.

She led them down a small corridor with three doors.

'Have you kept Alberte's room intact?' Carl asked cautiously.

She shook her head. 'No, we've fitted it out for Sara and Bent, and for the baby, when they visit. They live in Sønderborg, so it's nice for them to have a bed when they come to town. Alberte's things are in here.'

She opened the door to a broom cupboard where a pile of cardboard boxes threatened to collapse.

'It's almost all clothes but in the box on top we've got it all, drawings and postcards.'

She took it down and got on her knees in front of the box. Carl and Assad knelt on the floor beside her.

'This is what she had hanging on her wall. She wasn't your average girl, as you can see.'

She unfolded a few posters of pop stars and celebrities from the time. Very average, actually.

'And here are the drawings.'

She laid them in a pile on the floor, looking through them so slowly that their knees began to ache. Technically, they were very accomplished, sharp pencil strokes and contours, but as far as the subject matter was concerned, you couldn't mistake the lack of maturity. Floating young girls with long legs and fairy costumes draped in stardust and hearts. She'd clearly had a period where her romantic side was given free rein.

'She hasn't dated them. Were they drawn at the school?'

'No, they never sent those. I think they might have been part of an exhibition,' she suggested with pride in her voice.

'And here we've got the postcards.' She pushed the drawings to one side and pulled three postcards from a plastic wallet, handing them reverently to Carl.

Assad read along over his shoulder.

They were three glossy and well-read postcards with images from the town square in Rønne, Hammershus Castle Fortress and a summer scene from Snogbæk with a smokehouse, seagulls in flight and a view over the sea. Alberte had written short and sweet descriptions of what she'd seen on a couple of trips around the island, nothing else, in capitals with a ballpoint pen.

All ending with: *I'm doing fine. Hugs from me.*

Mrs Goldschmid sighed, her face contorted. 'Look, the last one is dated just three days before she died. It's so awful to think about.'

They got up, rubbed their knees and said thank you.

'What's behind the other doors, if you don't mind me asking, Mrs Goldschmid?' asked Assad, glancing down the corridor. It was uncanny how polite he was suddenly being.

'Our bedroom and then David's room.'

Carl was puzzled. 'And David's room hasn't been turned into a nursery?'

She looked tired again. 'David moved away from home when he was eighteen, leaving everything such a mess in there. He lived in Vesterbro, not one of the better places, I have to say. When he died in 2004, we got all sorts of things sent out here from his friend. We just put it all in the room.'

'So you've never looked through it?'

'No, we weren't up to it. Not his things, too.'

Carl looked at Assad, who nodded back.

'I know it might seem strange and maybe also out of turn, but might we be allowed to look at those things?'

'I don't know . . . what purpose would it serve?'

'You said David and Alberte were very close. Maybe she was in contact with him while she was at the folk high school. Maybe she wrote to him, too.'

Something happened with her face. As if a painful recognition tried to reach her consciousness, but she wouldn't let it. Had the thought really never crossed their minds?

'I'll have to ask my husband first,' she said, not wanting to meet their eyes.

Here in this room where dozens of boxes stood lined up against the wall and on the bed, there was plenty of evidence of the family's Jewish roots, in contrast to the rest of the house: Star of David on the wall, the poster of the terrified little boy from the Jewish ghetto in Warsaw, photos from David's own bar mitzvah in brown sandalwood frames, the scarf he'd worn over his shoulders for that occasion, all pinned to the wall with decorative tacks. Above the desk hung a small wooden bookshelf in teak holding literature by Jewish authors such as Philip Roth, Saul Bellow, Singer and the Danish Katz and Tafdrup. You couldn't say it was a stereotypical collection of books for a young man. But what characterized the room even more was the colourful collection of revolt and undisguised aversion to the suburban environment and the safe, taken-for-granted boundaries it represented. There were Warhammer Fantasy battle figures on the windowsill. On the walls, posters from Roskilde Festival and a few others featuring George Michael and Freddie Mercury. CDs lay on top of the small stereo, consisting of everything from Judas Priest, Kiss, and AC/DC to Cher and Blur. There even hung a rusty machete and a pretty good copy of a samurai sword crossed together on the wall. It wasn't hard to see that there had been significant distance between David and his plump father Eli sitting in the armchair.

They went through the boxes starting from one end, finding evidence of David Goldschmid's alternative life in the first box they unpacked. A mass of colourful shirts, tailored jackets and at least as expensive suits, ironed and dry-cleaned as if they were totally new. This was a man with style and taste, and to a certain extent a man with a wallet to match. They saw his diploma from business school with fantastic grades and reports, and the letter of appointment with a secure job in a distinguished company. Definitely a boy you ought to be proud of.

Unpacking the third box, Assad found something.

Most of the postcards in the cigar box were from a guy called Bendt-Christian, who'd sent greetings from Bangladesh, Hawaii, Thailand and Berlin, among others. They always started with *Dearest Davidovich* and contained a few tender remarks here and there, but other than that were relatively neutral. When they got to the postcards from Alberte, there were a few reminders of the cards she'd sent to her parents. Just plain descriptions of the day the card referred to and lots of assurances that she missed her brother.

'There doesn't seem to be much to go on here,' Assad said just as Carl pulled out a postcard with Østerlars Round Church on the front, with a red heart drawn above the cross on the spire.

He turned it over and skimmed it.

'Hang on a minute, Assad, not so fast,' he said. 'Listen to what it says here:'

Hi bro. Trip to Østerlars Round Church this time. It's meant to be fantastic with Knights Templar and everything, but the best thing was I met a sweet guy.

He knew more about the church than the guide, and he was SO hot. Meeting him tomorrow outside school. More about that another time. Hugs and kisses, your sis, Alberte.

'Bloody hell, Carl! What's the date?'

He turned it over and over but didn't find anything.

'The mark from the stamp, can you make it out?'

They both squinted and scrutinized the stamp from all angles. There appeared to be a number 11, but it wasn't possible to read any more.

'Then we'll just have to ask the rector couple when they went on that trip.'

'Carl, I'm thinking. There must be someone from the school who took photos that day.'

Carl wasn't sure. Compared to today's digital reality, where everything was endlessly documented and where everyone with even an ounce of self-respect had their smartphone ever at the ready to capture all sorts of trivia and selfies, 1997 seemed like the Stone Age.

'Yes, let's hope so. And that someone caught the guy she's speaking about in the picture.'

They rooted around in the boxes for another half-hour, but didn't find anything else they could use. No name, no later postcard that could uncover the next chapter in this catastrophic saga, nothing.

'Did you find anything?' asked the man of the house as he followed them to the door.

'You had a son you can be proud of, that's what we found out,' said Carl.

He nodded quietly. He knew it only too well. That's what made it all the worse.

*

They reached Stefan von Kristoff's studio at least an hour late, but the man was evidently not the type to worry about trivialities such as clocks and normal conventions.

'Welcome to the darkness,' he said, pulling down on a gigantic lever that turned on the lights in the machine room where, before the world had gone mad, at least sixty men had stood working metal.

'Big,' said Carl. And it damn well was.

'And a great name,' added Assad, pointing up at a welcome sign in metal, hanging under the glimmering fluorescent lights: *Stefan von Kristoff – Universitopia*.

'Well, if Lars Trier can adorn his cap with borrowed feathers, so can I. The name's Steffen Kristoffersen, the "von" is just for show.'

'I was thinking of the name of the studio.'

'Oh, that. Everything in my world is called something with "topia" at the end. You want to see *Fateopia*, I understand?'

He led them down to the far end of the machine room, where a pair of projectors lit up the back wall to a level verging on daylight.

'She's here,' he said, pulling the cover from a man-sized installation.

Carl swallowed. In front of them stood something nearing the most disturbing sculpture he'd ever seen. For the uninitiated, probably nothing special, but for those who knew of Alberte and her fate, it was heavy going. If her parents ever got wind of the monstrosity, the lawsuits would be never-ending.

'Great, isn't it?' said the artist.

'Where have you acquired all these things from? And how did you get information about what things you thought were important to include?'

'I was on the island when it happened. I have a summerhouse and studio in Gudhjem, and there was a lot written and talked about in relation to the case, as you can imagine. Absolutely every car was searched, including mine, so you couldn't exactly ignore the furore. In Gudhjem alone, all the men from the National Guard ran about searching without even knowing what they were looking for. And so did the rest of us, for that matter.'

Carl glanced over the monstrosity. Everything was built around a woman's bike with buckled wheels and twisted handlebars. Reinforced crossbars were welded to the frame, pointing out in all directions like bundles of rays. And at the end of each crossbar, evidence hung of the specific details and other related misery.

It wasn't badly made, just a tasteless jumble of different techniques. Around the bike, in the middle of the installation, there were etchings in metal and brass, depicting all sorts of imaginable car accidents. In addition, there was a colourful rendition of the checks at the ferry in enamel, and etchings in copper of a pixellated image of Alberte, probably taken from the local paper. There were casts of bone remains, branches and leaves and, not least, hands outstretched in an attempt at protection. But that wasn't the worst of it. The worst was the plastic vessel he'd placed under the etching of Alberte's smiling face, and that it was filled with blood.

'It's not human blood, unfortunately,' laughed Kristoff. 'It's pigs' blood that's been treated to stop it rotting. It might smell a bit sweet just now, but I do change it sometimes.'

If they hadn't been on duty, it would've been irresistibly tempting to dip his laughing face in the stuff.

Assad snapped away at the sculpture from every possible angle, while Carl stepped closer to the bike to assess it further.

It was a cheap bike, probably Chinese. Big wheels, huge prop stand and high handlebars. Rust had eaten most of the yellow colour away, and the rear rack was dangling. It wasn't a very good bike.

'What have you done to it? Did it look like this at the time?'

'Yes. Apart from the fact that I've put it upright, it's just as I found it.'

'Found it? You just as good as stole it from the police station in Rønne, didn't you?'

'No, I found it in a pile of junk in a container on the road in front of the station. I actually went in to the guard and asked if I could take it. The lads in the office just said that if I did myself any injury getting it out, it was on my own head.'

Carl and Assad gathered their thoughts. On the last day in her life, Alberte had sat in this saddle and probably imagined that it would be a happy day.

Carl thought it was a good thing that people didn't know the day or the hour when their time would come. It was a sad sight. Just as morbid as those plasticized bodies you could visit all over the place at almost no cost at all.

'You look like you want to buy the installation,' said Kristoff with a cunning smile. 'I'll do it at a mate's price. What would you say to seventy-five thousand kroner?'

Carl smiled cynically. 'Err, no, thank you. Right now we're almost considering whether or not we should confiscate it.'

21

October 2013

'I feel you all,' chanted Atu over the crowd in the hall.

'I feel you all, and you feel me. We feel Malena today, and we feel her pain and bring ourselves together now to pull it out of her.'

Pirjo was puzzled and looked around the assembly for Malena. She wasn't there.

What on earth did Atu mean when he said *feel her pain*? Did it mean that right now that mare was lying in his chamber, trembling with desire? Was this a warning that those two were about to attach themselves more to one another than Pirjo could allow. Maybe it'd been a mistake not allowing the black woman to challenge that relationship.

She stood for a moment with her eyes tightly shut, pondering the thought.

She shook her head. No, it hadn't been a mistake. Wanda Phinn had had to disappear. It couldn't have been any different.

'Behold my hands,' said Atu, and everyone looked up.

'Those of you who in spite of the soul hours still feel inner unrest,

I implore you to stretch your arms out in the air and prepare yourself to receive ablution.'

There were nine or ten people who reacted.

Then Atu moved his upper body back and forth with very small movements, while his arms hung still in the air.

'You who are ready, I implore you to channel your anxiety, anger and broken meridian lines into my hands. Be at ease. When you sense warmth and peace coming to you, set yourselves free and let go.'

Now those who had been asked rocked back and forth, breathing heavily, and then collapsed, one by one.

'Abanshamash, Abanshamash, Abanshamash, Abanshamash . . .' chanted a few of the bowed heads. The miracle had again been revealed to them.

Atu let his arms fall, smiling gently to everyone in the room. Then he turned his palms to face up to the bundles of rays that hit him, which usually indicated that the séance was almost over. Sometimes it took ten minutes, other times half an hour. You never knew.

'Now you will return to your refuges to collect your best energy and direct it to Malena, who is in dire need of them,' he said finally. 'After that, search the path to deep and unaffected balance and peace of the soul following the usual instructions. Do it with humility and pride in your heart, then you will be channelled towards all that nature has to offer. Draw the world's particles to you. Absorb everything from which you come and what you will be. Let the light burn the loathing and hatred out of you. Let the darkness envelop all your uncontrollable thoughts so they wither away, and liberate yourselves. Let the sun and all its energy reign.'

He spread his arms out to bless and received with bowed head their parting greeting: 'We are ready, Abanshamash, and we see. We see and we feel. Abanshamash, Abanshamash, Abanshamash.'

Pirjo nodded while the assembly collected themselves and slowly turned towards her. There were always many – perhaps especially male disciples – who treasured this tête-à-tête, and Pirjo relished it. When Atu couldn't show her interest of the flesh, it was something that at least some of the others could. But Pirjo knew well enough that there was nothing wrong with her appearance, and that power and beauty in equal measure were the best cocktail when it came to awakening desire. Her problem was just that she only wanted him, and he didn't want her enough.

'I think you look beautiful and serene today,' said a female voice in the crowd to her.

Pirjo caught Valentina's face. She was the chameleon and IT genius of the centre, sometimes in an ecstatic rush of happiness, sometimes short-haired, long-haired, dishevelled, or maybe outright the neatest individual, who could float across the blazing floor of the hall. This time she was on top. That much was clear. A man from the newly arrived recruits was standing with his hands on her shoulders, so there were obviously already new sensual vibrations to get used to. Good for Valentina, even though they didn't allow the disciples to have sexual contact before their auras had been directed toward each other and subsequently joined in a sun ceremony.

'You seem so serene and pure,' continued Valentina. She'd always had a desire to stick out from the crowd, but perhaps that wasn't so strange for someone with her past.

Pirjo straightened her back and smiled mechanically back at her. 'Go in peace, all of you,' she said as always. 'When your absorption is complete, the kitchen team from Fire House can go to the kitchen and start preparing.'

*

Like a cat creeping up on its prey, he was suddenly standing there looking over her shoulder.

Pirjo got a shock.

Just ten seconds earlier and he would've caught her red-handed deleting the day's recordings from the cameras that monitored the driveway and the Stable of Senses. If it had sparked any questions, it would've paralysed her.

She composed herself and turned slowly around in her office chair, looking reproachfully at him.

'You'll give me a heart attack, creeping up on me in the office like that. I've told you before, Atu.'

He threw his hands in the air; it was a habit he had consciously adopted years back in place of saying sorry.

'We missed you this afternoon, Pirjo. Where were you? We looked for you.'

It was an awful question. Not because she hadn't prepared an answer, but because it was Atu who asked, and because he had X-ray vision when it came to what she was thinking. She was like an open book to him. There was a risk that even the simplest lie would be found out.

She realized that she had to turn the situation around so he didn't probe any deeper, wondering if the time had also come to confront him with her desires.

'I just needed to get away for a bit from the academy,' she said. 'Why do you ask? Haven't you had enough of your own work to keep you busy?'

He sighed. 'It's been a terrible day, but maybe you don't know? Malena aborted a few hours ago, and you weren't there when I needed you. You should've gone with her in the ambulance to the hospital.'

'Aborted?' Pirjo averted her eyes. What should she think? Had Atu got her pregnant? Her? Malena?

She sat for a moment, trying to let it sink in. It couldn't be true, not now. She couldn't allow it, not any longer. It was serious now. Was she to share him with others while her fertility waned and the clock ticked faster and faster? No, not any more. It was her child Atu should father. Her child who should be his successor. Her child who should be the new saviour.

'She aborted and bled uncontrollably,' she heard Atu say.

Pirjo pulled herself together and tried to look neutral.

'Did she?'

'Yes. It was serious, so we needed you, Pirjo. Where were you?'

She blinked a couple of times before she directed her eyes towards him. Under no circumstances would she look remorseful, certainly not because of Malena. He just needed to think she was upset about it.

'I feel your energy. You aren't feeling well,' he said. The message had been received.

'No, that's right, I'm not feeling well. That's why I drove up to Nordodden today. I do that sometimes when I'm feeling a bit down.'

'A bit down?' He said it as if it ought to be the last thing she had any reason to be.

'Yes, despondent. But I don't want to discuss it with you, Atu. Especially not after what you've just told me.'

'What do you mean?'

'You know fine well.'

'We two can't have secrets from each other, can we?'

And he asked that now.

'Since when?'

'What are you implying, my friend?'

'Shouldn't you at least have told me that you were ready to impregnate one of your disciples? Didn't we have an agreement that I'd be the first to know when you took that decision?'

'We certainly have an agreement that if something's bothering you, you'll come to me straightaway, right, Pirjo?'

She hesitated momentarily. 'Why do you think I was up at Nordodden today? Can't you figure it out?'

He reached for the door to his own room. 'You're my vestal, Pirjo. I cherish that, and that's how I want it. And tomorrow you'll drive to the hospital in Kalmar and look in on Malena. Can we agree on that?' He said, giving her a hug before disappearing into himself.

Pirjo nodded very slowly. She had to go into town anyway to remove Wanda Phinn's suitcase from the locker. She was finally going to get a chance to be alone with that French gold-digger.

She sat for a moment, contemplating her ammunition. It was sure to use up some of her resources, but what did it matter as long as the bitch disappeared from her life.

For a moment she found herself laughing out loud.

Was it really now that Lady Luck had decided to smile down on her?

Would she really manage to rid herself of her two worst rivals within the same day?

22

Tuesday, May 6th, 2014

'Welcome to the meeting, my honoured guests, your drinks are served,' said Assad, pouring some sort of blend that smelled less of coffee or mint, and more like the hair of a goat, or worse.

Carl returned Gordon's worried expression, which Assad noticed with a smile.

'It isn't actually one of my recipes, it's Rose's,' he assured them, as Gordon stuck his nose in the cup and seemingly came off all right.

Encouraged by that, Carl took a sip, which led to less than happy memories of his and Vigga's trips to May 1st meetings and their ethnic cafes flashing painfully before him.

'Mu tea,' said Rose unashamedly, placing her notebook on Assad's Bollywood-esque tray table. Only the crakow shoes were missing.

Carl pushed the cup discreetly away from him. 'Right. Since we've got a so-called situation room, I assume the idea is that we'll meet here occasionally and brief each other. Shall we get started right away?'

He stood for a moment considering the order.

'It'll be a week tomorrow since Christian Habersaat took his own life,' he began. 'And while we've made some progress in relation to the investigation, it's rather small, to be honest, but let's cling to it.'

He nodded to Assad when he noticed that even he found it difficult to swallow Rose's brew. It was about time he got a taste of his own medicine.

'Most importantly, we now know precisely when Alberte met the man with the VW for the first time. If it *was* him she met, but it probably was. In relation to that, I'll shortly be calling the former rector couple from the folk high school, who'll hopefully confirm the date of the school trip to Østerlars Round Church. We expect it was November 11th, 1997, due to the imperfect dating on Alberte's postcard to her brother, but we're not sure.

'I'll also ask the couple to tell me what's become of Alberte's drawings. Not because I think it's relevant that we see them but because they never came to the parents, so it'll satisfy compassion and curiosity.' He tried to emphasize his empathetic qualities, but it apparently didn't make any further impression. 'Right then! Let's see what comes of that. And finally, I'll have a word with Lars Bjørn.'

'You don't think I'm the one who should contact Bjørn? Isn't it just a bit crazy and idiotic?' Gordon protested cautiously.

Carl shook his head. There was no way he'd let Gordon do that. It was one thing that Bjørn had thrust the man on them, but he shouldn't be his spy and snitch, too.

'Fine,' he said hesitantly. 'But then maybe you'd like me to call the automobile club that organized the classic car festival?'

'No, I'll take care of that, too, Gordon. I've got a bigger task in mind for you. I want you to trace the current addresses and telephone numbers of all the students who attended the folk high school in the autumn of 1997.'

There was a gasp. In a moment of desperation the guy clung to the sight of the teacup, evidently to have something or other to fortify himself, but he gave up that thought quickly. Apparently, he'd also had enough.

'But Carl, there were fifty students!'

'Yes, and . . . ?'

'And among them four from Estonia, two from Latvia, four from Lithuania and two Russians,' he said, his face looking more put-out than it normally did.

'There, you see. Look how well informed you are. You *are* the right person for the job.'

The poor guy looked as though he might cry. 'Not to mention that many of them have probably changed names.'

'Well, then, stop talking about it, Gordon,' said Rose angrily. But then he hadn't wanted to drink her tea either.

'Right,' said Carl. 'Of all the students, we've already spoken with Kristoffer and Inge Dalby, and for obvious reasons we don't need to talk to Alberte, so you're already down to forty-seven.'

Was that a quiet *hallelujah* from the man?

'How's it going with the technicians?' asked Assad.

'Laursen's on it. He'll get further with them than me. But you, Assad, keep hunting those shelves to see if you can find a photo of that board the boy found by the Camel Heads.'

'Hunt?'

'Hunt, search, look, same thing. Just an expression, Assad.'

He nodded, and Carl turned to Rose.

'And you're already in full swing calling the Bornholm societies that work with mystical phenomena?'

She confirmed.

'We need to assume that people behind these sorts of ventures have day jobs to have something to live off, so you might need to work nights. Spend the next few days on it, Rose. Then we'll see if anyone remembers something about the hippy commune at Ølene, and who might be able to provide information about the man with the VW Kombi.'

Strangely enough, she seemed satisfied with the job. She certainly offered the mu tea around a second time.

'Hello, Carl Mørck. You called the club chairman but you'll have to make do with me because our chairman is travelling.' The man introduced himself as Hans Agger, deputy chairman of Bornholm Classic Car Enthusiasts' Club. 'You see, I *am* the right person to talk to anyway, because I'm in charge of the club archives. And that's a job I've done since I stopped as chairman.'

Carl thanked him. 'Have you received the photo I mailed to the chairman?'

'Yes, the chairman's wife forwarded it. And what I can tell you about it is that a policeman by the name of Christian Habersaat asked me the same thing a few years ago. But unfortunately we don't know who took the photo. So I'll tell you what I told him, that where the man was parked was an area reserved for participants in the race, and a VW Kombi from the seventies didn't belong in that category now, did it?' He laughed so heartily that Carl had to move the receiver away from his ear.

'Which meant?' he asked.

'Well, we had to quietly and politely ask the man to park somewhere else, but the situation was such that he *couldn't* because the engine wasn't doing too good, to put it mildly.'

Carl pulled himself to the edge of the table. 'OK, you can actually remember that. Can you remember the man, too?'

He laughed again. 'No, not really. But I can remember that Sture Nielsen sorted out the little problem for him, just something with the distributor. It almost always is.'

'Sture?'

'Yes, Sture Kure – funny name, isn't it. He was our handyman. A wonderful mechanic up from Olsker, but he died shortly after, unfortunately. Maybe that's why I remember it.'

Damn it, could no one manage to stay alive until you needed them! Carl sighed. 'And Habersaat never managed to speak with him before he died, I suppose?'

'Not that I know of.'

He put the receiver down with an annoying feeling that didn't get any better after the call to the rector couple.

Yes, they remembered the trip to Østerlars well, because after Mr Mørck and his assistant's visit, their curiosity had been awakened and as a result they'd read everything there was about that fall in Karina's diaries, explained the rector. The trip was on November 7th and they'd visited several round churches. But other than that, Karina hadn't written anything of interest. Trips like those to sights on Bornholm had taken place as part of almost every course, so the novelty value had faded as the years had gone by.

Afterwards, Carl reflected over what had been said. Alberte met the man on November 7th and not the 11th, the two number ones on the postcard must be from the month, which meant that she'd only known him for less than two weeks when she was killed. But what could she have done to that man that led him, if there was any substance to Habersaat's theory, to choose such a fatal ending to their relationship?

And who was she, then? This girl who suddenly began to challenge her surroundings with her female presence? The girl who sang like an angel and drew almost as well?

He hit his forehead. The drawings! He'd forgotten them.

The second time he called the rector couple was altogether more successful.

Yes, confirmed the former rector. He was certain that Alberte's drawings were lying around somewhere up at the school. As he remembered, there should've been an exhibition of student work the day before Alberte disappeared, but then they had a visit from the Rhythmic Folk High School, and that had been excellent, but as a result the exhibition was put to one side and never came to anything.

'I think the drawings must still be lying in a folder somewhere down in the school basement, but you'd need to talk to the school secretary about that.'

'I'm nipping up to Bjørn, Assad,' Carl informed him five minutes later. 'I have another job for you. You were so taken with the school secretary on Bornholm, so give her a call and ask her to look for some drawings from what should have been a student exhibition on November 19th, 1997. We want to see Alberte's, and we'll pay for the postage and return them when we're finished with them – say that. Are you with me?'

'Err, yes, maybe. But what does *taken with* mean?'

Up in the Department of Violent Crime, the atmosphere was no longer like in the good old days when Marcus Jacobsen had been at the helm. Chief of Homicide Lars Bjørn really did try to create some form of cosy atmosphere with a pair of explosively abstract paintings by Annette Merrild and a few coffee cups with coloured dots on them, but it didn't change the fact that deep down Carl thought that the head of the department was a boor and a man who could only show affection if you were in his immediate family.

'Who the hell is that?' whispered Carl to his favourite secretary, Lis, in reference to an unknown face behind the desk.

'That's Bjørn's niece. She's temping for Mrs Sørensen while she's away.'

'Is the battleaxe away?' Strangely enough, he hadn't noticed. 'And why is she away?'

'Oh, you know. Menopause. She has hot flushes and she's a little hysterical at the moment. We've agreed to call it influenza.'

Carl was shocked. Had Mrs Sørensen been fertile right up until now? It certainly wasn't an obvious thought.

She pointed over towards Bjørn's door, from where a few new faces emerged.

They whispered a little as they walked past Carl. As if he gave a damn.

He pushed open the door to Bjørn's office without knocking first.

'Do we have an appointment, Carl Mørck? I don't recall that,' said Bjørn when Carl slammed the photo of the man with the VW on the table in front of him.

Carl ignored both question and tone. 'Here we have a photo of a man who very likely killed a young girl on Bornholm. I'd like your permission to put out a missing person's report on TV2's *Station 2*.'

At this, the chief of homicide bared his annoyingly white teeth somewhere between a smile and a laugh. 'Thanks, keep trying, Carl,' he said. 'I've already heard enough. We wouldn't be talking about the case from 1997 that Bornholm Police dismissed fifteen years ago by any chance, would we? Because if we are, then there's neither a murder case nor any suspicion about anything special. So, thank you for your time, Carl, and I'll see you at the general briefing.'

OK, so that snitch Gordon had managed to get here before him.

'I get the message, Bjørn. Gordon's obviously been here whining about his workload. If that's the case, you're more than welcome to take him back again. Just say the word.'

'Gordon has done nothing of the sort, Mørck. But you must understand that in my position as chief of homicide, I speak regularly with my colleagues on Bornholm. If you've otherwise forgotten, they are still closely connected with the department here.'

Sarcasm. Great.

'Thanks for the information. But let me tell you, since you have such a great need to keep informed about everything, that we've found new leads in the case, which your good friends on Bornholm haven't found, and that no matter what you say, I intend to follow up on until we have someone sitting safely behind bars for either murder or manslaughter and hit-and-run.'

'That same old tone again, Mørck. I've got one thing to say in response to that: you won't engage the whole of Denmark in guessing who this man might be. The man in that wretched photo has never been charged, and besides, he could be anyone at all. We'd receive tons of useless calls, hundreds of man hours would be wasted and, to be honest, Mr Mørck, we have more serious things to concern ourselves with up here on the second floor.'

'Fine, at least we know where we stand. You just divert all the calls down to the less serious Department Q in the basement, Mr Chief of Homicide. We wouldn't want to disturb Sleeping Beauty's beauty sleep up here.'

'Good day, Carl.' He waved him towards the door. 'You can forget any idea about a missing person's report on the TV. Maybe you don't recall a fairly recent case where some of the tabloids hung a person out as guilty in a murder case and shortly after came to eat their words. Compensation responsibility – do you know that expression?'

Carl slammed the door, making everyone in the reception area look up.

'Goddamnit, Carl,' sounded the voice behind the door. At least that provided a bit of amusement.

'Yeah, you've never exactly been in Bjørn's good books, have you, Carl?' said Lis just loud enough so everyone in the vicinity stopped. 'But on a different note, are you and Mona Ibsen back together again?'

Carl frowned. Why on earth did she mention that?

'I'm just wondering because she's been asking after you today. She stuck her head in for five minutes before she dashed over to a preliminary hearing.'

'She's back, then?'

'Yes, the reassignment was only until April. Then she took her holiday over on the west coast, and now she's back again.'

'She was only asking so she was warned if I should come barging in,' he suggested.

But it was definitely strange. As was the sinking feeling in his stomach that crept over him.

'I haven't found any photo of the wooden board, Carl, and I think I've been through most of the shelves.'

Assad looked done in. One of his bushy eyebrows appeared to have given in and covered half his eye. 'I know that I need to check once again, but I don't think I'll find it, Carl.'

'Are you OK, Assad? You look a bit bleary-eyed.'

'Just didn't sleep too well last night. I had a call from an uncle, and there are big problems.'

'In Syria?'

He looked blankly into space. 'He's in Lebanon now, but . . .'

'Is there anything I can do, Assad?'

'No, Carl, there's nothing we can do. Not you, anyway.'

Carl nodded. 'If you need a few days off, we'll work something out,' he said.

'That's the last thing I need, thanks all the same. I think we just need to move on and into that situation room. Rose has news for us.'

It was the usual. As direct and present as Assad could be on his best days, he could be just as distant and unreachable in moments like this. Carl had no idea what was going on with him. If he mentioned the situation in Syria, Assad sidestepped the issue. And yet it was as if all the serious events down there didn't really affect him. Actually, he never discussed Syria or other events in the Middle East. Sometimes a random word could open a wound, but other times it was like water off a duck's back.

Carl gave him a pat on the shoulder. 'You know you can always come to me with anything, right?'

Rose stood waiting by the whiteboard, and Gordon was about to sit down when they came in. Funnily enough, it meant that they were suddenly exactly the same height.

'Relax,' was the first thing Rose said when she saw Gordon's expectant face. He'd probably hoped that there'd been a breakthrough and that the mind-numbingly boring job of making contact with all the old folk-high-school students would be rendered superfluous.

'You can't get to Rome in a few hours now, can you?' she concluded mistakenly, as she pulled some of Habersaat's brochures with hearts, crystals and radiant suns down from the wall.

'So far, I've only managed to get in touch with the people behind these three alternative offers, and all of them work full-time with their different treatments, which they've done for nineteen, twenty-five and thirty-two years, respectively. But it was only Beate Vismut from Heart of the Mind, who mainly works with the symbiosis of body and nature, who could remember the young guy with the VW Kombi. She told me that she didn't have anything to add to what Christian Habersaat had already pumped out of her.' Rose smiled. 'And yet I still managed to squeeze something new out of her.'

'Good, Rose. Is it the guy's name? A description? His background?' tried Carl.

'No, she didn't remember the name, he possibly never mentioned it to her, and we never got to the rest. Beate Vismut doesn't like to know anything about her clients' past or data, which she explained by telling me that she was born blind and therefore works on a totally different level to the seeing.'

'Is our best witness blind?' He shook his head. It was all too much.

'Yes and she only wants to *feel* her clients, as she puts it. But she did manage to give me an idea about what the man stood for.'

'Stood for?'

'Yes. Beate encourages her clients, or students, as she prefers to call them, to rid themselves of anything that can remove them from nature, and that's quite a radical demand, let me tell you. Personally, for example, she won't have her home heated, because she doesn't like winter and summer blending together. Neither will she have nonorganic building materials, so she lives in a house built from straw bales, which she did long before it became fashionable.'

'She has a telephone.'

'Yes, and other things that can help her as a blind person. She's still dependent on the world around her. But here it comes.' The self-satisfaction radiated from Rose's pale face. 'The guy agreed with her about many things. He was also extremely preoccupied with nature as something sacred and healing, but they had discussions about the extent of self-sacrifice, she remembered. For example, he didn't think that he could do without his VW Kombi because . . .' She smiled and took a long pause. 'Because he had a great need to be free to travel to places where, through the ages, people had worshipped the sun, elements and supernatural phenomena. And he couldn't do that without a form of transport.'

'OK, so now we know that it's him with the VW Kom—'

'*And* . . .' she interrupted, 'because of that he'd spent the past few years travelling a lot around Europe with a few of his followers, among other places to Gotland, Ireland and Bornholm. He sought out sacred places there, of which there are many on the island, and he'd been very interested in the rock carvings on Bornholm from the Bronze Age, traces of ships in Troldeskoven, the monoliths at Hjortebakken, and the cult sites at Rispebjerg and Knarhøj . . .'

Knarhøj? Where had Carl heard that name before?

'Yes, and *not* least . . . the Knights Templar myths from Østerlars Church. What do you say to that?'

'Great. So we've connected the VW, the man and Alberte to each other,' said Assad.

'Yes, probably,' agreed Carl. 'Good work, Rose, but what now? We're no closer to knowing the man's identity. We don't know where he came from, or where he went afterwards. All we know is he's a man on the move, so now he could be anywhere, if he's even alive. He might be on Malta or in Jerusalem – they had Knights Templar there. Maybe he's sitting humming weird sounds at Stonehenge, in Nepal or in the Inca city of Machu Picchu. We don't know. Maybe he's moved on from all this nonsense and is right now assistant chief in the Department of the Interior with ten years of service and a pension ahead of him.'

'Beate Vismut said that he was a real crystal, so I don't think you should be worried about the Department of the Interior idea.'

'A real crystal, what on earth does she mean by that?'

'That he'd seen the true light and mirrored himself in it, and had probably never been able to live without it since.'

'God almighty, it gets more and more weird. And what does that mean?'

'If you ask her, she assumes that he's still active in the game, and probably more than ever.'

23

October, November and December 2013

Shirley was disappointed. Disappointed with Paco Lopez, the hot Spaniard who'd promised her the world, and went home with her every night for a week to have sex and home-made food, and then finally pulled his worn engagement ring out of his pocket before saying goodbye and thank you. Disappointed with her employer, who fired her instead of the new cafeteria woman who'd only been there for three months. Disappointed with the diet that'd guaranteed her a weight loss of ten kilos but seemed to do almost the opposite, and disappointed with Wanda Phinn, who despite all her grand promises had never even favoured her with so much as a simple postcard.

The first month she was a little concerned for her lapsed friend, but then that stopped just like everything else.

Such was her life.

She tried to forget her by telling herself that she'd just been a cow like everyone else, while trying to calculate how long she could last without work, with only her measly benefits and £1,006 in the bank.

Not exactly a positive future financial outlook, even though her standard of living had already been reduced to nada, as Paco always said, and nothing indicated that it could change.

'No, you're too late for that job, someone got it yesterday,' was the general answer she got when she did finally stumble across something.

So Shirley was standing on the edge of the most desperate and humiliating decision that an uneducated and moderately over-weight forty-something could take: to be forced to move back to the apartment in Birmingham where she was born and where her folks still lived.

She called her parents to test the water. What would they say to her coming home for a few months because she missed them so much?

Unfortunately it wasn't reciprocated, so they'd obviously seen through her plan: Shirley wasn't just fishing to celebrate Christmas and New Year's with them.

So there she was, stuck in a wretched apartment block in one of the most deprived areas of London, waiting for nothing, while the Christmas lights flickered in the shop windows and all the children were smiling.

Shirley thought that she should've done the same as Wanda because she must be happy where she was, seeing as she hadn't heard from her. And the more Shirley thought about it, the more she pictured Wanda's life on the mystical island, where Atu reigned, as a fairy tale come true.

Had Wanda had more money than her when she travelled? Not as far as Shirley knew. And had Wanda had an invitation to go over there? No, not even that.

So the question of why she couldn't just do the same filled her thoughts, shutting out the reality of her miserable situation over the coming days and nights.

While Shirley thought about these essential questions, she sat by the table covered with the oilcloth next to the gas heater, shuffling her greasy playing cards so that they could give her answers. Her preferred game of solitaire at the moment wasn't the easiest, but, on the other hand, it carried more weight if it worked.

Shirley decided that if she completed this game of solitaire, she'd seriously consider whether or not to leave. So when she *did* actually complete it, a whole new set of questions was set in motion. What now? Should she inform Wanda or the Nature Absorption Academy first? What was the most sensible approach? Just pack her bags and say goodbye to it all?

After spending half a weekend where she completed game after game, she subsequently decided that she *knew* that she would go, which left her only to answer the definitive question: to wait or go now.

And then it happened: she completed the seventh game in a row.

Now she knew for sure that she should leave her current life. And it had to be now.

Thoughts about how they'd receive her at the Nature Absorption Academy preoccupied Shirley for the entire journey. She was sure that the friendly people she had met in London would welcome her with open arms, but would Wanda? Wasn't there more than a hint that their friendship was history?

Shirley could imagine Wanda's reaction. Here she came from London, disturbing her routine with all her nonsense and chatter about the old days. No, Shirley didn't harbour any grand illusions about that welcome, but that shouldn't stop her. If Wanda could make the leap, then Shirley could, too. After all, she was the one who'd introduced Wanda to Atu Abanshamash Dumuzi's heavenly universe. She shouldn't forget that.

When she arrived, she took the bus from Kalmar train station out to the island as far as she could, travelling the rest of the way on foot.

When she finally arrived, she was greeted by the impressive sight of a cluster of newly built houses leaning out towards the sea.

Even from a distance the academy appeared magical with its many white buildings crowned with pyramid roofs with coloured glass inlay, glistening solar cells on several buildings and enormous windows. It was bigger than she'd expected. Much bigger. And from up on the road you got the impression that once you were here you didn't need anything else. Shirley hadn't seen much in life, and definitely nothing like this. It was as if the whole area quivered with energy. As if all sorts of currents glided through this landscape of exotic growth, work of human hand and mysterious signs.

The first thing that indicated what you had arrived at was a large enamel sign with the words:

Nature Absorption Academy
Ebabbar

A speckled tiled path led past it and up towards a few smaller houses and two pavilions joined together facing the water, with new meticulously painted signs written in several languages: *The Academy's Communal Heart.*

There was quiet activity in the reception, where people clothed in white appeared to glide across the floor in a state of inner peace as they nodded to her in a friendly manner.

She straightened her flower-patterned dress and smoothed down her blouse. She just needed to try to look decent amid all this stylish purity.

She thought that she could easily be happy here, as she stepped further toward the door where a sign read:

Arrival and Registration.
Pirjo A. Dumuzi

*   *   *

Malena was looking paler than the white lab coats worn by the nurses in the sterile-looking gynaecological ward on the fourth floor of Kalmar Hospital, when Pirjo suddenly stood at the end of her bed.

Pirjo smiled to herself. Of course the woman had hoped that it would be Atu who came to show his compassion and how much he cared, but then she obviously didn't know him well enough.

'How are you?' asked Pirjo.

Malena turned her head to face the wall. 'Better. They stopped the bleeding last night, so they'll discharge me later today.'

'Thank goodness, that's good news.'

A twitch of discomfort went through Malena's body when Pirjo took her hand. She tried momentarily to pull away but Pirjo didn't let her.

'What do you want?' Malena turned her head as the silence between them became more deafening. 'What do you want to say, Pirjo? Have you come to gloat? Does this suit you just perfectly, is that it?'

Pirjo frowned in consideration, not too much and not too little. The game had begun.

'No, is that what you thought? You're wrong, Malena, it's not like that at all. I'm truly sorry that this has happened.' She let her head drop slightly, pressed her lips tightly together and looked away, as if she was concentrating on something else she had on her mind. She could sense that it confused Malena. Things were just as they should be.

Pirjo let go of her hand, breathing deeply a couple of times before turning once again to face the woman lying there.

'You need to get away, Malena. When you're discharged, you need to get as damn far from here as you can, do you hear me?'

She pulled her purse out of her bag and produced a wad of notes. 'Look! Here's eight thousand euro. That should keep the wolf from the door for a few months. I've packed your things. They're out in the corridor in your suitcase.'

It was hard to gauge what Malena's face reflected, but it was probably a mixture of loathing and distrust.

'OK. You're really trying to get rid of me now, aren't you, you stupid bitch. I hadn't seen this coming despite it all. But do you really think you'll get me to leave that easily?' she said as she pushed the wad away. 'Atu's mine, do you get it? He doesn't want anything to do with you. You're just his skivvy, bowing and scraping wherever he spits. He told me that himself. So get lost and take your ridiculous money with you, Pirjo. You'll see me at the centre in a couple of hours, back in the position I've fought my way up to. I can find my own way there.'

Sometimes in life, there are moments where you know deep down in your soul that just one misplaced frown or careless smile will have totally unforeseen consequences. So Pirjo concealed what she knew in her heart that Atu felt and had always felt for her. And her anti-venom was to ignore Malena's outpouring and maintain her totally fixed and worried expression. If this was going to work – and it *had* to – Malena needed to have complete faith in her in order to prepare for her world to crumble in a few moments.

'I know better than anyone how much Atu has felt for you, Malena. And I've been happy for both of you, you mustn't think otherwise. Of course you've felt that I'm also very fond of Atu, but as the years have gone by that's changed and become something different for me than for other people, and that's something I came to terms with a long time ago. But you need to understand that in my time with Atu I've seen more than anyone else. There's a dark side to him that I need to warn you about, and I'm worried it'll come as a shock for you.'

The woman smiled. Everything that was enthralling about her radiated defiantly now. The dainty lips, all too white teeth, high cheekbones. 'And what might that be, then?' she asked, full of distrust.

'It's hard to talk about when you care for Atu as much as I do, but I'll try and be direct. You, Malena, are the third woman whose pregnancy with Atu has ended in a miscarriage, and he's both devastated and angry about it. Atu has no children, and he's over forty now, and that's a fact. Hasn't it struck you as odd that he's childless when we all know how many women would do anything for him? Maybe you think he doesn't *want* children, but I can tell you that he does. There's nothing he wants more. And now he feels let down and betrayed again. Yes, you heard me right, let down and betrayed.'

Pirjo squeezed her hands. 'Atu sees your miscarriage as the opening to an abyss of negative energy, and he's shaken up by it, really shaken up. He simply can't tolerate it, I can tell you that much. I know through experience.'

The woman in the bed sneered at her. 'Right, well, I think he can come and tell me that himself.'

Pirjo's eyes were severe now. 'Haven't you understood what I'm saying, Malena? Then let me be totally clear: if you come back to the centre, Atu will sacrifice you.'

Malena pulled herself up on her elbows, smiling mockingly. 'Sacrifice me? Could you really not think of anything better, Pirjo?'

'He'll sacrifice you to the sea, Malena. He'll drown you, just like the other two who lost his offspring. If you stay here, you'll be found bloated and naked on a beach far away from here, I guarantee you.'

She wrinkled her nose, but the words still hit home as hard as she had intended. She had sown both doubt and shock. And when doubt and shock gave rise to feelings of powerlessness and fear, it wouldn't require much before the time was right for a final twist of the dagger.

'They found one of the girls, Claudia, right down on the Polish coast . . .'

Pirjo paused, as if she needed energy again to prepare herself for what she was about to say. 'I don't know what happened to the other girl, Malena, I just don't know. But I don't think they ever found her.'

Malena shook her head. Maybe it was just a reflex. Maybe she just didn't want to hear more. But she was silent.

'I don't think Atu felt he did anything wrong. He was certainly calm when he confided in me. How he'd sent the first woman back into the cycle of nature because she couldn't fulfil her bodily mission. I tried to warn the second one – Lonny, her name was – but she wouldn't listen. You have to listen to me, Malena, please?'

Wrinkles gathered between her eyes. She tried to rub them away, but they wouldn't budge.

'It's a big risk, you know, me sitting here telling you this. I'm worried Atu would do the same to me if he knew I was telling you. Do you understand, Malena? Do you understand what I'm saying?'

She shook her head. But she did.

Following her successful mission, Pirjo drove back to the centre and told Atu that Malena was recovering and would be discharged in a day or two. It gave the girl a head start.

Needless to say, Malena never turned up at the centre and Atu was left wondering why. Why couldn't he get any answers as to why she'd left the hospital, or where she'd gone? He tried to track her down for a few weeks through all sorts of contacts, but it was as if she'd just been swallowed up.

Pirjo offered authentic accounts of the types of depression miscarriage could lead to, and the irrational decisions that might be taken by a woman who'd experienced such a severe and unfortunate event. Atu listened, sad and disheartened, but eventually resigned himself to the situation like the pragmatist he was after all.

One morning, when he'd gone out early as usual to chant, looking out to sea, Pirjo came to him. She brought warm tea and a damp cloth, and without so much as a word began to wash and massage him gently, before slipping off his trousers and straddling him. So simple when the opportunity finally arose.

Perhaps the surprise aroused his desire, perhaps it was her scent, perhaps it was a recognition that he owed her as much. Whatever the reason, he allowed himself to be carried away and gave her what she wanted.

He looked her straight in the eye when he came, and Pirjo trembled. It wasn't just an orgasm, it was something much deeper. Years of deprivation were released in the look she directed back at him. And something else, too.

Pirjo's menstruation cycle was under control, and always had been. Her ovulation was completely regular, and when she knew that she was at her most fertile, the feeling could be so strong that it almost scared her. These days could be a nightmare, but this time she felt the opposite.

It was fast approaching Christmas before she dared to find out for certain the cause of her absent periods. She'd read a lot about what the desire alone to be pregnant could do to a woman's body, so she wanted to be totally sure. The test she'd bought at the pharmacy was positive, and she almost fainted when she saw the result. But she still wanted to get a doctor's opinion of what she hoped the situation was and, if she was right, what measures she needed to take. She was thirty-nine, after all.

When she arrived back from the same gynaecological ward where two months earlier she'd visited Malena, it was with the deepest feeling of happiness.

Atu would be surprised but he'd also be happy, she was sure of it. When it came down to it, she'd proved long ago that she was worthy to bear his child, and that she was the one who had the necessary genes.

When she stood in front of the door to *The Academy's Communal Heart* she had to stop for a moment and compose herself to prevent her emotions from getting the better of her. She didn't want to stand in front of Atu crying. She wanted to say it to him calmly and with a smile. He was used to her that way and this was the way things would continue. Pregnant or not: Pirjo was Pirjo.

But she did smile, perhaps a little too much, as she walked past the disciples in the reception area and entered her office, from where she'd call and ask him to come in to her for a moment.

So her surprise was understandable when she found Atu already standing in her office, with a woman sitting opposite him in flat shoes, heavy make-up, and a dress that was too tight and garish, and which couldn't hide either her age or overweight figure.

'Here you are, Pirjo, just in time,' he said, smiling, nodding towards the woman. 'Shirley has arrived unannounced from London. She took part in one of the sessions over there this summer and would like to join one of our groups. I'm sure we can find room for her, don't you think?'

Pirjo nodded. It wasn't quite how she'd imagined she and Atu would meet in regard to her totally overwhelming news, but it would have to wait. It was a minor setback, but nothing that couldn't be remedied.

'Tell Pirjo what you just told me, Shirley.'

She smiled and said hello in relatively flat Cockney English. 'We were on your course in London, my friend and me, and both became very fascinated with nature absorption. So much so that my friend came over here a few months ago. Or at least I thought she did, but I haven't heard from her since, and Atu Abanshamash Dumuzi . . .' She took a short pause. Just saying his name made her blush. '. . . and I've just been told in reception that she never arrived. It's really strange. I'm actually quite worried now.'

Atu nodded gravely. 'It is odd, you're right, but as I said, she isn't here. I can actually remember her well, Shirley. She was a very attractive girl. Wasn't she mixed race?'

The woman shrugged, and Pirjo's skin suddenly turned ice cold.

'I've never thought about it, actually, but she was definitely very brown. She came from Jamaica, and you can find people of every colour there.'

Atu raised his head. 'Does any of this ring a bell, Pirjo? The girl wrote to us, apparently. What did you say her name was, Shirley?'

Pirjo didn't hear the answer. She already knew it, after all.

She only thought about her next move.

24

Wednesday, May 7th, 2014

'I have a really ridiculous problem with the former students at the folk high school, Carl,' said Gordon. It was incredible how much he could hunch himself up to show his suffering.

'When I finally get hold of some of them, they can't remember anything, and even if they try, they mix things up. One of them had actually been to five different folk high schools since Bornholm, and she couldn't differentiate one from the other. Another one, one of the ones from Lithuania, and the only one funnily enough who still lives at home, couldn't speak a word of English, so how she managed to survive five months on Bornholm is a mystery to me. And then there are the addresses! Apart from this one from Lithuania, there wasn't a single person with the same address as they had then, and that goes for most of the parents, too.' He sighed. 'It's an altogether hopeless job you've given me, Carl. The few I have managed to contact mostly remember something because Habersaat was so annoying, but otherwise only just the name Alberte and that she was found dead. That's all. So, to be honest, and to put it a bit bluntly, her death obviously didn't leave any lasting impression on them.'

Carl reluctantly focused again. When Gordon ranted on, he really had an uncanny ability to make people think about something else.

'Gordon,' he said so loudly that it caused the man to jump, 'you just need to find *one* person who remembers and wants to talk. And when you find him or her you transfer them to Rose, who has all the old student interrogations. She's the one who needs an overview, OK? So give it your best shot. Of course you can find them.'

He left Gordon with his head right down on the edge of the table, Assad giving him a gentle pat on the back. If he was to have any hope of being included in the team, he'd better lift his head up quickly.

Things were quite different in Rose's office. Masses of paper piled high with notes, masses of scrunched-up paper in the bin, and masses of wrinkles on her forehead. She was busy, that much was clear.

'Anything new from the alternative world, Rose?' he dared to ask.

She shook her head. 'I'll need to call around in the evening, Carl. As we discussed earlier, the majority also have a more normal job. But I've been looking through the interviews with the folk high school students, and I stumbled across one that I think Gordon should try and make an appointment with. Read it for yourself. Here's a transcript of the interview.'

'Can't you read it aloud for me?'

'Just read, Carl. Go into your office, light a cigarette and read. But remember to shut the door. All these papers from Habersaat stink enough of smoke already.'

Carl sniffed as he went past the shelves and on to his office. Apart from Rose's perfume, which both made his nose itchy and eyes water, he couldn't smell anything.

He put the paper down in front of him on his desk, obediently took a cigarette as suggested and read Habersaat's transcript.

12/19 1997. Interrogation of Synne Veland, 46 years old, autumn semester student. Middle-school teacher currently on leave from Hvidovre Municipality. Social security number 161151-4012.

Transcript excerpt 12/10 1997.

Carl stopped. A thought came to him, but was it really imaginable that the man was so blindingly stupid? He tried to imagine Gordon at work. God almighty, it could just be.

He pressed the intercom.

'It's coming from here,' shouted Assad into the intercom on the other side of the corridor, his own voice drowning himself out.

'It's not you I want to talk to, Assad. Are you listening, Gordon? Are you there?'

Something squeaked. Was it the chair or an acknowledgment?

'You *have* made sure to get a list of the social security numbers of all those at the folk high school, right?' He caught himself nodding, but knew that it couldn't be the case.

'No,' he confirmed. 'The school said they couldn't give them to me.'

Now Carl lit his cigarette and inhaled deeply. What a tool, and definitely not the sharpest one in the shed!

'Are you a total idiot?' he shouted. 'That's the first thing you do. Damn it, Assad, tell him that he's got direct access to all civil registration details, and that he has every right to those details from the school if anyone has, and that he can otherwise find all the social security numbers on Habersaat's interrogations, if he bothered to look. Tell him to get on with it. And that means *now*, tell him!'

'Do I need to when you've just said it, boss?' Assad grunted back into the speaker.

Carl took a deep drag and coughed a couple of times. 'And what are you up to, Assad?'

'I'm sitting with something I've just found. I'll be in with it in a minute.'

Carl hung up. Why couldn't anyone think for themselves?

But then maybe he should've seen this coming?

He shook his head and continued reading Habersaat's report.

. . . 161151-4012

Transcript Excerpt 12/10 1997.

Synne Veland's statement about Alberte:

'Yes, I didn't really know her like many of the others did. We seniors aren't with the young ones as much. The average age this year is roughly twenty-six and a half, raised by the group of over-forties, who I have more to do with, of course, so we feel a bit past it in relation to the others. And on top of that, you need to remember that Alberte was one of the youngest. Younger than my own daughter, in fact, and not much older than those I normally say goodbye to when they leave tenth grade. But I talked with her, of course, and I noticed her too. We all did because she was so beautiful and full of life. I also noticed that some of the other young girls seemed somewhat jealous of her because all the boys, and the men for that matter, were always glancing over at her, but I didn't think it was anything serious. It's natural at that age.

And I remember that the day before she disappeared we had a visit

from the Rhythmic Folk High School, and with Alberte being as inter-
ested in music as she was – she actually had a sweet and adorable voice,
too – I thought it was strange that she wasn't there at the end of the
afternoon and that she wasn't at the party in the evening, either.

One of the guys, one she'd flirted with, Kristoffer his name is, said at
one point that she'd found herself someone outside the school, and I'd
noticed that she'd been a bit distant over the last few days. You know
how a girl in love can look – (she laughs). And she was also distant in
another sense of the word. We took glass work together, but she didn't
turn up to lessons for most of the last week.'

(Q: Did you ever see the man or the young guy?)

'No, but it struck me that Alberte had said one day that she'd met the most
mystical and fascinating person ever. Nothing specifically about being in
love but she was obviously very taken with him. Naturally, we asked who
he was but she just giggled, she often did, and said he was just someone
she'd met and that he sometimes drove past the school after lessons.'

(Q: So you didn't ask if they met to talk out by the road or
if they went for a drive together?)

'No, unfortunately.' (Synne Veland seems regretful and perhaps also a
little sad.)

(Q: Are there others you can think of who might know
more about it?)

'We have spoken about it since. Maybe Kristoffer, but otherwise, no, I
don't think so.'

(Q: But isn't it just the sort of thing you'd expect the girls to talk about?)

'Yes, but I think Alberte was well aware that the other girls had had enough of all her flirting. So she just kept quiet, I think. Maybe to try and avoid provoking them more than was necessary.'

(Q: Maybe it was a sort of game for her with this guy? A secret game?)

'Yes, that could be it.'

Carl read on. There was absolutely nothing explosive in this interview.

He pressed the intercom again. 'Rose, would you come in here?'

'You can just as well come out to me instead!' she shouted from the corridor.

Carl stuck his head out, and there she was, sitting on the floor with all the transcripts piled in between her legs.

'Wouldn't it be more comfortable to sit in your office and read?' he tried without getting an answer. 'Right, well, why do you think this interrogation is something special? Apart from making me aware of Gordon's ineptitude, I don't see anything in it that we didn't know before. Maybe you want us to talk to the woman? Because from this, I don't think there's any point. She must be about sixty-two now. It's almost twenty years ago, so why should she remember something useful now that didn't come out in the open then?'

'You're saying that because you're a man. But men are sometimes so blind. Notice how simple the questions are that Habersaat asks her. If it had been you, would you have asked her the same?'

'Well, he certainly wasn't an investigator, but otherwise mostly the same, I reckon.'

'But the details, Carl. What about them?'

'Such as?'

'Listen, if it'd been *your* case, and if it'd been fresh, you would've asked about lots of things that you can't think of right now, but that a woman naturally thinks of even after such a long time.'

'Details? About Alberte, you mean?' Carl looked at the tightly packed shelves with tons of paper. As if they didn't have enough details to deal with.

He sighed. 'You mean footwear, clothes, hair?'

'Yes, that and a whole lot more. New movements, different make-up. Everything that tells us something about how a young woman feels. It can be expressed through things like that.'

He nodded, she was right. He'd had cases where women remembered everything about other women's plucked eyebrows, but nothing about where they'd seen them, or in what connection.

'Hmm. And I suppose now you want us to find Synne Veland and ask about these things seventeen years later?'

'Of course we will. Synne Veland has an artistic nature. She discovered the creative side of herself at folk high school, appreciated music, took glass craft. She must have noticed things like that.'

'And so what, even if she did? Maybe those signs will tell us that Alberte was in love or maybe just out to have a good time, but isn't it irrelevant now? I think the lead is a bit thin.'

'Probably. But we can talk about that afterwards.'

'Right then. There's another lead you might also check. Since you named Knarhøj yesterday in connection with the guy we're looking for, it's been on my mind. We've come across it before, someone who was digging there.'

'Hmm, yes, now that you mention it . . .'

Assad's dishevelled body appeared from his office, his hands full of paper and, unfortunately, also a steaming cup of tea. This would be good.

'I've found this here, Carl,' he said as they sat down in Carl's office. 'I wonder if it might be along the lines of what we're looking for.'

He put down a few sheets in front of him with graphs and numbers, placing the steaming cup next to them.

'I thought you'd be in need of a pick-me-up, Carl.'

Oh God! The cup was for him.

'What is it?' It didn't smell like it normally did. Better, actually.

'It's chai. A great recipe. Indian tea and ginger. It's good for everything.' He pointed to his crotch with a cheeky grin.

'You've been having problems with your waterworks, perhaps?' Carl said ironically.

Assad gave him a nudge with his elbow and winked. 'There's talk that Mona's been asking after you.'

Damn, word got around quick here! And what was the idea – was his libido to be pumped up by a strange-smelling tea?

'Forget it, Assad. Mona's well and truly in the past.'

'What about Pristine, wasn't that the name of the last one?'

'You're thinking of Kristine. But yes, what about her? She's gone back to her ex-husband. I don't think your tea can help much with that.'

He shrugged his shoulders. 'Look at this. Christian Habersaat has made a plan of the tree, the road past the tree and the bike in the thicket. It needed to be very precise, so he probably hasn't drawn it himself. I think it must've been the technicians.'

Carl turned the drawing a little and looked at it. Yes, not dissimilar to how he'd also envisioned it.

Assad produced another piece of paper. 'But I've also done a drawing. It's meant to be a vertical section of the accident site and surrounding area.'

He pointed to the different elements as he named them each in turn. 'As you can see, it was approximately here that Alberte was hit to enable her to end up in the branches.' His finger followed the trajectory that Habersaat had drawn. It looked reasonable, if slightly steeper than Carl had imagined.

'On this third drawing he's added what he thinks might've thrown her up in the air. Notice the angle of the whatsit. It's at an angle and only seven to eight centimetres above the surface of the road.'

Carl nodded. 'Yes, the shovel blade that threw Alberte up in the tree must've been at about this angle. I can see where he's coming from. But why did it kill her? I don't think it looks deadly.'

'Maybe the shock killed her, Carl. When you shoot people through the heart, they immediately die from the shock. This is probably similar.'

Carl shook his head. 'Yeah, maybe, though I've got my doubts. But if Habersaat's drawing is right, and there's good reason to believe it is, then she was almost shovelled up into the treetop. Of course you'd get some nasty bruises and definitely some lesions, but would it kill someone?'

'Just a moment.' Assad disappeared out the door, and Carl stared at the cup. The combination of words like 'libido' and 'Mona' made him suddenly thirsty. A little sip couldn't hurt.

He felt the steam and the smell of distant, exotic coasts and dived in. He thought it tasted rather good until the effect kicked in.

The combination of neck arteries suddenly opening, oesophagus collapsing, vocal cords scratching like hell and not being able to feel his uvula all made him instinctively grab his throat with one hand and support himself on the edge of the table with the other. If there'd been acid in the cup, it wouldn't have felt much different.

He wanted to swear but not a word came out, only tears and saliva from the corners of his mouth, and he had an unusually keen desire for revenge and ice-cold water by the bucketload.

'What's wrong, Carl?' asked Assad as he came in with the report. 'Was there too much ginger?'

Just as Police Superintendent Birkedal had told them, the autopsy upheld that Alberte's body showed both fractures and internal bleeding, though not so severe that any single injury could be deemed to have been the cause of death.

Carl summed up: 'We can conclude from the autopsy that Alberte was still alive when she was flung up in the tree, and that she was alive for a good while afterwards. The shinbone and calf bone were broken in both legs, as well as additional fractures elsewhere, but the lesions weren't individually so serious that they would be fatal. Not immediately, at least. She hung in the tree with her head down the entire time, so she lost blood. Not litres, but enough.'

Carl put the report down on the table. Alberte Goldschmid had hung there for a long time before she died. Poor girl.

'What do you say to that, Carl?' asked Assad.

'Nothing other than that Habersaat's drawing may well be correct. She was shovelled up there and during the collision sustained fractures and internal lesions, and a couple of deep wounds on her shinbones, from which she bled. So it's a collection of injuries that took her life. And time, of course.'

'Awful,' said Rose, standing in the doorway. 'If only someone had seen her hanging there a bit earlier, she might have been saved.'

She stood there thinking for a moment, as if a new possibility had come to her.

'What is it?' asked Carl.

'I'm not sure. Maybe there is something, then, that suggests it could have been an accident.'

'How's that?'

'Well, if it was a premeditated murder, the murderer would surely have made sure that she wasn't still alive afterwards and able to testify against him. If it'd been one of you who wanted to get rid of her, wouldn't you have made sure of that?'

'Yes, I would,' came the prompt reply from Assad.

Carl frowned.

'Well, just speaking hypo . . . Oh! You know, just if I had to imagine it, Carl.'

'Thank you, Assad, we get it. But, Rose, the vehicle didn't stop at the scene. So a lot could've happened that we don't know about. Maybe the driver parked the car on the main road and walked back to check that she wasn't moving. Maybe the driver observed it from the rearview mirror. Maybe the killer was in a situation where logic went completely out of the window. Killers don't often think rationally, Rose, you know that. So we can't allow ourselves to conclude that this one did.'

He collected Habersaat's drawings together. 'Assad, scan these drawings and send them to the technicians, and tell them that Laursen will call tomorrow and follow up on it all. Talk with Laursen – he can make things happen quicker than others. Over and above those questions already asked, the technicians should check what there is in their archives on the analysis of the wooden board. And we'd also like to know, insofar as Habersaat's theory about the shovel blade holds, how thick the board would need to be to ensure it wasn't completely smashed up during the collision. We'd also like to know if a board like that could be securely attached to the front of a vehicle like the pictured VW Kombi, and without leaving marks on the body of the vehicle. At the same time they can probably tell us, using Habersaat's drawing and the probable speed of the vehicle, whether it's possible that Alberte's body was thrown up towards the vehicle's windscreen and subsequently broke it. And finally, ask if they can do anything to make our photo sharper of the man with the VW. Of course, we'll keep trying to find the photographer and perhaps the negative, but they shouldn't count on it, tell them that. Laursen is already acquainted with most of it, but we've got a bit more to go on now, so bring him up to speed on where we're at.'

He turned to Rose. 'You still there? Do you have something else for me?'

'I've found what you're looking for, Carl.'

She looked so damn sure of herself.

'Found what? A sworn statement from the murderer and an admission of guilt?' He laughed.

'The thing about Knarhøj!'

'Good, what was it then?'

'It was where the young scout Bjarke Habersaat went digging together with a man. You remember, the odd guy on the bench in Listed mentioned that June Habersaat met a man up there on the same occasion. Up by the maze, isn't that what he said?'

Assad nodded like crazy, but then he had written it in his notebook.

'Right, that was it. But you look like you don't think they were digging a fire pit. Let me guess. You think it's the man from Ølene they met? Perhaps you've found his diaries?'

'Funny, Carl. I just know that it *could* be the same man, nothing else.'

Carl pulled himself in over the edge of the table. 'And how do you know that?'

'I googled Knarhøj, and I didn't get any hits. However, I found out that there are a lot of mazes on Bornholm, one of which should be situated just west of Listed. So I called a gallery out there, and they were able to tell me that it was actually the owner who made the maze, but that wasn't until 2006. The mound this maze is built on is called Knarhøj. And the gallery owner had chosen to put it there because of the interesting history of the area. There was a Bronze Age settlement there actually, called Sorte Muld, and there have been a lot of good finds, including several thousand guldgubber, indicating a cult centre.'

'Guldgubber?'

'Yes, thin pieces of gold embossed with figures, used as offerings. And the gallery owner had found a sunstone, and that type of find had never been heard of before. I've investigated it and it squares up. So it really is a special place.'

'Sunstone, you said. What on earth is that?'

She smiled. She'd been expecting that question, too. 'It's a sort of crystal, used by the Vikings to determine the exact position of the sun in the sky in overcast conditions. It's got something to do with polarizing sunbeams. Actually, they use something similar today when flying in the polar regions, so I read. They weren't stupid, those Vikings.'

'Sunstones, Vikings, guldgubber . . .' He needed to collect his thoughts.

'So in your opinion we've now got a connection not only between June Habersaat and the man we're looking for, but a connection between Christian Habersaat's interest in occult phenomena and the man from Ølene who took part in nightly naked dances and so on. Is that what you're trying to tell me?'

'You're not as green as you look, Carl Mørck, but that would've been a shame. It was actually you who caught the connection with Knarhøj. And if it is the same man Alberte met, then it's even more necessary for June Habersaat to tell us everything she knows about the man.'

Carl sighed again. 'Yes, and more besides. Much more. I know where this is going, Rose, and you're right. But you won't get me back to Bornholm to twist June Habersaat's arm behind her back. Do you want to go? Or you, Assad?'

You couldn't exactly say that he emanated enthusiasm.

Rose shrugged. 'OK, fair enough. Then she'll have to come to us.'

'How in the world will you make her do that? We've got nothing on her that can force her.'

'As I see it, that's your problem, Carl. Aren't you the boss?'

Carl put his head in his hand, and, God help him, now Gordon was there knocking on the door frame. They might as well invite the police choir and the Salvation Army brass band. There wasn't anywhere left to get a moment's peace anyway.

'Sorry, Carl,' said Gordon. 'I totally forgot to tell you that someone called Morten called. It's probably the guy who lived with you once. He said that Hardy hasn't come back.'

'What did you say?'

'That Hardy's missing.' All the idiot needed was to start bleating, he looked so sheepish.

'When did you find out?' asked Assad, looking worried.

'Almost two hours ago.'

Carl took out his phone and looked at the display. The sound was turned all the way down and there were at least fifteen messages and missed calls from Morten.

Now he stopped breathing.

25

They'd looked everywhere, Morten said, when he stood outside the terraced house with flushed cheeks that showed clear evidence of tears. Hardy had driven off in his electric wheelchair while Morten had been inside checking the weather forecast, and now he'd been out wearing only a shirt in the pouring rain ever since.

In spite of his confusion, nerves and chattering teeth, he just about managed to tell them where he and Mika had looked. 'We've been everywhere within a kilometre and a half of the house, Carl. He's just disappeared.'

'What about the phone? He can activate it, right?' asked Assad.

'He hasn't got it with him. We always go out together, so mine was enough,' answered Morten.

'Is he in the Kvickly supermarket or maybe at Expert Radio? He's always listening to music, so maybe he's out looking for something new.'

'He's got an iPod, Carl. He uses Spotify. I pop the headphones in for him, and then he can easily while away a couple of hours before he asks me to take them out again.'

Carl nodded. Spotify? He'd heard the name before but had no idea what it was.

'What about the wheelchair battery?' asked Assad.

'It's enormous,' answered Morten. 'He can get right out to Frederikssund and back on a single charge.' He began to snivel again just at the thought.

'I was thinking more about the rain.'

'It doesn't matter, Assad, a battery like that is well protected,' answered Carl. He turned to Morten. 'It's been more than three hours, and the wheelchair has a cruising speed of twelve-point-five kilometres an hour. He could be thirty-five kilometres away. Have you called his ex-wife?'

'You don't think he's driven all the way into Copenhagen?' Now his whole body was shaking.

'Go in and ring, we just need to check. And ring Hillerød Hospital, too. Ask if he's been brought in.'

Never before had Rønneholtparken witnessed so many fine small steps run so quickly. Morten was gone before the sentence was even finished.

They decided to do a circle of the neighbourhood. Maybe someone had seen him. Maybe he'd said something to someone.

'We need to split up, Assad. I'll take the car and . . .'

'What about me?'

'You can take that, but you'd better put a raincoat on. There's one in the trunk. I can't believe how bloody cold this spring has turned.'

He pointed to Jesper's moped. A well-oiled 50cc, which Jesper hadn't ridden since he'd left home.

Assad gave a short contorted smile.

Since the public care system had been set in motion, and day-to-day life in Rønneholtparken home had been turned upside down,

Carl hadn't had the same long talks with Hardy as before. Morten was his day-to-day caretaker, Morten's partner Mika was Hardy's mental coach and physiotherapist, municipal home caretakers covered relief, and the wheelchair enabled him to get out. So Carl was suddenly on the sideline, and that's where he was standing now, wondering if it'd been in Hardy's best interest.

As the window wipers went back and forth, he asked himself where the old boy might have got to, as the glories of Allerød sped past.

Hardy had his thumb and a little movement in his wrist and neck and, with these extremely limited tools, a different life and an immense freedom compared to the years of bed rest he had left behind. In the beginning, he'd been totally ecstatic about his newly won movement opportunities, but lately he'd developed a greater and greater understanding of their limitations.

'Before, I felt sorry for myself, but I also felt I was something special, because I endured my life. Now I just feel like a deadweight for those I'm closest to,' he'd said, explaining that he was well aware how heavy the work with him was, and how little he could give back.

But while he'd spoken of suicide when he was at the back pain clinic every time Carl had visited him, he hadn't mentioned it since he'd moved into Carl's living room. The question was, whether those thoughts had begun to haunt him again.

'Have you seen a man in an electric wheelchair go past in the rain?' he shouted once in a while out of the window. People had an ability to look amazingly indifferent.

He stopped in the car park at the bottom of Tokkekøbvej and looked at the area of woodland with a worried expression. All things considered, they were on an impossible mission. People did disappear if they didn't want to be found, and is that what Hardy wanted?

He called Morten's number.

'What about you, anything new?'

He heard a snivel through the receiver. 'He isn't at any of the places I've called. Mika's asked the police to send out a search party. They wouldn't normally do it so soon, but when they heard it was a colleague who'd been paralysed in service, they made an exception.'

'Good. Say thanks to Mika.'

He closed his eyes and tried to recall something or other that might give him a clue about where Hardy might have gone. He simply had no idea.

There came a humming sound from his phone, and Carl lunged for it. It was Assad.

'Yeah!' he shouted. 'Have you found him?'

'No, not quite.'

'What do you mean?'

'Up where the town hall used to be, I met a cyclist who'd seen a wheelchair on Nymøllevej out toward Lynge. So I stepped on it.'

'Why didn't you call me straightaway?'

'Well, that's it. I've been pulled over by the police. They're standing here next to me on Rådhusvej, claiming that I was doing 115 on the cycle path. Will you come out here?'

It took a while for Carl to convince his colleagues to release Assad. Actually, it was totally without precedent for the two uniformed men to see a moped, which had a limit of forty kilometres an hour, get up to those speeds. And there were no mitigating circumstances however you looked at it, as they said. The result would be legal action and that would undoubtedly have consequences for Assad's driving licence, said one of the officers.

Carl considered the consequences. Assad was about to lose his driving licence! He could've almost been grateful.

'Who owns the moped?' asked the officer.

'It's mine,' said Assad courageously.

Jesper didn't deserve it.

'We've just had a call radioed in,' his colleague said from the patrol car. 'The man you're looking for, Hardy Henningsen, has been located by a couple of employees at Lynge Drive-in Cinema. Go straight on past the gravel pit and over the highway, and you'll find your friend in the cinema car park, sitting in his wheelchair looking at a white screen.'

They let Assad go, but confiscated the moped. And even though Carl was impressed with his stepson's technical talent and knowledge when it came to tuning a vehicle, it was only fair that he should pay for his illegal activities.

Then one of the officers tapped Carl's shoulder. 'Here,' he said, slamming a couple of bits of paper in his hand. Carl looked at him. It was the ticket with Assad's name on it. 'We know about Hardy Henningsen's case, so the man looking for him shouldn't pay for it. But don't tell him straightaway. Let him sweat a bit.' Then he put a finger up to his cap to say goodbye.

It took less than five minutes to get there.

A drive-in cinema without cars, and especially in the pouring rain, is an extremely dismal sight. This was Europe's largest outdoor cinema, and in front of the enormous screen, Hardy's wheelchair and the figure in it appeared immeasurably small.

Despite the blanket they'd thrown over him, it was a long time since Carl had seen a living being so drenched.

'What's going on, Hardy?' was the first thing Carl could think of to say.

Hardy's eyes didn't lose focus at all, but the mouth shushed them. So they stood there a further five minutes and stared at him before Hardy finally turned his head around, saying, 'Oh, so here you are!'

They got him home with disability transport and rubbed him so that his pale skin glowed copper red.

'What happened there, Hardy? You need to tell us.'

'I've decided to live my life again, as much as I can.'

'OK, I'm not sure exactly what you're thinking about now. But if you continue in the way you did today, it'll be a short-lived affair.'

'Yes, don't ever do that again, Hardy,' Morten agreed. A stout being like him wasn't cut out for that kind of excitement.

Hardy tried to smile. 'Thank you. But you interrupted me re-living a film I saw out there thirty years ago with my Minna. I sat imagining that I was holding her hand like I did back then. Do you understand?'

'I do,' said Assad, more subdued than usual.

'You're saying that you saw a film that wasn't on and held a woman's hand who wasn't there and who is living a different life now. That's a dangerous path, Hardy.'

He banged his head against the neck rest on the wheelchair a couple of times. A bad habit he'd adopted after he started sitting up. 'Easy to say, Carl. But what would you rather have me do? Just wait for death? I've got nothing to do.' He turned his eyes to one side. 'When I was lying over there on the bunk, at least I had your cases to speculate about. You never tell me anything any more.'

An hour and a half after the sun had set behind the heavy, grey overcast sky, Assad and Carl had remedied what Carl had neglected.

And when they turned the light on in the living room, it was possible to see clearly what effect the review of the Alberte Goldschmid case had had on their disabled friend. As always, his body was like a pillar of salt in the wheelchair, but his eyes were present and more than ready to overlook all his limitations.

'So this June Habersaat, now Kofoed, is perhaps your key to getting a name and a description of your prime suspect, or maybe even more than that?'

'Maybe, yes. Rose thinks so anyway.'

'Yes, and me, too,' Assad said, nodding.

'But she wouldn't talk with you, so she isn't likely to next time either.'

'Rose thinks we can threaten her but I don't agree.'

'And now you've more or less reached a stumbling block in the story.' He smiled. 'What is it they say when a story's reached a deadlock? You just need to introduce a unicorn, and then things take off again. Or a flying elephant, for want of something better.'

Assad nodded. 'Where I come from, we say that if you can't do anything else, then you have to ride your camel in the fifth way.'

At that, Carl lost the thread for a moment. He wasn't sure if he wanted to hear an explanation of either the first four or the fifth.

'Something to do with at the front, in the middle, at the back, or on the humps,' said Hardy. 'I've heard it.'

Assad nodded. 'And the fifth is with your foot firmly in its backside. Makes the animal run like crazy.'

Carl was somewhere else altogether. 'Say again what it was June Habersaat reeled off out on the road in Aakirkeby, Assad.'

He flicked through his notebook. 'I didn't manage to get it written down straightaway, but something along these lines: *Wish I had a river that I could skate away on. But it don't snow here, it stays pretty and green.*' He looked up at Hardy with a puzzled expression. 'Does that sound right?'

Hardy's face twitched. 'Just about,' he said. 'It's Joni Mitchell.'

Carl gawped. 'You know it?'

'Can you come and help me, Mika?' said Hardy.

Morten reluctantly let go of his muscular partner. Everyone was together, so the large ex-mama of the house was happy again.

'What was the title, Hardy?' asked Mika.

'The song's called "River". You can find it on the playlist on the iPod. Put it in the docking station so everyone can hear.'

Carl googled it while Mika scrolled through the playlists with thousands of songs.

'I've got it,' said Mika after scrolling for a moment. 'Joni Mitchell, "River", 1970.'

'Yes, that's the one,' said Hardy. 'It starts a bit strange.'

A few seconds passed and then came the first few bars of 'Jingle Bells', a bit jazzy, a bit discordant, but 'Jingle Bells' all the same.

Carl and Assad listened intently. When they came to the right part of the lyrics, Assad thrust his thumb in the air.

Oh, I wish I had a river I could skate away on . . .

It was sung by a crisp voice to a melancholy piano accompaniment. A whole four minutes on longing and loss.

Carl nodded to himself. It probably wasn't a coincidence that Hardy knew that song.

'Try and find one of those websites that analyses songs, Carl. There are loads of forums that do,' said Hardy.

Carl typed in the title and looked down over the page of links. The fifth one was a hit.

He read out what was written.

'Joni Mitchell is Canadian but moved to California to be a hippy and follow her musical career. The song "River" is about spending Christmas far from home in a strange place with strange traditions – without snow or ice-skating. To put it briefly, the song is about a desire to put the present behind you and return to more simple and innocent days.'

They looked at each other, until Hardy broke the silence.

'She sings beautifully, and it expresses a lot. It hits me right in the heart when I hear it, you'll understand. I just don't know what it means in this situation. I don't know this June Habersaat. What had you just spoken about when she quoted it?'

Carl pushed his lip forward. How on earth should he be able to remember that?

'She'd just said to me that I didn't know her dreams or how much she'd fought to fulfil them,' said Assad. 'When she said that, it was easy to understand why she'd recite something like this.'

It went silent again. None of them knew what they should make of it. It would've been a different story if Rose had been there.

'Would anyone like some soup?' Morten sang from somewhere in the region of the kitchen. It brought Carl to.

'If you think carefully about it, June Habersaat probably hasn't seen so many of her dreams fulfilled in life.'

'Not many, no. But, then, who has?' asked Hardy. 'But the affair with that young man, don't you think that was one of them?'

'Probably, yes. But it just doesn't add up for me that she'd suddenly blurt out those lyrics. I don't think June Habersaat is the Joni Mitchell-listening type.'

'There was nothing but easy listening music on her shelves,' added Assad. '*Absolute Hits* one to a thousand, stuff like that.'

'"River" is a very poetical, ethereal and ambiguous song,' said Hardy. 'If she isn't the sort who normally listens to that type of music, then no doubt there's someone else who put it in her head. Is it possible she learned the song from that man? He was also in search of bygone days, wasn't he? Occult sites from the Bronze Age, sunstones, round churches and Knights Templar, long hair and hippy dancing years too late.'

'And if that's the case, what would you use it for?'

'I'd try to ride the camel with the foot in number five,' said Hardy.

Assad gave him a thumbs-up. If it was something to do with camels, he was with you all the way.

Five minutes later three men were sitting around Hardy's wheelchair in anticipation. Morten's soup would have to wait.

'Dial June Habersaat's number, Mika,' said Hard#y. No sooner said than done. 'Are you ready with the iPod?'

He nodded.

Mika pressed the call button and held the phone five centimetres from Hardy's ear.

'June Kofoed,' answered a voice. Then Mika pressed PLAY on the iPod and Joni Mitchell's voice filled the room again.

Ever so slowly, Mika moved the phone toward Hardy's mouth.

For a moment, the paralysed man sat there without blinking, eyes unfocused. Now he was a policeman on the job, deep in concentration; a man who knew when the timing was right, the tone just so, and the voice suitably anonymous.

'June,' was all he said, while the music played in the background.

There was a silence that might've caused others to give up, but Hardy still didn't blink.

There came a sound from the other end, and Hardy's eyes jumped up.

'Yes,' he said, nothing else.

And again, sounds from the other end.

'OK, I'm sorry to hear that. I didn't know. How are you?' he asked.

A few further sentences were exchanged, and then he cricked his neck slightly. 'She interrupted,' he said. 'She was on to me in the end, that or she just didn't want to talk to the guy.'

'Out with it,' said Carl impatiently. 'Let's hear everything that was said, and as precisely as possible. Take notes, Assad.'

'I just said her name: *June*. And she replied: *Is that you, Frank?* And I replied *Yes*. Then she began to breathe deeply. It was very odd because I thought she was moved to be talking to him but what she said next was strangely harsh: *A strange way to contact me after seventeen years. I never imagined I'd be hearing from you again. Maybe you've heard that Bjarke's dead? He took his own life, is that why you're calling?* I replied that I was sorry to hear that and said I didn't know about her son. Then I asked how she was but she replied with a question about where I was. I asked where she thought I was, and then she replied: *You're playing the miracle man, aren't you?* Then I think I messed up, but you heard that, when I asked her what she thought I was called these days. It was very clumsy.'

'She just hung up?'

'Yes. But now we know that the person called himself Frank, that he was Danish and that he hasn't had contact with her for years.'

'But the question remains whether it's the same man we're looking for,' Carl said thoughtfully. 'Maybe it wasn't a coincidence that she mixed them up when I called to question her about the man with the VW Kombi.'

'It's him, Carl, I'm sure,' said Assad. 'He bolted from the island after what happened to Alberte. It's the same person that Habersaat was looking for, and who went to bed with both his wife and Alberte, and probably lots more besides. Kristoffer hit the nail on the head when he called him a Don Juan.'

'And June just called him a miracle man, which also fits in with our man. Good, let's go a little further with this assumption.'

Carl googled once more.

'He was called Frank. How many people do you think there are called Frank in the kingdom of Denmark who are also around forty-five years old?'

'I don't know very many,' answered Assad. Not an especially relevant observation in statistical terms.

'No, me neither. But right now there's a total of 11,319 registered with that name in Denmark. According to the Statistics Denmark database, there are approximately five hundred who've been given the name since 1987, so it isn't very popular any more. We don't know the exact age of the person we're looking for, but if we say, for example, that back then he was somewhere between mid-twenties and early thirties, we wouldn't be totally off. And then comes the next question: how popular was that name in the period 1968 to 1973? We can't just guess our way to the answer so you'll have to get in touch with Statistics Denmark, Assad. But I think it must be in the thousands. So what do we do if that's the case? We can't seek them all out and cross-examine them, can we?'

It was a rhetorical question but Hardy apparently didn't agree.

'We'll just have to roll up our sleeves. Well, I mean you'll all have to. I assume that I can be spared the cross-examinations,' he said, smiling.

Carl returned a surly smile, but despite everything this was quite positive. They had a name. And Hardy was back on track.

26

Monday, March 17th, 2014

Nothing happened for a long time. Pirjo kept to herself, regularly changing the frequency of her conscious energy with the help of the nature absorption methods, all the while keeping her body healthy to ensure optimal conditions for the new little person growing inside her. She took part in their communal assemblies inside and sun assemblies down on the beach, just as she normally did. She kept herself busy with her work and other administrative tasks. Made sure the upkeep of the building was taken care of, and that new guests settled in quickly. She wanted to be pregnant again in the future, and Atu shouldn't have any grounds for thinking that it affected her daily activities.

New Year's Eve had started as it usually did, under the open sky with Atu's praise of the year's cycle. They assembled in a ring around the fire on the beach, each person expressing in their own way a great sense of community in a common knowledge that life constantly offered new chapters. The coming year should be the one from which all their future deeds should emanate.

Pirjo nodded gently to herself with the realization that nothing in her situation could be truer, and that from now on she didn't need to be alone in that knowledge. So when the round dance was finished, and each person was heading to their room for the first quiet meditation of the New Year, Pirjo grabbed Atu's hand and thanked him for the person he was, and the person he'd soon be.

Then she led his hand down toward her abdomen and explained the situation to him straight out.

From that moment when his face began to glow, Pirjo felt that nothing in the world could threaten her newly won harmony and happiness.

The situation continued for her in this way for two and a half months, and then this inner balance was destroyed.

It was a Monday and Pirjo had had many calls on the Light of the Oracle telephone line. Yet another few thousand kroner had made its way into the account.

She'd looked at the clock and was talking with the last client of the day.

'I can sense by the colour of your voice and what you're telling me that you are an important force for change in the world,' she had said for at least the tenth time today. 'It seems as if there are extraordinary development perspectives for your personality. I'm actually feeling right now that a uniquely special personality like yours would obtain lifelong benefits from me referring you to the Holistic Chain. From here it will be possible to establish all your options and also show you the path to achieve the mental strength and stability required to ensure you get the full benefit of your obvious talents.'

They were the sort of declarations people wanted to hear. And when you first reached that point, they were insatiable, and that meant time, which in turn meant money rolling in.

Pirjo had enjoyed it. On an average day, her oratorical skills were limited mostly to practical information and a bit of haggling with the local suppliers, but she was in her element here.

'You ask which of your future perspectives I would accentuate, but it isn't such a straightforward question. If you look . . .'

At that moment a recognizable silhouette appeared over Pirjo's desk. Shirley's outline was absolutely unique among all the ascetic disciples, so Pirjo turned around to face her with one of her usual subdued smiles, despite the fact that Shirley had once again chosen to ignore the *Do Not Disturb* sign. This was the tone she'd chosen to adopt with this woman for the past few months now. The less contact there was between them, the less chance there was of questions being asked.

But this time, Pirjo's smile wasn't reciprocated.

'There's something I don't understand, Pirjo,' Shirley said in a more subdued manner than usual.

Pirjo raised her hand to signal that she'd have to wait a moment, and finished her conversation with an apology and a promise that she'd like to present all the wonderful things they had spoken about to the person in charge at the Holistic Chain. That way, they would be able to pick things up from there when she called on Wednesday. She then wished the woman good luck and turned toward Shirley.

'What don't you understand, Shirley?'

'This.' She held out something dark in one hand, passing it to Pirjo.

It was a belt with diagonal stripes in red and grey.

'A belt, OK?' said Pirjo, taking it as if it were a rattlesnake ready to strike. 'What about it?' she heard herself ask while all her senses revolved around trying to maintain her mental balance while also trying to work out what could've happened.

She'd emptied the box of all Wanda Phinn's belongings only a week after the murder, and then burned them. Could she have overlooked this belt? Could she have?

'What is it with this belt, Shirley? Is it yours? Maybe you think you've grown fatter or thinner than you anticipated?' she said, her own voice sounding somewhere far off.

Was it the same belt? She couldn't remember it. Maybe she hadn't even really noticed it.

'No, it isn't mine, but I know this belt,' said Shirley.

Could the belt have fallen down to the bottom of the removal box? But what business did Shirley have up in the highest loft space in the Stable of Senses? It didn't make any sense.

She was thinking so much that it hurt. She had burnt a belt. Hadn't there been a buckle in the ash when she threw it out in the sea? Or had there?

'You say you know the belt? Is it a special brand, perhaps?' Pirjo turned it over a few times, shaking her head at the same time. 'It doesn't ring a bell with me. Not other than that it's a pretty belt.'

'Yes, I know it,' said Shirley. She seemed genuinely shaken. 'I bought that belt, but not for myself. It was a birthday present for my best friend, just before she left London. The one you all say has never been here. Wanda Phinn, don't you remember, I asked about her when I arrived?'

Pirjo nodded. 'Not quite the name, but yes, you mentioned a friend that you thought was over here. But belts look alike, Shirley, don't they?' She smiled as best she could. 'Well, I don't know so much about clothes. I mean it's not so often we wear . . . you know.' She let a hand slide down over her modest robe.

Shirley pulled the belt back. 'It was very expensive, not some-thing I can normally afford. I'd never buy it for myself, but I really wanted to give it to Wanda, and I managed to get it a bit cheaper because of this.' She pointed to a long and very superficial scratch on the belt.

Pirjo shook her head. 'I don't understand how it got here. Where did you get it?'

'From Jeanette.'

'Jeanette?' Pirjo could sense now that desperation was setting in. She had to pull herself together. Not one evasive glance, not one unintentional look must give her away. 'But Shirley, she isn't here. Jeanette left this morning. Her sister is very sick, you know. That's why she's left us, to look after her. I don't actually think Jeanette will be coming back.'

'She told me that, I know. And she collected her old clothes from a removal box up in the loft, just where she'd left them three years ago. But she noticed that her belt was missing and that this was in the box instead. So she took it. I helped her to pack and noticed the colours, the buckle, and the scratch when she bent over her case.'

'Don't you think it's just a coincidence? Scratches like this . . .'

'Jeanette's own belt was missing; she's sure because it was black and this one's two-tone. The brand is also the same as I bought. And the scratch, look. It's very distinctive. And then there are the holes.' She pointed at the second-to-last one. 'Look, that hole is stretched, so that's the hole that's been used. And when Jeanette put it on she had to move it out at least two holes, but Wanda was very thin around the waist.' She nodded with pursed lips. 'This is Wanda's belt, I just know it.'

Shirley's otherwise pale face now turned darker. She was

obviously frustrated and irritated and scared, all at the same time. A very dangerous cocktail.

Something began to stir in Pirjo's diaphragm. The nerves and unpleasant feelings might not be visible, but she could feel them. She pushed her lips forward in thought. Not about how the belt could have ended up at the centre, as Shirley must be thinking, but about how she would solve this problem, and if it couldn't be sorted, about the safest way she could get rid of this life-threatening person.

'Can *you* understand it, Pirjo?' Shirley said, sounding suddenly lost.

Pirjo grabbed her chance and Shirley's hand.

'There must be a natural explanation, Shirley. You're sure Jeanette found the belt here at the centre?'

She pointed over her shoulder. 'Yes, up in her box in the Stable of Senses, like I said. Totally sure.'

'Did you see her get it?'

She pulled back a little. Maybe the tone had been a bit too harsh. It mustn't sound like an interrogation.

'No, but why should she lie?'

'I don't know, Shirley. I really don't know.'

'Are you telling me that Shirley is here on a covert mission?' asked Atu. He pulled himself in to Pirjo's body and caressed the downy skin around her belly button.

Pirjo put her hand against his cheek. When they were lying together like this, it was solely about their unity in relation to the baby in her womb. Even though Pirjo wished for it more than anything else, she and Atu had never been intimate since that one time they'd made love. Instead of lusting after her as a woman, he treated her like a delicate crystal, almost as if she was something sacred. Pirjo was no longer just his vestal and squire, but also the symbol of the incarnate fertility that would provide him with life and intimacy, not sex.

But Pirjo had her own ideas. When she'd given birth to the baby she'd implore him to impregnate her again. And she'd make sure it wasn't successful straightaway, so she would get what she wanted. But first, threats had to be eliminated.

'I think it's all an elaborate lie,' she said, putting her hand on his. 'Jeanette must've been mistaken about the belt, and Shirley grabbed her chance. How much do we actually know about Shirley? She has to all intents hidden herself behind a mask of joviality and a sweet smile. She's the woman who wants to find a new side to herself, or so we think. But she's different from the others, Atu. She doesn't have a spiritual character. She could be anything. Maybe even cunning, without us seeing it. A sly petty criminal with a plan. Maybe this business with Jeanette's belt was just the chance she was waiting for ever since she got here. I've heard about other spiritual centres that've been subjected to threats and extortion, so why couldn't it happen to us? She knows that there's money in this venture.'

'All the same, don't you think she's too naive for that? I see her quite differently.'

'I'm worried that Shirley will end up threatening us with all sorts,' continued Pirjo. 'She's indicated that she'll request to be accepted as a disciple when her course is finished, and now she knows there's an empty room since Jeanette left. But we simply have to reject her when the time comes, is that OK, Atu?'

He nodded. 'And when will that be?'

'In less than two months. She's worked for us throughout the whole of the last period, so her course was extended. Don't you remember her application? It was you who granted it.'

'Maybe we should wait and see. No doubt she'll realize the business with the belt was a mistake before we take action.'

Pirjo nodded. That was Atu. In his elevated universe, and bordering on naivete, he saw the best in all people. But Pirjo knew better, and two months was too long when the questions were beginning to pile up. Of course, they could deny again and again all knowledge of the case to Shirley, but to what end if she got the police involved? And what if they found the body anyway? Through Shirley there was suddenly a link between Wanda Phinn and the centre. It was there the belt had been found.

She breathed deeply. 'If Shirley's insistent, I think we should stop her course immediately.'

'On what grounds, Pirjo?'

'That she's disturbing the peace here. That we can't find the right direction for her. That she doesn't have what it takes, which I actually don't believe she does.'

'Of course, I'll listen to what you say.' He closed his eyes and pressed his cheek against her stomach.

The signal that he would leave the decision to her had been given.

That gave her room to manoeuvre.

27

Thursday, May 8th, 2014

The area that Assad, Rose, and Carl had agreed to meet in front of wasn't the sort of building you'd expect an artistic sort like Synne Veland to have settled down in. Out here in the petty bourgeois idyll of Vægterparken on Amager you weren't met by graffiti on the walls or Christiania bikes in the bike racks. Instead, there was a local billiard club, trimmed hedges, integrated daycare centres, yellow walls and row after row of townhouses.

Carl had never been there before but his colleague Børge Bak had, he knew that much. A knife attack after a party, as far as he could remember, but the reputation of the area was otherwise impeccable.

'My daughter lives down in number 232,' the woman said of her own accord, before asking them to leave their shoes by the door. When had it become acceptable to ask a man on official business to expose his faded socks? It took the sting out of his authority.

'My daughter's divorced,' she explained. 'I moved out here so that she had me at least. But otherwise it's not a bad place to have your practice.'

Carl wondered why she called it her practice. Had he missed a sign by the door?

She smiled and led them into a living room where there was no doubt what you were letting yourself in for if you wanted to be treated by her. There were diplomas, human anatomy posters, flyers for any number of homeopathic treatments and other natural remedies, and, of course, the price list. It wasn't exactly expensive but, seen in light of the wage bracket of an experienced policeman, it was definitely a lucrative little business.

'I only have a few clients left. There comes a time when you can't be bothered any more, you know,' she said with a smile, as if she'd read their thoughts. 'Early retirement is calling and I'm about ready to answer. So, I just have my fifteen to twenty regular clients a month now.'

More than a few then, thought Carl. Who on earth frequented a clinic like this?

'You call yourself a Heilkunst practitioner?' asked Rose, who was of course better prepared than Carl.

'Yes, I trained in Germany, so I've practiced iris analysis and homeopathy for almost twelve years now.'

'You were a schoolteacher before?'

'Yes.' She laughed. 'But the need for a change of scenery makes animals and humans alike get off their backside once in a while, am I right?'

Carl scratched his eyebrow, wondering what on earth iris analysis might be. He looked at Assad's brown irises. If you were to try to infer anything about his constitution from those almost coal-black splotches, you'd have to be eagle-eyed. No, the socks with holes and protruding big toenail said far more about the man.

'I understand that you've come to talk about Alberte. It was a long time ago. You have to admire the police force. You certainly don't give up so easily.'

'Then perhaps you know that the investigator you spoke to back then has committed suicide? That's why we're stuck with the case now,' said Carl.

Judging by her expression, this news had no notable impact on her. Maybe she only remembered him vaguely.

Rose also noticed the reaction, so she gave a short summary of the case and Habersaat's interest in it and referred to when she'd been questioned. Apparently there was nothing wrong with her memory because she nodded almost every other second and seemed so engaged that in the end Carl had to look at the floor to stop himself from nodding along with her.

'So, what do you want to ask me about? I'm fairly certain I told the policeman everything I knew back then.'

'Two things,' said Rose. 'Can you remember the way she dressed? Did anything change around the time she met that man, anything come to mind?'

She shrugged as she sat looking at the raindrops running down the windowpanes. 'That's not exactly what you remember most after seventeen years.'

'Did she adopt more of a hippy style? Colourful and baggy knit-wear, for example? Did she put her hair up in a different way? Any sudden preference for Rastafarian hairstyles or large African jewellery? Things like that.'

'A hippy style? No, she was actually rather normal, in my opinion.'

Rose sighed blatantly, as she always did when she was out on a limb, and Carl wasn't any the wiser about where this was going. Of course a significant change in dress could give away that the young woman had been heavily influenced by the people down at Ølene.

But would that sort of knowledge bring them any closer to the man they were looking for? Carl had his doubts.

'We're looking for even the slightest lead that might tell us something about a man who, when it comes down to it, we don't know anything about other than that he was called Frank.'

'Frank?'

'Yes, that was the other question. Does the name mean anything to you? Did you hear Alberte mention anyone by that name?'

'No, sorry. But going back to your first question, I can remember that at one point Alberte started wearing a badge.'

This could be the first link to the man with the VW, which also had badges on it. A bit of a long shot, and yet . . .

'What was on it?'

'A nuclear sign.'

'One of those *Nuclear Power? No Thanks* badges?'

'No, not one of those. It was the logo from the disarmament demonstrations. The peace symbol: a ring with a vertical line in the middle and two diagonal lines facing down this way.' She drew it in the air.

Carl nodded. It was a good while since anyone had seriously rallied around that sign.

'And she didn't wear that badge in the beginning?' asked Rose, looking her straight in the eye. Just now you'd be forgiven for thinking that she was the one who analysed irises, not the other way around.

'No. Only in the last few days, I think.'

'Do you think she got the badge from the man she began to see from outside the school?'

'I couldn't say. But there wasn't anyone else at the place wearing one, as far as I remember. But I'm thinking that she could have had it with her from home, of course.'

Carl nodded. That idea sounded particularly unlikely, but they'd have to check, of course.

'One more thing,' said Rose. 'Back then, you told Habersaat that Alberte was a good singer. She didn't happen to sing a song by Joni Mitchell called "River", by any chance? Does that ring any bells?'

'No, not that I can say.'

Rose pulled out her little orange iPod and pressed it. 'This song,' she said, and passed the earphones to Synne Veland.

The woman listened without moving for a moment, mesmerized by the beautiful voice. Then she began to move her head from side to side and a couple of lines around her mouth became more distinct.

'Yes, of course!' she shouted, the music still playing in her ears. 'You'd better not hold me to it, but I think she did go about humming this song.'

Then Carl's mobile rang. He moved slightly to one side. It was his mum.

'You are coming on Saturday, aren't you, Carl?' she said without as much as a hello.

He took a deep breath. 'Yes, I'll be there.'

'I thought I'd invite Inger.'

'Inger? Inger, who's that?'

'It's the daughter from the next farm. Well, I say daughter, but she's getting on a bit now. But she's the one managing the farm, so—'

'Mom, don't invite Inger. I've got no idea who she is, I've never met her. I'm a policeman, and I'm not thinking about becoming a farmer or anything else for that matter up by you. Is this Dad's idea?'

'Well, but you're coming on Saturday, right?'

'Yes, yes, I'll be there. Bye, Mum.'

There was no knowing where this nightmare would end.

Ronny, Ronny, Ronny. Couldn't you just have stayed in Thailand?

It was an obviously exhausted Gordon that waited for them in the situation room, and judging by the colour of one of his ears it would appear that the phone had been stuck to it for hours on end. He tried to liven up a little when Rose sat opposite him with her legs stretched out at a right angle, but even then he quickly gave up again.

'It seems I'm not very good at this,' he said.

Well, well, the man was displaying a sense of self-awareness.

'I've called at least a hundred different numbers and so far only spoken with seven . . . eight people from the school.'

Carl leaned forward in his chair. 'And?'

'I haven't found out anything new because they all say the same. None of them could stand Habersaat, who was evidently quite insistent. They say Alberte was a beautiful girl who flirted with the boys and then one day began flirting with someone from elsewhere. A couple of those I called said that Alberte spoke about a guy who she said was more interesting than the guys at the school, and who could do things.'

'Could do things? What do you mean?'

'I don't know. That's just what they said.'

Carl shook his head. What did Gordon expect? That they'd shove a hand up his backside and ask for him like some sort of ventriloquist?

'Have you got a list?'

He nodded and Carl grabbed it out of his hand. There were only a very few notes in the margin.

'You check these, Rose. Knock it out of them. We need to know what that guy from outside the place could do.' He turned to Assad.

'Anything new on the name front? How many people are there called Frank in the years we're focusing on?'

'There isn't anything registered year for year before 1989 so we have to make do with the status from each decade, from which point it all goes a bit wrong, doesn't it?'

'Why?'

'Because you want to know how many people called Frank were born from 1968 to 1973, and there were 5,225 in the sixties and 3,053 in the seventies. And when you put those two numbers together and divide by four, because you only want those five years, we're left with 2,070, but that could easily be more if he was born before 1968.'

If you were travelling to Mars, a few centimetres' miscalculation at the beginning could mean that you raced thousands of kilometres past the planet, which obviously wouldn't be good, Carl was well aware of that. And out of respect for the significance of alarming figures like that, he didn't intend to put himself forward as an astronaut, if anyone had thought of suggesting it. On the other hand, if it was about the number of Franks in the kingdom of Denmark, he couldn't care less if it was a figure of 1,812 or a few thousand more Franks that had to be sniffed out. Some would certainly be dead, others would have emigrated. But no matter how you looked at it, there were just too many.

'Thanks, Assad. Then I think we'll let that line of investigation rest. Otherwise we'll be at it until the cows come home.'

'Whose cows are coming home, Carl?' he said, looking puzzled.

'It's just a figure of speech for something taking forever, Assad.'

'Whose?'

'Whose what?'

'Whose figure?'

Carl took a deep breath and shoved his hands in his pockets in defeat. 'Just forget it, Assad.'

Carl hesitated. What were all these bits of paper doing among the fluff in his pocket? He pulled the mysterious bits of paper out and looked at them. That was right – they belonged to Assad.

He passed them to his curly-haired assistant. 'Here. That's that taken care of, easy rider. You can thank the patrol police for that.'

Assad looked at the torn-up speeding ticket and smiled. 'I think you'll be happy about that, Carl. It means I can drive the car whenever you're too tired.'

Even if it meant he had to swallow sixty-four caffeine tablets to keep himself awake, he'd make sure that he was never in that situation. Best to change the subject, and quick.

'Did you get hold of Alberte's parents?' he asked.

'Yes. They'd never seen a badge like that in their house.'

'And the Joni Mitchell song?'

'I hummed it for them, but they didn't recognize it.'

'*What* did you say?'

'I hummed it for them, but they—'

'Thanks, Assad. I got you.' Those poor old people definitely had the odds stacked against them. Even a wooing tomcat had more musical sense than Assad.

'Right, so Alberte didn't have her anti-military impulses from home. Then let's assume for now that she got the badge from the guy she met outside the school, and the fact that there were several people who went about humming that Joni Mitchell song at the same time can be put down to coincidence. Maybe it'd been played on the radio a lot. Maybe it's back in the charts after being in the shadows for years, who knows? Maybe Joni Mitchell toured the area. There could be many reasons why Alberte and June Habersaat went about humming that song.'

Assad nodded.

A beep came from Carl's mobile; he'd just received a text, and that didn't happen so often. He took it out to look, butterflies in his stomach. Could it be from Mona?

It wasn't, he saw that after reading just the first word.

Carling, when are you going to visit my mom? You're late again, and you know it. Remember our agreement! Vigga xx

He was stunned. Not because it was from his ex-wife, not because of the message, though it was bad enough, not because he was eternally stuck with his ex-mother-in-law and her explosive and unpredictable dementia, but because of the form of the message.

He stared out into thin air for a moment, reflecting on the thought that suddenly came to him. Strangely enough, it was almost impossible to remember those sorts of things even though they were trivial.

He looked at Assad. 'Can you remember when people began to send texts to each other in Denmark?' he asked. 'Were people doing it in 1997?'

Curly shrugged, and he was right. Where on earth should he know that from? According to him, he first arrived in the country in 2001.

'Rose!' he shouted out in the corridor. 'Can you remember when you got your first mobile phone?'

'Yes,' resounded her grinding voice. 'When my mom moved in with her new guy on the Costa del Sol. It was in 1996, May 5th to be exact. So there were a lot of reasons for my dad to fly the flag at full mast.'

'What reasons?' he shouted back, regretting it immediately.

'Liberation Day, stupid,' she replied expectedly. 'And my birthday. I got the phone from my dad that day. All us sisters did that year.'

Was her birthday May 5th? OK, he didn't know that. In fact, he'd never thought of his colleagues as people who celebrated special days. For six to seven years these three had plodded around down there in the basement without ever really celebrating anything even once. Maybe it was about time they did?

He looked at Assad, who appeared equally in the dark as he shrugged his shoulders. He obviously hadn't been any the wiser about her birthday.

Carl stood up and went out into the corridor where Rose was in full swing digging around in Habersaat's remains.

'So it was your birthday on Monday?'

She brushed her hand through her hair like an Italian diva emerging from a pool, her eyes confirming both the answer and the stupidity of the question.

What on earth had they been doing on Monday, and why hadn't she said anything? Carl felt awkward. What were you supposed to do in this situation?

'Happy birthday to you . . .' came the frightening noise from behind. Carl turned to face Assad, who resembled an opera star, flailing his arms about as he kicked out his legs, bringing back distant memories of something Vigga had said about Greek dancing.

But Assad made Rose smile. Thank God for that.

Temporarily sidetracked by his gratitude to Assad, Carl tried to remember where he'd come to.

'Yes!' he shouted, as if it was something the others had been waiting for. 'What about those texts, Rose? Was it something you could do back when you got your mobile, can you remember?'

She frowned, thinking. 'Text? No, I don't think so.' She stood for a moment, staring. Apparently there was nothing that could jolt her memory.

'By the way, weren't you supposed to call back those students Gordon talked to earlier today, Rose?' asked Carl.

She just looked at him again, this time her eyes telling him that she couldn't be bothered and had her hands full with other things.

Speak of the devil. That second Gordon came out from Assad's broom cupboard, beaming with triumph from head to toe.

'He could bend spoons,' he shouted as if he were a ringmaster. The silence was deafening in the narrow corridors of Department Q.

'Let's sum up the events of the last hour,' said Carl while Rose passed around the brochures from the alternative therapists on the wall. 'You start, Assad.'

'I've spoken with Alberte's mom, and she says that Alberte didn't have a mobile phone. Then she cried a little and said that if only she'd had one, the accident might never have happened. That she might've spoken more with her daughter and perhaps sensed if something was wrong or if there was something her daughter should've been careful about.'

Carl shook his head. Those people would live with their self-reproach for the rest of their lives. Terrible.

'She could have borrowed one from one of the other students,' said Rose.

Assad nodded. 'Yes, but I've been told that texting was first introduced to Denmark in 1996, and that there were only limited networks supporting it back then. Plus the coverage on Bornholm was bad back then, so it's unlikely that Alberte communicated with the Frank guy that way.'

'But she could have called if she'd borrowed one,' insisted Rose.

Carl considered that while she did have a point, it didn't add up. 'Then those who had mobile phones would've been able to say more to the police because they would've been able to see the call lists on the display.'

Rose sighed. 'And the police could've been sent lists from the provider of all the calls made from the landline at the school, I assume.'

Assad nodded rather convincingly. It seemed that Alberte and the man from outside the school must have communicated some other way, just like Assad said. The questions remained how and how often. Did they talk together daily? Did they have rituals?

Then it was Gordon's turn, as he pointed out impatiently, going on to say that one of the girls, a Lise W. who now lived in Frederikshavn and had graduated as a high-school teacher, had given three bits of information that he deemed worth pursuing.

'Firstly, she'd luckily enough taken pictures of Østerlars Church on the trip. She'd no idea what had become of them, but she'd be sure to have a look for them. Secondly, she told me that it was when they were there that they'd met a man who'd boasted that he could bend spoons. She thinks this was the man that Alberte dated. He laughed because they didn't believe him and because he called himself Uri Geller the Second. But she still doesn't know why. Do you have any idea?'

Carl shook his head. Couldn't that man ever do a job right and finish it? If he'd looked the name up on Google . . . He sighed. 'He was a guy who could bend spoons through the power of thought back in the seventies. He demonstrated his talent and a lot of other tricks in the media. I don't remember if he was ever exposed as a fraud, but that was certainly his name.'

'He bent spoons? What a weird thing to do,' Assad added. It was evident that if he'd been gifted with supernatural powers like that, he wouldn't start by massacring the contents of the cutlery drawer.

'He held the spoon carefully with two fingers and rubbed it a little.' Carl demonstrated. 'And ta-da! It went soft right where he was holding it and bent. If our man could do that, then maybe he was actually a bit of a miracle man. But it's odd that Habersaat hasn't noted anything about it. Did he fail to ask the right questions or was it his insistence that made people clam up?' He turned to Gordon. 'Well, what was the third?'

'She said there was also someone else who took pictures at Østerlars Church.'

'OK, who?'

'Inge Dalby.'

They all looked at him, speechless.

'Are you sure? Did you ask her if she was positive?'

He nodded with a wry smile, as if asking them what they took him for. Maybe he was beginning to get the hang of it after all. 'She was sure because she remembered that the guy had talked with Inge Dalby, almost as if he already knew her,' he added.

Carl snapped his fingers at Rose and just ten minutes later she returned with a message that Inge Dalby wasn't home because she was on a study trip.

Carl noticed his jaw muscles tense up.

'Damn it, in what country?'

'In Denmark, actually. According to Kristoffer Dalby, she's flirting with the idea of taking a course to be a teaching assistant over here in Copenhagen. I think all our talk about the old days opened up something that shouldn't have been opened up, and definitely not on top of her seemingly leaving Kristoffer, too. He certainly seemed pretty down.'

'In Copenhagen? Couldn't she take that course on Bornholm? What about all the children she normally looks after?'

'As far as I understood him, she didn't have any more children after May 1st. That seemed to shake him just as much, as if now she was ready to leave the island. He didn't think it could've been planned. But now she's living with a brother out in the new district in Sluseholmen on Dexter Gordons Vej. The school is on Sydhavns Plads, just a ten-minute bike ride from her brother's apartment.'

'Well, I'll be damned.' Carl tried to imagine Kristoffer Dalby alone among all the toys in that little house. It must've been quite a shock for him.

'OK, now she's living with the brother, you say. And his surname is Kure, I assume, because wasn't that Inge's name when she was younger?'

'Yes, Hans Otto Kure. Owner of Kures' Advanced Automobiles.'

'Doesn't ring any bell.'

'It's the biggest workshop in the city for higher-end vintage cars. Ferrari and Maserati and Bentley and so on. He's a trained mechanic, following his dad and uncle.'

Rose looked at Carl for some time before he realized what she was thinking.

'Do you think . . . ?' he said.

'Wow,' said Assad. It'd clicked for him, too.

Gordon's face had the usual appearance of a slapped arse.

'You're telling me she grew up in a family where they fiddled about with cars?'

Rose raised her eyebrows a couple of times. 'Yup. And of course

I then asked Kristoffer Dalby if his wife could also do that sort of thing, and he answered that she was born with a wrench in her hand and could weld with the best of them. He said that until she starts her course she's working as a mechanic in her brother's workshop. Seems she's made of stronger stuff than you first thought, wouldn't you say, Carl?'

'Yes, but then the question is how much stronger. I can see you're all thinking the same as me. We certainly can't ignore the fact that she could've been capable of attaching a shovel blade on a vehicle and even driving it on a very early November morning in 1997. Do we know if the students were asked to account for their movements that morning? What do the reports say, Rose?'

'Nothing. They've been asked if they heard anything and if they had any specific suspicions, but not about their own movements.'

Assad nodded. 'She goes on the list of possible suspects then, right, Carl?'

The lanky guy next to them stared goofily over. 'Sorry, I don't quite follow. Suspect for what? Was she at that classic car show on Bornholm you're always going on about?'

They looked at each other.

28

It was a fantastic new city space for Copenhageners. For once the architects had bucked their own trend and created something homogenous and almost attractive. It was as if the rare rays of sunshine shone down from every angle, causing the glass and concrete to melt together with the landscape of bridges and canals that ran directly out to the harbour area. Even though the area had existed for a few years, Carl had never been there before, and he liked what he saw. If it hadn't been for his thoroughly pitiful financial situation, this would really be something for him. Maybe he should talk with Hardy about whether he might want to chip in a bit.

'They'll be home in five minutes,' said a very dark-skinned woman in an unmistakable Jutland dialect, as she led them through the apartment's micro-kitchen and down some stairs to the living room. It was at least six metres to the ceiling, and large glass panels revealed that only a small pontoon ramp separated the apartment from one of the canals. Three small floors on top of each other, stairs here and there and everywhere. Definitely not something for a man in a wheelchair like Hardy. So much for that dream.

'The water got a bit too close when the storm came here last December. The water was just this far away from reaching the window.' She demonstrated with her fingers what couldn't have been more than five centimetres.

Carl nodded. Another reason to stay in Allerød. There at least you were sixty metres above sea level. So when the catastrophe came, which was bound to happen sometime or other, it would take a significant glacial melt or tsunami.

'Good thing nothing happened,' he said, looking at the flat-screen and all the other electronic equipment. 'When Inge Dalby arrives, can we talk to her down here in peace and quiet?'

She gave him a thumbs-up. She and her husband could go for a walk. No problem.

Inge Dalby didn't look happy seeing the trio standing at the bottom of the stairs down in the living room, waiting for her.

'Sorry we've come unannounced, but we were in the area and have a few questions we think you might be able to help us with,' said Carl as the brother gave him a very firm handshake. A friendly man who also got a suitably impressive shake back when it came to Assad. Just enough to crush.

After five minutes, a few of these questions had been answered.

'Yes, that's right,' said Hans Otto Kure in an authentic dialect. It begged the question whether a Bornholmer like him could ever learn to speak real Danish. 'My dad took care of the work with the motors while Uncle Sture took care of everything else, apart from anything electrical, which they had an assistant for. I've been to lots of those classic car events, and so have you,' he said to Inge.

Then he and his wife left. 'We have to go Irma supermarket and buy some groceries,' she said simply, and that was that.

Inge Dalby sat with her back to the panoramic window and

rubbed her head with a rough hand that already seemed grey with oil and rust. Was she even aware where all this might be leading?

When their eyes met, she seemed calm, but a pulsating vein on her wrist told a different story. The next half-hour would be interesting.

'You might well have questions, but I'm done talking about that time. Kristoffer and I have been doing that for an eternity. It's just all a bit passé for me.'

'I understand,' said Carl with a nod. 'But I'm sorry to have to tell you that doesn't work with the police, Inge. We have grounds to believe that you withheld evidence last time we spoke so I've got four or five questions I'm going to ask you to answer, and I mean all of them. If you don't, we'll have to take you down to the station for questioning, understood?'

No reaction.

'Are you ready, Assad?'

He took out his notebook and lifted his pen, which strangely enough tended to get people talking.

'So, I'll ask: do you have a photo of the guy that Alberte was seeing? We know that you took photos at your trip to Østerlars Church where she met him, and that you most likely have a photo among them of the man we're looking for. We also know that the man had contact with several of you students. You were one of them. So a second question is why you haven't told us that. Was something going on between the two of you? Is that why you were so quick to forgive your boyfriend after his involvement with Alberte? Because you were both as bad as each other?

'My third question is equally important. You're good with your hands. You're interested in cars. You've been to classic car events, as your brother so kindly informed us, and probably also the event where the photo of the man with the VW was taken. We're convinced that you actually met the guy *before* that day at Østerlars Church. Can you confirm that? And finally, isn't it the case that you were fuming over Alberte stealing *both* your guys? First Kristoffer, whom you'd been together with for half a year, and then also the guy you'd had an affair with in the summer of the classic car event? Are you aware what sick minds, like the sort detectives have, make of that? We think that you're the one who rigged the van and drove it into Alberte. You simply couldn't stand that she outdid you *twice*, so you're the murderer, Inge. And now you've left your husband because he was getting too close to the truth, is that how it is? Yes, sorry, that makes it six questions.'

Carl had been watching her carefully during this tirade. Not once had she reacted. Not to the hypothesis that she knew the man earlier. Not even at the accusation of murder. Nothing. Just those black hands half covering her face. Had he played his cards too early?

Carl nodded to Rose, who moved closer. 'We're listening, Inge,' she said.

'Yes,' added Assad. 'We're old ears.'

At that the woman lifted her head and looked directly at him. 'It's "all ears", mate. What planet are you from?'

Did she have enough energy to laugh just then?

Rose put a hand on the woman's shoulder. 'Will you answer or do we need to take you down to the station, Inge?'

'You can do whatever the hell you want. You won't believe me anyway, no matter what the hell I say.'

'Try us,' said Carl.

They sat for several minutes in silence before she got her act together. Against all expectations, she appeared surprisingly unaffected, but concentrated as if she were passing a busy road with traffic coming from all directions. What was it that was making her so alert? Fear of being misunderstood or of saying too much?

'I know there were lots of things I could've told Habersaat back then, and that I didn't. Did you know the man?'

'No, we didn't,' answered Carl.

'Then let me tell you, he was strange. I didn't like him at all, and I felt like that from the beginning. It was as if by any means possible he wanted us to point to someone among us who could've done this to Alberte. And when it didn't work the first time around, you could be sure he'd be back, no doubt about that. And he was. Lots of times.

'If I'd told him everything I knew back then, he'd have pinned it on me, I can promise you that. He was obsessed with finding someone he could charge for what happened to Alberte.'

'So what was it you didn't tell him, Inge? Does it answer some of our questions?'

'Not all. But some of them.'

'What ones doesn't it answer?' threw in Assad. Always so impatient.

'Who did it. Because it wasn't me.'

'You met Frank before you started at the school, isn't that right?' asked Rose. A gamble with the name.

Inge sucked in half her bottom lip and started to bite it while looking over to the side. That concentration again, which experience said usually accompanied lies. Carl was really on alert now.

'How do you know that?' she asked.

She would have to make do with silence. Should they have blurted out that it was all guesswork? That they actually weren't even sure of the guy's name?

But they were just about to be.

She took a deep breath. 'I met Frank at the beginning of July, the day before the classic car event. If that photo had been taken ten seconds later, you'd be able to see that I was on the other side. Yes, we had had sex in the van. I'll tell you that right out. We did for a while. It was my idea that we should park down there at the back of the grass area because it was so secluded. I didn't think we'd be kicked off or that the classic cars would turn up so early. But I let Frank deal with the business of being parked somewhere he wasn't allowed, and I made my escape. I definitely didn't want my uncle catching me with that hippy.'

'But you were also seeing Kristoffer at that time, weren't you?' asked Carl.

'Yes, but Frank could do things Kristoffer couldn't, and never learned. He could make love so it blew your mind.'

Carl decided it was a subject best left alone.

'Then it wasn't guesswork when you described the VW Kombi. That black arched line that came up from the roof, what was that?'

'There was a large peace sign on the roof, and the circle around it went down the sides of the van a bit.'

'Anything else? Anything inside the van that could give us a clue so we can find the man.'

'I didn't see much other than him. But there were posters stuck on the walls. Don't ask me what they were meant to be. Some more peace stuff that the van's owner had put up way back when.'

'And you're sure you can't remember what he called himself when he was with Alberte?'

'He only used Frank when we were together. That's why it took a day or two before I found out that it was him Alberte was seeing. I don't know why he used that other name when he was with her. He was a bit special.'

'Special?'

'Yes, he had a lot of ideas, I think, but for us it was just sex.'

It was hard to believe when you looked at her now.

'Tell us about him, Inge. Where did you meet him, and how were things later?'

'I met him in Rønne. Even then, I already knew who he was because I'd been down to Ølene once with a friend to see the hippy house, and he was there, walking about shirtless, looking hot. My friend and I were curious because there wasn't much going on in those days on the island, and there still isn't. And after Rønne, we began fooling around a bit. Nothing Kristoffer knew about. I mean, I knew the thing with Frank was something that would end suddenly, so it was good to have someone like Kristoffer to fall back on. Someone from the island.'

Carl mulled over what she'd said, *fall back on*. He'd felt like that himself once in a while. Not a feeling he wanted to repeat.

'And Kristoffer never found out?'

'I don't think he ever suspected until you'd been to see us.'

'Why's that?'

'Because of the business with the VW. He didn't think you could see those stripes on the side. Not from the distance I said I'd seen it from, and he might be right. I should just never have mentioned it, and Kristoffer kept digging until I got pissed off. I hate it when people pick away at what I say.'

It wasn't hard to imagine.

'And what about you and the guy, then?'

'Well, we continued until the thing with Kristoffer and Alberte, and at the time I thought maybe that was good enough. Yeah, at least it wasn't me who broke up with him, even though that wasn't what I wanted.'

JUSSI ADLER-OLSEN • 310

What a nerve! Carl looked over at Rose, who just raised her eye-brows as if it didn't surprise her one bit. Maybe the method was common practice among women. He knew damn all about that sort of thing.

'And afterwards Frank began to see Alberte. Were you just frozen out from one day to the next?'

'Yes, it was the same for Kristoffer as for me.' She took a cigarette from her bag and lit it. The no-smoking-outside rule had obviously been dropped. Was she smiling ironically through the smoke?

'They dumped us both at the same time, leaving us in the lurch, despondent and unable to do anything about it.' She laughed out loud. 'But Kristoffer felt so guilty that I thought it was a situation I could use to my advantage for years. I had him over a barrel ba-sically, without him even knowing that I'd been much worse than him. Poor Kristoffer. If I'd had the chance, I would've escaped from the island with Frank.'

Carl nodded, Yes, poor him.

'It isn't true that you couldn't do anything, is it?' said Assad. 'As I see it, you were sick with jealousy and full of hate, so you killed her. You made that board thing from something or other from your dad's workshop and secured it on the front of the vehicle and killed her. Once she was out of the picture, you could pick up where you left off with the guy. But you just didn't get him to take you off the island because he disappeared, ironically enough. You might as well just admit it now.'

She leaned her neck back a little and looked down her nose with contempt, pointing at him with her smouldering cigarette. 'It's really wonderful to talk with you again after so many years, Habersaat,' she said.

She turned to Carl. 'Wasn't that what I said? That's why I kept my mouth shut about all this to Habersaat. I didn't want be accused of something *I* haven't done, like Mustafa's doing now.'

'My name isn't Mustafa, but I do know someone by that name,' Assad said drily. 'And he's a good guy, so don't let me stop you.'

There was no love lost between those two.

'OK, so we believe somewhat in your motives for not saying anything back then,' Carl cut in. 'Now I'm going to ask you a lot of questions and you'll answer briefly, agreed?'

'Yeah.'

'What was the guy called other than Frank?'

'I don't know. We were only on first-name terms.' She smiled cheekily.

'Can you tell us where he came from?'

'He mentioned Hellerup and Gentofte. We never talked about it.'

'Do you know what became of him?'

'I've tried to google him, but I don't know.'

'Do you have a photo of him we can see?'

'Yes, but it isn't any better than what you've already got. It was a really shitty camera. But I caught him by the church, that's true enough.'

'OK, while we're at it, you must have noticed that Alberte made passes at him when they first saw each other. What did you do about it? Did you try to stop it?'

'How could I? But I harassed her, which was fun because she was too stupid to work it out. It's true; I couldn't stand that Copenhagen bitch, but I didn't kill her. I had the room next to hers and could hear her talking to herself when she put the lights out. It was really pathetic. She was almost like a kid. She lay there touching herself, pretending he was there, but he wasn't.'

'Harassed her?'

'Yes. Washed her clothes with something where the colour would run. Encouraged her not to wrap up when we were outside so she'd catch a cold. Threw salt on her food when she wasn't looking. She was really very naive.'

'But that didn't stop them meeting, did it?' said Carl, all the while thinking what a bitch she was.

'I didn't know how much they saw of each other, to tell you the truth.'

'How did Frank end the relationship with you?'

'We just used to meet at certain places that we agreed on from time to time. Before the folk school we met at the square in Rønne. And at the folk school, before he dumped me, we met over in Ekkodalen valley. You can get down behind the school, it takes about five minutes. Then one day he just didn't show up as agreed. I went down there a few times but he never came again.'

'Do you think he also met Alberte down there?'

'Stupid question. Then I would've found out, wouldn't I? I don't know where they met or how. Only that she stood out on the road a lot.'

'Do you think Frank killed her?' asked Rose.

She shrugged as if she couldn't care less. 'No idea.'

'Was he the sort you think might be capable of it?' asked Rose again.

She shrugged again. 'I don't think so, but maybe. He certainly had a very strong personality.'

'What do you mean?'

'He could almost hypnotize people with a look. He had interesting eyes and interesting ideas. And he was strong and handsome. Charismatic, you might say.'

'And could bend spoons?'

'I never saw that. That was just a rumour.'

'Would you say he had psychopathic tendencies?' asked Carl.

She hesitated for just a second. 'Who doesn't?'

Was that self-awareness, or what?

'Do you have anything that might put us on his trail? Special characteristics, a completely general description, licence plates, something he said? Something about what sort of environment he came from or what his dreams were for the future?'

'His dreams? Not other than that he knew with certainty that he'd be something big, something that could change people's lives for the better.'

'OK, so he wasn't someone to hide his light. Change in what way, for example?'

'He believed that he could heal. That he had special energy and abilities, and I believe it. He certainly gave me some orgasms that I've hardly got over yet.'

Rose smiled at that. She was the only one.

'I'm afraid we'll have to take you down to the station anyway, Inge.'

That made her start. 'Why? I'm telling you everything I know.'

'It's taking too long, Inge. You've got time to think in between, and that gives you time to make things up, which isn't the point. If you want the chance here and now to avoid a normal hearing, you need to just list everything you can think of in relation to that man. Are you with me? And remember that you've said you saw him down at Ølene, so for that reason alone you must've seen more that can help us. So let's get going.'

She seemed a bit shaken, and Carl could understand why.

'I was damn well in love with him, OK! So you don't notice anything. I've thought about it a lot since, but I do remember a bit.'

She lit another cigarette and nodded quickly to her sister-in-law and brother, who were coming in the door with full plastic bags.

'His name was Frank and he was quite handsome with fine, strong features. He was six-one, six to seven years older than me, bit of a husky voice, but warm all the same. He was tanned but light-skinned under his clothes. His hair was long, down to his collar and almost ash blond, not red like you might have thought. And then he had a little dimple in his chin, which stood out when you saw him in a certain light.' She pointed to her own chin with a smile. There was certainly no dimple *there*.

'No visible scar or mark on his body? Hair, tattoos?'

'No, he did talk about wanting to get a couple of tattoos right enough, but he didn't really know what he should get. It wasn't nearly as fashionable as it is now.'

Carl nodded. No, people thought better of it in those days, which was unfortunate from an investigator's point of view.

'What about the eyes and eye area?'

'His eyes were blue, eyebrows very dark, front teeth rather wide, and a little white mark on one of them. He called it a sunburn. He was generally very preoccupied with the sun. That's why he was on the island, he said.'

Carl looked at Assad. Once she started there was no stopping her. It was just a case of hanging in there.

'He'd found two different sunstones within a week of each other, he said. He was really excited about it. First, one like those used by the Vikings for sailing. And then afterwards, one like those found in the sun cult area on Rispebjerg down by Dueodde.'

'Sun cult! I think you'll have to explain more about that, Inge.'

'I don't know so much about it. Just a place on the island where altars had been erected for offering things.'

Rose had already made a start with her iPad, he noticed.

'Do you have any idea what the man lived off?'

'Unemployment benefits, I think. The van certainly wasn't his. He'd borrowed it from someone he knew. Someone who'd been in the peace movement or something, way back when. And Frank did go about with those peace symbols on badges.'

'What did he wear?'

She smiled. 'Not much when we were together.'

Assad's glaring eyes and raised eyebrows expressed a wholehearted *Touché!*

Then her brother moved closer to the banister that separated the upper kitchen area from the living room below.

'Who're you talking about, Inge? No one I've heard of, is it?'

She hit out at him in the air. Apparently there was a sort of inside talk between those two that others couldn't or shouldn't follow. Rose saw it, too, noticed Carl.

'He was called Frank, Hans Otto,' said Assad. 'Someone you've met, maybe?'

He smiled and shook his head. Why wasn't he surprised? Was Inge Dalby more experienced than you might think? Did the brother have a hand in it with the Frank guy?

'I think I can sense from your brother that there might have been more than just Frank along the way. Am I wrong, Inge?'

She leaned her neck back and sighed. 'We're island folk. If fresh blood comes to the quay, you taste the goods, right? In the old days they did it to mix the DNA up a bit. Think of the Faroe Islands or Iceland. Nowadays, we just do it for the fun and kicks. Yes, of course there were others.'

Rose shook her head. Obviously not a lead worth following. 'We were talking about his clothes, Inge,' she said.

'Oh, yes. It was a bit wrong for the time, but actually really cool: bead necklace round his neck, loose-fitting woven shirts, and jeans. Really big boots. Not cowboy boots but some sort of home-made kind with soles that were a bit too wide. They weren't very good but they looked cool on him. Sometimes he looked like a Cossack.'

They listened to her for a further twenty minutes. Small things that were noted down. Remarks between Frank and her. What they did when they weren't together in the van. All commonplace things that from a policeman's point of view weren't exactly leading anywhere. But the appearance of the man was clearer now.

'We'd ask you to let us know if you're thinking about going anywhere, Inge.' Carl gave her his card. 'You're not a direct suspect in the case but you could prove to be very important if we run into questions later that we can't answer immediately. And you might be called to identify him if we find him. And just one more thing. We'd like you to get your husband to find the photo from your trip to Østerlars Church, OK? Because you're not going back to the island just now, are you? I thought you might have to go out there to be together with your kids.'

Strangely enough, that made her frown in a way that ruled out scepticism, resentment or any other negative responses. She frowned in the way people do just before they're about to cry.

'Maybe you don't see your children any more?' suggested Carl.

'Yes, of course I do. They're both at a residential school in Slagelse. We'll be together again this weekend.'

'You seem sad. Have we worried you?'

She shook her head. 'Sad? No. I'm just thinking that Frank couldn't have done what you think. And if you find him, I'd like to meet him again. I really would!'

They were already on their way out the door when Carl turned around and used his final ammunition. If it could work for Columbo, then it could work for him, too.

'Just one more question, Inge. Did Alberte have a mobile phone?'

She shook her head. 'No, but then not many of the girls did.'

'Did Frank?'

'Not as far as I know. He wasn't particularly materialistic. More the opposite.'

'OK. And then there's the thing with Frank's name again. When we visited you on Bornholm, you said that Alberte had mentioned another name for Frank, but which you couldn't remember. Probably something biblical or similar, you said. Short, like Eli or Job. Do you remember saying that?'

'Err, yes, of course.'

'Good.' He looked at Rose. 'So what can we conclude from that, Rose?'

'That it's extremely hard to believe that Inge Dalby wouldn't know what her boyfriend went around calling himself. And if for some strange reason she should only have heard it through Alberte, it seems extremely unlikely that she should have forgotten it. She'd definitely take special notice of something like that, if you ask me.'

Carl turned toward Inge Dalby. She seemed rooted to the spot, as if caught red-handed. 'What do you have to say to that, Inge?'

29

End of March 2014

After Shirley had spoken to Pirjo, she rolled up the two-tone belt and placed it on the windowsill. It lay there beside her toiletry bag and all the books she'd brought from home. Neither intrusive nor forgotten.

She calmed herself with reassurances that Wanda must be in Jamaica. Right enough, she'd tried to contact people there, but were they the right people, the right telephone numbers, the right questions and answers? When she thought back to her memories with Wanda, there seemed to be fewer and fewer details about who she was – her background and future ambitions – that she could be totally certain of. Wanda had *said* that she wanted to go to Öland, but she'd always been a warm-blooded and spontaneous woman, so how could Shirley know with any certainty that something or other hadn't happened in the meantime that changed her plans? She couldn't.

Nevertheless, from time to time she couldn't resist letting something slip about the Wanda mystery if the opportunity presented itself.

She told in colourful detail about how her best friend had become fascinated, yes, almost seduced, by Atu's personality and presence, and about how she'd totally unrealistically thought she'd become his chosen one. In the beginning, the other disciples laughed a little at this ambitious story, but after a while, as it became more and more worn, interest decreased and irritation grew.

'Some of us think that you should choose your words more carefully, Shirley,' said one of the men who worked with the carpentry team. 'The story with the belt is creating unease and a lot of unsubstantiated speculation. We're not happy about it. Maybe you should consider leaving the academy if being here gives you so many negative feelings.'

They weren't necessarily harsh words, but Shirley was paralysed by them. Was she making herself a pariah? Did people really think that the place would be better without her?

Shirley didn't want to be a pariah, she wanted to be popular and liked, and so for that reason she buried the story of Wanda Phinn.

When her course period was successfully completed, it was her intention to apply for permanent admission, and her innermost desire was for this to be granted. As the months had gone by, she imagined with more and more certainty that it was here she should spend the rest of her life. Yes, and it was maybe even here that she'd find a life partner.

Valentina was one of the ones she could talk about her future dreams with, because in that respect they weren't much different. At a few communal assemblies she'd seen her with a guy who she'd seemingly set her eye on, but that had come to an end, and afterwards the two women had begun to chat together. Throughout most of Shirley's course period, Valentina had worked with the centre website and advertising, but at her own request had been moved to internal maintenance, suddenly making her much more visible and present.

They told each other about their unfortunate backgrounds. About how they'd escaped both bullying and harassment and been elevated to a new and better life.

Shirley was astonished when Valentina began telling the story of her miserable time in Spain, because when Shirley looked around among all these well-functioning people, it had never crossed her mind that most of them had had experiences similar to her own before they came here. She'd seriously imagined that she was the only person here that fortune had never smiled down on. And now she'd found a like-minded friend, who was also able to tell her that her story was far from unusual.

'Everyone here has skeletons in their closet they don't want to be confronted with, Shirley. Remember that, and listen to Atu next time he says he "sees you". He knows who you are, and he accepts you for who you are.'

It was with that realization that they came to be really close to one another in so many respects. Not since Malena had Valentina had such a good friend here as Shirley, she told her. And Shirley was flattered and moved.

Naturally, it wasn't forbidden to talk about life outside the centre, but for many it just didn't seem natural. This certainly wasn't how Valentina and Shirley felt, with many common interests and favourite topics of conversation being the order of the day. 'Even though you grow up in Seville, George Clooney can still give you as many steamy dreams as someone who grew up in Birmingham,' as Valentina put it. Just like Shirley, Valentina loved Enrique Iglesias more than his dad, Julia Roberts more than Sharon Stone, beer more than wine, and musicals more than opera.

They rattled off hundreds of things they either hated or loved, and every time they ended up in stitches over how similar they could be in spite of significant cultural differences.

Disciples didn't normally sit in each other's rooms. Even so, there were times when these two women sneaked into each other's room so they could hang out together and have a laugh.

It was on one of these evenings that Valentina noticed the belt on the windowsill and was given the true and unabridged version of what had gone through Shirley's mind when it turned up.

Valentina listened to the story with great interest. It was obviously the first time she'd heard it.

And when Shirley was finished, shrugging her shoulders over how stupid it had been of her to have such thoughts, Valentina turned her head away and sat staring out of the window without saying a word for a long time.

Shirley thought she'd behaved like an idiot by transgressing an inviolable boundary. That she'd violated the confidence and friendship that Valentina had shown her and that it was now irreparable.

She was just about to say sorry and that it was all just nonsense, and that over time she'd become totally convinced that Wanda Phinn was now living her own peaceful life somewhere else in the world, when Valentina turned towards her with a look that you didn't normally see in that place.

'It reminds me of a strange and very unpleasant dream I had the other day,' she said with dark eyes. 'But I don't know if I should tell you about it.'

30

Thursday, May 8th, and Friday, May 9th, 2014

'Put it on speakerphone, Carl,' said Rose.

Carl hesitated. He knew who he was dealing with.

'We'll keep our mouths shut, right, Rose?' said the mind reader Assad.

She nodded slowly with her chin right down on her chest.

Carl dialled the number. It was a bit late in the day, but experience told him that all museum directors were geeks and found it hard to go home. Not least one like this one.

'You say he's a specialist of everything when it comes to the sun cult on Bornholm?'

Assad nodded. 'He's an archaeologist, Carl. He's the one who dug the rubbish up.'

Carl gave him a thumbs-up. It had been an oddish sort of grey day, but good nevertheless. Inge Dalby had talked ten to the dozen, and they'd managed to get through to her. She'd been able to explain somewhat plausibly that she didn't know Frank's alias. They'd had sex together, nothing else. That Alberte had been closer to him and could say things about him that Inge didn't know about had just been an extra thorn in her side.

All things considered, Inge wasn't a particularly attractive woman inside.

'Bornholm Museum, Filip Nissen,' came the voice from the receiver. They were off. The man was still stuck behind his desk.

Carl looked at the photo of him on the computer screen. A little too rotund, beard a little too scraggy, glasses a little too heavyset. A real geek, if you asked him.

'No, I'm afraid I can't talk just now, the museum is closed. You'll have to wait until the morning. I'm going skateboarding with my sons, you see, and they're waiting outside.'

Proof you shouldn't judge a book by its cover. It must be an extremely sturdy skateboard. Custom built, maybe.

'We just need to know if you can remember a hippy guy who was interested in your excavations back in 1997, and who was also very interested in sun cults and sunstones?' Rose blurted out. How long had she managed to contain herself? Approximately twenty seconds?

'No, sorry,' he said, panting. Was he already on his way down the stairs with the skateboard and everything? If so, then he had call redirection to his mobile, in which case the office hours were irrelevant.

'His name was Frank,' shouted Assad.

Then there was a pause in the panting. Had he stopped to think or had he already hopped on the board?

'OK, Frank, you say! Frank Scott, perhaps? Is it him you're thinking about?'

Rose gave Assad a high five, one–nil to him.

Rose turned immediately to the PC in the corner. Now she had a real name.

'A tall guy with long hair and a dimple in his chin?' Carl asked.

'Yes, yes, that's him. But why do you call him a hippy when he wasn't?'

'Because of his clothing.'

He laughed at the other end. 'He only had the same damn ugly gear as the rest of us. But maybe *you* wear Armani when you're lying in the mud scraping away?'

'I can't say I do, no. Have you had any contact with him since then? We'd really like to get hold of him.'

'Hi, boys,' they heard at the other end. 'I just need to finish up here, is that OK?' But it didn't sound like they thought it was.

'Contact?' he returned to the call. 'Well, not really. He disappeared from the island but we corresponded for a while. For a few months actually, I think. Frank had all sorts of theories and was very serious about the discovery of the sun cults that he could link with some theories about all religions originating from the same source: the sun, the seasons and the zodiac.'

'You corresponded. How? Letters? Emails?'

'Letters. He was very old-school. But I don't have them any more, I can assure you. I have enough old papers in my work.'

'Never emails?'

'No. Hang on, yes, maybe once, when he was visiting a colleague somewhere or other. Don't ask me about what or where. They had a quick question they thought I was the man to answer. Something or other about timber circles, I think.'

'Hopefully you've still got that email?'

'It would be quite strange considering we've changed computers at least three times since then. No, of course I don't have it.'

'Printouts?'

'I belong to that rare group who've avoided maximizing their use of paper in the digital age, so no.'

'Any address for Frank that you can remember?'

'I don't think I ever had it.'

'Think?'

'I never had it. I know he lived near Copenhagen. After all, that was where he could search for most of his information.'

'What information?'

'National Museum of Denmark, the Royal Library, Open University, that sort of thing. He soaked things up like a sponge. He was very inquisitive when it came to the sun cult's roothold here on the island and parallel events like that, which is understandable enough.'

'Absolutely,' answered Carl.

Even Gordon began to smile now. An atmosphere like this would be welcome on a more or less permanent basis in the situation room.

'Can't we talk together tomorrow? The boys are tugging at me. They're a little impatient,' insisted the man.

Carl shook his head automatically. Hell no.

'Do you have pictures of the guy? You must've taken loads of pictures in connection with your work on the site.'

'I really don't know. Maybe a few where he's standing in the background. But it's such a long time ago, and even if you're an archaeologist, we don't go around preserving everything that's old.' At that, he laughed out loud and then just as suddenly stopped again when Carl fired off the next question.

'This is a murder case,' he said drily. 'So will you tell your boys to go on ahead? We've got to get to the bottom of this.'

*

'*Damn it!*' shouted Rose a little later. 'There's no Frank Scott in Denmark to be found, according to the civil registration list. Damn it.'

Carl fumbled for the cigarettes in his breast pocket, but stopped when Rose pointed to a sign on the wall written in capitals:

SMOKING DOESN'T JUST KILL YOU BUT THOSE AROUND YOU TOO, YOU FUCKING MURDERER!

It couldn't really be put any more charmingly than that.

Carl pushed the cigarettes back. 'The museum director must've heard the name wrong, or else doesn't remember it right,' he said.

'Yes, or the man's had a permanent name change or moved abroad,' suggested Gordon.

Rose threw him a look of resignation. 'If there's been a man at some time or other in the more recent past living in Denmark under the name of Frank Scott, you can damn well bet that I'd have found him.'

'I didn't mean . . . I . . .' He looked around to find some sympathy. Christ, what a fool.

'Maybe he's not a Danish national and never has been,' he dared to continue. 'He could've belonged to the Danish minority in Slesvig. Or maybe he was Swedish or something.'

Carl nodded over to Rose. It was a possibility of course, so he gave Gordon a pat as high on his back as he could from where he was sitting, while Rose began typing like a lunatic.

'There was something that was weird about that museum director, Carl,' grunted Assad. 'He could remember Frank and a load of other details about how he helped at digs, and all sorts of things they talked about, but he didn't remember Alberte.'

'That's how it is with professional geeks, Assad. They can't see past the end of their own noses.'

'No, I don't think he seemed like an end-of-the-nose type. He remembered all sorts of things. How the weather had been, what Frank's van looked like, how they discussed the size of the timber circles and the old sun-worship sites they excavated. He could remember that Frank was a vegetarian, and that he used his left and right hands equally well. He could also remember that he once had one of the girls from their camp down to the excavations, and that she spoke Swedish with a Finnish accent. He had a very good memory in my opinion, and the Alberte case was big news. All the vehicles on the island were checked, and that most certainly includes the four-wheel drive from Bornholm Museum that they used at the dig.'

'Where are you going with this, Assad?'

'I know,' said Gordon with his hand in the air like a schoolboy. Wasn't he aware that you asked to speak *after* you put your hand in the air?

'He was most likely not on Bornholm at the time it happened, if you ask me.'

He got another pat on the back. This time from Assad.

'Exactly, boss,' said Assad. 'We forgot to ask him. It's possible this Frank borrowed the Rover from the museum and used it in the crime if the museum man had left it at his disposal while he was away.'

Carl clicked his fingers at Assad, who immediately went over to the corner and tapped on his phone.

'What about you, Rose, any luck?'

She shook her head. 'I think Frank was much better at using other people's names than his own.'

'So, suddenly we know almost nothing again,' said Carl. 'When we pressed Inge Dalby last, she thought he'd changed his name to something very short that most likely started with "A", the rest of which was something oriental. But what the hell can we do with that? And now Filip Nissen says Frank was called Scott, but of course no such person exists. How far did you get, Rose?'

She drew a circle in the air. Meaning all possible neighbouring countries.

Assad flicked his mobile shut. 'Filip Nissen was off travelling for part of that fall, he says. But the museum car had definitely not been left at anyone's disposal.' Assad sighed, and it was contagious.

'I'll call round the alternative therapists one more time,' said Rose. 'Maybe there's someone who can connect Frank with those two sunstones.'

She was already sitting in her seat when Carl turned up the next morning. Tousled hair, same clothes as the day before, and loud snoring was emanating from Assad's office, which Carl could immediately eliminate as coming from Assad. You didn't need to be much of a detective before you began smiling over the probable cause.

'Well, well,' said Carl. 'There seem to be a couple of you who slept in the situation room last night.'

'Yes,' answered Rose with her back to him. 'We have to get going with this lot, so I've caught those people on Bornholm in their beds before they went to work.'

Carl had a cheeky smile on his face as he thought that this wasn't the only thing that had gone on, and that they weren't the only ones who'd been in bed before they went to work.

'And Gordon?'

'Yeah, he obviously needs more sleep than I do.'

Poor guy. No doubt she'd sucked all the energy out of the beanpole. 'Any results?'

Now she turned around. Seldom would you see a more triumphant Rose. Even her running coal-black mascara glowed.

'Several things. I called around some more of those alternative therapists and have finally managed to sort them. Half are too young to be able to give information about something that happened nearly twenty years ago, a quarter are too far gone, to put it mildly, to be able to get anything concrete or meaningful out of, and the last quarter are trying as hard as they can because they've got the right age, expertise and wherewithal.'

'And?' he said impatiently.

'I got lucky twice this time: an esoteric astrologer and an Aura-Soma therapist, who both remembered Frank and his sunstones and keen interest in sun cults.'

Carl clenched his fists. Finally, they were off. 'Do we have a name or address?'

'No.'

'Thought as much.' He relaxed his hands and stroked his neck. 'So what have you got?'

'The description matches Inge Dalby's. They both agreed on that. And they added a number of other characteristics. For example, this Frank guy was totally disconnected from modern technology.'

'No mobile phones?'

'No mobiles, no PCs. He wrote everything by hand, and with a fountain pen. The car he drove around in was borrowed. He didn't use a credit card, always cash.'

'And for the same reason, he hasn't left any traces anywhere, right?'

She pointed directly at him. 'Not directly, no, and yet, yes.'

'What do you mean?'

'One of them thought that his special knowledge about the cults on Bornholm was just the tip of the iceberg. That he also had an extensive and more general knowledge about astrology, theology, astronomy and ancient history. He was very interested in the religions of different ages, and what had been passed on from them. So he was always open to a good discussion about such things. The esoteric astrologer also thought that his theories were very epochal.'

'How does that help us? And what the hell is an esoteric astrologer?'

'It's something to do with finding the power to reveal the soul's hidden intentions in the current incarnation. Something with helping the soul to fulfil its full potential with the incarnation.'

Carl tried to find a suitable grimace for the occasion. This was apparently outside his comprehension. 'But again, why's it important that his theories were . . . what did you say, epochal?'

'That means that his enthusiasm was infectious. The people living at the Ølene camp were one way or another part of his spiritual family, sort of his disciples, and that included the Aura-Soma therapist. Once, when Frank was with her to strengthen his aura, one of the other disciples was with him.'

'Disciple, how? I mean, how could anyone know that's what they were?'

'Relax, I'm getting there now, Carl. The reason that Frank contacted so many of these alternative therapists was because he wanted to learn from them, of course, to know their secrets. It was as if he wanted to merge all the alternative knowledge and techniques in the world and try to find a common denominator for them. For healing, for religion, for all the ancient sciences: alchemy, astrology, channelling, electromagnetic therapy, clairvoyance and so on and so on. Don't ask what it was he was striving for; that was a whole science in itself, and that was the crux of it.' She pointed tellingly at him again.

'What?'

'That Frank was in the process of establishing his own spiritual philosophy. He wanted to collect everything useful and combine it, and the man he had with him was a witness of truth, as he put it.'

'Damn it, that's some really weird stuff. But *did* he establish himself?'

'Yes, they both thought so. And what's more, the Aura-Soma therapist could remember the name of the man who was with Frank. His name was Simon Fisher, which they all laughed about because it couldn't really be more symbolic, could it? So Frank was a messiah and the man just a follower. And then one of the therapists said that Simon Fisher showed a keen interest in her garden with its medicinal plants and said that he'd like to have a garden just like it. And *now* comes the final thing, Carl!' Again, the pointing finger. It almost made you want to find a pair of scissors and cut a bit off it.

'Well, fire away, damn it. What next?'

'The man called Simon Fisher *got* his garden centre. It's in Holbæk in an area called Tempelkrogen.'

'Tempelkrogen? Yes, of course. Why doesn't that surprise me? One final question: what's an Aura-Soma therapist?'

'That's a bit of a weird one. I didn't want to ask her so I looked it up. Partly, it's something with bottles that contain healing colour vibrations, but I didn't quite understand it.'

Carl fumbled for his cigarettes. This was really a long detour on the road to finding out something that might lead them to the right track.

*

'Wasn't it wrong that we didn't bring Rose with us, Carl? It was her after all who found the man,' said Assad as his jaw tried to get the better of the chewing gum he'd shoved in his mouth fifty-five kilometres back.

'Have a look at the GPS, Assad. I think we need to go down past Eriksholm when we pass Munkholm Bridge, what do you think?'

'I think it was wrong that we didn't bring Rose along. And yes, when we're over the water, you need to take a left.'

Carl looked out south over the glistening fjord, winding in and out between small islands and headlands. As far as he could see, it must be over on the other side of the water where a white house on a peninsula in lonely majesty almost seemed to lean down over the low-lying pasture.

'You'll see, she'll be fine as long as she has Gordon to . . .' He turned his attention to a kiosk where he and Vigga had so often stopped when they travelled by motorbike out in the countryside on the weekends. They were good times when they couldn't afford anything else. How far had he come in life since then?

'I'm beginning to think about quitting the service, Assad,' he said after a sudden impulse. 'It would make Lars Bjørn's day, but still.'

He didn't need to look at Assad to find out if it had caused him to stop chewing. He could hear it.

'That would be absolutely the worst thing that could happen for me,' said Curly in a flawless accent, prompting Carl to turn to face him instantly.

'You need to turn here, Carl,' he said. The accent had returned. 'I don't understand. What'll you do?'

'I'll open a Syrian cafe with you, Assad. And we won't serve anything other than sticky mint tea and pastries. Sticky tea, and Arabic music blaring out.'

Now the guy began to chew again. He didn't believe he was being so serious any more. Good, it would've been a shame.

They took a few small roads past farms and turned to go through a village and further down towards the house.

'Deep in the countryside,' observed Assad, when the scenery opened up in all its rain-soaked splendour. He'd never been in Vendsyssel, it would seem.

Carl had yet another impulse. 'Assad! Would you come to my cousin's funeral up in Brønderslev? You'd be able to meet my parents, too, and the rest of the not so merry band.'

'Band? Will there be a band?' he asked as the house appeared at the end of the road. Water on two sides with the bridge in the background, and forest and road on the other two. A golden vision in the landscape. A rarity on earth.

It all seemed so accessible and friendly, but the Holistic Garden Centre wasn't just quite so easy to conquer. Two growling devils – the kind that'd been set on the unfortunate Christians in the Colosseum in ancient Rome – stood pawing at the floor as if they could jump over the fence at any second.

A small sign stated: *Birtemaja & Simon Fisher. Ring first.* Observant, thought Carl, as he pressed the bell right down and held it there.

'Hate and Skoll, down,' shouted a voice over the courtyard. A man, his trousers tucked down in his clog boots and wearing a baggy smock shirt, danced over a couple of deep puddles and edged towards them.

'Customers in the shop,' he shouted back toward the house.

Carl put his hand in his pocket to get his ID, but Assad put a hand on his arm to stop him.

'Nice place you have here,' Assad said to the man, giving him his hand over the fence. 'We've come to get some help with a few things.'

He opened the lock while the dogs began to growl at Assad.

'They're not used to dark skin.'

'No problem. I've got them under control,' answered Assad, at which the dominant dog lunged towards him ready to bite.

Carl jumped to the side but Assad stood his ground and that very second, as the gardener tried to stop the beast, he let out an infernal yell that made both dogs sink to their knees like puppies and piss themselves like they'd never pissed before.

'That's it,' said Assad, slapping himself on the thigh and calling the dogs to heel.

When they crept over to him and let him pet them, both the gardener and Carl stood speechless, watching.

'Where did I get to?' said Assad, the dogs on either side of him, as if they'd found a new master. 'Yes, we need a little assistance. Firstly, we need to buy something or other that can help me sleep.'

Carl couldn't believe his own ears. If Assad slept any deeper than he had in the hotel in Rønne, he'd damn well never wake up again.

'And then we need something that can revitalize my friend here. Afterwards, we'd like to ask you a couple of questions, if that's OK with you.'

The ID card never materialized from Carl's pocket.

31

'That looks fine. Those herbs will do the trick with your sleepless-ness,' Simon Fisher said to Assad. 'And now your friend here.'

He went over to the corner of the room, a bomb crater of the im-pacts of time, where nothing matched. Furniture that a flea market would reject, rugs consisting equally of dog hair, old coffee stains and, last but not least, a myriad of coloured posters of Hindu gods among pictures of Danish nature in gold frames. In this corner he opened a drawer in an exact copy of the bureau Carl's granddad had had in the tailor shop in Risskov.

He was just about to ask him where he'd got the bureau from when the man passed Assad a pendulum and briefly instructed him in how to use it.

'Do the same as your friend,' he said to Carl. 'Hold the pendulum still in your hand, and calibrate it with your energy. Afterwards, hang it over the plants you'll make your tea from, and then we'll see if I've chosen the right herbs.'

Carl took the chain and tried to stop himself from frowning. Now the pendulum just needed to damn well behave so they could get on.

He pulled the chain up and down to help it along.

'No, no, you have to sit totally still, and it'll decide for itself. It will detect the energy around you,' said the man as a woman in grey glided in behind him. They nodded to her but weren't so fortunate as to get any acknowledgement.

Carl looked down sceptically at the dead-still pendulum. Apparently there wasn't so much energy in the plant stuff he'd selected.

'No, it won't do. We'll have to calibrate the pendulum again. Now do what your friend here did so well. First, hold your other hand under the pendulum, and ask it to respond to a movement for yes.'

Carl turned his head to face him. Was he crazy, or what?

'Come on.'

Carl let the pendulum hover a few centimetres above his free hand. 'Respond to a movement for yes,' he said, almost whispering, but still nothing happened. Of course not.

'Give it here,' said the gardener, at which he pulled the pendulum up to his mouth and began to suck in the air around it in short bursts. He did this a few times in deep concentration, then raised it in front of his eyes and blew out hard after an extra-large intake of breath.

'There. Now it's cleansed,' he said. 'Try again.'

There was one other time, when he'd dived from the five-metre diving board at an outdoor swimming pool to impress Lise, only to end up with his trunks around his knees midair, that he'd felt more stupid than just now. Was he really sitting here trying to convince a metal cone that it should make a start and move?

And then it did.

'OK, good,' said the gardener. 'Now hold it over the herbs and ask the pendulum if they're good for you.'

He only did it because Assad poked him in the leg under the table.

'Thought as much. They're no good for you. You need something a little less potent, or we'll have you running around like crazy.'

Carl nodded and said that was exactly what he needed. That way he could be free from playing Dr Mesmer again.

'OK, but you've been warned,' he said.

Did the man think that he'd ever consider making soup from his stinking crops?

'Put the pendulum in your pocket. It'll help you another time when you need it most. I'll put fifty kroner on top of the price of the plants. That should keep us straight.'

Carl tried to smile and thanked him. 'But actually we're also here to talk to you about that time you were over on Bornholm with Frank in the Ølene camp. We mustn't forget that.'

He looked thoughtful. 'Frank?'

'Yes, that's the name we know best.'

'And why are you asking?'

Assad took over. 'We're interested in his philosophy about sun cults and the like. We'd like to talk to him ourselves but we don't know where he's gone. Do you know maybe?'

The grey lady in the background took a few steps forward, which didn't go unnoticed by the man.

'How did you find me?' he asked with his eyes fixed on the woman.

'From one of the alternative therapists that you visited together. She remembered your name, and she's been a customer of yours.'

He nodded when Carl said her name. 'Yes, that's right enough. I lived in the Ølene camp for the whole summer. They were good times. We had a difference of opinion, Frank and me, but our conversations were actually really fantastic.'

'What did you discuss?' asked Carl. 'Sun cults, religion and that sort of thing?'

'Yes, and a whole lot more besides. Frank and I were both part of the excavations at Rispebjerg, but Frank in particular felt a special affection for the place because of the sun offerings and extensive evidence of strong cultures that had been there thousands of years before. Actually, he stole one of the sunstones we excavated, but we only talk about that under our breath.'

He laughed for a moment but stopped again when he caught his wife's eye.

'Do you know how he got this interest?'

'I think it was just something he'd always busied himself with. And the Open University, of course. He took a couple of courses the year before while he was working in Copenhagen, so he told me.'

'What courses, do you know?'

'There was a lecturer from the theology faculty in Copenhagen, a visiting lecturer. I don't know his name but he was a professor, Frank said. It was apparently quite epochal, something to do with the origin of archaeoastronomy and religion.'

'Archaeo-what?'

'Archaeoastronomy, the significance of the zodiac for prehistoric peoples.'

Assad noted it down. 'Do you have contact with any friends from Ølene?' he asked.

'No, not apart from Søren Mølgård. But he's really gone to the dogs of late.'

'Søren Mølgård. Can we have his address?'

'It's a while ago and, to be honest, I've dropped him. Too many drugs, you understand. It's not really compatible with what we work with here, is it, Birtemaja?'

She shook her head, lips pinched. Just as well it wasn't her they were trying to squeeze something out of.

'I seem to recall that he moved to a commune with some Asa followers, just south of Roskilde. Probably what was needed if he didn't want to go totally under.'

'And who is this Søren character?'

'Nobody special. Just one of the people who lived at Ølene for a while. As far as I've heard, quite a few of us from there have ended up in the alternative world and made a good go of it, but Søren lacked the talent. He was just a hippy who happened to come past. He apparently tried to become a numerologist just like Birtemaja, but didn't really understand what lay at its core. We like some sort of order in our worldview, you understand, and that wasn't something for him.' He laughed.

Carl nodded. As far as he could tell, the order of the worldview hadn't quite made it into this room here.

'And what about you? Where are you two from?' he asked.

Now Carl pulled his ID card from his pocket, in spite of Assad's intense look.

'We're from Copenhagen Police, and we'd really like to talk with Frank about an accident that took place when you were living on Bornholm. We believe him to be the only one who can help us reach an understanding of what happened.'

Simon Fisher's eyes fixed on the card. He hadn't seen this coming. 'What accident?' he said with a look of distrust. 'While we were there? I don't know anything about an accident?'

'No, but then that's not what we're here to talk to you about. We just hope you'll be able to tell us Frank's surname and what name he's using at present. Do you know where he's based at the moment?'

'Sorry,' he said briefly.

*

'Honestly, Assad, can't you just hurl those plants out the window? It stinks so much it's making me sick.'

'I paid fifty kroner for them, Carl.'

Carl sighed and pressed the passenger window down.

'It's too cold and it's pouring down, Carl. Can you shut it again? The seat's getting soaked.'

He ignored him. Either the plants went or Assad would have to put up with it. And when they got back, he'd be keeping well clear of everything Assad might think to conjure up from the stuff.

Carl pressed Rose's work number on his phone and asked her to find a man who'd taught at the Open University in Copenhagen in the years just before 1997, a theologian whose passion was apparently comparing religions and constellations.

Afterwards, there was silence in the car for the next twenty kilometres. Really nice atmosphere when you were driving on a motorway where it seemed like half the population of Zealand had decided to head off in the direction of Copenhagen.

When they trudged past Roskilde in a traffic jam at ten kilometres an hour, surrounded by seriously irritated drivers, Assad put his feet up on the dashboard and looked away. Then it came.

'That was a bad move back at the house, Carl,' he said.

Just what Carl had expected. No further explanation necessary.

'You saw that the wife had seen through us, Assad. She was already about to stop him. They didn't want to help us, couldn't you tell? We wouldn't have got the information anyway, so now we'll have to bet on Søren Mølgård. But if there's something fishy going on, you can bet he's been warned.'

'Something fishy? I don't always understand what you're talking about, Carl. What are they doing with the fish?'

'An expression meaning that there's something suspicious going on, Assad.'

'Why fish?'

'I don't know, Assad.'

'Why not something—'

'Are you listening to me, Assad? I've got a distinct and very well-founded suspicion that there's something wrong in this case. All this stuff about sun cults and sunstones, it puts me on edge.'

'On the edge of what?'

'*Stop!* I can't think when you're interrupting all the time. I don't like it, OK?'

The telephone rang. It was Rose.

'The course was called "From Star Myths to Christianity" and it took place in autumn 1995. The lecturer came from the Faculty of Theology in Copenhagen and is now professor emeritus living in Pandrup. His name's Johannes Tausen.'

Johannes Tausen. You couldn't really get a more theological name in Denmark.

'Pandrup in Vendsyssel?'

'Is there another one?'

'OK, text me his full address and I'll drive out there tomorrow after the funeral in Brønderslev. Thanks, Rose.'

She hung up before he even managed to blink.

'You're planning to talk to the professor tomorrow?' asked Assad.

Carl nodded. He was still thinking about the impression Simon Fisher had left on him. Why hadn't he and his wife been cooperative? Was there something he hadn't understood when it came to people like those from Ølene?

'Then I'd like to come.'

Carl looked absently at Assad. 'Good. Thanks,' he answered.

'I can see you're not really here. You're thinking of the motive, right?'

'Of course I am.' Carl rolled the window up, which resulted in a deep sigh of relief from Assad. 'I feel more and more that we're on the right track. I'm afraid Habersaat was right about Frank being a megalomaniac. Saw himself as some sort of messiah, and maybe everything was going to plan before Alberte came along and blocked his path somehow or other.'

'How do you mean?'

'That she became a deadweight for him. But there is another possibility, and more uncomfortable to imagine in my opinion. Maybe it was simply a case of sacrificing Alberte. A murder that Frank and the others from Ølene didn't want to be connected with the sun cult. A sun sacrifice that curiously enough must've taken place at the very moment the sun was rising.'

32

Friday, May 9th, 2014

She had felt the pain in waves. Strange short circuits where the diaphragm contracted, like when you sit in a draught or when something you ate the day before begins to take revenge. Of course it worried her, just like any other irregular bodily sign. But she'd been for a check-up the day before and everything was as it should be. The gynaecologist had nodded authoritatively and declared the pregnancy to be exemplary, leaving Pirjo both relieved and happy. More than six months in and the baby was declared healthy and viable, so she dismissed the discomfort as random and harmless.

Just as the pain seemed to disappear completely, the phone rang.

The voice sounded familiar, but it was only after the usual introduction that Pirjo began to smile.

'Simon, Simon Fisher! It's been a long time,' she exclaimed, trying to remember when they'd last had contact. Was it five years? Or ten?

'Is everything OK over there, Pirjo?' he asked.

She was puzzled by his tone. Simon wasn't exactly a natural when it came to perception, so why was he suddenly calling to ask? Could it be Birtemaja who'd sensed something?

'Why are you calling to ask that?' she asked cautiously.

'It's Birtemaja.'

She knew it.

Pirjo looked down at her hands and noticed that they were already shaking. How could Birtemaja know? How could she know that Pirjo's entire world could come crashing down around her in an instant if someone caught a whiff of what she'd done to Wanda Phinn?

'The police have been here asking about Atu. Well, the policeman and the immigrant he had with him as an assistant only knew him as Frank, but it *was* him they were thinking of. It was about something that happened over on Bornholm.'

For a brief moment she was relieved, and then she realized what he'd said. It wasn't Wanda Phinn. It was even worse.

'Bornholm?'

'Yes. They're investigating something about a girl who disappeared. What was her name again, Birtemaja?' he called out to the living room.

Pirjo knew the answer well enough. But what was going on just now? It was almost twenty years ago. The dust should have settled on that case long ago.

'Alberte was the name, Birtemaja says. And while they were here, Birtemaja sensed that it could be fateful for you. She felt it so strongly that we had to warn you. That's why I'm calling. Does any of this mean anything to you?'

Pirjo took a deep breath. 'Bornholm, you say? A case with a girl? Did you say her name was Alberte? No, it doesn't ring any bells whatsoever, it must be a mistake. Did you tell them where we're staying?'

'Why should I do that? But I did refer them to Søren Mølgård. That soon got rid of them.'

Pirjo shook her head. The idiot had referred them to an even bigger idiot. This wasn't good.

'Right, well, that can't do any harm, can it?' she said with a certain degree of scepticism.

'No, I can't see why it would,' he answered. 'The man is so spaced out that he can hardly remember what he did the day before.'

Something was mumbled in the background. It sounded like a woman's voice. 'Birtemaja is asking how things are going, Pirjo. It's all going splendidly, I imagine.'

She momentarily considered saying yes. Telling them that there was an heir to Atu's kingdom on the way, and then a twinge went through her from her lower back, crossing down through her abdomen. She pushed the telephone away from her mouth for a moment so she could counter the pain with deep breathing.

'Thanks for the warning, Simon,' she said afterwards, her breathing more relaxed. 'Don't think any more of it, it's just a mistake. And yes, everything is fine here. Say hello to Birtemaja and cheer her up for me. She must have misread her hunch this time.'

She hung up quicker than was called for, leaning back in the office chair with pain that went under her breastbone and awoke foreboding.

For a moment she prayed to Horus and the higher powers. First on behalf of the fetus, then for herself and finally for Atu. Pregnancy had changed her order of priorities. And after a couple of minutes the pain let up.

She promised herself it was nothing when she felt the baby kick inside, telling herself that it was just her body trying to keep up, reminding herself that she wasn't exactly young any more. And anyway, maybe this is how it was meant to be for some people.

Søren Mølgård, Simon had said. Should she call him and try to shut him up? Could she?

She shook her head. The risk that he might blurt out that she'd called was too high. Søren Mølgård had been the weakest link in their commune. Always the one who fell for temptations and succumbed. So what could a man like him say? Absolutely nothing. Wasn't she the only one from the commune at Ølene who knew anything about Alberte, apart from Atu? Yes, she was.

She shook her head yet again and began to relax as the stomach pains subsided.

Then there was a knock at the door.

She straightened her robe. 'Come in,' she said.

Valentina stood looking utterly apologetic, with a grip on the door handle as if she had no intention of coming in, but Pirjo waved her closer. Her role was to be every disciple's mother, and this office was their confessional, counselling and advice centre. Nobody was turned away who had problems, and Valentina evidently did. It almost radiated from her.

'Is something worrying you?' she asked even before the woman had sat down. She wanted to get it over as quickly as possible so she could have peace to think. So she used the same questioning technique as when giving advice: straight to the point. 'Are you disillusioned about something? Or is it powers fighting against the love around you that have put the worry lines on your face today, Valentina?'

She shook her head. The first time Pirjo saw her, she was marked deep in her soul from intense bullying from colleagues and physical abuse at the hands of a partner who'd treated her like a whore or an animal. When she finally decided to come to the centre, she saw herself as a commodity with limited use, and who after a while should just be broken in two and thrown away. Suffering from a sense of inferiority and hate, a desperate desire for acceptance was her only driving force at that time.

And now, sitting there with her eyes lowered, it was almost as if the nearly two and a half years she'd been with them had never existed. It was definitely not the Valentina they knew at the centre.

'It started with a dream, Pirjo,' she said after collecting herself for a moment. 'The other night I dreamt that an angel with black wings flew over my room. After a while it dived through the roof and down to me, where it placed a hand over my eyes. It burned intensely, but not as if it could harm me, at least not before I thought that I needed to wake up. But then the angel rose again through the hole in the roof, and up above it a massive hall floated, lit by projectors. It felt as if the entire building vibrated when the angel disappeared into it. As if it could almost explode with the presence of that being. And the second after, the walls of the hall suddenly disappeared so you could see that the interior was full of yellow blobs. And then I woke up.'

Pirjo smiled. 'OK, that sounds very special. But you know that dream analysis isn't my strong side, Valentina. I'm sure that your dream can be interpreted better and more precisely by some of the others here. It seems to have made you feel uncomfortable, but maybe in reality it's a tremendously good dream. I don't think you should worry about it.'

'It isn't the dream that worries me,' she said as her eyes slowly moved up until they caught Pirjo's. 'I've already mentioned it to several people, and some thought it was an illustrative dream that revealed a lot of nonsense about myself, while others said that it was an advisory dream, telling me something about my actions and unresolved conflicts. If was only when I spoke about it with Shirley that I understood it might be a warning dream.'

Pirjo tried to maintain a look of calm.

When she talked with Shirley, she said!

'I know now that it was a real event that triggered the dream, and that's what's troubling me. That's why I'm coming to you, Pirjo.'

'A warning dream? Warning about what, Valentina? Has something in particular happened here? Because if it has, we'd better ask Atu to attend. It can't be right now because he's—'

'I don't think you'll want Atu to be here,' she said in an unexpectedly harsh manner.

Pirjo turned her head a little, maintaining eye contact all the while. The warning signals were clear. What was Valentina up to? If Atu shouldn't be here, was it because she was about to negotiate something? But what could she demand, and for what?

'Why shouldn't he be here?' she said with as much authority in her voice as the situation demanded. It didn't work that way here. You couldn't just keep Atu out of affairs without so much as a by-your-leave. Valentina should know that.

She wiped a drop of sweat from her nose and straightened up. 'Shirley didn't understand the dream. She doesn't actually understand very much at all, I've realized that. But she made me remember something important and understand that I'd seen things that could be read into more than I'd initially thought.'

'I don't know what you're talking about, Valentina. What have you seen?'

'It would appear I've seen many things, now that I think about it,' she said, breaking away from Pirjo's inquisitive eyes in favour of resting them on the wall behind her. 'Just before telling Shirley about the dream, she'd told me about her friend with the belt and the time when Jeanette had to leave us. And when she told the story, she said something in particular that I noticed, as a result of the dream I'd had.'

'Well, what did she say, Valentina?' Pirjo smiled. It was the only defence she had now. The pain in her diaphragm was pulsating just under the surface. First Simon Fisher's call, and now this.

'Shirley told me something about her friend Wanda, that's connected with the day when Malena went to the hospital.'

Pirjo shook her head and raised her eyebrows a little, intended as a display of ignorance and uncertainty as to why all these things were being connected.

'It's also so strange that Malena disappeared the way she did the day after being admitted. Did you know, by the way, that she was my Latin soulmate? Yes, she was, Pirjo. There were so many things we had in common, Malena and me. So why didn't she give me so much as a hint before she disappeared? I've thought from time to time that maybe she wasn't in a position to do so.'

'I don't think she was either, Valentina. The doctors said that she just discharged herself and left. Yes, and before she was ready to do so. Maybe it was a sort of birth trauma, even though there wasn't actually a real birth. No, I don't know, Valentina. But how is that connected with your dream? Is she the angel?'

'I thought maybe she was at first, but the wings were black, and Malena's couldn't have been.' She lowered her eyes again but kept them fixed on the wall. 'It's happened before.'

'What's happened before, Valentina?'

'That one of us has just disappeared without any warning.'

'Yes, unfortunately. You're thinking about Claudia? But she drowned, Valentina. They found her down on the coast of Poland, we know that. She'd become so depressed that we couldn't help her out of it, no matter how much we tried.'

'No, I'm not thinking of her. I'm thinking of one of the people who was on the same course as me. Iben Karcher. The German girl that Atu was so fond of.'

'You know what, Valentina, I don't understand what it is you want to tell me. Iben was a strange girl, and we have to face the fact that all sorts of people seek us out. We offer our disciples peace in their soul and a new understanding of the world. That's all we can do. There are some people we can't help, and Iben left of her own accord.'

'That's what you keep saying, and I've always thought so, but then there's the dream.'

Pirjo sighed. 'Out with it. What is it that's worrying you, Valentina?'

'Shirley mentioned the episode with the belt, which Jeanette found in the loft of the Stable of Senses. Well, that building isn't as light as all the others here. It's darker.'

'Err, yes. But I don't understand where you're going with this. It's just rose-coloured, isn't it? White or rose, what's the significance? I'm totally confused now.'

'It was a similar light red hall that the angel disappeared up into, so it was precisely that hall I dreamt about. And the angel with the black wings was you, Pirjo. I saw you that day. I saw you from down on the beach when you drove into the Stable of Senses on your yellow scooter. It was the scooter that left the yellow blobs when the walls in the dream disappeared. And it was the same day that Malena miscarried. I know because several of us were looking for you even though it was during meditation hour. Atu wanted you to take Malena to the hospital. I was glad when I saw you come home because I knew that things were just as they should be and Atu would be relieved. Afterwards, in the assembly hall, you looked so beautiful. It almost felt as if an angel of deliverance had returned. From that moment, I knew that you'd help Malena while she lay in the hospital. At least I thought so.'

'What do you mean that you saw me? Should that be something out of the ordinary, perhaps? I remember the day well, Valentina. I wasn't feeling well and took a ride up to Nordodden to meditate, and it helped. Afterwards, I parked my scooter in there on a sudden impulse because I wanted to charge the battery, that's all. And yes, of course I helped Malena when I was there. How could you think otherwise? She was given every chance to either come back quickly, so we could look after her, or stay at the hospital until she was back on her feet.'

'Do you know what's weird, Pirjo? Now we're getting to the thing with Shirley's friend. Shirley told me precisely what day her friend Wanda left from London. So I was able to work out that she must have come on exactly the same day that Malena miscarried, the same day as you and the scooter and the Stable of Senses. I *know*, Pirjo, because I'll never forget that date.'

Pirjo nodded. She looked serious now. 'Strange coincidence.' She pressed her lips and thought for a moment. 'We don't know what this Wanda Phinn has actually done. I'm inclined to think that she spun Shirley a story and that right now she might be living in . . .'

'You were the angel, and the hall was the Stable of Senses, and the black wings a warning that something unspeakable has happened. Am I right, Pirjo? I'm telling you now because you've always lifted my spirits when I've needed it.'

Pirjo smiled. 'Thank you, Valentina. That means a lot. I don't know what to believe. The dream is very strange. May I have time to think it over? Maybe I need to talk to someone about it before I believe, as you do, that it means something that shouldn't be ignored. I've had a similar dream, I don't mind telling you. But in mine there wasn't an angel. It was a large bird with wings of two different colours, red closest to the body and grey on the tips.'

Valentina looked at her sceptically. She squinted her eyes slightly, raising her head to face her directly.

'That's what I meant before when I said it was a strange co-incidence, Valentina. The night after Malena's miscarriage, I lay tossing and turning in a dream. I woke up bathed in sweat and remembered everything. That the red-grey bird was cawing up over the Stable of Senses, that it flew in over our timber circles and disappeared out over the sea. Now that you mention your dream and Shirley, I think that the bird's colours refer to the colours of the belt. Don't you think?'

Her confusion was obvious.

'Yes, it's suddenly dawning on me now. I'm thinking, maybe Shirley's the bird. That maybe she had some reason or other to create unrest here at the centre. Do you think that could be it? Has she said anything that could be interpreted as negative tensions? An energy out of sync with ours?'

Valentina shook her head. Obviously totally disarmed.

'Can this story about the friend be something she's plucked from thin air? Do you think so? We don't really know anything about her, do we, Valentina?'

She shook her head again, more slowly this time.

'I don't know what to say, Pirjo. I'm spinning. I'm sorry about all this. I'm obviously still shaken by Malena abandoning us without any warning. And when I had that dream, and Shirley told me about Wanda, who . . .'

Pirjo stood up, went around the table and placed a light and comforting hand on Valentina's shoulder. It was quivering.

When she'd left the office, Pirjo sat down heavily, supporting herself against the table. Her fists were clenched.

If the police in Denmark found them, as they were guaranteed to, it was only a matter of time, there mustn't be the slightest thing at the academy that could cause them to doubt that everything that happened here at the centre was born of purity of soul and ethical thinking. That those who stood for the management – herself, Atu, and their closest helpers – had always worked with the people's best interests at heart. That in every respect it was unthinkable that any of them, even in the distant past, could have been behind anyone coming to harm.

And for that reason alone, neither Shirley nor Valentina could be there when they came. No matter what the cost.

She straightened up and placed her hands comfortingly on her pregnant womb. 'Mum's looking out for you and Dad. I promise you, darling,' she said. 'No harm will come to you. Mum will make sure of that, no matter what.'

Pirjo was well aware what the consequences could be if she didn't. She didn't consider Valentina to be any significant problem. She could always be sent abroad on some mission or other. It was more difficult with Shirley, especially if she was making friends at the centre, and especially as she was clinging to her theories and mistrust.

She looked up as there was another knock at the door.

The electrician who had come to check out the solar power system in the control room at the end of the corridor looked at her with a worried expression.

'This stinks,' was his initial reaction when they stood in there, and with good reason, as long as it was his responsibility and the warranty still covered them, because it was now the third time he'd had to change the power inverter. In fact, there were still tools and masses of cables and bits and bobs on the floor from the time before.

She pushed a few of the tools under the bench fastened to the wooden wall so they wouldn't trip over them. What on earth was he going to use a huge wrench for on this job? And a rubber mallet?

'The system should never have been built in this room. Do you know why there are metal walls on three sides in here?'

'Yes, I do. This room used to be the cold store for the manor. Carcasses were hung here on hooks, so I imagine that the metal walls were for hygiene reasons.'

He nodded. 'Possible, yes, but we should've taken them down, because for some reason or other they have a ground connection. At any rate, something strange is going on in here.'

'What seems to be the problem with the system?'

He explained a little about the installation on the wall. Something was faulty, whether it was the junction box with all the cables from the different panels, or the inverter.

'We're always getting problems reported from here, and I don't quite understand it,' he said. 'The inverter is sending so much power up and through your mains that a normal HPFI residual-current device doesn't register that there's a faulty current. Of course, it isn't the biggest problem on a bland, grey day like today, where so little power is generated.' He pointed up to the skylight, where dark clouds drifted past. 'But in a few days the weather will hopefully be much better, and then you'll see. I'm afraid we'll have to rethink the whole installation. I'd better talk to my boss about it.'

He unscrewed the cover plates off the junction box and the inverter, and having studied the interior for a couple of minutes, scratched the back of his neck. 'Yes, I can't really see that anything is wrong. Your system is producing a heck of a lot, even though the sun can't really break through at the moment,' he said. 'Well, that's something at least. But still, the direct current is very unstable. I'll just make a few adjustments so it's not quite so intense. Whatever you do, you folks mustn't fiddle about with this yourself, Pirjo.'

As if they would ever do that.

'You could cause yourself serious injury if God's lamp was giving it full throttle from behind the clouds up there.'

'What could happen?'

'Good question. There's no power switch on the sun or the power that comes directly down from the panels, so what *could* happen? That depends on how long someone intended to stand here with the cables in their hands.' He laughed.

Pirjo nodded, staring at the boxes and gauges. Maybe it would be a good idea to get Shirley involved, considering how ungainly and clumsy she could be.

Pirjo smiled to herself, watching the workman's body and strong arms at work. She looked at the power metre beginning to rise. There was a little sunshine again. The temperature was also rising, she noticed, when her eyes caught the black patches spreading between the electrician's shoulder blades.

She followed the black patch down his back to his slim waist.

'That's a special belt you're wearing. Where did you get hold of that?' she asked by way of changing the subject. He turned around and grabbed the buckle with a smile.

'What, this? I found it on the Internet. I liked the fact that it looked like a zipper, it tickled me. I buy almost all my work gear and clothes online.'

Pirjo nodded.

There were suddenly so many possibilities.

33

The drive along the dirt road to the farm was the ultimate challenge for the worn-out police car, and not least for Assad's jaw that bounced up and down like an out-of-control yo-yo.

Scattered along the rain-filled, deep tyre tracks there were monoliths with carved runes and coloured Celtic and Norse symbols. There could be no doubt that this was the entrance to a world parallel to the one where politicians strutted in borrowed plumes and people bought even the most obvious lies.

As a result, the farm itself, with its traditional four wings, was disappointing overall. No Viking gates and oak timbers or anything else Norse; only the sign above the gate suggesting that they weren't about to meet ordinary farmers after all.

Einherjer Farm, read the sign.

'Hi. What does that mean?' Carl asked a woman who was crossing the yard. He hadn't seen someone like her for a long time, straight out of the seventies, with loose-hanging breasts under her T-shirt and wild, unruly hair.

'Hi.' She smiled and shook their hands. 'Well, the *einherjar* were warriors in Valhalla who defended the gods against the *jötnar*. So there could hardly be a more fitting name for us, seeing as we've all been soldiers or married to soldiers in Afghanistan at Camp Bastion. My name is Gro, by the way,' she said. 'I knew you'd be coming, because they called from the Holistic Garden Centre, whatever that is. Bue, my husband, is on his way.'

He was a bear of a man, but apart from the thin braid in his beard, and a couple of huge tattoos twisting round his bare arms and reappearing as flames on his neck, this man looked nothing like what Carl imagined the leader of a so-called *blótlaug* would look like. No Viking horns or sheepskin clothes, just the usual farmer's outfit: dungarees and the compulsory green wellingtons.

'No, I don't personally know the man you're talking about,' he said after they'd stated their business. 'But Søren Mølgård has talked a little about the time when he was on Bornholm, based on what his tired-out brain can handle. Enough anyway to get the idea that it was a pretty interesting time that I would've liked to have been part of, if I'd been old enough.' He laughed, leading them across the yard and out through a gate to the other side of the wings.

Carl looked around. It was hard to see how the symbol-laden monoliths on the road to the farm were connected to this ordinary bit of Denmark. Everything here bordered on being clichéd and dull: slurry tank, compost heap and scratched agricultural machinery being operated by men who looked nothing like Rambo or Thor, the god of thunder.

'Everyone here is a member of our *blótlaug*. We aren't associated with Forn Siðr, though, if you know what that is. We interpret the Asa-faith in our own way. And even though I'm their *goði*, we're all equal here.'

Carl tried to smile. He had no idea what the man was talking about.

'But you do arrange *blót*?' asked Assad.

Carl turned towards him. Was he at it, too?

Bue nodded. 'Yes, four times a year, at equinox and solstice. We drink a few horns of mead – actually, we brew it ourselves. Perhaps you'd like to take a couple of bottles with you?'

Carl gave a very vague nod. At least he knew what mead was. And it really tasted like piss.

'It's very different from the dishwater you can buy in shops,' said Bue, as if he'd read Carl's mind. He turned toward the peoples. 'Any of you seen Søren?' he shouted.

Someone pointed at a smallholding behind a windbreak, half in ruins.

'There's smoke coming from the chimney, so he's probably in today; he usually is,' explained Bue.

Carl nodded. 'But why is he staying here with you? He hasn't been in Afghanistan like the rest of you, has he?'

'No. But Søren's son Rolf was with us at the camp. Rolf was a good soldier, but also reckless and unlucky, and fell victim to a roadside bomb. When we returned home, Søren came to us in despair. I warn you, he's a bit odd.'

Assad turned around to watch the people working for a minute. A gentle rain had started to fall again. Apparently it didn't bother them. 'I understand you're all former soldiers. So why did you come here?'

It was clearly a question Bue had heard dozens of times before.

'We'd already founded a *blótlaug* at the camp, so it seemed the obvious thing to do. I've practised the Asa-faith since I was a boy, and out there in the war zone I found comfort in my rituals. It was obvious that I got along better on a day-to-day basis than most of the others, so it wasn't long before there were many of us who found peace in the faith. When you're up against a movement that builds on faith as much as the Taliban does, quite honestly you begin to feel poor without something, especially when you're so exposed and far from home. So we rooted ourselves in the past that we've inherited in the north. Does that make sense?'

He pointed at a stack of wooden boards that led across a muddy ditch to Søren Mølgård's small shanty, then turned to face Carl.

'Without our faith and the sense of community it gives us, I'm sure some of us would never have come back, at least not as whole people. Now we're a family, and the family of Asa-faith is growing across the country. I'm actually talking on the radio about it in a couple of days. I have a sense that you belong to that part of the Danish population that's struggling to accept people like us, so you'd be welcome to come along. People who call the show could ask what you think, and you could ask them anything. If you're lucky, someone might be able to help you find the man you're looking for, if Søren can't.'

'Oh, well, I don't know.' Carl hesitated. To be a guest on a radio show with an Asa follower in order to gather police information? He could just imagine the reaction at HQ if he did.

'So you're professional soldiers?' asked Assad.

'Most of us, yes. I was a captain, and there are other officers here, too, although most of the people on the farm were PFCs.'

'A captain! So you've seen your share of the hot spots, I imagine?' said Assad.

Bue nodded. 'I have, in fact.' He gave Curly a friendly smile, but then a furrow suddenly creased his forehead, as if he was trying to remember something specific at the sight of Assad without being able to.

Assad turned toward Søren Mølgård's house. 'He's standing in the window watching us. Have you told him we'd be coming?'

'No, I didn't have time. Sorry.'

Carl would've probably preferred that the red-eyed and quite spaced-out Søren Mølgård had been warned beforehand. In any case, he seemed more scared than was good for him when Bue introduced them as investigators from Copenhagen Police Headquarters.

He glanced around his small, low-ceilinged, hash-smelling living room, clearly uncomfortable with the situation, probably checking if there were any drugs lying around.

'I see you smoke a few chillums now and them,' said Carl drily. Now at least the cat was out of the bag.

'I guess, but I don't sell it, if that's what you think. I grow a bit out the back, but not enough to . . .'

'Hey, relax, Søren,' interrupted Bue. 'They aren't from narcotics. They're from homicide in Copenhagen.'

The man seemed a little distant due to the significant influence of his homegrown crops, but the word 'homicide' almost seemed to make his heart stop. Not very unusual, if you thought about it.

'Homicide?' He stared into space before nodding in recognition, a hint of seriousness showing on his face. 'Is this about Rolf?' he asked, his lips trembling. 'Was he killed by his own?'

Carl frowned. The man must be fairly gone.

They asked him to sit, and explained their business, which didn't seem to calm him.

'I don't understand. I don't know anyone called Alberte, except that singer. Why are you asking me about it?'

'We're asking if you know where Frank is now, and what he's doing.'

He turned his head towards Bue, shrugging. 'I won't be coming out in the field today, Bue. I've got a bit of trouble with my lungs, you see.'

'That's all right, Søren, but you might want to answer the question for the police.'

He looked confused. 'About Frank? Yes, that's his name. And he was a jerk, I think. I haven't quite made up my mind yet.'

'What do you mean?' Carl nodded to Assad, who showed that he was ready with his notebook.

'He always had to dictate everything. I didn't want to put up with that, so I left.'

'When did you leave?'

'When we returned to Zealand. He wanted to go to Sweden or Norway, do something that would earn him some money. A sort of course centre. Can you imagine me out in the woods or the wilderness? Ha!'

'A course centre? What do you mean by that?'

'Just somewhere he would get to decide everything.'

'Do you know what he calls himself nowadays, or where he ended up?'

He shook his head, looking longingly at the silver foil and the cigarettes on the desk.

'Do you think it might help you to remember if you rolled a joint and took a puff?' asked Assad, but Bue shook his head. Apparently that wasn't worth wishing for.

'Frank was only interested in Frank,' he said. 'He didn't give a damn about anything else.'

'Not even women?'

At this, the man let out a deep sigh. He seemed to think that was enough of an answer.

'Do you remember if he had relationships with any of the girls?'

'Relationships!' he snorted. 'He screwed them all, but relationships had nothing to do with it. That's just how it was.'

'Can you remember their names?'

He closed his eyes halfway. It wasn't possible to see whether he was thinking or on his way to dreamland.

'They were called all kinds of insignificant shit,' he drawled. Then he drifted off.

'I'm sorry,' said Bue, handing them a couple of soda bottles filled with golden liquid as they said their goodbyes by the car. 'Actually, it's one of the few times I've heard Søren answer any questions. He's probably severely brain-damaged. We've discussed whether it's because of all the joints or if it's something else he uses. We tend to think it's the latter. He's simply ruined most of his brain cells.'

Carl nodded. For some reason, the notion of dead brain cells made him think of Sammy and Ronny. But the cremation service was tomorrow, and a long drive up to his family in Vendsyssel, and the professor who'd taught Frank way back, lay before them.

'You're still welcome to participate in my radio show if you'd like,' said the giant. 'You might be lucky. I'd be surprised if there wasn't at least one listener who had some useful information.'

34

Saturday, May 10th, 2014

There were two women crying in the front row. Not Ronny's wife, who wasn't even there, or his sister or, for that matter, the girl who lived on the neighbouring farm and who for some bizarre reason had always dreamt of being his. No, these were two other women, who stared up at the casket at regular intervals, and just as regularly and mechanically reached for the handkerchiefs in their laps to dry their eyes.

'Who on earth are they?' Carl asked the people in the pews in front of, behind and next to him, but no one knew. The only thing anyone knew was that nobody else in the church was crying, not during the hymns and not during the odd collection of sentimental sentences about a time with Ronny long past, read out by the vicar in accordance with his testamentary wishes.

'They're hired mourners,' whispered Assad. 'I asked them. I was curious because they're sitting in the front row.'

Carl frowned. Hired mourners?

'Yes. They said it was written in Ronny's will that someone had to be hired to cry in church. It was kind of expected, he wrote. So that's them.'

Carl nodded and looked up at the casket. Exotic, maroon, probably heavy as hell. Only half covered in flowers. No flowers in the aisle. Twenty-odd people in the church, and two of them hired, with a third only there as Carl's companion.

Carl thought to himself that hiring mourners showed dedication to the Old Testament, and that Ronny was to be congratulated, because who else would have cried for him? He considered how Ronny had killed his dad, or at least claimed he had, and walked all over people like a complete bastard all his life. How he'd lied and cheated and left people in a mess, so who would cry? His mother? She died long ago – could that have been Ronny, too? His airhead of a soya-sauce-coloured brother who only cared about what this show might wield? Other family members? Nope, Ronny had got it right. He'd had to hire a couple of mourners. That was good thinking, and Carl thought he ought to respect him for that at least.

Carl was staring out into space for a minute while the organ player changed register, now playing at full blast, which had an immediate effect on the mourners' performances.

Who knew what would happen someday, when it was his casket lying there. Who would cry then? His indifferent stepson, Jesper? His ex-girlfriend, Mona? His ex-wife, Vigga? His parents, who would probably be long gone? Unlikely. His older brother, who was completely lacking in emotion, and various hangers-on? Hardly.

But Hardy, then? If he was still alive, and someone would do him the favour of arranging the transport, wouldn't he be there? Wouldn't he at least show some sign of sadness? Morten certainly would. As soon as he saw the casket, he'd collapse on the floor, wailing with bloodshot eyes. But then again, he acted that way when he saw a fluffy kitten being licked by a puppy on YouTube. Somehow it didn't really count.

And then of course there was Assad.

He looked at the man, who was innocently trying to sing along. Touched, Carl automatically put his hand on Assad's arm and patted it gently. Yes, he would be the only one there.

Assad stopped his song practice. 'You're patting my sleeve, Carl. Is there something you'd like to say?' he whispered.

Carl felt a smile creasing his cheek. He'd probably said all he would and could for now.

Restaurant Hedelund was the place where Carl had given the first and only speech of his life. Newly confirmed, his hair held in place with elbow grease and brilliantine, shaking slightly, and anything but *almost an adult,* he'd turned towards his parents to thank them for the party and cassette recorder. They'd smiled, his mother had even shed a tear, and that was it.

Here they were in the very same room, on an overcast day, with trays of open sandwiches and drinks ad libitum, pretending that time hadn't passed and that the occasion was less unpleasant.

Ronny had been taken to the crematorium, but with Ronny, dead or alive, there was no way of knowing when lightning would strike.

Carl looked around the group, wondering who Ronny had assigned to detonate the bomb. Who would get up in a minute, a piece of paper in their hand, to read out Ronny's crafty accusations against the bereaved? When would the scoundrel be laughing from the great beyond, while one or more members of the family, Carl most likely, took a beating?

'He's a very likeable young man, your new partner,' said his mum later, nodding towards Assad, who was squeezed in between Aunt

Adda and some friend who was just as old. 'You said he's called Assad. Isn't that strange, given the Syria thing?'

Carl shook his head. 'As far as I know, it's a very common name in the Middle East, Mum. But yes, he's all right, otherwise we wouldn't have worked together for . . .' He counted on his fingers. '. . . almost seven years now.'

Heads were nodding around them. Seven years was a long time, even in Vendsyssel, so he must be all right. Which was why no comments were made on his origin or skin colour, even though the urge was there. That's how people were in those parts. They could hardly help being folk of few words.

There was a clinking on one of the beer bottles, and one of Carl's second cousins on his mother's side got up. Definitely not one of Ronny's acquaintances, so he was probably just there to get the numbers up.

'The family attorney has asked me to read a brief statement that was enclosed in Ronny's will.'

Here it came. Of course it did.

He cut open the envelope.

'It's very short, so Ronny doesn't intend to intrude too much on this splendid event. And while we're at it, let's raise our glasses and thank the staff at Hedelund for the great food, and toast Ronny, who opened his wallet for the cause.'

Most of the guests laughed and toasted politely, but not Carl.

'Anyway. Ronny writes:

Dear friends and family. Allow me, here from my newly acquired Buddhist temple, to thank you for coming. I've always been a party animal, so raise your glasses to a quick toast.'

There was a brief pause. A bit too brief for anyone to grant the wish.

> '*As some of you might know, I hated my dad from the bottom of my heart. Every word he ever managed to say confirmed that his surroundings were better served if he descended straight to hell.*'

People began shifting in their seats. Especially Carl's dad, who was poking the tablecloth with his fork, eyes fixed on the reader.

> '*Well, some might think that was a modest wish. But I congratulate myself for making it come true. Yes, I killed him, might as well just say it how it is in front of this closed company.*'

'Would you stop that filth!' shouted Carl's dad, while the rest of the guests made their discomfort known by mumbling and complaining.

'Let's hear it,' shouted someone else. It was Sammy, Ronny's brother, half out of his chair. 'I've a bloody right to know what this is about. He was my dad, too!'

'Well, I guess I'll continue,' said the second nephew nervously, his eyes seeking Carl's dad. 'Is that OK, Gunnar? Now that Sammy's asking.'

All eyes were on Carl's dad. Farmer, tough as leather and tired to the bone, yet still straight-backed and determined. Carl saw his big brother put his hand on their dad's clenched fist, something Carl would have never dared. But then again, the two men at the end of the table were birds of a feather, the mink breeder and the farmer, who never asked anyone for favours and rarely offered. What an alliance.

Carl braced himself. In a minute, the mood would turn a hundred and eighty degrees, directly against him. There was no need for intuition, he just *knew*.

'I guess I'll carry on, then,' said the second nephew. 'Ronny continues:

I've described the circumstances in detail in my will, so I won't tire you with them, but I would like to thank my cousin Carl from the bottom of my heart for . . .'

He knew it. Now all eyes were on him.

'. . . *making it possible for me to get rid of the old man. And for that same reason, I'd like to ask you all to raise your glasses and toast Carl, who I'm convinced Aunt Tove has made sure is present on a day like this. To Carl, who did me such a great favour in life.'*

Carl shook his head and spread his arms out wide. 'I have no idea what the man is on about. Did he have a brain tumour or what?'

'Is there more?' shouted Sammy.

'Yes, here it is,' said the second nephew, and continued:

'*Carl was my best friend. He taught me karate, so I knew exactly how and where to paralyse my father with one strike, without anyone being able to tell. I let him tumble in the river and left him there, it's as simple as that. Carl looked away, and I thank him for that. That's why I leave him everything that's left after my wife has taken her share.'*

For a moment the temperature in the room dropped to below zero. No one cleared their throat, and no one could be heard breathing. It was the unpleasant calm before the storm. The silent storm moved at full speed around the room. In a minute he'd no longer be sitting in its eye; he'd be feeling all the forces of hell pounding away at him. He had no intention of waiting for that.

'That's a pile of rubbish and damned filth,' he shouted, letting his eyes wander over the shocked, weather-worn faces of aunts and uncles and people he didn't even recognize. 'I remember it as if it happened yesterday, of course I do. It was a really sad day for all of us. I saw nothing because I was walking over to two cute girls standing at the side of the road with their bicycles. I didn't look away from anything, because I was never looking in that direction. I'm as shocked as you.'

'Wait a minute!' shouted the second nephew. 'There's more:

And if Carl claims anything different, he's lying. We were in it together, which will also become clear from the memoirs I've sent to some of the big publishers.'

Carl fell back in his chair. This was a clean knockout. How was it in any way possible to defend himself against the words of a dead man? And what were the consequences if he didn't succeed? His family would cut him off; he could live with that. But to have it made public would ruin his career, and even worse: It would brand him forever. The man who joined the police force after having been an accomplice to murder. The investigator who was no better than the people he put behind bars.

'Come on,' said a voice behind him.

Carl looked up. It was Assad, hair neatly combed, black jacket.

He tugged gently at Carl's chair. 'Come on, we're leaving, Carl. You shouldn't put up with this.'

But as Carl pushed his chair back, Ronny's callous brother came tearing along the wall, straight into his side. The impact of his oversized shoulders made Carl's ribs rattle against each other. The punch from his fist, fingers tattooed, came from below, hitting Carl cleanly on the jaw. And while he fell backwards groggily, he could feel one arm supporting him from behind and another swinging past his head to hit Sammy's scorched forehead with a sound that would be hard to forget for some time.

He heard protests and shouts behind him, while Assad dragged him out along the backs of the chairs, and Sammy, half unconscious, caused the table underneath him to collapse and the tableware to spread all over the floor.

It was total chaos within a few seconds. What the hell had he expected?

'What now, Carl?' asked Assad, driving up through Bredgade past the church where Carl had been confirmed and Ronny's funeral service had just been held.

'I can't just leave. I need to speak to my brother or parents about this. I can't live with suspicion running wild.'

At the roundabout for the road to Aalborg, he pointed to the highway going north.

'Take the first left, just after we reach the state hospital on our right. We won't drive all the way up to the farm. We'll wait on the dirt road, and then I can decide what to do when the others arrive.'

He looked melancholically up towards the farm when Assad pulled over. This was where he'd grown up. This was where his sense of justice and struggle against wrong had begun. This was where he'd had a pitchfork stabbed halfway into his thigh, and where he'd taught his brother that you're not necessarily weaker just because you're younger. This was where he'd been given his first dog, and where his dad shot it.

This was where he'd had his first orgasm, in the hay bales with an old *Varieté* magazine on his knees.

Johanne Farm. The root of his existence.

They waited in silence for half an hour, before the mist from a four-wheel drive speeding through puddles rose in the rearview mirror.

'They'll drive past me, you can be sure of that,' he said, stepping out of the car to stand in the middle of the road. He did hear Assad's warning shout when he stretched one hand out towards his parents' advancing vehicle. He also heard the cursing from inside his parents' car when it finally stopped a few centimetres from his shin.

What he chose to ignore was his mother's pleading with him to go back home, as he flung open the door to the driver's side. He simply *refused*.

'I'll tell you this in a few, unmistakable words. I had *nothing* to do with what Ronny suggested in his filthy letter. Far from it, I'm as appalled as you are, but first and foremost because I cared more about his dad than about anyone else in this world. So let me put it to you as it was and is, since it can't be any other way: Birger Mørck gave me more drive and self-respect than you ever did, and I loved him for that. Your brother was funny and a real judge of character, Dad. You could've learned from that. Then maybe our relationship might not have been as awkward as it turned out.'

'You've always been like this,' said his father with contempt in his voice. 'Always contrary, nobody should tell you what to do. Always wanting to provoke.'

Carl managed to hold back his next salvo. 'And why's that,' he said instead, so quietly it was almost inaudible. 'Why, Dad? Isn't it obvious? Because you paved the way to independence for me. But so did Uncle Birger, and I'm still cut up about his death. That's my defence. And as long as you still have one grain of common sense in you, I think you should leave me in peace with that.'

'You ploughed the meadow, even though I'd said you couldn't. You hit your big brother and you turned your back on the farm.'

Carl nodded. 'And you don't think Ben did the same? A mink breeder in Frederikshavn isn't a potential farmer in Brønderslev, remember that. And if you think my brother is ready to take over when you kick the bucket, I think you need to have a serious talk with him before Mum is left alone with the problem. Why would I have taken over back then? Did you ever ask the question? Did you ever ask me to? Not that I know of.'

'I asked in my own way, got it? You'd think a policeman would be able to figure that out.'

'Now that brother of Ronny's is coming,' shouted Assad from the police car.

Carl looked down the road. The pickup truck was a classic case: fog lights all round, extra-wide tyres and lots and lots of chrome all over a crappy car that could be purchased for less than half of what the extras had cost. Inferiority complex at full blaze.

'I'll call, Mum,' he said, slamming the door shut. If they hurried, they'd be able to make a U-turn and escape via the dirt road towards Sjerritslev, before Sammy managed to cut them off.

But then something strange happened. Fifty metres away from them, Sammy stood on the brake, causing water to splash over the car, jumped out and shouted as loud as he could, 'There was nothing left.' Then he laughed hysterically. 'Ronny owned nothing. Everything was in his wife's name. So you get nothing, Carl, zilch. So you can just drive home to bloody Copenhagen and feel miserable, you dirty cop.' And then he laughed again until he doubled over and almost fell on his side.

If Carl could've been bothered, he'd have arrested Ronny for drunk driving.

'That was strange. Your father suspected you, just like that. Do you know why he would do that?' asked Assad.

'I'm afraid he always has. Isn't it sometimes the easiest thing to do, Assad?'

He was nodding for a long time, but never answered.

'We need to turn off here,' said Carl, surprised at how painless the drive had been. Not once had Assad's driving been unsafe. Not one misjudged brake, not a single hazardous gear shift.

'Say, have you been taking driving lessons lately, Assad?'

He smiled. 'Thanks a lot for the compliment.'

The compliment! That was another word Carl had never heard him say before.

35

Saturday, May 10th, 2014

After Shirley had confided in Valentina, and Valentina had told Shirley about her dream, they drifted apart, which was definitely not what Shirley had wanted.

'Couldn't we meet up tonight and have a little chat?' she asked her in the days that followed, but after several rejections Shirley got the message.

Valentina's dream had made an impression, so Shirley had started looking at Wanda's belt on the windowsill with renewed and strengthened suspicion. Was it really out of the question that it *was* Wanda's belt? When they'd last spoken, Valentina had mentioned other incidents here at the Nature Absorption Academy that seemed suspicious.

And why had Valentina so suddenly and irrevocably rejected her? To her, the complete change of heart almost made it seem like she was under the influence of something or someone.

Could she have talked to Pirjo? Was that really possible, given that Valentina's dream specifically accused Pirjo, and that Malena's sudden disappearance from the hospital preoccupied her so much?

Could Valentina and Pirjo have a new, hidden agenda? Shirley tended to think they might, since Valentina preferred to sit at the opposite end of the assembly hall now, as far away from her as possible, where Pirjo entered.

She had a surprisingly strong feeling that a kind of bond had been formed between the two, beyond what was normal for a relationship between Atu's right-hand woman and one of the common disciples.

At the same time, Shirley could sense Pirjo's eyes resting on her in a completely different way whenever their paths crossed. Eyes seeking information but not contact. In fact, Pirjo didn't speak to her at all during that period. She might greet her with a nod, sometimes even feign a smile, but that was all.

Shirley had thought several times that she'd have to talk to Atu about it, but that type of request always went through Pirjo, so how should she go about it?

Once in a while she both feared and believed that Pirjo was out to get her. And if she was, Shirley had no future at the Nature Absorption Academy.

That was why she found herself in a terrible dilemma. Because no matter what her position was, and regardless of what means Pirjo used to mark her territory, she'd decided to stay at the centre, whatever the cost. What else should she do with her life?

Should she go back to London and certain unemployment, lousy housing, the same habits and mischief as before – casual, bad sex with strange men whom she didn't even want to wake up next to? No, that wasn't going to happen, under any circumstances. And would anyone lament the fact that she didn't return? No, that wasn't going to happen either. Actually, she couldn't think of anyone except her parents who would have any idea she'd been gone. And looking at it objectively, not even her parents wanted anything to do with her. They'd made that quite obvious. During her stay here at the centre, she'd written to them at least ten times, and the only answer she'd ever received was a postcard that stated in a few, precise words that as long as she stayed at this unchristian place, she shouldn't bother writing again.

Her decision deeply rooted inside, Shirley tried to catch Pirjo's eye at the Saturday assembly, so she'd know that she needed to get in contact. Only for a moment did she succeed, when Pirjo looked directly at her without noticeable aversion.

Perhaps for a second there was even a hint of a reconciling smile on her lips.

Shirley went cold all over when the smile froze.

Was she looking at a female spider that felt her web vibrating?

36

The house was situated on the other side of town, so close to the coast that it wouldn't take much in terms of climate change and rising sea levels before it disappeared. It was clearly dilapidated and useless as a permanent residence, so the loss would be insignificant.

'It smells like camel shit here,' was Assad's comment on the place.

'It's the North Sea and the seaweed, Assad. And this is nothing.'

He pointed towards a figure appearing in the door, trying to look imposing despite the hunched back.

'Johannes Tausen, Assad. That's what a genuine professor emeritus of theology should look like.'

'Emeritus?'

'Former, Assad. In other words, retired.'

'Pardon me, I shake hands with my left,' said the professor, offering them a talon that was so gnarled from rheumatic arthritis that it was like shaking a clenched fist. Carl looked at the other hand, which was even worse, useless in fact. It really broke his heart to see.

'Apart from the pain, you get used to it,' said Tausen, and invited them in.

His hand shook as he poured tea that smelled pleasantly of Earl Grey, before sitting in front of them with the alertness of someone who was about to unravel the mysteries of the universe. And after he'd been talking for a while following their explanation as to why they'd come, Carl realized that in fact that probably was also the case.

'Yes, I gave a short series of lectures at the Open University during that period in autumn 1995, so everyone could go along.'

'It was called "From Star Myths to Christianity" – is that correct?' asked Carl.

'Yes, exactly, and there was quite a turnout, due to the highly controversial topic. Nowadays, you can find all kinds of interpretations of these topics, so no one is trumpeting them in the same way. They were originally theories taken up by a young American woman at the time, and they caught my interest. She challenged established science and created a good deal of controversy in the American Bible Belt, which was actually rather refreshing. I've heard that you can find an account on YouTube that is a bit similar to my own, if you're interested; *Zeitgeist*, I believe it's called. I haven't seen it because I don't have the Internet out here, but that doesn't really bother me.'

He pushed the sugar bowl over to Assad and followed with interest how it was slowly emptied. 'I have more in the kitchen,' he said, his voice full of respect.

Assad held up his hand; he'd had his fill.

'I think I do remember the man you're talking about. In relation to which, you should probably know that even though the topic probably wouldn't cause raised eyebrows in this country, a course of that kind will always attract lots of sceptics and, perhaps especially, the opposite. It's a topic that easily becomes dogmatic in itself. I think that might have happened to the young woman I mentioned, and I'm afraid it happened to Frank as well.'

'Can you remember his last name?'

He smiled. 'You should be glad I even remember his first name. No, we didn't use surnames. Of course it would've been on the list of my students, but I didn't look at that.'

'The list. Does it still exist?'

'Gosh, no. I don't make a habit of saving paper.'

'Do you think the university might have kept the lists?'

'Definitely not. They wouldn't keep them for more than ten years. I would say less. They probably throw them away after five years.'

'Does the name Frank Scott mean anything to you?'

'Scott?' He mulled over it for a minute. 'No, not Scott. Is that what you think he was called?'

Carl shrugged. 'It's the only name we've heard. But no one in Denmark is called Frank Scott.'

He smiled. 'I guess it's wrong, then.'

Carl's head did a little jig. Made sense. 'What kind of a person was he, do you remember?'

'I do, because Frank was different from most people. I think it's safe to say that he experienced a kind of awakening, as I recall it. And that's probably why he became the most inquisitive student I've ever had. You don't forget someone like that, because we lecturers like to have someone to help keep the discussion going.'

'Was it this guy?' asked Assad, handing him the photo of the man with the VW Kombi.

He was already squinting before he reached out for his glasses on the table and put them on.

'Well, it has been more than eighteen years, but it could very well be.'

They gave him plenty of time, while he nodded to himself.

'Yes, I do believe it's him. At least, I remember the man much better now and there must be a reason for that. As I said, it could very well be him.'

'We're investigating him in connection with an accident on Bornholm, and we'd be thankful for any information that might give us an idea of his whereabouts. So what do you remember about Frank?' asked Carl.

The thin skin around Johannes Tausen's eyebrows contracted slightly. His concern was whether he would end up saying something that was incorrect and might cause someone harm for no reason. Carl had seen it a thousand times before.

'Just tell us what springs to mind. We'll make sure to filter the information properly, I promise you that,' he said, knowing full well that it wasn't possible. Once said, things couldn't be unsaid.

'I see.' He swallowed with difficulty a couple of times. 'Then I do actually believe I remember him telling me at some point that my lectures had changed his life. That they had given him a clearer picture of the path that was laid out for him.'

'Which was?'

'I think I'll have to quickly go over what the series of lectures was about,' he said. 'Then you can deduce from that what you will. A lot of it consists of somewhat bold interpretations. It's not something I've excelled in since, but it was good fun.'

At this, his eyes shone brighter. Maybe because for once he got to be a lecturer again, or because what he was about to tell them meant something special to him.

'You are familiar with the star signs, aren't you? Leo, Scorpio, Virgo and so on. Twelve star signs, each connected not only to a season but also to the movements of the Earth. These star signs are ascribed special meanings in horoscopes – a bit of hocus-pocus, if you ask me, but still with a basis in some form of worldly reality, at least if you look at the northern hemisphere. Aquarius, for instance, representing the time of life-giving spring rain.'

'I'm a Leo,' interjected Assad. 'And funnily enough, my name also means lion,' he added.

The professor smiled. 'All these astrological signs create a circle around the Earth called the zodiac. Over the course of a year, the Sun moves through this circle in a great ring, while the Earth rotates around its own axis once a day in a small cycle between the four points that consist of sunrise; zenith, which is the highest position in the sky; sunset; and finally nadir, which is the lowest point. Do you follow?'

Carl nodded. It was quite elementary. 'I call that morning, noon, evening and midnight,' he said drily.

The professor smiled. 'And in an astronomical understanding, these points correspond to the solstices, midsummer and midwinter, and the equinoxes, spring and autumn. Now, if you draw the two axes between zenith and nadir, and between ascent and descent – or, in an astronomical sense, between the two solstices and the two equinoxes – a cross will appear across the circles drawn by the Sun, known as a sun cross.'

He lowered his head and raised his eyebrows. He was probably getting to some kind of point.

'Some call this cross *the crucified sun.* You can actually find it carved in rocks all the way back to prehistoric times, and this is where we find the foundation of a number of religions and theses that all have the Sun and zodiac as their point of origin.'

Out of a yellow box, he managed with a bit of trouble to fish a small Ga-Jol licorice lozenge, which he chewed on for a moment to stimulate saliva.

'To cut a long story short, many religions can be defined on the basis of the stories inspired by the constellations of celestial bodies, and that was the crux of my lectures. The Sun, which is a circle like the zodiac, has from ancient times – and quite understandably, given its life-giving properties – been a representative of the Creator and God, the light of the world and the saviour of humanity. Countless world religions would later see a transformation of the star signs and the Sun into a number of stories of sun gods and other mythological figures. My lectures demonstrated that all these stories are more or less identical throughout the ages, regardless of the religion.'

'The Egyptians had the sun god Horus,' commented Assad.

The old man thrust his crooked index finger towards him.

'Exactly, my friend. You've hit the nail on the head. Three thousand years before Christ, people worshipped Horus, who stood for light, and Seth, who stood for darkness. The legend of the two gods tells that every morning Horus, the good god of light, wins the battle against Seth, who can be simplified as the evil god, darkness. Translated to other religions, you talk about God and the Devil and lots of other things. But the hieroglyphs that tell us about this account in such detail, and as early as fifteen hundred years before Christ, also recount a number of other stories that may surprise you. Actually, the fact of the matter is that almost every figure in the Old Testament appeared in detailed description already then. Moses in the bulrush basket was known as Mises in Egypt, and is known as Manou in India, and Minos on Crete, for example. The hieroglyphs also reproduced the story of Noah and the flood, which can be read in the earliest known great work of world literature, the Babylonian epic of the hero Gilgamesh, twenty-six hundred years BC. People of the Jewish faith will probably claim that they have the exclusive rights to these stories, but the funny thing is, you might say, that many of the stories in the New Testament are *also* found in these hieroglyphs.'

'You mean the story about the prophet Christ,' ventured Assad. 'The three wise men, the Star of Bethlehem and all that?'

Carl was speechless. He may have grown up in Vendsyssel, where boys were quick to learn scripture, but that Assad, being Muslim, was just as familiar with Christian history was something else.

Again, the professor pointed at Assad with his left index finger. Definitely a habit he'd acquired over a long life as a lecturer.

'Correct. And the aforementioned Horus was born on December 25th to a virgin. His birth was predicted by a star in the eastern sky. He was worshipped by three kings. He became a teacher at twelve, and at thirty he was baptized, after which he was joined by twelve followers – disciples, you could say – that he travelled around with, performing miracles. He was betrayed by Typhon, crucified and resurrected after three days.' He turned to face Carl. 'Sound familiar?'

'Well, I'll be damned,' Carl burst out mechanically.

'Maybe not the most apt expression in this context – rather the opposite, I should think,' the professor said with a smile.

'But what's it got to do with this Frank person?' asked Carl.

'Just a second, there's more. When you look at the most prominent figures in different religions throughout history, you'll see that there are a number of completely generic characteristics. I've mentioned the similarities between the lives of Horus and Christ, but the exact same elements appear in a number of other religions: the time and date of birth, the wise men, the guiding star, the disciples, the miracles, the betrayal, the crucifixion, the death and the resurrection, just to mention the most important ones. All these stories are similar in relation to the Greek god Attis; the Persian god Mithra, twelve hundred years BC; Krishna in India, nine hundred years BC; Dionysus in Greece, five hundred years BC; and in lots of other countries, including Hindustan, Bermuda, Tibet, Nepal, Thailand, Japan, Mexico, China and Italy, to name but a few. Each and every time, the same story with a few modifications.'

'Modifications?' Assad looked really puzzled.

'Changes, adjustments, you know.'

Assad nodded, an inscrutable expression on his face that Carl couldn't quite work out.

'I got the impression that this Frank person who we're looking for was a sun worshipper or something in that vein,' asked Carl. 'But maybe I'm wrong. How does he fit into the whole thing?'

Again the professor stuck his deformed finger in the air. 'Patience, Mr Mørck. We'll get to that.'

He fumbled after another lozenge. 'You'll have to excuse me. I've had a salivary gland removed on one side. Cancer, you see, so I need something to keep the remaining glands producing so my mouth doesn't get too dry. These licorice ones are really good. Please, help yourselves.'

He pushed the box towards them. Only Carl was polite enough to accept the offering.

'This is a complex issue, and I could talk about it for hours.' He laughed, so no doubt about that. 'But don't fret. What I'm trying to get at is that the common denominators of all the different religious histories descend from astronomical and, very often, also astrological phenomena.

'For instance, let's take a look at the birth sequence: born to a virgin on December 25th, sought out by three wise men, the three kings, who follow the star in the east.

'And here comes the astronomical explanation: the clearest star in the northern hemisphere in December is Sirius, which is aligned with the three stars in Orion's Belt, originally called . . . ?'

'The three kings,' suggested Assad.

Once again, the crooked index finger flew in the air. 'Exactly. So, the three kings are aligned with the clearest star in the sky, and at the same time these three kings point directly downward towards sunset on December 25th. Therefore, the three kings can be seen as following the star in the east towards solstice, the symbol of life and man's saviour. And above it all shines the constellation Virgo, which is also known as the House of Bread. Finally, we can look at the place of birth in our Christian tradition, Bethlehem, and translate the Hebrew, which means exactly . . .'

'House of Bread?' Assad beat him to it.

'Yes, that's it. And if we look at another common denominator in these different religions, the cross and the crucifixion, again we must turn our attention to astronomical explanations. On December 22nd, 23rd and 24th, the Sun is, as most people would know, at its absolutely lowest point in the year. Particularly we up here in the north know that, because these days are the darkest of the year, and in olden times they were experienced as death itself, because it wasn't known if the Sun would ever rise again. At the same time, on December 22nd, the constellation Crux would be extremely clear in the sky about two thousand years ago, and after three days of watching that constellation, the Sun – it's tempting to say, thank God – would once again start moving north. So, the Sun, the very symbol of the divine, has been hanging for three days under Crux, the cross, after which it is resurrected. Our Jesus Christ shares this fate with most other sun gods.'

'Is this something that's being discussed openly at faculties of theology?' asked Carl.

Johannes Tausen did a slight wave with his best hand. 'Of course, most of it is well known, but comprehensive astronomical interpretations like this have no place in theological studies.'

'Very strange,' said Carl, not knowing what to do with this knowledge. Perhaps it could've been funny to dish it out in his confirmation class, but the vicar probably wouldn't have thanked him for it.

'There are many other phenomena that suggest a correlation between the celestial bodies and the stories, as we know from the Bible and lots of other religions. But I promise to stop soon,' said Tausen, closing his eyes as if to make sure he'd remembered the most important facts.

'I can only say that if you look at Jesus on a general level as the giver of life itself, as the son of the Sun here on Earth,' he continued, his eyes still closed, 'then that idea has been passed on figuratively from ancient times in the sense that Jesus's head, with the corona around it and the cross behind it, precisely resembles the sun cross of the zodiac. Jesus is the son of God, the light of the world, fighting against the dark forces. And if you want to go into detail, the crown of thorns is merely the shadow that appears when the Sun shines through treetops.' He turned to face them directly. 'I can understand if this is difficult to take in. In fact, it is for me, too, and as a theologian and a man of faith I will admit that in many respects it's a hard pill to swallow. But that said, this is only a concentrate of a series of lectures, and maybe it all became too concentrated for the occasion.'

Assad kept a straight face, but that's how it was with scepticism – it had many faces.

'This all sounds completely . . . unbelievable,' said Carl quietly. 'These theories must have the potential to shake the foundations of almost any religious group.'

The old professor smiled. 'Not at all. You can also choose to say that this is the only narrative of any significance to mankind. The fact that it is repeated over and over is completely natural, given that mankind has always been in need of a saviour and reconciler. And that is how I look at it, too. A really good and in many respects well-founded story for all times.'

'And that's how Frank thought as well, I would imagine. Don't you think so?' asked Assad.

'Yes, absolutely, and that is in fact the essence. When so many known religions are based on astronomical phenomena such as the Sun and the stars, following their patterns, it's probably because all life on Earth and in the universe is the result of these constellations, and this in turn provides us with an explanation for the existence of everything – even the Lord himself, you could say.'

He stared into space for a minute, as if his last sentence had led to a minor epiphany. 'Now that we're talking, I actually believe I remember some of the things he said to me the last time we spoke.'

Carl held his breath.

'He said something along the lines of: *If you want to worship everything that's divine at once, everything you can't understand, you'll have to give in to the only thing we know for certain: that the Sun was given to us in the form of life, and that nature was given to us in the form of bread. Horus was the first sun god in the world, and therefore Horus is also the name of the primal instinct in man, commanding us to worship both the Sun and nature with respect and care. All the things we don't do today but ought to start doing.* And then I believe he added: *And as soon as possible.*'

'And that's the last thing he said?' asked Carl, slightly disappointed.

'Yes, and then of course he thanked me.'

'Do you think it made him neo-religious,' asked Assad.

'Why yes, it's very likely.'

Assad turned toward Carl. 'That's several times we've heard that, Carl.'

He nodded. People on Bornholm had seen signs everywhere. The man who found sunstones. And the blind woman Beate Vismut had sensed it, too.

'What was it Beate Vismut told Rose about it, do you remember, Assad?'

He leafed through his notebook for half a minute, the professor and Carl watching. 'Here it is. She said that Frank "was a genuine crystal", and that he'd seen the true light and reflected himself in it, unable from then on to live without.'

'There you are,' said the professor, nodding his head. 'You should look for a man who lives like that. A man who worships the Sun and nature, and Horus as the symbol.'

'We began with the question of what he wanted to do with his life before your fascinating account. Do you think the answer is that he might have wanted to become a new messiah, and that he found the tool through your lectures? Is that a possibility?' asked Carl.

The old man frowned. 'I doubt it,' he said. 'But you never know, do you?'

37

Sunday, May 11th, 2014

When Pirjo woke up, her body was quivering with an unpleasant sensation, like the kind you get before an exam you hadn't prepared for, or the morning after a quarrel you couldn't resolve.

She looked at the clock, aware that she might as well get out of bed and get it over with. In less than one minute the alarm would go off anyway. It was 3:59 A.M., forty-five minutes before sunrise.

She heard Atu's footsteps in the hall, heading as always for the beach, where he'd greet the first rays of the Sun with prayers, despite the presence of clouds pregnant with rain.

Like him, Pirjo also had her routines.

To begin with, she needed to wake up the newly arrived course members, and then go under the showers in the central courtyard to perform the usual personal cleansing process with communal wash-down and subsequent drying-off on the porch, gazing at the aura of the sun as it slowly edged its way up over the horizon.

After this, the new course members would go back to their cabins to perform a brief, silent exercise of chanting to the Celestial Sphere.

The permanent residents and temporary assistants were already working in their respective quarters, and now it was Pirjo's task to go from house to house and check that all residents were ready. From time to time, someone overslept, and sometimes someone was sick. If Pirjo wasn't there to check and help, the hour of awakening was at risk of being disturbed by latecomers who would suddenly turn up during the ritual. Atu had impressed on them that culprits who were late would have to find something else to do, but sometimes it happened anyway.

This morning, three people were sick. They'd been vomiting all night, and the air in their rooms was thick with the smell of sick and fumes from upset stomachs. Pirjo fetched herbal tea for two of them and let the third one sleep, which was often the best cure. Understandably behind in her routine, Pirjo stepped out into the hallway connecting the small cabins. Normally she'd be on her way down to the timber circle by this time, so she accidentally overheard a conversation that wasn't meant for her ears.

The men were out in good time before the assembly, and therefore they were shuffling slowly through the hallway. The light was still dim, but she recognized the footsteps and voices of two of the oldest disciples: one who looked after the crops in the greenhouses, and another who was helping to build a new timber circle to the north. A long, hard day's work ahead of them, it was understandable that they were taking it easy.

'Should we take this to Atu?' asked one of them.

'I don't know,' said the figure next to him.

'We can't take it to Pirjo. That would be like taking sides in advance.'

'But if things keep happening that shouldn't, and that Pirjo has some part in, then where will we find inner peace?'

'I don't think Pirjo has any part in it. It's Shirley who's ruining the harmony of this place, not Pirjo.'

'Yes, you're probably right. So you don't think we should go to Atu and ask him to stop the gossip?'

'No, why? Shirley doesn't fit in here. So it'll solve itself when she's gone.'

Pirjo stopped so they wouldn't see her when they turned the corner by the exit door.

'It'll solve itself when she's gone,' they'd said. The way Pirjo looked at it, that couldn't happen soon enough.

She turned off towards her office, walked past the door to Atu's quarters, and opened instead the next door that led to the solar-power-system control room.

It only took her a couple of minutes to remove the cover plates to the junction box and the inverter, laying bare all the cables.

So, she had paid attention after all.

The morning had been foggy, but just before the sun showed above the horizon, the clouds dispersed and everything suddenly became immensely beautiful.

Atu was waiting as usual, elevated seven metres on the platform in the timber circle, his hair glistening wet, his eyes turned to the sunrise in the east, consumed with the glow above the sea.

His hair was shining like gold, and his yellow robe was waving in the morning breeze. He was beautiful like a god.

He turned towards them, and everything went quiet.

'Let us greet the Sun with upward-stretched arms,' he said.

Thirty-five pairs of arms stretched out towards the sea, and they remained motionless like that until he told them to breathe deeply twelve times, and then let their hands glide down over their bodies so that all the dormant energy of the night would be activated.

'I feel you, and I see you. Abanshamash, Abanshamash,' he whispered, stretching his arms out in front of his body, causing the yellow sleeves to flap. 'I see you,' he whispered. 'I see you, and your souls are beckoning to me. You are ready.

'Today is the one hundred and thirty-first day of the year, and it has increased by nine hours and twenty-two minutes. Three days from now, the full moon will rise, and the Sun will gain strength through its arrival. Helianthemum, the flower of the sun, is in bloom everywhere, alongside potentillas and orchids. Just now, our greenhouses are bursting with green beans, onions and cucumbers. New potatoes and asparagus will soon fill our dining tables. Let us give thanks.'

'Horus, Horus, blessed by the star, infused by the Sun,' exclaimed the assembly with one voice, 'allow us to be your servants and bear witness to the power you bestow on us. Allow us to follow your path and worship it, so that our descendants may find comfort in your bosom. Let us be prepared when you go into hibernation, and let us never forget the reason for your presence.'

They stopped just as suddenly as they'd started, the same way they always did.

Atu stretched his arms out towards them. 'Let us remember that a guiding star is something we follow, and let us at the same time beware of bestowing on the gods a so-called existence. Let us live instead in eternal knowledge of our own ignorance regarding the universal, and care for our immediate surroundings. Let us, instead of always demanding, concentrate on learning and settling for less. Merely feel nature and give in to it. Merely realize that man is but an insignificant part of everything, and that the individual is only significant in terms of their humility in the company of others.'

He laid his eyes directly upon them.

When his gaze met Pirjo's, it was full of tenderness, and she put her hands under her pregnant stomach, knowing that she should feel happy. Instead, she had a sense of despair and unease. Something she had never before experienced during their assemblies.

If she didn't act soon, she'd lose her grip.

She mustered the newly arrived, one by one. All these trusting people who'd begin from the very first assembly to breathe deeper, simply because Atu spoke to them and because it felt so precious. Their faith and respect mustn't suffer. When she stood here in six months with Atu's baby in her arms, she still had to be as she was now, irreproachable and, yes, like an icon. The mother of Atu's child, the redeemer's son.

Now Atu was smiling up there, like a father at his children.

'To those of you who are new, let me tell you that you've reached the point where together we will go through a series of nature absorption exercises. And when we are finished with that, I'll ask you to come up here to me together with your tutors. You've probably already sensed that the spiritual paths many of you have chosen throughout your lives have no significance in this place. You have not come to engage in your own understanding of self, or to focus on what other spiritual movements focus on. You aren't here to concentrate on your own soul and consciousness, or to indulge in dogma or creeds. You're here for the sole purpose of learning to *be*. To us, Horus is everything, but not only because Horus in many respects represents millennia of different clever people's interpretations of, and wonderment at, the questions of where we come from and, especially, why. You may think that there is as much mysticism and hocus-pocus going on here as in other circles, but remember that what we are going through on a daily basis are merely rituals. It is our task here at the centre to ensure that you can achieve the required peace of mind by simple, durable means, and nothing else. By using the name of Horus we merely express our thanks for the gifts of life and nature, and that they are enough in themselves. If you can devote yourselves fully to this, you'll also reach a stage where you possess all the human characteristics that serve you best: compassion, love of your fellow human beings, and peace of mind to assess tomorrow's path and power to analyse yesterday without regret and despair.'

Then he asked them all to sit down on the ground.

'All science builds on comparison of the known and the unknown, so therefore . . .' he began.

Pirjo pulled Valentina aside when this part of the séance was over and the newly arrived were ascending the stairs to the timber circle platform, their faces expectant, while the permanent residents went to perform their daily tasks.

'Yes,' said Valentina, apparently not intending to allow Pirjo to drag her away.

'I have good news, Valentina. We've heard from Malena.'

Valentina's lips opened slightly and her hand moved up towards her chest.

'Malena?' she said, disbelief painted across her face.

'Yes, she called this morning, just before the assembly. I don't think she'd considered what time it was here on Öland, but never mind. She's in Canada, in a town called Dutton, she said. A small place in Ontario with a main street and a provisions shop where she can buy all the French specialities she enjoys so much. She's still travelling from place to place, making a living by writing texts for people. She just wanted to let us know she's doing well. She did sound happy.'

'Really?' exclaimed Valentina. She had clearly been hoping for more than that. A personal message, perhaps.

'I can see what you're thinking.' Pirjo smiled. 'And she did actually have a personal message for you, Valentina. She wanted to thank you for your friendship and everything you taught her. She asked me to let you know. She's very happy now, she said, and wanted you in particular to know that.'

'Friendship – did she use that word?'

'Yes, and her voice sounded very warm when she said it.'

Finally the woman smiled. 'Will she be coming back?'

'I didn't ask. Maybe, if she feels the need. I believe we'll hear from her again, when she needs to talk.'

For a moment Valentina stood staring into space, trying to replace her excitement with relief. 'Even though I don't really mean it, even if I never see her again, I guess it's for the best, as long as she's all right, isn't it?'

Pirjo took her arm. Now she'd captured her confidence and attention. Five minutes' research last night on some random French-speaking town far, far away had paid off.

'I have more good news for you,' she said.

Valentina touched her neck. Could there really be more?

'We have an assignment for you. You're going on a journey.'

'Would you come with me for a minute, Shirley, I'd really like to have a word with you. We've reached a point where we need to talk about the future, don't you think?'

The woman straightened her robe over her stomach and down the sides. It was a movement she'd carried with her from her former life, when she was still making an effort to look presentable despite her weight.

'That sounds . . . interesting,' she said.

She could bet it was going to be interesting, thought Pirjo, looking around her. The hallway down to the office was empty, as was the adjacent office. Even better, the rays of the sun were now streaming sideways in through the windows.

Wondering how long it would take, she thought it was best to let Shirley go in first. If she was paralysed by the first shock and fell on the floor, Pirjo wouldn't be able to lift her up again. But then she could get the cable kit in the garage and hook her up to it. That ought to do the trick, she thought, suddenly doubtful. Perhaps the fuses would blow, or something would short-circuit.

She hesitated and decided to walk more slowly. This plan suddenly seemed insane, but what other options did she have? The woman had to go.

'Come with me into the office, Shirley. Then I'll tell you what we had in mind. Yes, you go first.'

She pointed at a chair on the other side of the desk, just next to the open door to the passage and the solar-power control room.

'Oh, someone has forgotten to shut the door again, that's where that noise is coming from. Would you mind shutting it, Shirley?'

'What's in there?' she asked, her eyebrows lowered. A sign of mistrust or curiosity?

'Oh, it's just the control system for our solar-power system.'

'Really?' said Shirley, letting go of the chair she'd been about to sit down on.

Pirjo waited a moment before following her. 'If you like, I can show you what it's all about,' she said, pulling a rubber glove over one hand, while Shirley stepped into the control room.

Pirjo checked the gauge. Even though it was still early in the day, the production of power was steadily increasing. The sky had also started to look brighter and bluer through the skylight, she noticed.

'I must admit, it's a bit of a mess. Our electrician has removed the cover plates from the junction boxes, so we have to be careful,' she warned, getting ready to push Shirley's hand into the snake's nest of wires.

'Nothing much would happen,' answered Shirley, unimpressed. 'The effect isn't very high, and it would be very difficult to be killed by direct current. You'd have to be unconscious and have one negative and one positive wire attached to each side of your body. Then your insides would be more or less boiled. Like being inside a microwave.'

She said that in the very moment Pirjo stretched her arm forward, getting ready to press Shirley's hand into the trap.

So she let her hand drop. Unconscious, she said? Wires on each side of the body?

Shirley looked at her authoritatively. 'Didn't you know that the first electric chair was supposed to have used direct current, but that Thomas Edison guy warned the authorities, telling them that direct current wouldn't kill without excessively prolonged torture? He was the one who suggested alternating current instead. Crazy, isn't it? Edison himself! No, this direct current would only sting a little. Perhaps it'd be different later in the day, when the sun was at its strongest, but not now. Shouldn't I screw those cover plates back on for you, by the way? After all, it isn't completely safe if worst comes to worst.'

Pirjo was stunned. 'Er, yes, please. How on earth do you know stuff like that, Shirley?'

'Oh, my dad was an electrician. Guess what he entertained the family with over dinner, the few times he preferred to spend time with his family rather than his pals down at the pub.'

Pirjo tilted her head to the side. Shirley's father was an electrician. Had she mentioned that when she filled out her enrolment papers?

'No, just leave it – the electrician can fix that when he comes back. I'll lock the doors so no one gets hurt in the meantime.'

So, Pirjo's plan A had been replaced by a plan B by the time they sat down in her office.

'Listen, Shirley,' she said after a brief pause, 'I'm afraid we've decided not to accept you as a permanent member of the academy. I'm sorry, because I know how disappointing it must be for you,' she said, expecting a reflex protest. Nothing happened.

On the contrary, Shirley just sat there, her eyes and face expressionless, wringing her plump hands in her lap. Judging by her quivering lower lip, the message had taken her completely by surprise.

'Yes, it's a shame. But we simply don't have any free places. Otherwise there might have been a chance. So it won't happen for the time being, Shirley, I'm sorry.'

'But I don't understand. Jeanette's room is still free,' she said, still with a hint of hope in her voice.

'Well, that's true, but Jeanette's coming back, Shirley.'

Shirley sat still for a minute. Her hands were resting now, her expression no longer lost.

'That's a complete lie, Pirjo,' she suddenly snarled.

Pirjo was just about to explain Jeanette's situation, but the words stuck in her throat. She'd also have clarified that there was a slim chance of Shirley being accepted later, if she could remain patient, but now the gauntlet had been thrown down instead.

'I don't know why you're snarling like that and calling me a liar, Shirley. It's actually quite hurtful,' she said. 'I think I need to remind you that I'm the chief administrative manager of this centre, so the decision about your future lies in my hands, no matter what you say or do. So why don't we—'

'That may be, but you're lying, and I'm not going anywhere.' The last sentence came out as a shout.

'I see. I'll choose to ignore that,' said Pirjo coldly. 'But we do have an offer to make . . .'

'People are starting to doubt you, Pirjo. They're beginning to put two and two together. You seem so cooperative, but you're just yanking our chains. Right now I feel the same way about you as when a man pulls the chair out from the table for you, expecting that'll buy him the right to touch your breasts. You feel you've been taken for a ride, but not just that. You also feel incredibly manipulated, and of course I can only speak for myself, but I really hate that.'

'You always seem to speak for yourself only, Shirley. Maybe that's actually one of the reasons why it'll be hard to find a place for you.'

At this, Shirley got up suddenly to point an accusing finger at Pirjo, her entire voluptuous body quivering.

'If you think you can stop me by sending me away, you're wrong.'

Pirjo squinted. 'I don't get it. Stop you how?'

'Here we go again. You're just being manipulative. Stop me before I tell the world that you know what happened to Wanda Phinn, of course.' She pinched her lips, trying to compose herself, but her anger and all the thoughts she was grappling with made her burst out crying.

Pirjo breathed a sigh of relief. Just a few tears and she knew she'd have the situation under control.

'My, oh my, Shirley, are we back to that story about the belt? Come over here to my side of the table and I'll show you something.

Then you'll see that you're completely wrong about me and the whole situation.'

When Shirley didn't show any sign of obeying, Pirjo turned the screen towards her.

'Look what I found online. I felt I had to, after our last talk about that belt.' She clicked on the first link, and a webpage called Fashion Belts appeared.

'See how many belts look like the one you said Jeanette brought down from the attic.' She pointed at a few. 'Look, diagonal stripes in red and grey.' She clicked on another link. 'And this company also has some that look like the one you gave Wanda Phinn. Six months ago that was how belts should look. It's a completely common belt.'

Shirley huffed. Her eyes were glistening. At that very moment, they were balancing on a knife's edge, and they might both fall, so Pirjo had to be extremely careful to maintain the balance. Keep Shirley convinced that they were fighting for the same cause.

'I know what you're thinking right now, Shirley. The belts on the Net aren't used, and the scratch on the buckle and the dent in the belt can't be explained by this. But look what I also found.'

She clicked on a couple of links to pages where women sold clothes from their own wardrobes. On two of the pages there were used belts for sale that looked more or less like the one Shirley was talking about.

It had taken her all night to find them.

'Look, Shirley. One of these belts has a scratch, and they both have dents around the hole that are actually identical to the one you showed me. Can you see the resemblance? Four holes in and there's the mark from wear, exactly like on the belt you thought was Wanda's. They're just pretty ordinary marks of wear and tear on a belt, don't you see?'

Shirley's eyes fixed on the screen and her tears began to flow uncontrollably, both from sadness and relief.

Pirjo let her cry while she considered the situation.

Just now, the woman was both disappointed and confused, but the problem was that in a few days she might not be confused any more, only disappointed. Perhaps she'd be sitting in London, imagining that somehow she'd be able to track Wanda down. That she had a mission. And when another month or two had passed, and she'd talked to every Tom, Dick and Harry, including Wanda's parents, and found out that the girl in fact *had* disappeared, her alarming ideas would reemerge.

And then what? Would her suspicions also reemerge with renewed strength? Pirjo was certain that they would.

Of course, it would take convincing proof for Shirley to be able to substantiate her accusation against Pirjo and the centre, but what if her timing proved fatal? If she launched her attack just as the Danish police drew in? There might only be a slim chance of that happening, but the baby was growing and kicking inside Pirjo, and she'd made a sacred promise to this child.

Nothing would ever be allowed to harm them.

She looked at Shirley for some time, and then placed her hand on hers. 'I feel the same way as you, Shirley. I don't like it when people turn their backs on me either. When they suddenly show sides of themselves that couldn't have been predicted. When they flush me out of their lives, coldly and cynically, as if I'd never been a part of it. Yes, I really do understand you, Shirley,' she said, when their eyes finally met. 'But listen, why don't we forget about what happened between us just before? I know you're very disappointed with our decision that you can't stay, and that we can't accept you into our inner circle, but we do still have a suggestion for you, Shirley.

'You see, Valentina has been given an assignment today. She's to go to our office in Barcelona to recruit local course members. Perhaps you could do the same for us from our London office? Do you think that could interest you? It would be wonderful, because I actually think you'd be really good at it.'

Pirjo sent her a hesitant smile. If the gullible woman was ever going to buy it, it had to be now.

'I know you'll be out of a job when you return. But the job I'm talking about will be paid. I know the salary is commission-based, but we usually have a lot of applicants in London, which would be to your benefit. And it's important to remember that there's also a small apartment that comes with the job. What do you say – wouldn't that be exciting?'

Shirley remained silent.

'But before we can do this, you'll have to be led through our purification process, just like the one Valentina went through about a year ago. As always, that requires you to be isolated for a month, so you can forget about everything that's worldly and spend all your energy on letting the nature absorption settle within you – become neutralized, as we call it. If you're willing to do that, and if you accept the job, I see no reason why we shouldn't begin straightaway.'

Pirjo scrutinized her face. Often, the order in which the parts of a face reacted would give away whether or not an answer was honest. Smile lines around the eyes, for instance, would often be the result of cool calculation; it was the same with smiles, so you couldn't trust that kind of reaction, just like the far too short answers OK, or just yes. On the other hand, if there were signs of the person being touched, before the smiles or short answers, then you were on fairly safe ground.

At the moment, Shirley's face was completely blank. It was

impossible to tell what was going on inside. Would her next sentence be a burst of anger or a declaration of surrender?

Pirjo waited, aware of the seriousness of the situation. Their eyes were almost united in symbiosis. For a moment she thought Shirley would get up and slam the door, but then the corners of her mouth moved downward, as if she was about to start crying again.

That's when Pirjo knew she'd won the battle.

'Is Atu OK with this arrangement?' asked Shirley quietly.

Pirjo nodded. 'Yes, of course. We've been talking about it for some time. Actually, I believe you'll be able to recruit many new people with your fine, gentle nature and honest face.'

That brought the smile out. Not too much, not too little, and at the right time.

'Well, in that case I'll accept,' she said, her eyes avoiding Pirjo's. It was difficult to tell what that indicated. Maybe it was a sign that she was ashamed of having attacked and accused Pirjo, but of course there was also the possibility that she was trying to memorize the sight of a place she wouldn't be seeing for some time now.

Pirjo smiled.

If it was the latter, then she had no idea how right she'd turn out to be.

She'd certainly never see this room again.

This room, or any other room like it for that matter.

38

Monday, May 12th, 2014

Carl looked over at the TV, where the usual bunch of laughing hosts and overly energetic chefs were trying to teach Denmark how to make a salad of pointed cabbage and sesame seeds, boldly arranged around a small, balsamic vinegar–marinated filet mignon aux pimentos, or whatever the hell they were saying. Carl glanced despondently down at his pale scrambled eggs and Hardy's stale oatmeal porridge. What a bloody nerve TV2 had to abuse bachelors and other poor souls at seven in the morning with that sort of utopian dream.

Hardy certainly looked less than enthusiastic at the spoon Morten was about to shove into his mouth.

'But the porridge will get the peristalsis going, Hardy. So won't you please open your mouth and wipe that frown off your face?'

Hardy swallowed the lump, and breathed deeply. 'If you'd eaten as much porridge as me over the past seven years, Mr Holland, I'd like to see who'd be doing the whining. And allow me to quote Assad: It tastes like camel tonsil hockey.'

'Tonsil hockey . . . ?'

'French-kissing an eager camel.' He tried to laugh, but didn't have sufficient air in his lungs.

Carl put his newspaper aside, and looked at the glowing screen on his phone. It was one of the local numbers from Police Headquarters.

He glanced at Hardy a couple of times as he read the message. No doubt his old partner had understood what was going on.

'It's about our case, isn't it?' he said when Carl put his phone back down.

Carl nodded. 'Yes, there's been a new development in the nail-gun case.'

Morten put a hand on Hardy's shoulder. He was having a hard time coping with that case; everyone knew that.

'It seems they may have found the firearm that killed Anker, and nearly us, too,' said Carl. 'Apparently there's been a raid somewhere, and because a Danish policeman was killed with the weapon, Lars Bjørn has called a press conference.'

Hardy didn't say anything.

'In an hour and a half,' continued Carl.

Still not a word from Hardy.

'Damn it, Hardy.' Carl could see the pain in his eyes. Even though it hurt to think about the bloody weapon, it also felt good to be given just a little bit of hope that this might be over soon, and the murderer brought to trial.

Carl walked around Hardy's wheelchair to give him a hug.

'They wanted to send a car so you could come. Do you want to?'

Hardy quietly shook his head. 'Not until it's definitively over,' he said. 'I'm not being put on display.'

*

Lars Bjørn reached over Carl's head to point at Head of Communications Janus Staal, who thanked everyone for coming. Then he presented the agenda and sat down, leaning over towards Carl.

'You didn't manage to get Hardy to come?'

Carl shook his head.

'I can understand him, but it was Bjørn's idea. A man like Hardy is great publicity.'

'What the hell is this about?' whispered Carl, looking around him. Anything and anyone who could creep and crawl in the world of crime reporters was present, and TV2 News had already started filming. The crime reporter from DRTV already had his microphone out, and even a couple of tabloid magazines had turned up, as always with *Gossip* in the front row.

'It's not my case any more, so why did I have to come? What's happened, Janus?'

Staal raised a hand in the air, pointing to his watch. 'We begin in twenty seconds, Carl. Then you'll know everything. Good thing you made it.'

Was it, though? Carl placed his briefcase on the floor next to his chair.

'Thank you for turning out in force,' began Lars Bjørn. Then he introduced the gathered assembly to Carl Mørck, followed by his head of communications, and his Deputy Assistant Commissioner Terje Ploug, who'd been in charge of the investigation of the case since Carl and his team were shot down.

After this, he turned towards a man Carl definitely knew, although he couldn't recall his name or where he'd last seen him.

'And this is Hans Rinus, who's been in charge of a similar case in a suburb of Rotterdam in the Netherlands. Carl Mørck was our observer in connection with the Dutch case, and he'll tell you what happened there. Would you start, Carl?'

Yes, *now* Carl remembered him. The policeman who'd trampled through a crime scene with a lack of overview like a Danish politician on a bad day, wearing something that looked like safety shoes. What the heck was going on, and why was that buffoon here?

'Sure,' said Carl, quickly recapping his visit to the Netherlands and the description of the two men who'd been shot with a nail gun with ninety-millimetre Paslode nails, their mouths stuffed with cocaine of legendarily poor quality.

'We were unable to establish a link between the crimes in Denmark and the one in the Netherlands, so we handed over the Schiedam case to our Dutch colleagues, who continued work on it as a local case.'

'Which was a mistake,' added Terje Ploug, with ill-concealed innuendo that it wasn't *his* fault. 'But Hans Rinus can tell you much more about that, which is why we've invited you here. The murder of Anker Høyer, the permanent physical damage to Hardy Henningsen, who unfortunately couldn't make it today because he is still extremely marked by the episode, and the shooting of Carl Mørck, all of which happened on January 26th, 2007, more than seven years ago, all these crimes were committed with the same weapon, of which we're now in possession.'

There was bustling among the reporters when he pulled a heavy semiautomatic pistol from his lap and held it up in the air. Carl slowly turned his eyes towards it, feeling the pressure rise in his head, and a couple in the crowd got up.

'How does it feel to see the weapon, Carl Mørck?' one of them shouted, the result being that Lars Bjørn asked everyone to remain calm and sit down.

How did it feel? Right now the muzzle was pointing straight at him. It was the same muzzle from which five 9mm projectiles had been fired, ruining life for quite a few people, including his own. How did it feel?

He raised his left hand and pushed the muzzle away with his index finger. There was a sound of at least twenty-five clicks from digital cameras all at the same time.

Terje Ploug put the pistol on the table with a clunk. 'We're dealing with a pistol of the type PAMAS G1, a variety of the more widely known Beretta 92, which was produced for the French Gendarmerie Nationale. Automatic, semi-heavy. The serial number has been filed off, and given that quite a few of these pistols have disappeared from military arsenals over the years, we've got no chance of establishing the history of this one. What we *do* know with certainty, because it's been confirmed through our ballistic investigations, is that this is the weapon that was used in the shooting of our three colleagues in 2007.'

At this, Janus Staal pressed a key on his laptop, and a PowerPoint image of the pistol and a data sheet of its properties were projected onto the screen above their heads.

If Carl's arms and hands had been allowed to decide, they would've been shaking. His forehead felt like ice, while his body was almost boiling. They could've spared him this.

Now Lars Bjørn took over. 'Obviously, we've called this press meeting today to impress on the public that when police officers are killed on duty, it will always take very high priority in our investigations, and that we won't stop until the perpetrators have been brought to trial. Apart from that, we wanted to inform you that we're now in possession of the knowledge that the nail-gun murders in Schiedam, Netherlands, and those on Amager and in

Sorø, here in Denmark, are likely to be connected after all. And now I'll pass you over to Hans Rinus.'

The man cleared his throat a couple of times. Carl remembered him clearly now. His English was worse than Assad's Danish the first time Carl had met him.

'Thank you,' he said in some kind of Danish, and then went on to butcher what was supposed to be English.

'I am police in Zuid-Holland, and the murders in Schiedam are mine. For a long time it wasn't certain who had the kill, and it still isn't, but now we know, hmmm, what do you say, that the dead man was also someone that the Danish police was after.'

You'd have to look far and wide to find worse gibberish than that.

Lars Bjørn gave a friendly smile and put his hand on Hans Rinus's arm.

'Thank you very much for your splendid work,' he said in English, before continuing in Danish. Thank God.

'Three days ago, Daniel Jippes, a twelve-year-old schoolboy out riding his bike in a suburb called Vriesland, south-west of Rotterdam, found a body in a canal called Meeldijk. He was on his way into a park area, where the canal runs under the bicycle path through a drainpipe.'

He pointed at the head of communications, who pressed another key. This time it produced a screenshot from Google Maps showing the location. Park trees, the canal running into the drainpipe where the body had been found, and the cycle path that led over the dike that the pipe went through. Everything was very, very green. *Park Brabrand* it read underneath.

'The body was a male, found with sturdy string tied around his right foot. The string went all the way across the cycle path, down on the other side and under the cycle path through the pipe, where the other end was tied to his left wrist.'

Janus Staal produced a slightly blurred photo that showed both the string on the cycle path and what was presumably the body in the drainpipe. That was probably the closest the Danish press would come to a photo of the deceased.

'There were clear signs of defensive bruising on the body, and the technicians assume he was tied while lying on the cycle path, then the string was pulled through the pipe, and finally they dragged him in the water and through the pipe where he drowned.'

Carl frowned. Why not make a clean kill if they'd wanted to eliminate the man anyway?

'We can't rule out the possibility that he was dragged back and forth a few times before they finally decided to let him die.'

'They were probably trying to get something out of him,' interjected Terje Ploug. Lars Bjørn gave him a penetrating look.

'Yes, as Terje Ploug said, we can probably conclude that someone tried to get something out of the man.'

The journalists started to raise their hands in the air, but the head of communications stopped them before the questions piled up.

'You won't have an opportunity to ask questions today, but you will all be given a printout of all the available facts.'

They grumbled. Carl could understand them. How the hell could they sell the story if they all had the same poor starting point?

'The man has been identified,' said Terje Ploug, once again using PowerPoint to show a photo of a balding man in his forties, with blue eyes and an annoying, droll smile.

He was clearly well-dressed. Ray-Ban sunglasses in his hair, pressed white shirt and a Hugo Boss-type jacket signalled that he was someone who wanted to exude that he had things under control. Which probably wasn't what he felt just before he was pulled down into the drainpipe.

'We're dealing with a Danish citizen living in the Netherlands, by the name of Rasmus Bruhn, forty-four years of age, several prior convictions. Over the past few years, he also worked as a journalist under the pseudonym Pete Boswell.'

Carl frowned. What did he say?

Ploug lifted his eyes toward the assembly. 'Some of you probably recall that this was the name given to the dismembered body we found in a box out on Amager, when the barracks were torn down where the shooting of the three Danish police officers took place years ago.'

Both Carl and the people from the press were confused. 'So why did you assume back then that the dead man on Amager was called Pete Boswell?' someone shouted.

'An anonymous tip,' Bjørn broke in. 'We were given several leads, but the decisive factor was a fleur-de-lis branded on his right shoulder. We didn't go public with it for several reasons and, furthermore, it took the medical examiners a few days to verify it due to the decomposition of the body. Admittedly, it was an assumption, but in our opinion a well-founded one. That's how it is with anonymous tips. The press hopefully knows that better than anyone. You need to take them with a grain of salt, am I right? And this tip unfortunately turned out to be misleading.'

Carl clenched the cigarettes in his jacket pocket. Just knowing they were there was better than nothing. Damn it, there was so much he could discuss with Bjørn and Ploug. He just didn't have the energy.

'Our Dutch colleagues have checked up on the man's background, and there are several striking facts. Firstly, in his capacity of travel correspondent, he had ample opportunity to act as courier for people – by this we are mainly thinking about precious stones – and secondly, his network was so extensive that he could easily have connected people and passed on messages that way.

'He has travelled in many countries in East Asia and the Middle East, but also in Africa and the Caribbean.'

He nodded to their Dutch colleague. 'And now our colleague Hans Rinus will explain the results of the technical examination of the body and the search of Rasmus Bruhn's home.'

A lengthy, complicated account followed, but the meaning was clear enough. The body had been in the water for some days. The tongue, which was hanging out of the mouth, was no longer blue, and his irises already slightly blurry. There were scratch marks on the inside of the pipe, and the silt on the bottom indicated that he'd tried to drag himself out. He'd dressed young for his age, and had nothing on him except a business card which – despite days in the water – was still readable and led them directly to his residence at Haverdreef in the neighborhood of De Akkers, just north of the crime scene. That was also where the pistol was found, the magazine full and his fingerprints on it, along with 250 grams of poor cocaine and some notebooks containing names, including some relations in Denmark. More precisely, these relations lived in Sorø, and even more precisely, one of them was the younger of the two men who were murdered with a nail gun in a car repair shop in town. He was the nephew of the man Carl, Anker and Hardy found murdered with a Paslode nail in his temple on Amager.

Carl looked over at Lars Bjørn, who was watching his head of communications switch between different effects on the screen with a straight face.

All this ought to feel like a relief. A chain of information that put things into context and triggered new possibilities for investigation. Still, Carl felt nothing but displeasure, his jaw muscles now working away uncontrollably.

How long had Lars Bjørn kept this knowledge to himself? How many times had he chosen not to inform Carl? Why hadn't Carl been the first person he went to?

While the people next to him talked their way through a series of possible scenarios and motives, which they knew absolutely nothing about anyway, rebellion started to stir inside him.

Weren't they just sitting there presenting unsubstantiated hypotheses to gather points in the great performance lottery? Was it the case that Lars Bjørn wanted to demonstrate that despite his anonymity, he was a man of leadership, impact and perspective? That he was a worthy successor to Marcus Jacobsen, the man who hadn't granted Carl as much as a few minutes to explain himself in one of the TV police report programmes?

'Do you have anything you'd like to add?' Lars Bjørn suddenly asked his colleagues. Carl must've been in another world for a minute, because their Dutch colleague was already standing.

Carl bent down to pick up his briefcase.

'Yes,' he said, 'I do.'

He rummaged through the briefcase before he found the right papers.

'I'm investigating another case, a road casualty, and in that connection we're looking for this man. About five-nine, dimple in his chin, husky voice, blue eyes, strong features, dark eyebrows and wide front teeth with a small light mark. He speaks fluent Danish.'

Carl avoided Bjørn's eyes, but noticed Terje Ploug sending him a worried look, while he held up his photocopy of the man next to the VW Kombi directly in front of the TV2 News camera.

'This is the man. Please note the VW Kombi, light blue with a wide fender. What you can't see is the big peace sign painted on the roof. We know he's called Frank, and that he's since changed his name to something more exotic.'

Bjørn grasped his forearm. Rather hard for a white-collar worker. '*Thank you*, Carl Mørck,' he said. 'I think that's enough already! Today we're talking about another—'

Carl freed his arm. 'He was staying on Bornholm in 1997, and took part in the excavations of timber circles. They were a type of platform resting on thick posts, designed for sun worship and offerings of stone and animal bone. We know for certain that he was a sun worshipper, and that he might still be practising as one. All tips in regard to this—'

'Stop right there, Carl Mørck!' Bjørn held his hand up towards the press. 'We'd like to save this case until we have a bit more to go on. Allow me to thank you all for coming. Regarding the nail-gun case, we'll get back to you when there is progress in the Danish part of the investigation. Meanwhile—'

'You can contact Department Q directly. The phone number is here under the photo.' Carl pointed. 'We're working at full throttle, waiting only for *your* tip.' Carl looked directly into the camera and held the photo right in front of it.

If he'd had the chance, he would've liked to show other items from his briefcase, but he reckoned he'd pushed his luck enough if he wanted to hang on to the hope of still having a job tomorrow.

Carl left his copy of the photostat on the table in the briefing room for everyone to see, but Bjørn managed to remove it before the journalists got to it.

'My office, immediately,' he ordered Carl.

39

Sunday, May 11th, 2014

'A penny for your thoughts, Shirley,' said Pirjo. She took her arm and leaned into her. It felt good. 'Are you happy?' she asked.

'Happy? Yes, I think so.' She nodded.

It all felt so strange. Only nine months ago, she'd walked up the staircase in one of the flashiest houses in the exclusive Chelsea area with Wanda by her side, excited like a child before Christmas. And what she'd experienced there had been wondrous, a big leap forward in her life. That day she'd really felt that for once it wasn't just some silly fad, like doing courses in stress management, or trying to communicate with spirits, or something like that. This time she'd decided that she was really going to challenge herself, and listen to the ideas and instructions of a great man about how you could turn your life around completely. And afterwards, back in the apartment, she'd been joking with Wanda about the fabulous impression Atu had made on her. She'd really felt in mind and body how the encounter with Atu's world had satisfied her expectations, but for Wanda there'd been more to it than that. In fact, she'd been completely absorbed.

And now *she*, Shirley from Birmingham, was the one who'd walk those stairs every day. Now *she* was Atu's appointed one, who'd welcome new applicants like Wanda had once been welcomed. *She* was the one who'd arrange Atu's stays and make him feel comfortable when he visited the London office.

Wasn't that reason enough for her to feel proud and happy? Yes, why not? And yet, there were still some big, unanswered questions. Where was Wanda? What had become of all *her* dreams of lasting change?

And what about herself? Was this what she'd wanted most, only a few hours ago? After all, she'd hoped to be invited permanently into their circle here at the Nature Absorption Academy. But then again, wasn't it true what Pirjo had made her so painfully aware of – that it wasn't for her?

When you thought about all the unjustified words and the suspicion, all the venom she'd brought to this glorious place, it probably was true.

And still they'd shown incredible faith in her with this assignment. Was she really worthy of it?

She thrust her lower lip forward, and looked at Pirjo. Seeing her there, so fine and immaculate, how could Shirley ever have thought she could have done the things she'd suggested? Done what? Shirley didn't even know. All she knew was that Wanda had gone missing, and that a belt that looked like hers had been found. Why would she ever have pestered these wonderful people with her unfounded and horrible ideas? Why would she even have pestered herself with them?

And now they rewarded her with this trusted assignment.

Shirley grabbed the bag, which they'd packed together, looked over her shoulder and said goodbye to her small room. Side by side, they stepped out into the sea air and headed for the place that would help Shirley achieve a purer attitude towards life.

From this moment on, she would do anything to deserve Atu and Pirjo's trust and put all her strength into developing spiritually and rising to the occasion. From now on, she'd simply be as irreproachable and loyal as the cream of the crop here at the centre – no more, no less. She promised herself that.

She put her hand on Pirjo's arm. 'Yes, I'm happy, but that's such a small word. I can hardly describe my true emotions.'

Pirjo smiled. 'Then don't, Shirley. I can tell by looking at you.'

She pointed out towards the meadow area, where a cluster of pointed houses were being built. In this area, they would be building a second centre with its own timber circle, assembly room and eating facilities. This would enable them to accept more than twice as many course participants, explained Pirjo. And the plan was that the course members and permanent residents in the old centre would only meet those in the new centre during the morning assembly. It was a wide-scale project.

'They'll soon have the timber circle finished over there,' said Pirjo, pointing at the half-finished roof that rose above the grass field. She nodded with contentment. 'And when they're finished in just over a month and a half, the team will continue finishing the houses and the assembly rooms down here. For the time being, you'll actually only need to stay in the finished purification house in the new quarters. And it's a very nice house, let me tell you. At least, no one's made any complaints yet. Perhaps because you'll have the privilege of breaking it in.' She let out a little laugh.

And it *was* indeed a privilege, Shirley clearly sensed that. Still, she had to stop for a moment and compose herself when Pirjo unlocked the door to the high-ceilinged, wood-clad room.

'Yes,' said Pirjo. 'The light streaming in from the ceiling, the pale woods, the beautifully coloured tiles, and all the details are fantastic, don't you think?' asked Pirjo. 'And it's thermally built, so it conserves heat in winter.'

'Yes, it really is very beautiful,' said Shirley quietly. She'd already noticed the things Pirjo was talking about, but she'd also noticed that apart from the skylights about seven or eight metres above the floor, there was no light coming into the room. In other words, she'd be spending weeks without being able to see what was going on outside. Every day, no colours other than these yellowish walls and grey-speckled tiles.

'It's pretty bare,' she said, slightly worried.

Pirjo gently patted her shoulder. 'You'll be all right, Shirley, I'm sure you will. Your senses can rest here. By the end of your stay, you'll look back on this as one of the best times in your life. Find peace, read your texts, meditate on the creeds and think about your life. You'll see. Time will pass much quicker than you think.'

Shirley nodded and put down her bag on the small bunk, beside which there was only an unpadded chair and a round pinewood table in the room. At least there was somewhere for her to play solitaire. 'You've got the toilet and shower out here, and it's also where you get your water from,' said Pirjo, pointing at a door. 'We'll bring clean clothes, towels and bedding once a week. And like the rest of us, you'll eat three times a day. I'll probably be the one who brings food over to you, although it might also be someone from the kitchen team.' She smiled, taking Shirley's hand and putting a small blue, handwritten notebook in it.

Shirley opened it carefully, letting one finger, light as a feather, slide across a page.

'It doesn't look like Atu's handwriting,' she said.

'No, it isn't, but Atu dictated it all, word by word. All his clear instructions to the purification-period rituals are here,' said Pirjo. 'They're very easy to follow, as always when it comes to Atu's thoughts. If for some reason you should have any questions, it isn't unknown for Atu himself to come over here to ease the way to a better understanding.'

Shirley pulled her head back. She was astonished. Would Atu really do something like that?

'Well, in that case there'll probably be a lot I don't understand.' She allowed herself to shake her head slightly and smile at her own joke.

Pirjo smiled, too. 'I think you're good to go, don't you, Shirley?'

Shirley hesitated. 'Yes, but what if I can't go through with the purification. Can I stop?'

'Let's not meet trouble halfway, Shirley. I'm sure you'll manage. Otherwise Atu wouldn't have appointed you. He *knows* things like that. He has *seen* you, Shirley.'

She smiled. Had he really? It felt so good.

'Give me your watch, Shirley. Otherwise you're just going to look at it every fifteen minutes for the first day. I'd like to spare you that.'

Shirley took off the watch and handed it to Pirjo. She felt naked now that time had also been taken from her.

'I'm just thinking, Pirjo . . . what if I get sick? I mean, not that I plan to,' she said with a smile. 'But can I get in contact with someone? Will anyone be able to hear me from outside if I shout when they walk past?'

Pirjo put the watch in her pocket, stroking Shirley's cheek. 'I'm sure they will, sweetie. Take care till I see you again.'

And then she said goodbye and left.

She locked the door behind her, turning the key twice, which seemed a bit exaggerated.

Shirley was all alone.

40

Monday, May 12th, 2014

'Have you gone completely insane, Carl?' The attack was launched already in the reception area.

All his colleagues were staring at him. Some faces showed how happy they were that they weren't in the line of fire. Across others, the word 'idiot' was painted, and Bjørn's niece behind the reception desk even had the nerve to laugh, but he could deal with her when he came out again.

'You're *this* close to a suspension, Carl,' was the first thing the chief of homicide said once they were in his corner office, demonstrating the statement with a paper-thin space between his long, sinewy fingers.

Then came the tirade about lack of loyalty and a sense of priority, followed by disobedience and disrespect for the work of his good colleagues. Carl didn't utter a word. He was only thinking about how many people might have been watching TV2 News at this ungodly time of day.

'Are you listening to me, Carl?'

He looked up. 'Yes. And I'd like to know if *you* would've seen it as an example of a good sense of priority, respect and loyalty if you'd been dragged out of your bed and into the spotlight, and confronted with the weapon that ruined several of your friends' lives, not to mention your own?'

'Don't try to sidestep me here, Carl. You've disobeyed my orders, and I'll need to consider what to do about that.'

'You could begin by giving me better working conditions and thanking me for taking the investigation of our cases so seriously.' He turned towards the door. He wasn't going to take any more from that idiot.

'Stop right there, Carl.' Lars Bjørn's face was white, his voice icy. 'You and I are not on the same level – I'm the one who manages your professional life, and you're the one who has to comply with that. If you ever humiliate me in public again, or speak to me again in that manner, I'll send you straight back to the sticks where you came from, is that understood? There are still good positions vacant in Ølsemaglegård, from what I hear.'

When Carl was eventually kicked out, the niece was still there, ready to flash both teeth and dimples.

Carl stepped over to the reception desk and looked at her with dead eyes.

'My sweet little troll. I assume you're showing your pretty, porcelain-covered front teeth so clearly because you want to announce that you enjoyed the show. That it was great fun to see Uncle Bjørn so hot under the collar, isn't that right? Because if not, then . . .'

'You're completely right,' she continued with a smile. 'It was hilarious. My mum is going to love it. She can't stand him either.'

Carl's eyebrows shot up. 'Your mum?'

'Yeah, my dad is Lars's brother, and he's just like Lars. That's why he and Mum got divorced.'

Lis, the uncrowned queen of reception, patted the girl's shoulder. 'You can go and help out downstairs now, Louise. I can hear Catarina, who you're filling in for, coming up the stairs.'

Both the niece and Lis flashed smiles at Carl: an effective way to turn stiff legs to jelly.

The change of guard between temporary and permanent secretary, on the other hand, was not particularly pleasant. From Miss Baywatch behind the reception desk to Ilsa, She Wolf of the SS, with her shining forehead, moist eyelashes, flat greasy hair and eyes that could suck all joy out of you from far off.

Her eyes commanded him to stop staring. Actually, he'd sooner throw himself off a bungee jump with a barrel over his head than clash verbal swords with the irritable Catarina Sørensen during a hot flush, so Carl gave up on his compulsory flirt with Lis and ducked.

'It's not amusing to feel like I do just now, if you were in any doubt, Mr Protruding Front. Why don't you speak to our head psychologist about it?'

Carl frowned. Was that how Mona felt? Was it the menopause?

He looked down at himself. Protruding front? Was she being naughty, or was his shirt just too tight?

There was a vibration in his back pocket. He took out his phone, and looked at the glowing display. It was Hardy.

'I saw it all on TV2 News,' he said.

'I got quite an earful for it afterwards,' answered Carl. 'But I suddenly had a chance to call for witnesses who might know something about the guy we're after.'

'Yes, you took a chance of course, and you'll have to live with the consequences. But I was talking about the press conference. The murdered man in the drainpipe, Rasmus Bruhn – doesn't that name mean anything to you?'

'Not a damn thing.' He looked at Mrs Sørensen, who commented on his language by rolling her eyes.

'I'm surprised, Carl. It worries me.'

'What do you mean?'

'I was wondering why you didn't comment on it when they showed the photo of the dead man on the screen.'

Carl pulled away from the reception desk. 'Comment? How? I've never seen him before, Hardy.'

'Yes, you have. You burned his driving licence in the middle of the street.'

'I did wh . . . ?' Carl waved at the women behind the reception desk, and they disappeared out into the stairway. 'Help me out here, Hardy. I only have a vague recollection. Was it during an arrest?'

'Oh, come on, Carl. You and me and Anker were eating roast pork ad libitum at Montparnasse. Your birthday in 2005, Carl. We wanted to celebrate, but Vigga had just moved out. You were pouring your heart out when this drunken man sat down at our table and began tugging at Anker's sleeve.'

'It's slowly coming back to me. Then what happened?'

'He was drunk as a lord, talking a lot of bull that only Anker could understand. Then Anker slapped him, and you separated them. You and me, together with one of the waiters, managed to get him out on the street, but then he tried to punch us and began threatening us with his car keys.'

'Yes, and I took them from him, I remember it vaguely now. Did I give the keys to the waiter?'

'You did, so the jerk could come and get them when he was sober.'

'And then he punched me in the eye. Damn it, it's coming back to me ever so slowly.'

'That's good, Carl. Anything else would've been strange.' He sounded sarcastic, Carl didn't like that. Did he think he was lying? 'You punished him by taking his driving licence and setting it on fire with your lighter.'

'Was that him? Are you sure?'

'Absolutely.'

Carl nodded to Bente Hansen, one of the best investigators at headquarters, who walked past him and down the stairs. She'd gained a bit of weight on the backside after her last pregnancy, he noticed with a hint of sadness. She used to flirt with Anker. That was a long time ago. It all was.

He tried to concentrate. 'Hardy, you mentioned long ago that you suspected Anker had some part in the shooting out on Amager.'

'Yes, and I'm more convinced now than ever. There's just one thing I need to add to the story.'

'And what's that?'

'You know what.'

'Not at all.'

'When you burned his licence, Rasmus Bruhn pointed straight at you. Don't you remember what he said?'

'No.'

'He threatened you, shouting *I'll remember this, Carl!* He knew your name, and I know for certain it hadn't been mentioned at any time during the incident.'

Carl closed his eyes and leaned against the wall. Why the hell had Hardy never mentioned that before? If they'd talked about it back then, he would've been able to find an explanation.

'Listen, Hardy. If Anker and that man had some unfinished business, we might both have been mentioned as his colleagues.'

'He didn't know my name, Carl. He told me to stay out of it, but he just called me *man*.'

'Listen to me, Hardy. I think you're starting to go cuckoo. I don't know the man, and I didn't recognize him today, OK? It's been a long time, Hardy, and unlike you, I have to constantly take in new inf . . .'

There was a sigh at the other end, and then Hardy hung up.

Damn it, why did he have to say that!

'Lord almighty, here's my hero!' Those were the words Rose welcomed him with in the hallway. Had she gone mad? Had Assad's incense sticks, Gordon's horniness and all her strange ideas finally caused the circuits in her weird, winding brain to short? Because it couldn't possibly be . . . admiration?

'That was brave, Carl. We've already received a few calls because of what you did. One of them looks promising. Assad is talking with her now.' She pointed at the door opening, where Assad could be seen with the receiver glued to his ear.

'OK, that sounds good. Did she recognize the man?'

'No, but I think she recognized the VW.'

'What do you mean? There must've been hundreds like it.'

'Not with a peace sign painted on the roof.'

Carl stepped into Assad and Gordon's broom closet of an office. 'Let me talk to her,' he whispered, but Assad waved dismissively with his free hand.

Across from Assad, Gordon leaned over the table. 'Carl, I've connected our phones to our respective computers,' he said quietly. He pointed at a thin cable that went from the audio exit socket on the phone to the PC. 'Just click on the arrow there on the screen, then it records.' He pointed at his screen. It looked fairly simple, so Carl nodded knowingly.

'I also have something else for you,' he said, pushing a note over to Carl.

It read:

1) Health & Well-Being Fair, Tuesday May 13, 2014 to Friday May 16, 12–9 PM, Frederiksborg Sports Centre, Hillerød.

2) Laursen will come down to your office if you call him.

Carl nodded, and then Assad put down the receiver.

'Hey, what are you doing, Assad? I would've liked to talk to her.'

'I'm sorry, she's a surgical nurse and was calling from work, so it wasn't possible, Carl. Kitte Poulsen – funny name, isn't it? She lives in Kuala Lumpur, and the only TV she watches is TV2 News on the Internet during her lunch break. So we were very lucky there.'

Kuala Lumpur? How lucky was that really?

'The Kombi probably belonged to her father. She told me he was a very active peace activist up until the mid-eighties. He was called Egil Poulsen. He died way back, but his wife still lives in their old house, and Kitte said that the last time she saw the Kombi was when she came home for Christmas. It's been put on blocks in their garden in Brønshøj.'

Carl thought to himself that of all things true and holy at police HQ, this was the most amazing. What half the population on Bornholm and most of the island's police force hadn't managed to do in seventeen years, Department Q had done in less than two weeks. Only about an hour had passed since the press conference, and already they had a bite. It was going to feel wonderful presenting this to Bjørn.

Carl almost laughed out loud.

'Did the daughter know anything about the Frank guy?' he asked.

'No, but as far as she knows all the files concerning her father's peace friends and all the events he went to are still sitting on the shelves in his old office, so we can check ourselves.'

'Let's get going. Have you got the address, Assad?'

'Yes, but hold your horses, Carl. We'll have to wait till tomorrow.'

'Why?'

'Because the wife has just been to visit her daughter in Malaysia, and she's on her way back with British Airways. She'll be landing in Kastrup tomorrow at 12.50 P.M., so maybe we should pick her up at the airport.'

'All right, Assad. And you, Gordon, call Laursen and say that I'm in my office. He's welcome down whenever it suits.'

Gordon's, Assad's and all the other phones in the basement rang at the same time. Now the ball was rolling.

Brilliant!

A hundred and eighty calls and one and a half hours later, Carl was considerably less cocky. So was Rose.

'This is bloody awful,' she said, standing in the doorway when her phone rang again. 'There are all sorts of loonies calling, and they're getting on my nerves. Some call because they want to buy the VW, others to ask if we know the brand of the really cool classic car in the foreground. People are completely shameless, and stupid, and annoying. Can't we just take the receiver off the hook and leave it on the table, Carl?'

'Haven't you got anything more substantial?' he asked.

'Nothing.'

'OK. Then redirect all the numbers to Gordon, and go get Assad.'

Twenty seconds later he heard a roar from Assad's office. Apparently Gordon had realized that he was trapped now.

'I have a couple of assignments for you,' said Carl to the odd couple standing in his office. 'A call has been recorded confirming that the VW Kombi in Brønshøj is indeed the one with the peace sign on top. Listen.' He pressed the PC recorder.

There was the sound of someone clearing their throat and then a dark female voice. 'Hello, my name is Kate Busck – not Kate Bush, although I'm a good singer, too.' She laughed huskily, more like you'd expect from guys like Rod Stewart or Bryan Adams. 'I remember the van with the peace sign. It was used during the demonstration outside the American Embassy in 1981. I remember we used it as our administrative van. I think it was someone called Egil who owned it. Egil Poulsen, that's it, but I think he's dead now. He'd painted a peace symbol on the top. If you're interested, you can see it on the poster we made from an aerial photo of the American and the Russian embassies in Copenhagen. Funnily enough, and quite symbolically, the two embassies were only separated by a cemetery.' She laughed.

Carl pressed the recorder's stop function. 'The entire recording is over five minutes long, and concerns all kinds of other stuff, too. She must have had plenty of time,' he snorted. 'So I'd like you to call her, Assad, so we can check if she knows more. Maybe Frank was a volunteer at some of the demonstrations and met Egil Poulsen there. He can't have been very old in the early eighties, so it's not very likely, but ask anyway.'

Assad nodded. 'I've also had a call. I recorded the whole thing on this.' He held up his smartphone. So that was also possible?

He tapped the PLAY button, and a cranky woman's voice – the type you'd rather not listen to for more than a minute – delivered a torrent of complaints of the type Carl hadn't heard since his mom had explained to his dad why it wasn't OK to sit shirtless at the dinner table, even if it was 30 degrees Celsius.

'Don't I know that ugly car!' she jabbered. 'In fact, it's been parked right next to our hedge for God knows how many years, so we can't avoid the sight of rusty metal and dirty windows most of the year. I explained to Egil time and time again that he needed to get rid of that heap of junk, but did he do it before he died? No, he didn't. That's how he was with things like that, didn't give a damn. But now I guess you'll take it away, assuming it's been used for something illegal. Yes, nothing should ever come as a surprise. I expect you to handle this; what else are the police for? The tarp that used to cover it flew off in a storm and landed on top of the hedge, but of course not within reach. And that happened all the way back in . . . well, I don't know, it must have been in 2003, or was it later, I . . .'

Assad tapped the button. 'She screams like a camel that's eaten sand.'

Carl tried to imagine why a camel would ever do that, but gave up. He turned to Rose.

'Can I ask you to drive out to Alberte's parents in Hellerup? They called administration a minute ago and said that they'd received Alberte's drawings from that exhibition at the folk high school that never came to anything. Why the school secretary chose to send them to the parents is beyond me, when we were the ones to request them. Mr and Mrs Goldschmid sounded quite upset and wanted us to pick up the drawings as soon as possible. Tell them we'll make copies as they might want them back sometime anyway.'

She looked at her watch. 'If you want me to do it, I won't be coming back today,' she said.

He was sure he'd get over that.

*

When they had left, Carl quietly took the phone off the hook and put his feet up on the table. With Rose safely out of the building, it was time for a cigarette.

He switched on the flat-screen TV, turned to TV2 News, and saw his own face advertise a case that made Lars Bjørn's face turn the colour of some poor ginger sod who'd fallen asleep on a tropical island beach.

He didn't think he looked so bad himself. Maybe he should apply for a job as a TV host.

He scanned across his noticeboard, with all its possible and impossible leads. Newspaper clippings, various photos and excerpts from maps of Bornholm, all put up with coloured pins.

Hanging there, it all looked so simple: the photo of the scene of the collision, the community hall in Listed, the location of the folk high school and a number of other important places and people that were part of the investigation. A small story of a collision, and a man who wanted nothing more than to find the perpetrator.

The only problem was that when you looked at it like that, trying to create an overview, questions popped up that pointed in every possible and impossible direction. It was one thing that Alberte had cycled out early in the morning to a side road some distance from the school, obviously a place that had some significance to her. But why had she been there at that specific *time*? It was so tempting to imagine it was a meeting place, that she was meeting the guy she was infatuated with. Why else would she have rushed there at that ungodly hour? But was it all really that obvious?

How had she known where to go? Had the arrangement been made the day before? Or was it always the same time and place?

Carl found a compass in his drawer and got up.

Alberte cycled a lot, and someone had mentioned that she loved the nature over there. Who the hell was that again? He took a deep drag of the cigarette, which usually helped. When it didn't, he took another one. Wasn't it the caretaker at the folk high school? He nodded to himself. Yes, it was. He was also the one who'd said that Alberte was usually only gone for half an hour. Actually, that was quite observant of him.

Carl looked at the photo of the beautiful girl. Beautiful, young and strong, so all in all it wasn't unlikely that she could go at least twenty kilometres an hour on her bike.

In order to get to her destination and back within half an hour, the distance to the meeting place or the place where they left messages to one another couldn't have been more than five kilometres away, if she also needed to stay there for a few minutes.

He took the compass, measured five kilometres according to the scale of the map, placed the leg of the compass in the middle of the folk high school and drew a circle with a radius of five kilometres around it.

Yes, the tree was well inside the circle, so it could easily have been the meeting place and where they left messages to one another. Probably a very romantic place – until it went wrong, that is.

Carl scratched the back of his neck. Nothing but assumptions; the truth could easily lie somewhere else. The question was *why* she was there. If she was there to meet someone, it must've been arranged beforehand, either verbally or in writing. Of course, she might also have visited the tree that morning to see if there was a note from her secret lover. In that case, she'd gone in vain, because the police didn't find anything. Either that or the note had been taken afterwards, although it couldn't have been taken from her, given that she was hanging in the tree.

No, that was too many parameters. It didn't help to force it. He looked at the circle around the school, sighing. What the hell had Alberte been doing out there so early?

'Hi, big boy,' sounded a voice from the door.

Carl turned around. It was Tomas Laursen with a cup in each hand.

'Why've you put the receiver on the table? It's impossible to get hold of you.'

Carl put the receiver back, and only five seconds later the phone started ringing.

'That's why,' he said. 'It's redirected to Gordon and Assad. The poor guy in there's recording all the calls he doesn't have time to answer.'

'Any luck?'

Carl waved his hand. 'A couple of interesting calls, yes. Not bad at all.'

'Tell Assad he can stop looking for that photo of the plywood board.'

'Really. Have the technical department found it?'

'No.' He sat down, and pushed a coffee cup over to Carl. 'It's not boiling hot any more, but it's Jamaica Blue Mountain. You've never tasted anything like it.'

It smelled heavenly. Carl took a sip, and then the whites of his eyes showed. Fresh, slightly sweet, not a hint of bitterness. Damn better than Assad's camel sweat.

'I know, but don't get addicted, it's only a taster. It costs an arm and a leg, and I definitely wouldn't serve it to the mob up there.' He laughed. 'Anyway, let's get to it. Tech have dug out all the old examinations, and they can confirm the splinter that was found was plywood. But after a bit of a palaver over there, they can say for certain that the board found in the water wasn't the one that flung Alberte Goldschmid up in the tree. And the boreholes Habersaat described couldn't have been used to attach the board to a vehicle like the Kombi. It wouldn't make sense, unless there'd been hooks fastened through the holes. But where would they have been attached, that's their question. If they'd been attached to the furrow with the rubber gasket under the windscreen wipers, then both the windscreen and the board would've been flung all over the place, and the technicians would've found traces of them back then, even if someone had thoroughly cleaned up the crime scene, and nothing suggests that happened.

'Apart from that, the technicians claim that the fender alone wouldn't be enough to fling the woman up in the tree. It would take a well-adjusted shovel blade to do that, apparently.

'In other words, they don't believe that the board found could be the one used, but of course there could be another explanation.'

'I see. Then we're back to square one,' said Carl.

He took a comforting drag on his cigarette and offered one to Laursen.

It felt good for once to have a partner in crime.

41

Sunday, May 11th, and Monday, May 12th, 2014

For the first hour she was very unsure about her new situation.

Despite having been left to her own devices for most of her adult life, Shirley had always been a sociable person. Even when she was alone, there were many ways to avoid feeling lonely. Back home, when neither Wanda nor any of her other friends had been available, she'd listened to the radio, watched soaps on TV, talked on the phone or looked out the window. Here at the centre, she'd also had a few friends she could hang out with once in a while. Not an exciting life, but many people had it worse.

In the purification room, there were absolutely none of the things that would normally keep her occupied. No contact with anyone. No incoming stimuli. Only the small blue bible of the Nature Absorption Academy, a deck of cards and a hole up to the sky where she could watch the clouds drifting by. That took a bit of getting used to.

Surrounded by this void, Shirley began thinking her own thoughts – something she wasn't used to. Not about what she normally did, or pressing issues, but about the abstract and unusual situation of suddenly feeling privileged.

Little by little, she realized that she'd been appointed. Appointed to be the ambassador to London, and what a big thing that was. According to the very first page of Atu's manual, already on the tenth day she'd feel liberated from all the usual mundane and unnecessary distractions. On the twentieth day she'd feel purified, and when the entire period came to an end, she'd be reborn as a whole person living in harmony with nature and Atu's wisdom of life.

That was actually why she was here in this empty, wood-clad, neutral room, she needed to remind herself. She'd been appointed! Appointed! It was such a beautiful word, something she'd never felt before. Pointed at, yes, she'd experienced that! Pointed at and poked because she was too fat, too stupid, wore the wrong clothes, or maybe even sometimes the right ones.

Pointed at and appointed – what a gap there was between the two.

For some time, to her great surprise, Shirley felt that she was almost happy. The feeling continued until her stomach began to rumble and the sun had passed by the glass section in the ceiling long ago.

Shouldn't her food have been brought over quite a few hours ago? She would've liked to have her watch now. Wasn't it long past the time when the disciples were summoned to the late-afternoon meal and communal meditation? She could feel it both in her soul and her stomach region.

So where was Pirjo?

As evening approached, she decided that she must've misheard from the outset. Pirjo must've meant that Shirley wouldn't be catered to like the others until the second day. She was meant to fast a bit to kind of kick things off.

Having realized this, she took the academy bible and slowly read through what Atu intended for a disciple to achieve during this purification period, and especially what rituals you had to struggle through in order to benefit fully from the voluntary isolation.

Voluntary! That was a word she needed to chew on. Well, she supposed it had been. At least, she hadn't been forced in here. It *had* been voluntary.

Shirley read on, but couldn't find any procedure parallel to the one she was about to go through in Atu's instructions. Nothing about fasting, nothing about catering, laundry and all the practical details.

At first it puzzled her.

Then it worried her.

And when she came to page thirty-five, she was convinced that something was very wrong.

When the morning sun ricocheted across the glass surface high above her head, she thought about how they'd all be on their way back from the morning ritual by the sea.

The construction team working on the new timber circle would probably be there in a few minutes. Even though it was several hundred metres from here, they must be able to hear her if she shouted loudly enough.

She sat on the bunk, nodding her head. The question was how to interpret the circumstances. She *had* accused Pirjo of nasty things, and now she was here. Was it possible that this was a kind of revenge, or perhaps rather a tribulation, like the one God subjected Moses or Abraham to? Was it a trial of strength, like the forty-year walk in the desert, or Job's disasters? Were they testing her loyalty and faith in what nature absorption could do for her?

She frowned. Why *they*? Wasn't this more likely to be Pirjo's doing? Wasn't it her undisputed decision and act, and hers alone?

Shirley leaned her head back and stared up towards the drifting clouds, rocking from side to side. The greatest comfort during every tribulation had been the same throughout history: the bargemen's songs when they worked themselves into the ground along the shores of the river Don, the black slaves' gospel and blues out in the cotton fields, or the mother's comforting lullaby to her sick child.

After Shirley's mum had quarrelled with her dad, she'd always grumbled that singing drives sorrow away, adding that if you did it loudly enough you might drive your husband away, too. That proved to be true.

Shirley smiled as she remembered what her dad had answered when he was in a decent mood again: 'Easy for *you* to sing, you're not the one paying the taxes, said the farmer to the lark.'

And then one day there had been no more singing in their home.

Shirley was humming and listening for signs of life for about fifteen minutes. Then she concluded that as she couldn't hear any sounds of hammering or shouting from the timber-circle construction work, they probably couldn't hear her either.

Perhaps it was too early to raise the alarm anyway? Yes, probably.

She thought of how her dad had said that hunger could be driven away with laughter and singing, when she'd been grounded in her room without any dinner. After that she sang loudly and uninhibitedly for about an hour.

She had drunk litres of water from the sink in the bathroom, trying to ignore the hunger. She'd done everything to avoid thinking wicked thoughts, and she'd read the entire manual several times. Gone through all the rituals, said her mantras, prayed to Horus, repeated the tenets of nature absorption over and over, and tried to sink so deep into meditation that it would make up for sleep.

After having spent thirty-six hours doing that sort of thing, she began to seriously cry for help.

When her vocal cords no longer obeyed her, she stopped.

42

Monday, May 12th, 2014

'Now I've talked to that Kate Busck woman!'

Carl blinked a couple of times. Had he nodded off?

He looked down at himself. One foot in the drawer, the other in the bin. Yes, he must've been dozing.

'Kate Busck?' He squinted toward Assad, trying to return to reality. Had he just been dreaming about Mona? And who the hell was Kate Busck?

'Kate is the one who knew the man with the VW, Egil Poulsen. The one from the peace movement,' said Assad without being asked.

Was he a mind reader or what?

'I told her how important it is that we find the guy in the photo. I sent her a scan of the photocopy, and she was looking at it on her computer while we were talking.'

'Good idea. And . . . ?'

'She did remember a youngster who helped collect leaflets for the demonstrations. A handsome guy who prattled on and on about peace. And yes, he was apparently called Frank, but they called him

the Scot. She didn't know why because he spoke perfect Danish.'
Assad made a long pause, allowing the information to sink in. So
there was something about that name.

'She recognized him in the photo, even though she'd only seen
him as a boy, you said. Does that seem very likely?'

'Well, she said she was positive he *could* be the person in
Habersaat's photocopy.'

Carl stretched. 'That's fine, Assad, thanks. Let's just hope we'll
find something in Egil Poulsen's widow's house that can bring us
a bit closer,' he said, fumbling with his cigarette pack. 'Would you
get Gordon in here?'

He took a few drags on his wake-up cigarette.

Maybe all these small steps would lead to a breakthrough for
them. Maybe the man would suddenly be right in front of them.

And then what?

Gordon looked more than tired when he stood in front of Carl's
desk. So tired, in fact, that his incredibly long legs were about to give
out from under him. How on earth one small heart could transport
blood through that entire system was a mystery. No wonder the
brain was in short supply and the legs a bit heavy.

'Sit down and shoot, Gordon. What do *you* have for us?'

He shook his head, sinking into the seat.

'I don't really know what to say.' He took out his notes. 'I could
begin by telling you that I've managed to get hold of four or five
more students from the folk school, and that they had nothing to
add to what we know already. They all referred me to Inge Dalby,
whom they imagined would know more, given that she had the
room just next to Alberte's.'

Carl looked up towards the window. Those calls hadn't resulted
in much. Had Gordon been the right man for the job?

'And the rest of the students? How many are left on your list?'

He looked miserable. 'A bit more than half, I think.'

'OK, Gordon, we'll stop there,' he said abruptly and maybe also a bit too harshly. 'So what do you have for us now? The phone's been ringing almost constantly today.'

The beanpole took a deep breath, trying to express something that was meant to sound like the sigh of all ordeals. 'I've spoken to . . .' He held up his notepad, and began counting lines with the tip of his pencil.

'Never mind,' said Carl. 'Any luck?'

Gordon was still talking. He didn't even hear him. A sign that it was time to stop for the day.

'All in all, forty-six calls.' He looked around, as if expecting some kind of sympathy. Did he think he was the only one in the world who'd worked his socks off for a crumb of information?

'Anyway, I did manage to get hold of one person who had more to say. I have her number, so you can call her if you want to speak with her.' He handed a note to Carl. Apart from the number, it said *Karen Knudsen Ærenspris.*

'She knew the man we're after,' he added surprisingly.

'In here, Assad,' yelled Carl.

'They used to live in a commune together,' explained Gordon when Assad stood in front of the desk. 'It was in Hellerup – some kind of late-hippie commune with micro-macro food and shared economy and clothes. They called it Ærenspris, and everyone took that as their surname. As far as I could understand from her, she was the only one who kept the name in the long run. The commune wasn't particularly successful.'

'So they disbanded?'

'Of course – fifteen to sixteen years ago.'

Carl sighed. He was beginning to miss some bloody cases to do with the here and now. 'And when did our man live there?'

'She wasn't sure, because it was for such a brief period, but she believed it was 1994 or 1995. That fits in with her saying that he celebrated his twenty-fifth birthday there.'

Carl and Assad looked at each other. That would make him approximately forty-five today, as they'd already calculated.

'Out with it, Gordon, what was the man's name?' said Assad, shuffling his feet impatiently.

The beanpole pulled a face that didn't make him look any more attractive. 'Oh, the thing is that she didn't remember. We agreed that he was called Frank, but she wasn't sure about the surname. She could only remember that it wasn't Danish. Perhaps something with Mac, given that they called him the Scot. But whether it was because he used an Apple computer, which none of the others did, or he actually did have a Scottish name, she couldn't say or remember if she'd ever been told.'

'*Shit!*' shouted Carl. He looked at the note, and dialled her number. 'She'd bloody well better be in.'

She was, and while he introduced himself, he put her on speakerphone. The information they got was more or less the same, so the crucial, epochal piece of information wasn't easy to drag out of her, if there was one.

'What did the guy do? Did he have a job?'

'He was a student, I think. Perhaps he lived off a state education grant. I don't know.'

'A student of what, and where? Daytime or evening classes?'

'It certainly can't have been in the mornings because he was usually having it off with one of us at that time.'

'What do you mean? Are you talking about sex?'

She laughed, and so did Assad. Carl waved his hand dismissively. He'd bloody well better keep quiet while the conversation was rolling.

'Of course I am. He was a pretty hot guy, so most of us girls allowed him to take us in turns.' She laughed again. 'Nothing the guy I was dating at the time knew about for certain, but still it upset the apple cart. That's why he was kicked out. And probably also why my guy left, and the commune disbanded in the end.'

Carl asked her to describe Frank in more detail, what kind of person he was, but nothing new came of that. Inge Dalby had described him in almost exactly the same way. He was a man without marks or visible blemishes, tall, beautiful, wonderful and charismatic.

'Well, not many of them around in Denmark today, so we'll easily find him,' said Carl caustically. 'Can you tell us what kind of interests he had? What he talked about?'

'He was actually quite good at talking with us girls, which was probably what gave him such easy access.'

'About what, for example?' The woman had to give him something to work with.

'Back then, everyone was talking about the situation in the Balkan region, and many of the guys were obsessed with sport. Tour de France, stuff like that,' she said. 'But Frank would talk just as much about how terrible it was that the French were throwing nuclear bombs on Mururoa, or about girly stuff like the wedding between Prince Joachim and Princess Alexandra. That was probably cool calculation,' she said with a laugh.

Carl clicked his fingers at Gordon, silently mouthing the words 'the Mururoa Atoll.' Gordon turned Carl's laptop around and typed.

'The Mururoa nuclear tests! Are you sure he talked about those?'

'Absolutely. He painted some banners and tried to get the entire commune to come to a demonstration in front of the French Embassy in Copenhagen.'

'That was in 1996,' Gordon mouthed back.

Bingo! They had the exact year.

'I get the feeling he was into theology, is that right?'

There was silence at the other end. Was she thinking?

'Are you still there?' asked Carl.

'Well, now that you mention it, he was driving us all mental with some theories about all religions having the same origin. He'd talk about stars, and the sun, and constellations, that sort of thing. It was a holistic commune, not a spiritual centre, so it ended up annoying and boring us. He probably went on about it because he'd taken a course at university that made him completely cuckoo. As far as I remember, he actually wanted us to build a sun temple in the back garden.' She laughed. 'When he began to rise with the sun and chant in the garden, one of the guys who had a real job, and didn't enjoy being woken up so early, wanted to kick his arse. That didn't end well for him, let me tell you. Turned out Frank had a hell of a temper, thrashed the guy to pieces. Literally. You didn't want to mess with Frank.'

'OK. Would you say he had psychopathic tendencies?'

'What do you want me to say? I'm not a psychiatrist.'

'You know what I mean. Was he cold, calculating, self-obsessed?'

'I wouldn't say cold. But he probably was. Who isn't in this day and age?'

That was the second time he'd heard that kind of answer to that question.

'You seem to think he had good reason to fight back. Do you know if he did anything similar on other occasions?'

'Not that I know of.'

'Did those of you living there have leases?'

'No, we didn't. I actually don't know who was in charge of the tenancy. Someone who'd lived there some years before, I think. We just paid to a communal fund, and then individually transferred the money every month. People were constantly moving in and out, so that was the most practical solution.'

Afterwards, Carl nearly asked Assad for a cup of mocha or tea to keep him going. This was such a mess. How in the world had anyone managed to drag him into this? If this was the kind of dreary nothingness they could expect, they might as well stop answering all the calls that constantly sounded from Gordon's phone.

'Now, now, Carl, we did get a year of birth,' said Assad, sitting down on the edge of the table. 'He was born in 1971, so he'll be forty-three today.'

'Yes, that's right. We also know that he's about six foot one, and lots of other stuff about his description that matches as thousands of people out on the streets. And we also have a decent profile, and we know a good deal about what drives and interests him, so *maybe*, if we're damned bloody lucky, we might find him despite the odds. But you know what? That leaves the big question: then what?'

'Then what *what*?' Gordon mustered the energy to ask.

'We know a lot, we've got a decent description, maybe we'll even have his name soon. And perhaps we'll learn something in Brønshøj tomorrow that'll give us the last nudge, but where does that leave us?'

'Nudge?' Assad had lost the thread.

'The final push in the right direction, Assad.'

He nodded, the corners of his mouth hanging down. 'You're right, Carl.'

'I don't understand what you're talking about,' said Gordon.

'That if we were so insanely lucky as to find him, what would we be able to prove?' He shook his head. 'I'll tell you. Zilch! You don't expect him to blurt out voluntarily that he was the one who killed Alberte, do you?'

'Not unless we break his arms,' interjected Assad.

They all sighed and got up. It was time to go home.

Carl put the receiver down, and the telephone started again, of course. He looked at it for a moment before picking up. *This* particular call might be useful, his intuition told him.

It was an irritating voice. 'Hello, Carl Mørck? Martin Marsk calling from *Formiddagsposten* newspaper. We'd like to know if you've been reassigned to the nail-gun case after today's press conference.'

'I see. Well, I haven't.'

'Shouldn't you have been, given that you might contribute to ensuring justice for your friends – or that they might even get their revenge?'

Carl didn't answer. Revenge? Who did they think he was – Clint Eastwood?

'You don't want to answer that, apparently. So, where's the case going from here?'

'Nowhere I'm going. You'll need to speak to the people up on the third floor. Terje Ploug is head of the case, as you well know, Martin.'

'Maybe you can tell me how Harry Henningsen is doing, then?'

'The next time you try to exude just the slightest hint of authority and thoroughness, Mr so-called journalist Martin Marsk, I suggest you do your homework properly. He's called Hardy, not bloody Harry. And if you want to know how Hardy Henningsen is, ask him. I'm not an information service for people who have all their marbles, and definitely not for those who don't.'

'So you don't think Hardy Henningsen has all his marbles?'

'Oh, get lost, you jerk. Goodbye.'

'There, there, hold your horses, Carl Mørck. What's happening with that case about the guy with the VW Kombi? If you want help from the press, we'll need some details. Is there a reward for information on his whereabouts?'

Apparently none of the others had put their receivers on the table, because now the ringing increased in volume. Just imagine if the press blew up the story, too.

'No, there's no reward. I'll contact you when there's a new development in the case.'

'You know you won't, so you might as well just spit it out now.'

If it hadn't been for Lars Bjørn, he would.

'OK, since you insist, here are my parting words: have a nice day, Martin.'

Driving up the Hillerød motorway, he thought of Hardy's face most of the way. A face that had forgotten how to smile, furrowed by disaster and hardship. If it were to change, he'd really have to become better at listening and talking with him about the bloody case, but he didn't feel comfortable doing that. He knew he had to, but the reality was that someone like Hardy, who was being confronted with the past on a day-to-day basis, was better prepared than Carl, who was trying to ignore it. And Carl was.

Every time the incident was mentioned, an uncontrollable electric pulse pounded through his body. It had caused a couple of meltdowns – Mona had called them mental breakdowns and untreated post-traumatic stress, but Carl didn't give a shit what they called them. As long as he could avoid them.

But now he and Hardy would have to talk about it again, and this time with a new agenda. It was necessary, but he wasn't looking forward to it.

His mobile rang. He was just about to switch it off when Vigga's name popped up on the display.

Carl filled his cheeks with air and slowly blew out before he turned on the speakerphone.

She was going at full throttle from the very first word. Unfortunately, he had no idea what she was talking about.

'I went to see Mum yesterday, and the staff said you haven't been there for a long time. I just think that's really unfair.'

He only knew one phrase that was worse than 'I just think that's really unfair,' and that was 'That really bugs me,' so she was well on her way to cornering him.

He couldn't be bothered with it.

'Apparently, I have to remind you about our agreement, Carl,' she continued nagging.

'No, thanks, that won't be necessary, Vigga.'

'Oh, it *won't*? Well, then let me tell you that—'

'I'm parked just outside the nursing home.'

He looked up the motorway in front of him. The exit to Bagsværd was just ahead, damned lucky for him.

'That's not true, Carl. I'll call and ask them.'

'Suit yourself, my conscience is clear. I've even brought chocolates. Of course I'm sticking to our agreement. I've just been on Bornholm for some time. I'm sorry I didn't mention it.'

'Chocolates?'

'Yes, Anthon Berg filled chocolates. The best in the world.'

At least he could buy those in the SuperBest supermarket.

'You surprise me, Carl.'

Time to change the subject.

'Is Gargamel being nice to you?' he asked. 'It's been a while since I saw Jesper, so I never hear any gossip about you and your little shopkeeper.'

'He's not little, Carl, and his name is Gurkamal. And no, it's not OK, and I don't want to talk about it with you, not now anyway. And if you're stupid enough to expect anything from Jesper, I can inform you that *I* never hear from him either.'

'He's got a girlfriend. That makes us of secondary importance.'

'Yes!' Her voice sounded thick, so he'd have to stop there. He didn't want to get involved in her life.

'I'm on my way through the door to Bakkegården, Vigga. Have a nice time with Garga . . . Gurkamal. Everything will be all right.' He was turning off the motorway. 'I'll say hello to your mum for you. Bye.'

He felt good for a few seconds. He'd managed the balancing act, managed to neutralize Vigga. But while he was buying chocolates before setting course for the nursing home, he was once again overpowered by the feeling that things could've been different. That the past was weighing down on him, squeezing the air out of him. On the whole, it wasn't very pleasant.

Carl's ex-mother-in-law looked the same, except now only half of her otherwise raven-black hair remained black. Perhaps the staff had given up colouring it, or perhaps she'd finally realized she wasn't thirty and a treat for the opposite sex.

'Who are you?' she asked, when he sat in front of her.

So it had come to that. Dementia had permanently damaged her brain.

'Carl. I'm your former son-in-law, Karla.'

'I can see that, you idiot. But why are you camouflaged like that? You're not usually that flabby.'

That was also the second time that day he'd heard that. But when a half-blind, crazy, ancient fishwife observed it, there must be some truth to it. Damn it!

'What've you brought for me?' she asked blatantly, her hand stretched out. You'd have thought she was a ticket lady at some big venue.

'Chocolate,' he said, pulling the box from the plastic bag. She looked at it sceptically. 'Ugh, economy-size. I would never buy that, even if they offered it for free.'

He wondered to himself why he bothered coming, but he knew the answer. If he didn't live up to the obligations under the contract he'd signed, he'd have to pay compensation to Vigga. A big compensation.

'Anthon Berg, of course,' he added, slightly offended, which brought her greedy hands up to speed, and ten seconds later she was already in full swing.

After the third piece, she put the box down on the table between them, which Carl took as an invitation, so he took one. And when the box remained, he went for another piece, marzipan and dark chocolate, but quickly retracted his hand when she gave him a hard rap over the fingers.

'There's no prize for emptying the box,' she said. 'What else have you got for me?'

Thank goodness he didn't come here very often.

He searched through his jacket pocket, where there was usually something at least remotely shiny. A coin or perhaps a bottle opener. What he wouldn't do to make his demented mother-in-law put in a few good words for him.

The wooden figure Bjarke had carved was at the bottom of his pocket – he must remember to put it on the shelf with the other items from Habersaat's house – but next to it was something he couldn't decipher.

He pulled it out, recognizing it as the pendulum from Simon Fisher's holistic garden centre. It could've been shinier, but it ought to do the trick.

'Here, Karla, a pendulum. It's a magical little instrument that—'

'Know it. Good with spirits and that sort, but what would I want with that? I speak with the dead without that kind of nonsense. I do that every day. Last night, for instance, I spoke with Winston Churchill, and you know what, he was very, very charming. Much sweeter than you'd have thought.'

'Er, that's nice, but this pendulum can do something else. For example, it can tell you what'll happen in the future. You can ask anything you want, and the pendulum will answer. You need to hold it like this, and then ask your question. It just takes a bit of practice.'

She seemed sceptical, so he demonstrated by asking the pendulum if the weather would be fine tomorrow. As expected, the darn thing wasn't cooperative, so he had to help it along.

'There you see, it's moving around in a nice circle, so the weather will be nice. Now you try, Karla. What would you like to ask?'

She took it reluctantly and let it hover above her hand.

'Will we get cabbage rolls next week?' she asked after a minute's deliberation.

To his annoyance, although it was to be expected, nothing happened.

'It doesn't work. What a piece of junk you've given me, Carl. I'll make sure to tell Vigga.'

'No, Karla, try another question. I don't think you can ask things to do with food. Ask if Vigga will visit you tomorrow, for example.'

She looked at him as if he were off his rocker. Why in heaven's name would she ask that?

For a moment she stared into space, her eyes milky from cataracts, and then she smiled.

'I'll ask if that new nursing assistant wants to shag me black and blue.'

That seemed to set the pendulum on fire.

Could she be cheating?

Hardy was sitting in twilight when Carl let himself in.

There was a note on the kitchen counter from Morten.

He's in a bad mood, it said. *Have tried to get some booze in him, but he's gone into his shell. Have you been fighting?*

Carl sighed. 'I'm here, Hardy,' he said, and held the note in front of his face. 'Does that mean you're not having a drink with me?'

Hardy shook his head, looking away.

'Spit it out, Hardy.' Better to get it over with straightaway.

His voice sounded unused. 'I don't get you. Now you've got the chance to crack that case open, Carl, and you're not taking it. Why? Don't you know it means everything to me?'

Carl grabbed the wheelchair joystick, and turned the chair so they were face to face. 'It's Terje Ploug's case, Hardy. It *has* been opened, you saw that yourself.'

'I think your priorities are strange, Carl, and I don't like it. Why should a case about a girl who was killed by a car almost twenty years ago prevent you from working a bit on our case? Is it because you're scared of what might come to light?' He raised his eyes to meet Carl's. 'Are you scared of the consequences, Carl, is that it? I saw you on TV, you didn't give a damn. You could hardly be bothered to look at the pistol we were shot down with. Why, Carl?'

'It might sound a bit harsh, Hardy, but you're physically paralysed, and I'm mentally paralysed. I just *can't* cope with that case. Not now, at any rate.'

Hardy looked away.

They sat like that for a couple of minutes until Carl gave up trying to get anywhere with Hardy – or with himself for that matter. It just wasn't one of those days.

He got up and sighed. Maybe Hardy was right. Maybe he should leave the Alberte case to Assad and Rose, and join Terje Ploug's team, if they'd have him.

He poured himself a drink in the kitchen, and hung his jacket over the back of a chair. When he sat down, something was poking him in the back. He reached back to fish the object out of the pocket.

It was the small wooden figure he'd found on Habersaat's coffee table. The wooden figure that, according to Uncle Sam, Bjarke had carved.

The more he looked at it, the more he realized that it probably wasn't a coincidence that it'd been there on the table.

In fact, the more he turned it, and looked at it up close, the more convinced he became that the figure had a lot of features in common with the man they were trying to find.

This Frank, whom some people called the Scot.

43

'Thanks! Thanks, Simon, it was nice of you to let me know. But no, I've got no idea why the police want to talk to Atu or why it's so important that they're calling for witnesses on TV. Are you completely sure it was him you saw in the photo?' She held a hand against her chest but could hardly breathe.

'Yes, Pirjo. The policeman who also came here to the garden centre put it right up to the camera. In fact, I recognized Atu and the VW Kombi.'

The van. Oh God, that too!

'He gave quite a good description of Atu. Has he still got that light stain on his front tooth?'

'No, he had that removed years ago.'

'Anyway, now you're warned. I hope it's nothing serious. I can assure you they won't get anything out of me. I owe you that.'

'Thanks, Simon.'

She slowly put the receiver back. So, they were on their tail, but how far had they come? Could they be here any minute, knocking on the door?

Pirjo told herself to get a grip, she had nothing to fear. How much could the cops really have?

She went over it in her mind. What could they prove? After all, there *was* nothing to prove, and that was it. Maybe they knew that the girl had had an affair with Frank, but so what, that wasn't illegal. They'd stayed at Ølene for a couple of months, and then they'd left. There was no connection there.

Pirjo looked over at Atu's door. Should she tell him, or was it better not to? If she wanted them to be in this together, now was probably the time.

She shook her head. Why confront him with it? Why disturb his peace now that everything was working out so well? They'd never talked about it, so why now? If he was able to manage his own business, Pirjo could manage hers, too.

The child growing inside her was what mattered most. The child that would be born to greatness and adoration. Nothing must stand in its way, neither the police nor Shirley. Once the police arrived, things might soon be said that would raise suspicion.

She looked out of the window. Right now, the area was quiet, the hour of meditation still under way. But in ten minutes, everyone would gather in the assembly hall to receive Atu's weekly briefing. She'd speak to the assembly about Malena, Valentina and Shirley. She'd give them the same explanation about Malena as she'd given Valentina, and she'd make them all express how pleased they were that she was safe and well. After that, she'd bring them greetings from Valentina, telling them that she was in Copenhagen Airport, and that the day after, she'd be pulling the strings in their office in Barcelona. She'd say that the office had suddenly been unstaffed, and that they'd decided to give her the opportunity if she was willing to leave straightaway.

She'd tell them that there would be many tasks like that in the future as the teachings of nature absorption gained currency. She'd tell them that Atu's tenets were being translated into Italian as she spoke, and that they'd probably be opening an office in Assisi or Ancona, because that was close to Croatia, which was one of their potential target countries.

The assembled disciples were smiling, and the atmosphere was good.

With the sun shining outside, Pirjo stuck out her pregnant belly while she spoke to the disciples. Tomatoes had been harvested in the greenhouse, and Atu's lesson had been absolutely wonderful. The impetus for his teachings to reach the rest of the world was everyone's success, confirming that their life choice had been timely and right.

Pirjo smiled at Atu, who was listening silently on his podium. They hadn't discussed Valentina's task, the Italian translation, or the location of a possible new recruiting office by the Adriatic Sea, but that wasn't necessary. Pirjo was the entrepreneur, and he was the spirit hovering above it all. He seemed pleased with what he'd just heard.

'We've been given an opportunity to bring peace to the world with our teachings,' he often said. 'All religions will merge into one, and humanity will concentrate on working for one another, at one with nature and its whims and blessings.'

The sooner she sent disciples out into the world, the more consolidated Atu's position would become, and that would also benefit her and the child, which was kicking a bit too eagerly inside her as she was speaking.

'I also bring greetings from Shirley,' she said quietly, seeking a few faces of people she'd seen in Shirley's company.

'Shirley left us yesterday when I made it clear that unfortunately we can't accept her as a permanent member of our family.'

There was a stir among the listeners. Maybe they were more puzzled than was good. Maybe they wanted to ask questions, but she wouldn't give them the chance.

'Shirley is a wonderful, warm and unique person, and we'll miss her a lot. Yesterday, I asked her a series of questions, and presented her with a number of possible future tasks that would allow us to make up our minds about her future here. To my great surprise, it became clear during the interview that Shirley had a very specific plan. She'd developed an intense desire to take over functions that some of you are in charge of, believing herself to be more capable of performing them. During the interview, she turned out very surprisingly to be an exponent for ambition and selfishness, which doesn't harmonize with our ethos here. So I gave her the opportunity to go through a period of purification, which she rejected while also becoming increasingly angry. Maybe some of you heard her shouting in my office about it. At one point, I was about to call for help because she got so carried away that she threatened to hit me, but I managed to calm her down, convincing her to immediately pack her belongings and go home. I paid back part of her course fee, otherwise I don't think the situation would have been resolved so easily.'

She looked out over the assembly, who all seemed appropriately shocked.

'I really wanted her to say goodbye to those of you she meditated with in a nice and orderly fashion, and in the spirit of the Nature Absorption Academy, but she was far too uncompromising and just wanted to leave. She didn't even want a ride to the mainland, that's how angry she was. Well, apparently that's how she felt.'

'We should appreciate Pirjo's dedication,' sounded a voice from behind her. It was Atu, now standing. 'And we should appreciate her courage.'

He stepped over to her, and put his hand on her waist. 'We have a lot to thank you for, Pirjo,' he said, and turned to face the group. 'If anyone has any questions about Shirley's choice and new path, let's hear them.'

But nobody said anything.

For some time, Pirjo stood in front of the new timber circle, watching the men working, with all her senses alert. The distance from here down to the house where Shirley was locked up for the second day was several hundred metres. She told herself again that it was remote enough. In order for any sound to escape through the walls of the house and reach the timber circle, Shirley would need at least a foghorn. And as long as these men stayed near their work site, there'd never be any risk. But one of them had just left in the direction of the house to relieve himself, and if he did it, others might do it, too.

In other words, a silly coincidence could end up resulting in a keen ear hearing a desperate voice screaming for help, and she couldn't allow that. According to her estimate, it would be at least four to five days before Shirley was so fatigued that the shouts would no longer have any considerable effect. And at least twenty days before she died. That was a long time. Far too long, she knew that now.

She clapped her hands, and the workmen's flexed muscles relaxed. They all looked at her.

'I have a new project for you, which means that you'll have to suspend work on this for a week. We're going over to the other side of the centre, because it's my plan that we should all have bikes, so we can send people out to do missionary work on the island. There'll be great advantages to creating a closer connection with the local inhabitants, and I've already ordered the bikes. The materials will be delivered early in the morning, and then we'll start building bike sheds.' She looked at them questioningly. 'What do you say? Does that sound OK?'

She sent them a big smile, which helped.

With one hand on her stomach, she walked slowly through the long grass towards the house where Shirley would die. She'd considered speeding up the process by poisoning her. She'd also considered the possibility of knocking her unconscious, and then slitting her wrists. But then what if the body was found by some freak accident before she managed to get rid of it? Or what if Shirley had left incriminating messages somewhere in the house where Pirjo would overlook them? There was always a risk, and that was her main concern.

Shirley's weight was another worry. Even if she starved to death, she'd definitely still be a large woman, and Pirjo would have to drag the body a considerable distance to hide it properly. How would she manage in her state, and when could she do it so that no one would notice?

The plan was that Shirley would never be found alive, and that Pirjo couldn't be connected with her death. That was why her initial thought had been to wait until Shirley starved to death, and then kick the door in and put the key in Shirley's hand, so it would look like she'd committed suicide by not eating and drinking.

The only problem was that it took such a long time. That was why she went down to the house again. Not to kill Shirley, but to turn off the water.

As far as she remembered, there was a water main behind the house, and if she turned that off, it would have two positive long-term effects. First, it would mean a quicker death for Shirley. Second, it would give Pirjo better odds if she opted for plan B.

Without water, Shirley wouldn't be able to put out or douse the fire if the house was suddenly burning, and maybe that was the best way to end things. A few drops of surgical spirit and a match when everyone else was away from the centre. Only a question of timing.

Neither the police nor people at the academy would find any leads pointing to her.

All to protect what they had built.

44

Tuesday, May 13th, 2014

'What on earth happened to you, Gordon? Did you have an accident on your bike?'

Gordon automatically held a hand to his battered face. It looked like a complete massacre, a veritable orgy of colours. If his right eyelid swelled up any more, they'd be in danger of an explosion.

'No!' His good eye looked apologetically at Carl. 'I've been in a fight,' he said, not sounding proud.

'*You?*' Carl inspected his skinny upper arms, hunched back and hollow chest. One punch to the guy's stomach and that fight would be over. 'How in the world did that happen?'

'It began when the other guy hit back.'

Carl tried to smile at the old joke. Was the man being serious?

'The fact of the matter is that yesterday after work, I walked past Byens Bodega in Niels Brocks Gade. There were a lot of Danish flags outside, and a couple of our colleagues were hanging out around the tables, so I asked if it was anyone's birthday.'

'Fairly harmless, you could say.'

'Yes, but only until they began to slag you off and make fun of Department Q. They said you were a prick, and that your conduct on TV was a disgrace for HQ, and that they could understand why you didn't want to talk about the nail-gun case, considering what a coward you'd been seven years ago.'

Bull's-eye.

'What did you do then?' sounded Rose's voice from the door. She had her arms crossed. Her entire attitude was too relaxed, so you could only assume she'd had it off with some guy last night or had something else up her sleeve.

'Well, then I punched the man in the nose. What else could I do? It was goddamn *my* department and *my* boss he was talking about.'

'I'll be . . .' Carl looked at Rose. She also had a cheeky smile on her face.

Gordon had entered the world of men.

As predicted, Rose had something up her sleeve: four sketches made by Alberte's rather talented hand, as she put it.

'I've also received a copy of the list of all the drawings that should have been part of the folk school exhibition that was cancelled due to Alberte's death. The students gave their works numbers and names. You'll find Alberte's numbered twenty-three to twenty-six.'

Carl skimmed the page. There were a lot of drawings with titles like *Rocks on the East Coast, Sunshine on Gudhjem* and *Mist in Almindingen.*

'OK,' said Carl, stressing the second syllable, when he read the titles of Alberte's drawings. He could understand why Rose was squinting.

'Pretty erotic titles, if you ask me,' he said, picturing her parents. It must've come as a shock for them.

'They're erotic drawings, too,' said Rose, placing the pile in front of him.

The one on top, titled *Gentle Touch of Skin*, showed a close-up of a tip of a tongue just touching a nipple.

'I think it's a man's nipple,' said Rose, pointing out a few curly hairs around it.

'Well, well. That's not an entirely innocent situation for a young, Jewish virgin of nineteen.' He picked up the next drawing. 'And neither is the next one, I'll say.' It was another close-up. Two pairs of lips slightly parted, kissing with spit trickling from the corners. The title was *Surrender*.

'There's no doubt she was in a phase when she was being stimulated by something or other,' he said, pulling out a third drawing. This time, the motif was a nude woman looking intensely at the viewer with a sketchbook in one hand and a pencil in the other.

'Could that be Alberte looking at herself in the mirror?' he suggested. It was extremely detailed, enough to take his breath away.

'If that had been hung up as part of the exhibition, she would've been lynched by all the other women at the school,' he continued. He could really understand why Kristoffer Dalby, the groundskeeper and all the others had followed her so attentively.

'Well, who's to say that wasn't what happened?' said Rose.

Carl gauged her expression. You never quite knew when she was being serious.

'The last drawing is the one that's going to stick in your mind,' she said, pulling it out.

Carl held his breath, and it wasn't because it was almost identical to the drawing of the nude Alberte in front of the mirror, but because this time a man's face had been drawn behind her. By far the most detailed image they'd seen of Frank.

Carl turned to look at the photocopy on the wall. Finally they had a close-up of that face.

'The drawing is called *Future*, Carl. Notice Alberte's face.'

It was true, there was a difference. The face looked gentler than in the drawing before, but the situation was also different.

'I wonder if she drew the first ones before she met this Frank.'

Rose nodded. 'Yes. Here, in the fourth drawing, her expression looks kind of satisfied, and the one who has satisfied her is her chosen one, standing behind her. She seems strangely settled for someone that young.'

'Exactly. As if she's already prepared to commit to the man.'

'Of course, we have to take into account the possibility that she could've drawn his face from memory, so we can't be a hundred per cent sure what he really looked like,' she said.

'Very possible. It could also be that she drew herself in front of the mirror, adding him as a life drawing. In principle, she could've done that on any of their dates. In which case, I assume it looks like him.'

They both looked at the photo of Alberte on Carl's noticeboard. The resemblance between photo and drawings left no doubt she was talented.

'No matter what, I think we have a really good image of that man,' concluded Rose. 'I just don't understand why he allowed her to do it. Do you think he knew it was going to be part of the exhibition?'

Carl shrugged. 'There's still the possibility he never saw it.'

'At any rate, it's a shame you've already *been* on TV, Carl, otherwise you could've shown it. That opportunity isn't likely to arise anytime soon, as far as I can tell.'

Carl and Assad only had to wait ten minutes in Terminal Three before a neat woman with poodle curls, about seventy-five years of age, appeared from customs. She fit the description exactly of the widow of the owner of the VW Kombi, Egil Poulsen.

She seemed tired-out by lack of sleep and her twenty-hour flight, but she did stop when they addressed her.

'Dagmar Poulsen?' asked Carl, followed by five minutes of explaining and sceptical glances from her before she finally agreed to accept their offer of a lift home to Brønshøj.

'You could have warned me, but now you'll just have to put up with the state of this place,' she said, letting them into a house that had a sour smell of dying houseplants and more dust on the shelves than a twenty-day holiday in Malaysia could explain.

'Egil *was* going to get rid of the wreck out there, but in the end it couldn't even roll on its own wheels.'

She pointed out through the patio door toward an overgrown, decaying wooden fence. 'On the other side of the thicket down there,' she specified.

The wreck was difficult to see in the thicket, and it was still partly covered with bits of tarp, so the woman next door hadn't been entirely precise.

'Want to draw straws for who's going in there to rummage?'

Assad pointed at the broken windscreen, where heaps of leaves had blown in and were now rotting on what used to be the driver's seat.

'Draw straws, Assad?' Carl smiled. 'Do you know the one about the camel that thought he could fly and threw himself off a cliff?'

'No. What about him?'

'He wasn't very smart either.'

Assad sneered. 'So what you're saying is that I'll crawl in to check the glove compartment, while you'll check in the back?'

That earned him a pat on the shoulder. He wasn't so stupid after all.

Carl struggled with the sliding door, trying to ignore Assad's swearing and cursing as he climbed over the piles of rotten leaves.

Just as Carl was thinking that Assad's clothes would be all right with a quick dry-clean, the sliding door went up with a cracking sound.

There wasn't much light in there, given that the side windows were both frosted and filthy. He tried to get used to the darkness, and slowly a lot of cardboard boxes appeared. He opened a couple of the boxes, which had already been breeding grounds for generations of mice, and assessed the contents. Nothing but printed material from various peace demonstrations, similar to the posters that had been put up inside the van. Just like Inge Dalby had said.

Peace meeting read a poster hanging above a leather bag of the kind Carl had been carrying on his very first day of school.

He opened it. The mice had been at work in there, too, but a small ring binder with pamphlets from all different kinds of events, like the World Council of Churches' congress in Bella Centre, and years of Easter Marches, was still intact.

Carl leafed through it. No names of activists.

'Finding anything back there, Assad?'

He heard a moan.

'So, was it any help?' asked Dagmar Poulsen back on the patio.

'No, not really, but we got some photos of the van. Apart from that, all we found were mouse nests – and then Assad found this in the glove compartment.' He signalled for Assad to hold it up.

Mrs Poulsen's hand flew up to her chest in shock. A long, mummified grass snake like that was sure to scare anyone to death.

'We found it in the glove compartment. It probably fed on mouse pinkies, and then one day ate too many,' said Carl, and then changed the subject. 'Do you think your husband had lists of the activists lying around somewhere? Your daughter seemed to think so.'

She shook her head. 'I threw everything away when Egil died. At that point, I kind of thought the grassroots work had taken up enough of our lives.'

Assad was breathing heavily. He still hadn't recovered from the grass-snake incident.

'Throw it into the bushes, Assad,' Carl said, turning to face the woman again. 'You wouldn't happen to know a young guy who borrowed the van back then? He was called Frank, but I believe they called him the Scot.'

Surprisingly, she froze, and her hand flew up to her chest for the second time.

Was she blushing?

'He was called Brennan, Rose. Frank Brennan. And Dagmar Poulsen almost died when we mentioned his name. She'd had an affair with him. Her, too. He definitely didn't restrain himself as a youngster.'

'Fantastic!' she said, but it didn't quite sound like she meant it. 'Of course, you've checked up on him, and found him already, right?' she continued with a caustic undertone.

Carl controlled himself. How annoyingly perceptive she was. 'Well, we're working on it. Apart from that, Dagmar Poulsen confirmed everything we already know about him, both regarding his appearance and personality. She could also confirm that he used the VW from the spring of 1997. He didn't borrow it, he rented it. She thought it was because her husband had discovered the affair, so he didn't feel very friendly toward the young man. But she was never completely sure. It wasn't something they spoke about.'

'When did he give it back?' she asked.

'Around Christmas the same year, and Poulsen was furious with him because there was a dent in the fender. So they quarrelled, Dagmar Poulsen told us. And after that, they never saw him again.'

'OK, I assume you checked the front of the van. Did you find the dent?'

Carl stuck his Samsung in her face, and scrolled through his photos. Twenty images of a front that was completely corroded, and a fender lying on the ground. They'd turned it over, and there was a very small dent, but which fender in Copenhagen didn't have one?

'We can't use that for anything,' she said. 'Lucky that Gordon and I have something.'

She dragged them to the man behind the desk, who currently resembled a jammed contortionist.

Gordon looked at them with a blurry expression. Rose must have seized the chance, while the others were gone, to reward him for his black eye and his fight for the honour of the department.

Shame on him who thought badly of it.

'What's up, Gordon?' asked Assad, his eyebrows dancing a fandango. Gordon ignored it. He'd really built up some confidence.

'The man who took photos at the car show on Bornholm has called. He's a classic car enthusiast who can talk the hind legs off a donkey and insisted on showing us his entire collection of photos of old cars.'

Carl knew they had to avoid that fate.

Rose smiled assertively. 'He only took four photos on that occasion, so we have all of them. Actually, he's been missing those photos for all these years and would like them back. He doesn't know how they ended up in Habersaat's possession, but he probably forgot them after an exhibition at Rønne Theatre, which the Classic Car Enthusiast Club had arranged. All his photos are taken with an Instamatic camera, as we assumed, and the negatives have been thrown away. That's why Gordon kindly declined the offer to meet him.'

Just as well, thank heaven.

'As I see it, you've had exactly as much luck as we have,' said Carl, but it had no effect.

'We had a far more interesting call from another man. And this one we've agreed to meet.'

'All right. Mr Frank Brennan himself, I presume?'

That sarcastic remark also went in one ear and out the other.

'This man calls himself Kazambra, and we've looked him up.' She pushed a print of a leaflet toward him.

HYPNOTHERAPY! was written across the front in big, bold letters.

Carl frowned, folded up the leaflet, and read the headline.

Have you got a problem with quitting smoking? Lack of confidence? Fear of flying? Fear of heights? Involuntary urination? Nervousness?

All that was missing was bed-wetting, fear of water, arachnophobia and a few hundred other ailments. It almost sounded like he could cure anything.

Carl read on.

Albert Kazambra has the solution to these inconveniences and many others. Two or three effective but harmless sessions, during which you will be hypnotized and your problem dealt with and blocked, will be your safe path to greater personal freedom. Get rid of your problems. Visit my clinic, where you will be received with discretion and kind attention by our receptionist.

'Was he the one who called?' Carl pointed at the brochure photo of an elderly man with grey hair and penetrating eyes. There was definitely some photoshopping involved.

Carl studied the prices. Three thirty-minute sessions: kr 7,110. *Guaranteed effect or your money back*, it said, but nothing about what the effect would be.

He thought it was a heck of a price, puzzled at the last kr 110. Was seven thousand not enough?

Rose's eyes were glistening. 'Carl, he can provide us with facts about our missing person. He says he's met Frank. And he'll be at the Alternative Cosmos health fair in Frederiksborg Sports Centre in Hillerød. We're meeting him there later this afternoon.'

Carl smiled. Hypnosis? Kazambra? Just the name! Not since he'd been in a sports centre in Øster Brønderslev thirty years ago, looking at a man who called himself Humboldt and claimed he could put the entire audience into a trance simultaneously, had he met anyone who actually believed they could hypnotize people.

Actually, the man in Øster Brønderslev couldn't. At first, he'd wanted them all to jump at his command, and Carl had jumped as high as he could because he didn't want to be the only one left slouching in his chair. But when the man had wanted everyone to fall asleep, Carl couldn't be bothered, so he'd just looked around at all the others. Everyone with their eyes half-closed, wondering if they were the only ones it wasn't working on.

The world demanded to be deceived.

He turned towards Assad with a cheeky smile. 'Perhaps you should empty your piggy bank and see if you can get rid of your fear of dried-up grass snakes while we're there.'

Strangely enough, Assad didn't find that appealing.

Rose, on the other hand, was ready to go the whole nine yards.

'He's got a special offer at the fair. Two sessions for kr 2,370. That's exactly fifty per cent off. So Gordon's actually considering coming, too. Something about existential phobia, he said.'

Existential phobia? That sounded right on the money. Carl couldn't stop smiling.

A man was standing in front of Frederiksborg Sports Centre, waving a sign: *The Alternative Cosmos is humbug. Don't be seduced.*

'You'll be exploited and conned out of your sound sense of judgement. You'll be led astray from God by all the witchcraft!' he screamed, handing out leaflets with his free hand.

Only a few people took them, and those who did threw them in the bin by the entrance without reading them.

He should've known he wasn't going to be a hit here.

They showed their ID cards, but still the doorkeepers were unwilling to let them pass without paying.

'Try to say that one more time, and we just might provide you with free lodging on bread and water,' suggested Rose, overly cocky.

The doormen grumbled, but let them in.

Frederiksborg Sports Centre was bigger than it looked from the outside, and the amount of stands made the place seem chaotic.

'He's at stand 49E,' said Rose. 'We're meeting him in twenty minutes, so I'll have a look around on my own.'

Carl looked at her despondently. Twenty minutes here was an eternity.

He and Assad walked through the aisles, observing people sauntering around with dreamy, searching looks in their eyes. It wasn't hard to tell what they were searching for: a quick, easy and preferably cheap shortcut to a better and more settled life. The easy way to lots of happiness, personal satisfaction, increased harmony, better health, and last but not least better understanding of self, and access to the world beyond this and the secrets of the universe. The question was only at which stand they would find it, considering the vast amount of suppliers.

They slowly walked past hopeful people who'd already entered the small stands, and were doing strange things. It was a very peculiar experience for a man like Carl, who had grown up on a farm in Vendsyssel, where Kosmos was the name of the neighbour's tractor, and palm reading a conversation between deaf people.

Assad, on the other hand, was enjoying himself, now and again pointing at something that caught his interest.

Miracle Poul announced a sign at a stand where a middle-aged, somewhat tubby man was practising his healing touch. There was no limit to what he could do in half an hour, according to his sign, and the client definitely looked ready for healing of all kinds of things, from gas to divine guidance.

There were people chanting *hummm hummm,* people letting out guttural sounds that would scare even the bravest, and people holding their hands up in the air, twenty centimetres from each other, feeling one another's auras, soul energy, colour spectrums and spiritual potentials.

There was trance channelling, drum therapy, reincarnation sessions, angel dance combined with tarot reading courses, channelling of master energy, healing and hundreds of other incomprehensible things. Each and every one had their specific solution to oceans of problems, convinced that their path was the right one. It was enough to make you dizzy.

Carl had just spotted a draught beer dispenser that seemed to deliver on promise when Rose appeared, saying that it was time for them to meet Kazambra.

Stand 49E with Kazambra's imposing image was empty, but he shared the booth with a very lovely and active young woman, whose speciality was detection of earth radiation and water with willow twigs and pendulum.

Carl pictured his ex-mother-in-law.

'You should've seen my mother-in-law use a pendulum like that yesterday. She wanted to know if she'd be shagged by her nursing assistant. Yes, that's what she said. It really set the pendulum in motion.'

Carl laughed, realizing too late that an elderly woman had appeared behind him with a hurt expression on her face. Could she be one of pendulum-woman's clients?

'I saw how you acted up at the entrance to get in for free, and I've noticed the looks you throw around. You shouldn't be here at all,' she said, almost too quietly. 'What do you know about what these things mean to us? I'm sick, and if I didn't have my crystals and the metaphysical world to resort to, I'd be nothing.' She looked at Rose. 'You're young and healthy, but I'm worn down, and the crystals keep death from my door. Please try to put yourselves in our place.'

'Well, I don't actually feel—' Rose tried to protest, but the woman cut her off.

'Albert asked me to give you this. He's not feeling so well at the moment, so he had to give up on coming today. The address is on the card. He's waiting for you.'

Kazambra's house in Tulstrup was sparkling from a recent renovation, by far the flashiest in town. Hardly surprising, considering his extortionate fees.

'One at a time,' said the man, whose eyes looked completely normal, as he let them in to the corridor.

Carl shook his head. 'I think you've misunderstood. We've come to hear what you know about Frank Brennan.'

'We'll get to that,' he said, coughing. Hopefully it wasn't contagious. 'But I've agreed with the young lady here that I won't do it for free.'

'I see, but the Danish police don't pay for information,' protested Carl, throwing Rose a reproachful look. What in the world was she thinking?

'No, not information, I understand that. What you're paying for is half an hour of hypnosis each, and then afterwards we can talk about Frank. Wasn't that what we agreed – Rose, was it?'

She nodded. 'Yes, we all suffer from something we'd like to get rid of. Your fear of flying, Carl. My bad memories. And you, Assad, you know best what you most need to overcome. Personally, I think it's anxiety.'

She turned toward Carl. 'Take it easy, Carl, I found a loophole in the budget. You won't have to chip in yourself.'

This was outrageous.

First, it was Rose's turn, and then Carl's.

For some time, he and the coughing Albert Kazambra sat face to face in a dimly lit room with oakwood bookshelves from floor to ceiling, sceptically looking at one another. An annoying power struggle was taking place, while Kazambra whispered, growled and stared. Definitely not a comfortable situation for a deputy police superintendent with more than twenty years in the service. And then suddenly – everything disappeared.

Afterwards, when he and Rose were sitting in Kazambra's lobby waiting for Assad to come out, he felt strangely relieved, almost as if a load had been lifted from his shoulders.

He should probably feel good about the situation, but the truth was that he felt his soul had been violated. What the hell had happened? What had this man done to him? What had they talked about?

He tried to get Rose's attention as she sat staring silently out the window.

'What do you think happened?' he asked her a couple of times, before she finally turned toward him drowsily, as if she were under the influence of some kind of drug.

'Did anything happen?' she said, almost in a trance.

The situation didn't get much better when Assad came out. Basically, it seemed they would both benefit from going home for a good, long nap. At any rate, Carl thought he'd got through it with more energy than they had.

'Would you like me to book a couple of cabs, so they can go home?' asked Kazambra, when Carl had asked how long his partners might feel like this.

That was probably enough of an answer.

'Well, goodbye then, Rose and Said,' he said, when the taxis arrived. 'Please call me if you start feeling unwell. You might experience some nightmares tonight, but it's nothing to worry about. Tomorrow everything should be back to normal, except for the small adjustments we've made today.'

'You seem to have got over our session more easily,' he said, when he and Carl sat face to face again.

Carl nodded. Actually, he felt oddly light and comfortable. Almost like in the good old days, visiting his aunt on a warm summer afternoon, a pitcher of home-made lemonade in front of him. Out of danger, just happy and free.

It was a nostalgic, almost surreal feeling, he explained.

Kazambra nodded. 'Don't count on avoiding a reaction, but that's something we can get back to. After all, it wasn't peanuts what you've just been through. But we're on the right track, no doubt about that.'

Normally, Carl would've insisted on knowing what they'd talked about, and what the man had done to him, but right now it just seemed insignificant. It was the *feeling* inside him that counted, and he felt good.

'You wanted to ask about Frank Brennan, whom I understand you're looking for. Let me tell you straightaway that I haven't been in contact with him for quite a few years. He came to me as a young man and made a scary impression on me, which is why I remember him so well.'

'When was that, do you remember?'

'Yes, it was in the summer of 1998. My wife Helene had just passed away, so it was a year of pain I'll never forget.'

Carl could understand that. 'I'm sorry. You've been alone ever since?'

He nodded. 'We all have our crosses to bear.'

'True, true. You said he was scary. Why?'

'For several reasons. Firstly, he's the only person I haven't been able to hypnotize in my long career. But most of all, because I discovered that he'd come to me with insincere intentions. Usually, people want to get rid of something. But this Frank Brennan only wanted to be filled up, and that didn't occur to me until the second time he came. He simply came to watch and learn the art, but I could sense he didn't intend to use it only for good. I felt more and more that he didn't just see me to learn hypnosis, but rather to acquire a tool to dominate people around him. At any rate, I've never met anyone who could manipulate others like he could. You could also sense it on the woman who was following him. She was like a puppy around him, almost as if he'd hypnotized her.'

'A woman. Can you describe her?'

'Yes, you wouldn't forget her in a hurry either. She spoke Swedish with a Finnish accent, was slender and flighty, but also sinewy and slightly bony. I believe she was naturally blonde, but she was henna-dyed back then. A profound gaze, as if there were many things hidden in her mind that could lead to inner struggle. She wasn't in harmony with herself. That was the impression I got.'

'But you didn't hypnotize her?'

'No, that was never in the cards.'

'And then what happened?'

'The third time he came to me, I put my foot down, stopped taking him in. By then I knew with certainty that he'd been acting all along through our sessions, pretending to be in a trance. I also knew a good deal more about what he was doing, and I couldn't relate to it. Working in the alternative world, I meet lots of people who have other people's best interests at heart. In fact, that's by far the majority, and they very often help people to feel better. Often, I don't even understand myself how it happens, but does that really matter, as long as the effect is positive? Anyway, what *he* was planning to do in the alternative world made me nervous. Sometimes you meet people who want to found a new movement, gather followers around them, and when they succeed, these people are normally quite satisfied with the result. Perhaps they gather ten or a hundred followers, and that's the scope of it. But in Frank Brennan's case, I could see much greater ambition. He seemed to have an insatiable desire to influence people. He spoke about the disintegration of the great religions and new paths for humanity. Of course, we've heard it all before, but compared to most of the others, he was incredibly systematic and determined in his work. I believe that if he hadn't been the person he was, he wouldn't have come to me three times. He went very purposefully for the tools that could be used to carry out his plan, and he wouldn't be stopped by anything. That's why our work together had to stop. I was the one who decided that.'

The old man looked at Carl with eyes that were completely different from his professional gaze. He almost seemed relieved, as if he'd been in the confessional and obtained an indulgence for his knowledge and actions.

'We're searching full-out for him now, so I need to know more so we can find him,' said Carl.

'I know. As I said, I haven't seen him since, but for some time I followed him from a distance. I know he founded an academy, and that it's based in Sweden.'

He took a sheet of paper from his desk, and handed it to Carl.

The Nature Absorption Academy, run by Atu Abanshamash Dumuzi. Head office on Öland, Sweden, it read in the old man's neat handwriting.

Carl could have hugged him. No money had ever been spent better than the amount he'd been relieved of today. He sighed blissfully. The man called himself Atu. So it *was* a three-letter name.

The old hypnotist pulled back. His mission had been accomplished.

Carl shook his hand. 'You've been a great help,' he said. 'While we're on the subject of names, why did you call Assad Said?'

The old man looked down at his feet. 'That was a mistake. I accidentally overstepped my authority; client confidentiality is the cornerstone of my business, otherwise it's no good. But that was the name he used during the séance.

'Said, and a surname I never got.'

45

Wednesday, May 14th, and Thursday, May 15th, 2014

When three days had passed, Shirley was out of likely explanations.

She could've easily understood if Pirjo had been sick the first day, and the second, too. But after that, wouldn't she have found someone to take over, so Shirley got what she needed? What if nobody knew she was there after all? Pirjo could have forgotten, or she could have been so sick she was sleeping constantly. Because it wasn't possible that Pirjo was fine but had just left her in the lurch? Was it?

She'd comforted herself from the beginning with the thought that she wasn't in any danger. You could go three weeks without food. But when suddenly the water stopped running, it became a whole different story.

Initially, she thought that it would return. That it was only a matter of time. But as the hours went by, and she thought more about the course of events, she got scared. Really scared.

When the water supply stopped, it had happened suddenly. The flow hadn't decreased gradually, and there hadn't been air trapped in the system. From one second to the next, the supply had stopped, and precious drops had disappeared in the sink while she was looking.

She'd waited half an hour before turning both the cold and the hot tap, but nothing had happened.

Could something have occurred up at the building site? Had they cut a water pipe by accident? At any rate, the muffled sounds of hammering and shouting had stopped more or less at the same time that the water disappeared. Could there be a connection?

She'd tried a few times to scream for help as loudly as she possibly could, even though she knew it was pointless. She'd tried it before, and now her throat felt even more raw and dry.

She stared despondently at her playing cards and the manual that was meant to make her a better and more complete person. No matter how much her soul was thirsting for relief, and no matter what she believed the meaning was behind her being in this room, her body was thirsting more. If she didn't get help or water within a couple of days, she wouldn't make it, she just knew it. She'd never kidded herself that she was strong in that sense, because she wasn't.

In her daily life, it only took a few hours without food and drink to make her desperate. She was such a creature of habit. Always a bottle of water in her drawer, always an energy bar in her purse. It made her feel secure.

Once again, she let her eyes wander across the massive wood walls. Even though she tried really hard, she couldn't spot any screw holes or nails anywhere. The boards had probably been hammered in place so the nail holes had been covered, but if she could only pry one of the boards loose, it would be easier to grab the next one, and maybe then she could reach the insulation material and pull that out. Then people outside would definitely be able to hear her. Or even better, she might be able to kick a hole in the outer cladding.

For the thousandth time that day, she tried to swallow a little saliva but nothing came. Then she dug her nails in under the profile board where the gap was widest, trying to pull it loose.

The only thing that came out of it was two broken fingernails. Not that they were anything special. The women at the perfume counter in Liberty had made that clear long ago.

She rummaged through her bag. She had a pair of shoes with buckles and some things in her toiletry bag that might be useful instead.

After a minute's search, Shirley's lips began to tremble and her hands worked feverishly. Every nook and cranny in the bag was searched, until finally she stopped apathetically, her hands in her lap, the bag on its side on the floor.

She almost couldn't face it, but this was how it must be: Pirjo had helped her pack the bag, and now the shoes with the big buckles weren't there, nor were the nail scissors or file. It couldn't be a coincidence. In fact, not many things were when Pirjo had been involved.

The conclusion was horrifying. She wasn't meant to come out alive. She could sense that now.

Shirley nodded to herself. She should've listened to her inner voice. As she'd sensed, Wanda Phinn *had* been at the Nature Absorption Academy, and Pirjo had made her disappear. But how? And where was she now?

The outcome of an encounter between those two could easily have been fatal. Wanda wasn't one to back off, and neither was she one to roll on her back on Pirjo's say-so.

But what then? What had Pirjo done about it?

Had the worst imaginable happened? Was Wanda's body rotting away in one of the other houses? Had her poor friend been on the academy premises all along, while Shirley had been walking about, naive and oblivious?

There had been days when she'd almost taken her suspicion to Atu, and she regretted now that she hadn't. Atu would have done something, she was almost certain. Pirjo might have a lot of power there, even over Atu now that she was carrying his child, but Atu was so open and made you feel so liberated with his profound, clever gaze. He would've listened and understood. She knew that.

But what about Valentina? She'd also disappeared suddenly.

A terrible thought hit Shirley. Imagine if she'd put Valentina in danger. After all, she'd let her in on her suspicion about what had happened to Wanda. What if Valentina had passed it on to Pirjo? Was that why she was trapped in this sterile cabin? Was that why Valentina had pushed her away, and then she'd disappeared?

Shirley laid her hands over her face. She couldn't keep up. These thoughts were so horrible. If she'd had enough liquid in her body, she would have cried, but how could she cry without tears?

She felt the anger well up inside her with an intensity she'd never felt before. An anger that would make her strangle Pirjo if she ever got the chance. An anger she wished she'd had every time she'd been bullied, teased, pushed aside, abused.

She clenched her teeth and pressed both her fists against her lips as hard as she could. She pinched herself until her skin started bleeding. Scratched her cheeks until she gasped for air.

She needed the pain to feel alive, because she was alive, and bloody well intended to stay that way to make Pirjo pay for this.

Shirley tilted her head back, catching a few glimpses of the stars in the skylight.

In a couple of hours, the sun would appear there and heat up the purification room. The weather had been very changeable and mostly wet the last few days, but what if the sun returned with renewed strength? Her thirst would get even worse if the temperature rose even just a few degrees.

She woke up to a sky that was far too clear and a temperature in the room that was at least 8 to 10 degrees Celsius higher than the day before.

If the pores in her skin opened and she started sweating, how long would she last, given that her fluid balance was already so critical?

She got up and went to the bathroom, looking for the tenth time at the showerhead she'd sucked dry long ago.

Images of a breakfast table with bread, juice and coffee flashed in her mind's eye for a moment. No, actually not all that. Just the juice.

Shirley wrestled free of her imagination, and felt the heat grab her like a choke hold. Under no circumstances could she start sweating. Don't sweat, don't sweat.

She thought about iced drinks. Evening swims in Brighton that she'd refused because the water had been too cold, because she looked terrible in a bathing suit, because she'd been alone and everyone else had had things to do. She dreamt about cool breezes and soft drizzle.

Then Shirley took the decision to undress. Put all her clothes in a pile on the sink, feeling with satisfaction how her skin could breathe again.

She let her eyes wander down her pale, flabby body. How ironic that she, who had always struggled with her weight, was now dying of starvation and thirst.

Shirley shook her head. She decided that she couldn't allow that to happen. She wouldn't die without getting her revenge. She'd regulate her body temperature by dressing and undressing, so it was constant regardless of the weather outside. And at the end of the day, she still had a way to quench her thirst, even though it was far from inviting.

She looked down in the toilet, trying to gather courage. There was still water left in the S-trap, and the cistern wasn't empty either. She'd been smart enough not to relieve herself there since the water stopped. If she economized with the water in the pan and the cistern, and did her business on the floor instead, just like she'd done the last two days, she'd still have about eight litres of water at her disposal.

It wasn't inviting, though. There were still traces of feces and urine around the edge of the water left in the pan.

She thought to herself that there was no point in being picky, dipping her hand in the water and bringing it up to her mouth.

She gagged a couple of times, but when the water reached her lips, she knew she could do it.

When she swallowed, she stared down in the pan and began to gag again.

'Stop it, Shirley, you can do this,' she shouted, hitting herself hard on the side of the head. It hurt, but it felt good, too.

And she was still here.

Throughout most of Thursday, the sun had shone more and more unrelentingly, while Shirley scratched away at her wallboard. She hadn't managed to loosen it more than one and a half millimetres at the most. She'd admired the team working on the timber circle for their craftsmanship, but just now she cursed their skill. This was far too solid carpentry. It wouldn't budge.

Then the idea occurred to her that she could break off the drain-pipe under the sink. She must be able to use a metal pipe like that to punch a hole, as long as she hit long and hard enough.

She grabbed it with both hands, pressed her feet against the wall, and pulled with everything she had in her.

The pipe broke as if it were made of paper, which actually was the case, more or less. It was very thin plastic, covered with imitation chrome.

'*Damn it!*' she screamed, and slammed it against the floor in sheer frustration.

The splinters scattered across the floor.

After a couple of hours' futile work on the board, she gave up, then peed in the corner so she'd be ready to go to sleep and save energy.

Only a few drops of urine came, that was all that was left, and it smelled strongly and sharply. Her body odour had also changed over the last day. She didn't like that at all.

After a couple of hours' deep sleep, she woke up dizzy and dazed, feeling the need to pee again.

It was only after she'd flushed the toilet that she realized she'd used it.

She stood, shocked, and stared down into the pan in the half-darkness. What had she done? There was barely a litre left.

Now she genuinely cried, even though her eyes were still dry.

46

It was a hellish night, and the following day wasn't much better.

Carl had slept heavily, much more than usual. It ought to have felt good, but when he woke up his heart was pounding so hard he thought he was going to die.

He stayed in bed for a long time, one hand on his chest, staring at his phone on the nightstand, considering whether to call the control centre so they could send a doctor. What the heck was the new number? There'd been nothing but talk for the past few months about how bad the new service was, and now he couldn't even remember the number. Being a policeman, he should know it better than anyone. How embarrassing! He could die before he managed to remember it.

He counted the beats of his pulse, and when he reached a hundred in less than a minute, he stopped. That was far, far too many, almost like the time when he'd had his first anxiety attack. Only this wasn't an anxiety attack. It was something different. He could feel it. Something buzzing around in his head that he couldn't let go of.

A nightmare, most likely.

He threw his head back on the pillow and chilled out. 'Humm, hummm,' he chanted, the way he'd heard at the health fair the day before, and strangely enough it worked. People should know that; it would save them the money. Then he fell into a no-man's-land where sleep and a waking state fought against each other, creating completely uncontrollable dreams.

'Hello, Hardy,' he heard himself whispering out there somewhere. He saw himself standing with a mobile phone in his hand, trying to make his friend answer. Apparently, he desperately needed his advice and honest opinion. 'Why did Anker and I shut you out, Hardy?' sounded a voice in his head. Why? Did he dare ask? Did he even dare confide anything to Hardy? Confide – what?

'There's a casket in the attic, Carl,' laughed Jesper in the background, and Carl turned off the phone, but then he turned it on again, and called Mona. Nothing happened.

And then he woke up.

He staggered down to the kitchen, his head dizzy and heavy as if he'd only slept for an hour or was running a fever.

Maybe Morten and Hardy said good morning, he didn't know. All he knew was that the only thing he wanted was the oats Jesper had left in the food cupboard last time he visited, and for them to turn down the sound of the crap morning TV, where overly enthusiastic hosts were talking about trivial things while stuffing their faces with excessively hyped food creations.

Having sprinkled sugar and a bit of cocoa powder on the porridge, he ate the first spoonful, the taste of the everlasting mornings of the past almost like a jolt to his palate. All his senses were flipped upside down. His sense of smell was distorted, reviving smells of long-gone aunts and uncles. The sound of his chewing on the oat was enhanced. The sight of the box dissolved into images of a family silently and stubbornly hanging on to unsaid words.

Suddenly, he remembered that time when he and Ronny had been fooling around behind Ronny's dad while he was fishing. He suddenly remembered how he'd jumped around, punching the air, imitating Bruce Lee with savage karate kicks and horizontal chops.

Carl gasped, almost choking on the porridge. What was happening? Where was that coming from? Was he going crazy? Was everything inside his brain short-circuiting at once, or was it the opposite? No matter what, it didn't feel good.

'Someone named Kristine called, Carl,' said Gordon, his mouth lopsided, his battered face a palette of colours.

Kristine? No, he wasn't ready to renew contact with her, especially not at the moment. Anyway, why would he want to be with someone who'd left him for her ex-husband? The idea was absurd.

'She didn't leave a message, but said she'd call again.' The part of Gordon's face that was still able to express something changed character. 'And Rose hasn't come in. Do you want me to call her?' He sounded worried.

Carl nodded. 'Where's Assad?' he asked. 'Hasn't he come in either?'

'Yes, he's been here. He said he needed some air. But it's strange, because when I came he wasn't here either. I think it's the third time he's gone outside in the yard, and it's only quarter past ten.'

Carl thought he wasn't the only one who was at sixes and sevens today. He pictured Kazambra sincerely declaring that the side effects of the hypnosis would be minimal. Maybe Carl should give him a call.

'While I've got you, Carl, there's something strange going on with

Assad that I wanted to show you. His PC was on when I came in at seven, and I could see all sorts of stuff on his desk that suggested he'd been here all night. Three tea glasses, some empty peanut bags and a couple of empty halva boxes, and then the mail from you about that Atu-whatever guy. I think he'd been Skyping. I know you shouldn't spy on your colleagues, but I couldn't help looking at what was on the screen. It was Arabic writing, so I took a photo of the screen and mailed it to one of the Arabic-speaking interpreters here at HQ to find out what it said.'

'Hmmm,' said Carl. He had no idea what Gordon was babbling about. Assad outside to get fresh air? That had never happened before.

'It was Arabic, Carl, but there were phrases mixed in that weren't Syrian. Iraqi, more likely, said the interpreter.'

Carl looked up. He was slowly coming to. 'Say that again. What did you say? You've been nosing about in your colleague's computer? Repeat what you said a moment ago, and I'll give you a piece of my mind.'

Gordon looked slightly nervous now. 'I just thought that since we're all working, it must be work related. And then it must be of interest to the entire department. Or . . .'

'Go on, Gordon, say it again.'

Carl was listening. If the guy could do this to his office mate, he could do it to anyone. To be honest, Carl didn't like that. Only problem was that if anyone in the basement needed to know more about Assad, it was him. So when you did have a sneaky spy like that in your group, at least he could make himself useful. He could always be told off later.

'The interpreter didn't understand everything, but here's his suggested translation.'

He pushed it over to Carl.

Just drop it, Said. No one is interested in time contracting any more. You are like a feather on a fish to us. Accept it.

There was that name again, Said.

'Why do you think he calls him Said, Carl?'

Carl shrugged, but inside him it triggered a chain reaction of piled-up, unanswered questions.

'I don't bloody well know if that is what he's doing,' he said. 'Was that all it said?'

Carl cast a sidelong glance at Assad's computer. Except for the police-force icon, the desktop was empty.

'He closed down Skype when he came back, and he must've deleted the correspondence. I just checked.'

'Listen up, Gordon. You've seriously fallen short of the respect we treat each other with down here, and you're in deep shit if you ever do this again. I'll let you off this time, but next time you even *think* of doing anything like this, I'll make damn sure you're kicked the hell out. Understood?'

He nodded.

That was that, then.

Assad was standing at the back of the square-shaped courtyard, in the niche in front of *The Snake Killer*, the bronze sculpture with the swastika engraved on his glans, which policemen with contempt for death had teased the Nazis with during the war. If you didn't know any better, you'd have thought he was sleeping on his feet, although his eyes were open. Distant, but open.

'Are you OK?' asked Carl.

Assad turned around slowly.

'I've sniffed out the address for that Atu Abanshamash Dumuzi,' he answered. 'He's the leader of a centre on Öland. I've made enquiries about him.'

Carl nodded. Wasn't that the crucial information they'd been after? So why did they look like two piles of piss with no spark or zest?

'What's happening to us, Assad?' asked Carl.

He shrugged. 'Is something happening? In my case, I think it's just because I've been working most of the night.'

'Why are you out here? Gordon says you've been in and out all morning.'

'I'm just tired, Carl, and I'm trying to wake up so we can get going.'

Carl squinted. Should he ask about the name?

'Rose isn't on top form, Carl, so she won't be coming. I don't think that hypnosis was good for her. She was shaking all the way home in the cab, and when we dropped her off, she sat down and started rocking back and forth. I tried to call her just before, but she isn't answering.'

'OK. I don't feel too great either. I had nightmares last night, kept seeing things that I haven't thought about for years.'

'It'll pass, Carl. At least that's what he said to me.'

Carl wasn't convinced. 'What about Rose, then?'

Assad drew a deep breath. 'Rose? She just needs a couple of days at home and she'll be all right again.'

'You keep in contact with her,' Carl said to Gordon. 'We need to get her back on her feet. When you get through to her, ask if there's anything you can do, and by that I don't mean for yourself, Gordon, get it?' Carl gave him a stern look.

Gordon nodded. 'I can see it's 365 kilometres to the Nature

Absorption Academy on Öland. The GPS planner says it'll take you about four and a half hours to drive over there, so including a break you'll be there at three this afternoon if you leave now and drive fast. Do you want me to call and say you're coming?'

Had he been at the back of the queue when brains were handed out?

'Definitely not, thanks all the same. But we won't leave until tomorrow, Gordon. We're not on top form today.'

'OK. By the way, they called from Bornholm Police. They liked the missing-persons report on TV.'

'I think they should tell that to Lars Bjørn. You didn't tell them we've found the man with the VW Kombi?'

'My God, no! What do you take me for?'

Best not to answer that.

'And then the policeman said they'd started talking about the case in the cafeteria again, and that one of them remembers that a relative of the teacher who died at the school – the one with the pistol Habersaat got his hands on and used for his suicide – said that the dead teacher actually had two completely similar pistols.' He panted. That was some torrent. 'And that the other pistol had never been found after that. Not among Habersaat's possessions either.'

Carl shook his head. What bloody difference did one measly pistol make in Denmark today, when any idiot member of a gang with an ounce of so-called self-respect owned at least one?

The world had gone completely bananas.

And so had Carl's head.

He staggered to bed at four in the afternoon, and when he woke up the next morning, still feeling out of it, he called Assad to cancel the trip.

'It's probably just an after-effect of the hypnosis, Carl,' Assad said consolingly. 'You know, if you look a camel too deep in the eye, it ends up cross-eyed.'

Carl thanked him for the comparison and fell back on his pillow. Everything around him was shrouded in a haze. Thoughts as well as movements seemed to unfold in slow motion. And even when he tried to control them, they didn't obey. When he tried to think about the Alberte case, pictures popped up of Ronny's brother instead, racing up and down the dirt road to his parents' farm. When he tried to think about that episode, his mind was filled with memories of Hardy and Anker instead, on their way into the shed on the allotment on Amager where their fates were sealed. And then when he tried to think more profoundly about that terrible and fatal event, an unexpected stream of emotion and longing flowed through him. Suddenly it was Vigga, Mona, Lisbeth and Kristine he saw – and then Mona again. It was all completely crazy. He couldn't sort out his thoughts at all.

There was a quiet knocking, and before he'd mustered the energy to answer, Morten pushed the door open with a steaming breakfast tray.

'I can't remember when I last saw you like this, Carl,' he said, before helping Carl up and placing a couple of pillows under his head. 'Don't you think you should call someone?'

Carl looked at the tray, which Morten placed on his knees. Two fried eggs were staring at him, next to a couple of bits of the flat toast Morten knew he hated.

'Protein, Carl. I don't think you're getting enough protein. This'll help.'

Help what? Help make him even more confused? And then what should he do? Call for help, or struggle through this London breakfast extravaganza? What would come next? Warm milk with honey? A thermometer in his bum?

'I'll take Hardy with me to Copenhagen,' came the words from the mouth on the plump face. 'Don't wait for us.'

What a relief.

When Carl woke up, his duvet looked like a lunarscape of egg, toast, and deltas of spilled coffee.

'Ugh, damn it!' he shouted, and answered the call that had woken him up.

'I just wanted to let you know that Rose has come in. She doesn't look too good, but I don't dare say that to her. She's sorting the last shelf, and we've received Bjarke's old PC from the police in Rønne. Rose is already busy emptying the hard drive. Quite a few photos of naughty men in leather pants with their bare arses showing she told me to pass on to you. She'll continue working on it tomorrow, but she'll do it at home, since you and I will be gone anyway. I've calculated that if you pick me up at six, we can get there early. Are you feeling better now, by the way?'

At six in the morning! Fried eggs all over his bed, and a flood of coffee heading under his duvet. Was he feeling better? What the hell could he say?

47

Friday, May 16th, 2014

When she accidentally pressed the toilet flush, thereby sending valuable water down the drain, Shirley lost the last of that one thing that can keep people going: hope. Without that to cling to, she was nothing. Throughout her life, hadn't there always been a little bit of hope somewhere? Hope of recognition from her parents. Hope of weight loss. Hope that despite everything she'd find a partner, or at least a less ambitious hope that she'd be able to find a really good friend, male or female. Or even just a meaningful job.

But if she put all of these unfulfilled hopes in one equation, she had to admit that she'd never get the right answer. A hope in one direction had been constantly replaced by a new hope in another direction, which in turn was replaced by yet another. And now the final hope was gone. A small handful of water was all that was left in the toilet, and she'd been sparing with that, so what was there left to hope for?

No, she knew that even though this nightmare had lasted barely a week, it was going to be a short-lived process. All the stories about people who survived for weeks without food and for a very long time with only a very meagre supply of water, didn't apply to her. But strangely enough, it didn't frighten her.

Despite the extreme dryness in her mouth and an unpleasant smell from the feces and her body, her state of mind improved hour by hour. Over the last day, her body had almost reacted with a feeling of euphoria, presumably because her organs no longer had to work so hard at digestion, and probably for other reasons she didn't understand.

Since the fateful trip to the toilet in the middle of the night, she no longer felt the need to relieve herself. Her body was weak and tired, but her mind was more alert than it had been for years. She thought rationally and with a level head. She drew conclusions without sentimentality and inhibition. She was going to die, and the only thing she was going to fight for now was to make sure she didn't go quietly, and that all blame would point toward Pirjo.

Many hours had passed in trying to coax one board free so she could create a hole to the outer cladding, but when she finally succeeded in making a gap wide enough to enable her to see what lay behind it, she gave up her quest. She was faced with an aluminium sheet, and had no idea what it was for apart from that it might have something to do with the thermal properties Pirjo had talked about. Yet another sliver of hope disappeared as she realized the impossibility of breaking through that layer with the miserable tools she had at her disposal.

Of course it came as a blow for a while, because the alternative was certain death. And yet she quickly regained her courage, a condition probably triggered by the chemical processes now controlling her body.

She turned to the next plan and found her reading glasses from her toiletry bag. They were a hideous pair she'd bought in a Tiger discount store in the Southside Shopping Centre in Wandsworth, in the vain hope that she'd be able to apply her make-up so it looked more flattering.

Based on the sun's current position, it was time. The question was whether her venture could be done in a day or if she'd need tomorrow to help it along.

She got down on her knees and tried to catch the sun's rays in the glass to create a burning point on the wall.

For a while in her younger days, Shirley had had the idea that she should work as a volunteer paramedic, so she'd taken several first-aid courses as part of that plan. She found out, however, that she couldn't stand the sight of blood and so decided to abandon the idea. But during her training she'd learned that people who die in fires normally don't feel any pain due to being unconscious as a result of smoke inhalation.

If she managed to start a fire with her glasses, she'd jump into the bathroom and hope that someone would sound the alarm and come running over to the house before the fire was so strong that it took her with it. And if this didn't happen, then things would just have to run their course. The bathroom was a small room so the oxygen would quickly be used up.

Then she took Pirjo's blue notebook containing Atu's pearls of wisdom and ripped it apart, page by page, until there was a good pile of crumpled paper up against the wall that she could use as kindling.

When she had been sitting for five minutes and concluded that the burning point would under no circumstances reach the degree of warmth that a burning glass can reach under optimal conditions, she looked up at the skylight. In just under an hour, the sun would have passed far enough overhead that there would no longer be any direct sunlight entering the room, and her plan wouldn't be achievable before tomorrow. And when she thought about it carefully, the question arose of whether it would ever be achievable regardless of the sun's strength. Maybe the essential problem was that the windows refracted the light so much that it lost its power.

She pursed her lips. It just couldn't be right. Should she just sit here and wither away? Should Pirjo come one fine day and dispose of her mummified body, by that time light as a feather, and get away with murder?

Shirley clenched her teeth together and tried to judge the distance up to the skylight. She'd imagined it to be about six to seven metres, but maybe it wasn't even as much as that.

She turned to her toiletry bag again, emptying the contents.

She weighed the toothpaste, her face powder and her deodorant, judging that none of these objects was nearly as heavy as her jar of wrinkle cream. Actually, it was a relic from the days when she thought there could be a miracle hidden in the product. That ageing and loose skin would be a thing of the past, if only she remembered to apply it generously every day.

When she realized after a month that the only thing the cream did for her was to lighten her purse, she forgot about it in the bottom of her toiletry bag. You don't throw away that sort of cream, which cost almost two days' wages if not more.

And now it was finally going to live up to its cost.

It was one thing to throw six to seven metres horizontally, that much was straightforward enough, even if like Shirley you hadn't thrown anything since you were a child. But it was another thing altogether if you had to throw an object vertically up in the air with such precision and force that some of the windowpanes, which looked as if they could withstand more than a particularly heavy hailstorm, would smash.

Shirley's jar was also made of porcelain, so if she made a mistake the first time around, there might not be a second chance.

She sat thinking about her dad, the electrician from Birmingham, who'd always given as good as he got, unless it was about general knowledge because he didn't know so much about that.

'Try first,' he always said. 'Damn it, woman, if you're not sure, try first.'

Shirley smiled. He hadn't been happy to be reminded of that sentence when she dragged home her third guy within the space of a week. She grabbed her face powder and took aim. The interior mirror might get broken on the way back down again, but just now she had other things to worry about than seven years' bad luck.

The first throw hit the roof a good two metres from the skylight but didn't break. The second hit a metre to the side. The third throw never made it that far, and she already felt a pain in her shoulder.

When she and her cousin used to play around as children, they always took their old aunt by her forearm under the pretence of wanting to help her up. The loose wobbly skin she had there, and which they were free to fondle, could make them laugh for hours. It was all so funny back then, but just now she realized that she wasn't much better off than her old aunt had been. She certainly didn't have any muscles.

She took a pause, decided to drink the last of the water in the toilet, dried her mouth and stared threateningly at the window above.

She remembered how the mantra of every cricket coach at her school had been that success depended on putting a bit of your soul in the target and the rest in the ball.

So she divided her soul in two and rammed the face cream up to the skylight with everything she had.

She heard a cracking sound from up above, so she'd hit her target. Encouraged by this success, she grabbed the jar of wrinkle cream and did exactly the same one more time. Whether it was the windowpane or the jar that made everything in the room rattle when it all tumbled down, was difficult to say. But the hole in the glass was established and the direct rays of the sun caressed her face.

She closed her eyes. 'Horus, Horus, blessed by the star, infused by the sun, be now my servant, and show me the power you bestow on us. Let me follow your path and worship it, and never forget the reason for your presence,' she prayed.

Afterwards, she screamed as loud as she could in a final hope that someone would hear her now that there was a hole in the skylight. She stopped after ten minutes. The house was so well insulated that no one heard her.

Logically, the situation should have made her sad and afraid, but it didn't. Actually, she laughed about it for a moment. It felt totally crazy. If she'd known earlier what a feeling of euphoria came from hunger and thirst, and how light and free and strong you could be, she'd definitely have done it more often.

She got down on her knees, took her glasses again, and focused the rays of the sun on a small bright point, at first on the wall itself and then on one of the crumpled pieces of paper from the blue notebook that slowly but surely turned darker and darker.

*   *   *

When Pirjo was almost six years old, the summer turned out to be ideal for picking bilberries. The forests were abundant and Pirjo's dad suddenly saw the chance for increasing his earnings. As everyone knows, bilberries from the forest are free, so if you multiplied this hundred per cent profit with the expected daily sales to tourists from Tampere, it had to add up to many, many Finnish marks in a single season. In fact, Pirjo's dad sat every night working out what it might add up to *if* the hordes of tourists were supplemented by those from Turku and all the Swedes who sometimes strayed to these parts. The profit would be enormous, he said, as he dreamed of a delivery van and his own supermarket. Yes, he dreamed and dreamed, and all these profitable bilberries had to be picked for him by Pirjo and her mother.

They collected bucketfuls, despite nasty bites from gadflies, horseflies and mosquitoes, but the tourists stayed away, leaving the bilberries to sit and ferment.

'We'll make schnapps, cordial and jam from them,' said her dad, and sent Pirjo off on her own after more, now that her mother was busy in the kitchen.

When she came home with the next bucketful, her mother was sitting in the kitchen with her hands in her lap and had given up. She couldn't keep up, and the sugar was too expensive.

'Eat the bilberries you've collected today, Pirjo, so they're not wasted,' she said, and so Pirjo ate the bilberries until her fingers and mouth and lips were so blue that you wouldn't believe your eyes.

It backfired in the days following when Pirjo suffered from an abnormal constipation that cost money in medical assistance and gave her indescribable pain.

Though not an exact comparison, it was a touch of the feeling Pirjo had just now. The pain in her stomach was indefinable but worrying. If it continued like this throughout the day, she'd drive to the hospital.

She put her hand on her stomach and felt to see if the kicking from the child inside her had changed. She didn't think it had, even though it had become more moderate over the last few days. She looked out of the window, sure that this couldn't be so strange given that room was getting tight now.

Outside her window, in the empty space facing the highway, the team that was building the bicycle sheds had been hard at it all afternoon. The materials had arrived on time, and later in the week she was expecting the delivery of the first bikes.

It would be exciting to see if the project to missionize on the island would lead to anything. Pirjo wasn't a daydreamer like her dad, but if they could just recruit fifty people here on Öland it would be a success.

Four days had gone by since she'd turned off the water to the house where Shirley was locked up. And even though she'd heard faint scratching sounds on the walls when she went down there to inspect, there was absolutely nothing alarming about the situation. In a few days the sounds would stop, and in a week from now she would assume that Shirley was dead.

In the meantime she'd just keep to herself and let time pass.

She got up and looked out at the men, who one by one stopped with their work. It was time for the communal assembly.

She nodded with satisfaction. In many ways the small building was a handsome and presentable feature out towards the road, where before it had been a little too open in her opinion. If they planted dog roses up against the cycle sheds, the view from her room wouldn't just be beautiful and harmonious but it would also lessen the noise from the road significantly.

And while she stood thinking this over, a car with Danish licence plates drove very slowly past. The driver looked attentively out of the window towards the buildings but the car didn't stop.

It wasn't that unusual. An institution like theirs attracted a lot of curiosity due to the special buildings, the name of the place and all the people in white robes. And yet this man's gaze was more intense than they usually were. His age and type and the person next to him didn't point to them being tourists. So what were they?

She felt a twinge in her side and her pulse soared.

Could it be the men from the Danish police she'd been warned about? The man behind the wheel could easily look like someone of that sort.

Worried, she remained standing for five minutes to see if she had anything to fear, and if the vehicle would turn back.

She was just about to leave the room and head to the assembly hall, relieved that her mind had played a trick on her, when she saw a couple of figures on foot on the other side of the road.

This time she felt the rush of adrenaline that put her entire system on a state of high alert. There was no doubt that the taller of the two was the driver from before and that the man next to him was an immigrant.

They were undoubtedly the two policemen Simon Fisher had warned her about, she just knew it.

You just wait, she thought to herself.

No matter what or how.

They had to be stopped as quickly as possible.

48

It had been overcast all morning over Skåne and Blekinge, and the police in Sweden had already been informed about their business, so in that respect everything was in good order. Carl and Assad hadn't said much to each other, the heavy clouds being as evident inside as outside.

Carl was thinking mostly about Mona, but also about whether or not the time was right to find a different job. Would it even be possible at his age if he didn't want to end up as a security guard escorting half-drunk boys out of shopping malls?

'What are you thinking about, Assad?' he finally said after three hundred kilometres and with the bridge to Öland in sight.

'Are you actually aware why there are camels in the desert and no giraffes?' asked Assad.

'It's probably got something to do with food, hasn't it?'

He sighed. 'No, Carl. You're thinking too straightforwardly. You should try thinking more laterally for a change. It might work out better.'

God almighty! Was he going to be subjected to a lecture on brain geometry now?

'The answer is simple. If there were giraffes in the desert they'd die of sorrow.'

'Aha! And why's that?'

'Because they're so tall, they'd know that there was just endless sand as far as the eye could see. Fortunately for the camel, it doesn't know this, so it trudges on assuming that an oasis is just around the corner.'

Carl nodded. 'I understand. You feel like a giraffe in the desert, right?'

'Yes, a bit. Just right now.'

The Nature Absorption Academy was situated beautifully with the sea just behind and with a number of architecturally well-designed buildings that sparkled with order and plenty. Between these clusters of houses with glass domes, close to the water's edge, you could see an open space and the centre of a timber circle, which apart from the size in every way resembled those they'd seen in pictures from Bornholm.

A group of men close to the highway were finishing their work of erecting the framework for some outhouses, as Carl and Assad quietly sauntered past.

'Let's park down the road, Assad. It looks a bit too sectarian for my liking with all those people in white. So if they aren't inclined to welcome our arrival we can make a quick getaway.'

'What's the plan?'

'I think we need to start by treating Frank Brennan just like any other witness. He knew Alberte right up until her death, and we'll ask him to elaborate on that. We need to see how he reacts when we present him with more direct accusations that he might have been involved in her accident. So we'll see if he falls in the trap. Until then, we won't give too much away about the case.'

'And if he doesn't fall in the trap?'

'Well, then we won't be going home anytime soon.'

Assad nodded in agreement. They just had to keep their wits about them.

An extended stay on a remote island would have to do, they were agreed on that.

In the reception, a woman sitting behind a desk covered with a white cloth asked them in Swedish that was both easily understandable and clear if they'd be so kind as to turn off their phone and leave them with her.

'Here at the centre, the residents need to be able to shut out the outside world, if that's what they need. We'll look after your mobiles in the meantime,' she said. She wasn't someone to be questioned.

They stated their business, saying that they were from the Danish police and would like to talk to Atu Abanshamash Dumuzi concerning an old accident. No indication that it was anything other than a routine case.

'Excellent. But our dumuzi is taking the communal assembly at present. In the meantime, we have a small anteroom for our guests, so you're more than welcome to participate, but with the understanding that you'll remain silent. So, if you'd like to come with me . . .' the woman said.

'Yes, we would. But I'd thought dumuzi was a name,' said Carl.

She smiled. It wasn't the first time that question had come up.

'We all have one or more names derived from the Sumerian language. For example, my name is Nisiqtu, "the appreciated", and which I'm infinitely proud of and grateful for. And so Atu Abanshamash Dumuzi is the Sumerian for what our Atu stands for. *Atu* means "guardian". *Aban* means "stone". *Shamash* means "sun" or "celestial body". *Dumu* means "son of", and *zi* means "spirit", "life" or "lifespirit". So the name in full stands for "Guardian of the sunstone, lifespirit's son".' She smiled again as if she had given them words of wisdom that could bestow upon them lasting power, lifting their souls up towards the infinite.

'What a load of bull,' Carl whispered to Assad as the woman led them into a small gallery from where they could observe between thirty and forty expectant and white-clad people sitting on the floor like snowflakes on a tarmac.

Everyone remained silent and reverent for a few minutes, and then a woman came in, preparing them for who was about to enter, saying, '*Ati me peta babka.*'

'It means: Guardian, open your gate for me,' whispered the woman.

Carl smiled to Assad but he was totally gone. Carl followed his eyes to a door that slowly opened and from where a man entered, dressed in yellow with colourful ornamentation.

Carl felt a shiver run through him.

The man was tall with dark eyebrows, light-coloured skin, long ash-blond hair and a dimple in his chin.

Assad and Carl looked at one another.

Despite the passage of time, there was absolutely no doubt. This was definitely the man they were looking for.

A collective hush went through the assembly when he spread out his arms toward them and began to rock back and forth while chanting 'Abanshamash, Abanshamash, Abanshamash' for several minutes, first alone and then – after a nod from the woman leading the séance – all together.

Carl looked at her with an odd sensation in his body when, as if she had a sixth sense, she unexpectedly caught his eye. Her eyes, intelligent but intense and cold, sent an icy shiver down his spine.

'Who's she?' he whispered to the woman taking care of them.

'That's Pirjo Abanshamash Dumuzi, Atu's right hand, our mother. She's carrying his child.'

Carl nodded. 'And she's been with Atu for many years?' he asked.

Nisiqtu nodded and held up a shushing finger in front of her lips.

Carl nudged Assad on the shoulder and pointed. He'd also seen her.

Almost the entire séance now took the form of a monologue in English. Atu gave the people his directions for how to live life in symbiosis with nature, and how they should renounce all dogmas and beliefs, surrendering themselves instead to the universe and the life-giving sun.

Then he turned to the woman who had begun the proceedings.

'Today, I have listened to Zini, spirit of the wind, through whom I have learned the name of our child.'

'When is she due?' Carl whispered to the woman.

She showed him three fingers. In August, so she was six months in.

'If it is a girl, we will call her Amaterasu,' he said, while the people folded their hands toward the ceiling.

'Beautifully thought,' whispered Nisiqtu. 'Amaterasu is goddess of the sun in the Shinto religion. The full name is Amaterasu-Omikami, "the great god of August who shines in heaven".'

The woman appeared to be totally elated now. 'It's exciting to know what he'll call the baby if it's a boy.'

Carl nodded. Probably not Frank.

'And if you favour us with a son, Pirjo, he shall be called Amelnaru: the singer, who will sing the message out across the whole world.'

He motioned her to come up and join him on the podium, and when she stood with her head bowed before him, he passed her two small stones he had in his hands.

'From today forth, I beseech you, Pirjo Abanshamash Dumuzi, to take my place as the guardian of the sunstones from Knarhøj that can guide in even the brightest of light, and the sunstone amulet from Rispebjerg that binds us together with our ancestors and their faith.'

Then he took off his cloak, leaving him barechested, and placed it over her shoulders.

The woman next to Carl covered her mouth. This gesture obviously moved her and everyone else in the assembly.

'What does it mean, what he just did?' whispered Carl.

'He's proposed to her.'

'Look at his shoulders,' said Assad.

Carl squinted his eyes. The tattoos on his bare shoulders weren't big but they were big enough. On one shoulder there was a tattoo of a sun, and on the other the word *RIVER*. The story was coming together now.

The woman on the podium turned to face the assembly, who began to rock back and forth in small rhythmic movements while chanting in unison. 'Horus, Horus, Horus,' they chanted endlessly, and almost as irritatingly as when a flock of orange-clad Hare Krishna followers went down the Strøget pedestrian area in Copenhagen chanting at full volume.

A whole spectrum of feelings came over the woman's face while she stood there, shivering, accepting the disciples' praise. Ever so slowly, her smile grew wider and wider and her expression more and more open. She had obviously been taken aback with the fulfilment of that one thing she desired most in the world.

And then she looked up and saw Carl and Assad.

From ecstatic happiness her eyes changed through all the alarming phases of expression that Carl had seen time after time in difficult circumstances in his professional life. Like when an accused, certain of being pronounced innocent, is handed a severe custodial sentence. Like when someone receives the worst imaginable news. Or when someone who loves passionately suddenly realizes their love isn't reciprocated.

The mere sight of the two men on the balcony caused the pain to tear right through her. All the pleasure and bliss she'd just received was taken from her in an instant.

Carl frowned. He interpreted the situation as an explicit signal that the woman down there saw them as the enemy, that she knew who they were, what they represented and why they'd come.

But how could she know? And was she really so involved in what happened back then that she knew the possible consequences if Frank, alias Atu, was found guilty?

They had heard of a woman who'd followed Atu for many years. Now Carl was fairly certain that it was her and that she knew what had happened.

After ten minutes they were led out because now the time had come where Atu concentrated on a special chosen few from the assembly. The end of his performance had been a display of demagogy, just like that used by politicians when they needed to convince people that their understanding of the world was so much better than others'. This seductive aspect of Atu was seemingly given with good intent, but you never knew what it could develop into. History had provided so many horrible examples of how it could go really wrong if a person like that was willing to do anything to uphold their point of view.

But it made sense that he appeared this way. Maybe Alberte had been someone who got in the way of his project. Had she suddenly become an obstacle that needed to be removed?

It was always about finding the motive. If only he knew that, their attack could be much more direct and effective.

In any case, Carl had now formed an opinion about what kind of person Atu was, and that it could very well be him they'd come to stop because of an unforgivable deed in the distant past.

'If you'll wait here, Pirjo will come and see to you.' Nisiqtu nodded. 'Yes, she's the one Atu just proposed to.'

She showed them to an office with several doors and a handsome view out over both the water and the courtyard. A sun worship business certainly wasn't a bad line to be in, not if you compared this view with the one Carl had down in the cellar of Police Headquarters.

'I don't feel comfortable with that Pirjo,' said Assad spontaneously when they were alone.

'What do you mean?'

'She looks like the sort who can run rings around people and cause harm. Didn't you feel it?'

'Maybe not quite that.'

'I've seen strong women in my time who've caused worlds to collapse, Carl. I just want you to know.'

They both stood up when the woman they were talking about entered the room. She'd removed the cape, along with the state of ethereal, stoic calm and sublimity she'd just been in.

She shook their hands, addressing them in a Swedish that almost made Assad dizzy.

'May we offer our congratulations,' said Carl.

She thanked them and asked them to take a seat.

'To what do we owe the honour of this visit? Nisiqtu from reception tells me you're policemen from Copenhagen,' she said.

Carl thought to himself that the bitch had known that right from the start. Nothing about this woman could soften his impression of her after the look she'd given him.

'We've come to talk with Atu.'

'About what, I wonder? Atu is a very solitary person, living most of his life here at the centre, so what could he have to talk about with the police?'

'I'm afraid that's a matter between Atu and us, if you don't mind.'

'As you saw earlier, he's a very open person and as such is also very vulnerable. We can't have him coming to any unnecessary harm. It would impact the whole spirit of the centre.'

'Did you also live at Ølene on Bornholm?' asked Assad directly. Definitely not according to the plan.

She looked at him as if he'd splashed water on her. Irritated and intimidated.

'Listen here, I don't know what your business is. If you want me to answer questions, then I should also have the right to ask some.'

Carl threw his hands out to the side. She could try. The cat was out of the bag now anyway.

'I'd like to see your ID.'

They showed them to her.

'What are you investigating that concerns Atu?'

'An accident on Bornholm.'

'An accident?' She looked sceptically at Carl. 'You don't investigate accidents. You investigate acts of crime. So what's your business?'

'Sometimes you have to investigate accidents in order to rule out crime. I suppose that's what we're doing now.'

'I think you're too far from home to be running around after something insignificant. So what type of accident are we talking about?'

Carl scratched his chin. This was a strange development. Was it really possible that she actually didn't know anything? Had he so misjudged the way she'd looked?

He tried to gauge Assad's mood. He also seemed unsure just now.

'We're investigating a hit-and-run case where the victim was a person who we believe that Atu, or rather Frank Brennan, as he was known then, was acquainted with.'

'Acquainted with? In what way?'

Her chest was heaving now, so she was tense. Did she think they wouldn't notice?

'It isn't pleasant to have to say it today of all days, when he's declared his desire to share his life with you, but it was a romantic relationship, we can say that much, can't we, Assad?'

Curly nodded. Like a cat keeping an eye on the mouse about to pop its head out of its hole, he watched this woman's movements down to the smallest element. Carl was certain that afterwards he'd be able to recall the whole course of events and her behaviour down to the last detail.

Carl decided to try the charm offensive. 'Believe us, we've come here to . . . what was the name on the sign? Yes, Ebabbar. What does that mean, by the way?'

She was ice cold. 'House of the Rising Sun.'

Of course it was so pretentious. Carl nodded and continued with a subdued smile. '. . . here to Ebabbar after a rather long search for Atu. I have to stress that we've only been looking for him as a matter of routine. We've got a lot of other leads to follow in this case, but the temptation to take a trip to this beautiful place was honestly just too great,' he said.

Carl thought to himself that the temptation to kick her out was just as strong, so they could be left in peace and quiet to wait for Atu alone. The questioning that lay in front of them would hopefully be quick, successful and result in Atu's arrest, which would be guaranteed to leave the woman here angry. Like a lioness, she would protect her mate, so they just needed to get her out of the way first.

'You need to understand that our work has many aspects. You could say that we're experts in distinguishing between secrets and what just remains unsaid. Because those things don't necessarily need to be the same thing, do they?'

She smiled drolly at them. Carl didn't like it. He felt as if she'd seen right through him.

'So what are we searching for, the secret or the unsaid?' she asked. 'Can you also differentiate here?'

'Yes, we think so, but we need more information. So I'd like to ask if we can have a little look around Atu's rooms while we're waiting,' Assad threw in.

Where on earth was he going with this?

'No, of course you can't. Not even I have that sort of access without his express authority and consent.'

'No, I thought as much,' said Assad. 'Incidentally, are you often visited by the Swedish authorities out here?'

She frowned. 'I don't really follow where you're going with that sort of idiotic and irrelevant question.'

'Right, but I can tell you that maybe Atu is hiding something from you and the Swedish authorities, something you can't even imagine, precisely because he is as he is. It could be so many things: tax evasion, abusing the women at the centre, being in possession of stolen goods. You never know what goes on in a place like this before you've checked, do you?'

Something was going on behind the look she was throwing them, and he couldn't work out where it might lead. Normally, a person would flare up at such an outrageous attack like the one Assad was carrying out just now, regardless of whether or not they were guilty. But she just sat there and observed them, as if they were worth less than the dirt on her shoe. She appeared completely indifferent.

'Just a moment,' she said, and got up, opened the door out to the corridor, and disappeared.

'What are you up to, Assad? You're right off with that tactic,' whispered Carl.

'I don't think so. I'm trying to stress her out. She's as cold as ice. I'm thinking that if she's like that, Atu probably is, too. So we'll be driving home in an hour without a leg to stand on, and what then?' he whispered back. 'You've said it before, Carl. We *don't* have anything to go on. No concrete evidence or witnesses. We need to stress her out and probably Atu, too, if he even . . .'

Carl only registered the shadow when he saw it swing a heavy rubber mallet towards Assad's head.

He was about to jump, but didn't make it before the next swing hit him.

He momentarily managed to catch a glimpse of her bending over him to pick something up.

When she lifted the small wooden figure, which he'd had in his pocket, up to her face, everything went black.

49

Pirjo was shaking all over.

She knew it was the most stupid thing she'd ever done. She'd overreacted and painted herself into a corner. Yet she still couldn't reproach herself.

Behind the door to the room with the electrical control system lay two unconscious men who'd just spoiled the most precious moment in her life. Ever. Two blasphemers who'd trespassed on holy ground at a moment that would shape her future. Maybe the one extreme attracted the other. All her life she'd dreamt of a future like this, and now that it was within reach she wouldn't let them get in the way.

But what should she do? They weren't just anybody. Not vulnerable or naive women who could suddenly disappear. They were policemen in the middle of an investigation, which she neither knew the extent of, or who was involved. This was information she simply needed to get hold of before she could assess the danger and how she should react going forward.

One thing was certain: they had to be stopped. The question was how.

She noticed dark red blotches spreading treacherously on her forearms, and how they began to itch.

It was the mixture of adrenaline and frustration, she knew it all too well.

In an hour Atu would be finished with his coaching and come in to her, expecting embraces and ill-concealed happiness.

In an hour.

Pirjo's head was full of what she had to find out and what she had to do. She had to force them to tell her what was lying in wait after them; how many she should expect and who they were; what they knew and how many people they'd told; and she needed to make it look like an accident – an accident that might well make you wonder, but not doubt.

She looked at the door leading to the control room. Now and again she felt stomach cramps, and the men were big and strong, so how could she neutralize them with such a disparity in strength. In better circumstances, the most logical thing to do would be to kill them with a tool that was heavier than a rubber mallet. The wrench lying on the floor in there, for example. But a blow like that would be deeper, and subsequently analysed as having been inflicted by a third party, so that wouldn't do.

'If only they hadn't been so insistent,' she snarled in frustration. They'd gone at her too hard. It wasn't how these things were supposed to happen. She'd expected questions and answers that she'd have been able to shoot down with ease. There were so very many ways you could get around that sort of thing, especially when the case was so old, but not when they were so aggressive.

Actually, she felt certain that the dark one would have taken it to extremes that a civilized police force couldn't stomach. And she was equally certain that the two men would've softened up

Atu in a confrontation. If they'd been successful in that, the whole truth would've come out and everything would've been lost on this otherwise miraculous day.

She looked at the wooden figure that'd fallen out of the Danish policeman's pocket, and frowned. Someone or other had carved a wooden figure many years ago of the man who'd just proposed to her. The likeness was uncanny.

Pirjo wondered how these policemen had come to be in possession of it, and why one of them had it in his pocket. Was that their tactic? To slam the figure down on the table in front of Atu, like a bolt from the blue, in the hope that it would shock him and knock him off-balance?

She imagined the type of questions they'd ask. Do you deny that the figure is carved in your likeness? Do you deny all knowledge of someone who has seen you so clearly and at such close quarters?

They'd try to soften him up with that figure, and it might work.

Pirjo had no doubt who the artist was. It was that bitch Alberte who used to plague Atu. It was her special form of voodoo doll, intended to bewitch him and keep him trapped in a net of stipulations and demands from which he couldn't escape.

Yes, she was certain that this was her doing, so it was good they'd managed to break the curse and get rid of her. There was no knowing what might have happened otherwise.

And the more she thought back to the time when it had happened, the more she hated the people that had brought back the memory of Alberte.

She clenched the figure in her hand and was about to slam it on the floor, but looked closer at the finely carved face and the beautiful mouth. It was almost like bringing back Frank as a young man, and that moved her. So simple and straightforward everything had been back then.

And yet so complicated that everything had gone wrong.

All because of Alberte.

She put the figure to her cheek, moved it a little, and kissed the lips in memory of lost days of innocence.

Then she heard a noise from the corridor behind her and put the figure down on the table. It was one of the two men out there, moaning.

In the following seconds she made some radical decisions and acted accordingly. When she stood in the control room she saw that both men were still lying spread out on the floor and that the immigrant was trying to lift his head a little. She'd need to deal with him first.

She rolled the cylinder with non-insulated cable forward, pulled the man's shirtsleeves down to the heels of his hands and wound the cable around his arms at least ten times so they were tightly bound together. She then pulled him up to the bench and tied him securely. First around his ankles, then his thighs around the bench and after that she bound his body tightly to a pair of old butcher's hooks on the wall. When she was finished with him, she did exactly the same with the other man. He wasn't much heavier than the immigrant, despite the difference in size, but he was completely limp, so it wasn't easy, not least because Pirjo was feeling sick. So she stood for a moment and recovered herself until her stomach didn't feel so strange.

Then she tied their bodies together with the cable and took a step back to scrutinize her work.

She went over the scenario in her head, wondering if she'd done anything wrong or overlooked any details.

It might be possible to trace the men via their phone signal, but the mobiles had probably been confiscated and turned off in reception. And then there was the car she'd seen pass by. It was probably parked some distance down the road, but it couldn't stay there; it was too close.

She fished out the car keys from the pocket of the larger of the two men, checking again to see if everything was as it should be. They were securely bound together, and nobody came in this room except her. The electrician wasn't expected back for a few days, so that gave her enough time. Next, there was Nisiqtu, who'd welcomed them, but then hadn't it been Pirjo herself who'd given her the name 'the appreciated'?

Yes, she'd definitely believe Pirjo when she claimed that the men had caused the accident themselves.

Now the immigrant was seriously starting to come round, so there was no time to waste. She judged the distance up to the junction box and cut two pieces of cable in lengths of three metres, winding one around the base of the immigrant's thumb and the other around the policeman's left ankle.

She looked at the junction box where all the different solar-system cables were gathered together, unscrewing the cap. Unknowingly, an electrician and Shirley had each told her how she could apply torture and much worse. The direct current would only cause a little stinging sensation for the person the current was sent through, so long as the sun was weak. But the stronger the sun, the more dangerous it would become. It would kill them eventually.

She nodded, taking a screwdriver with an insulated handle from the pile of tools under the bench, and loosened the two cable lugs that sent the current to the inverter. The direct current effect from the two cable lugs came from all the solar panels, creating an optimal effect. Were the sun to shine brighter, the voltage would be enormous.

She pulled the end of the cable that was wound around the immigrant's thumb up to the junction box, connecting it to the positive pole, and then similarly the cable from the big man's ankle to the negative pole.

In the same second that she connected the second cable, every muscle contracted in the two men's faces, and all four legs shot suddenly forward. The immigrant's leg kicked her hard in the stomach, causing her to sink to her knees.

She grabbed her abdomen, looking up at the men, who were both sitting with their eyes open, staring, while everything inside her was screaming that she had to get out.

She stumbled into her office and sat down for a moment by the desk, groaning until the pain subsided. She was momentarily scared, but then turned her attention to what needed to be done, looked at the clock and got up again.

'I'm just popping out for ten minutes to get some fresh air, Nisiqtu,' she said to the woman in reception. 'There won't be anything else today, so you can return to your room now. I'll serve tea for the men myself when I get back.'

They smiled to each other. No danger there.

The police vehicle was a short way down the highway, parked to one side but very visible.

She rooted about in the glove compartment, opened the trunk and checked the interior, but found nothing about the investigation that had led them here.

She started the car and parked it a few hundred metres down a small connecting road that nobody used any more. It gave her a bit more control over the situation. If more police turned up in the immediate future, she could maintain that they'd driven off but said they'd be back again.

No one should enter the centre and pry as long as those two men were still alive. And when they were dead, she'd consider whether or not it could appear to be an accident, or whether she needed to get rid of them. In any case, when the time came she'd go down and take the licence plates off the car and make sure it ended up in Poland or some other obscure place. The Poles and Balts who drove around begging to paint the houses red could have it for a song if they agreed to take it far away. They could have the licence plates from the old car sitting gathering dust in the back of the Stable of Senses. It wasn't going to be used again anyway.

She walked back towards the academy, looking up at the sky. The clouds were still heavy but an easterly breeze looked to be blowing them away from the coast.

She thought about how the sun would soon be shining again, massaging her stomach as she walked in the door to the reception. It'd been a long time now since the baby had kicked.

'Come on, sweetheart,' she whispered. 'Are you so tired? It's been a special day so Mum's a bit tired, too,' she muttered. 'Dad's chosen your name, so you can be happy about that. And when you're born, we'll name you on the same day as Dad and I are joined together under the sun in the timber circle. It'll be a great day, sweetheart.'

She screwed her eyes shut as sudden discomfort shot through her. It was a really nasty feeling, as if something in her body was completely off-balance.

She thought to herself that something really wasn't as it should be, as the sweat poured off her. She needed to get to the clinic in Kalmar and get it checked, but first she needed to know what she was up against. The men needed to answer her questions, and then she needed to get going.

They both sat with quivering jaws and tense neck muscles, staring at her as she entered the room.

The immigrant tried to hiss something at her, but the words became distorted by the contractions in his neck.

She took her screwdriver and unscrewed one of the cables from the junction box.

They both collapsed at once, their heads hanging on their chests.

'You should be glad that the sun isn't out at the moment,' she said, as they slowly lifted their heads.

She looked up towards the skylight and noticed as the men's eyes followed hers.

'You're crazy,' said the larger of the two. 'You could kill us.'

She smiled. Did he think she was crazy? Dear God, he had no idea how much was at stake. The whole world was waiting for this centre to spread the message so that all religions could be united and the world could live in peace. Who did these two insignificant people think they were that they could stand in the way of that vision?

Her smile hardened. 'What do you know?' she said, sticking the cable back in the cable lug with the effect that both men's legs kicked out and their backs arched. This time she knew from bitter experience to keep a safe distance.

'I'm well aware that the effect isn't much at the moment. Maybe it just feels like an internal massage, right? But just wait until later, when the sun comes out again. Then it'll be worse. Much worse.'

She pulled the cable to her again, causing the men to fall back, albeit not as much as last time. Maybe you could get used to this level of current.

'What do you know?' she asked again.

The big man coughed a couple of times before answering. 'We know everything and we aren't alone in that knowledge. Your Atu killed a girl in a hit-and-run years back, and now the past has caught up with him. So don't make it any worse for yourself than it already is. Let us go, Pirjo. We . . .'

She pressed the cable against the cable lug again and the whole scenario repeated itself. After a few seconds, she let them off.

If they wouldn't spit it out now, it would be the last time she'd try.

'Are there more of you?' she asked.

The big one tried to nod. 'Of course. Atu's been under suspicion for a long time. A policeman is dead as a result of this investigation. Atu's left a trail of death and misery. Why are you protecting him? He isn't worth it, Pirjo. There's no reason to . . .'

He gasped for air when she once again pressed the cable against the cable lug. This time she screwed it tight and turned her back on the men.

Now she knew that what would be, would be. The men couldn't say anything to her to ease her worry. The immigrant hadn't even said a word. He'd just stared at her with cold eyes, as if he might kill her with a look. No, she'd done the right thing.

She looked up at the floating clouds, and then the twinge came again, only this time like a knife being stabbed in her stomach. It almost felt as if the baby inside her turned right round with one jerk. As if it was the fetus rather than the men who'd been subjected to the current.

Pirjo staggered through the corridor, slammed the door behind her and fell down in the office chair. She took a few deep breaths, deep down into her lungs, in an attempt to get her pulse under control, but without success. Her arms began to shake and her skin became cold. Something was very wrong. Was it a psychological reaction to what she was about to do? She didn't feel anything about it, but could that still be the reason? Was her conscience awakening? Was it a type of trial or punishment? She couldn't believe it. She implored Horus as the pain in her abdomen increased, praying to him to deliver her from this tribulation.

'I'm doing it with the best of intentions!' she screamed.

And then it stopped as suddenly as it had begun.

It was with a sigh of relief that she went to stand up, but then she realized to her horror that her legs wouldn't obey.

Then she noticed the blood.

Blood on the seat of the chair and blood on the white robe.

Blood that ran warm down her leg, dripping on the floor under the table.

*　　*　　*

Carl could only think of three short words, the rest of him being no more than a body: *not long now.* In the beginning, it felt as if his whole body was bubbling, like when you have a dead arm, but then all his muscles contracted and seized up. Even the tiny muscles in his eyelids and nostrils tightened and stiffened. It almost felt as if his body was slowly burning up. Suddenly his heart was beating extra systoles, and his brain sporadically short-circuiting in flashes of light, while his lungs were increasingly ceasing to respond to the lack of oxygen. And the more light that the cloud cover let through, the stronger the effect of the current, and the more the words 'not long now' made sense.

Carl didn't feel Assad next to him at all. He only remembered in glimpses that they sat securely tied to one another. Only in glimpses did he remember where he was.

Then the current suddenly became weaker. He gasped, breathing heavily. There was still an electric trembling in his body, but nothing compared to before. He looked around in confusion. It was bright in the room. Maybe even brighter than before. What was going on?

He heard a moan coming from beside him.

He sat for a moment, trying to get his neck muscles to obey. They were still as hard as stone. With difficulty, he managed to turn his head toward Assad, seeing his grave face contorted with pain.

Carl coughed when he tried to talk, but he did get the words out. 'What's happening, Assad?'

A moment passed before he answered in short breaths.

'There's an earth connection . . . in . . . the wall.'

Carl turned his head a fraction more. At first he didn't understand what Assad meant. The wall was metal of some sort, he could see that, but what did that matter?

Then he noticed a faint smell of burning flesh and tried to work out where it was coming from.

Now he saw one of Assad's arms twitching. He'd raised his bound arms in towards the wall as much as he could, pressing his thumb, which the cable was wound around, against the metal wall.

A very weak trace of smoke rose up from it. That was what he'd been able to smell.

'The current . . . doesn't get . . . any further,' he mumbled.

Carl looked at the finger and the nail that was slowly turning brown, and the tip even darker. It was shocking to look at. Carl knew enough about current to know that Assad was sacrificing his finger for them. Just now, current was accumulating from a crazy number of solar cells down to the cable wound around Assad's thumb, and from there onto the metal wall.

Wasn't it his physics teacher who'd said that current always finds the shortest route to discharge?

'Can't you manage to twist your hand and press the cable directly onto the wall, Assad?' he asked tentatively.

Assad shook his head tensely. 'Arghh,' he mumbled, when a cloud suddenly drifted past over them. For one second the pain caused him to release his pressure against the metal wall, causing Carl to hit his neck against the wall and his arms to spasm.

Just until the next cloud came.

He noticed Assad twitching, and then the current disappeared again from Carl's body.

Assad gasped beside him. It was unbearable to watch. It couldn't continue like this for long.

Carl took a deep breath. 'When the sun breaks right through, Assad, let go. The pain will be over . . . in a moment,' he heard himself say. It was awful to think about, but what if he was wrong? If it wasn't over in a moment?

'But before you let go, I need to know, why . . .' He reconsidered for a moment. Did he really want to know?

'Know . . . what?' groaned Assad.

'Said! Why do they call you that? Is that your real name?'

For a moment, it went completely quiet next to him. He shouldn't have asked.

'It . . . it belongs in the past, Carl,' he struggled. 'An alias . . . that's what it is. Don't think . . . about it . . . now.'

Carl looked down at the floor. The shadows became more defined.

'The sun's breaking through. Let go now, Assad. Are you listening to me!'

The body next to him twitched, but Carl felt no change. He hadn't let go.

'Come on, Assad. *Let go!*'

'I'll . . . be OK,' answered Assad almost inaudibly. 'I've . . . tried . . . it . . . before.'

50

She leaned in over the desk and reached for the telephone. If the ambulance came quickly, she'd be lying in the gynaecological ward in Kalmar in forty-five minutes.

She told herself that if Atu came with her, everything would be all right again.

She was just about to smile at the thought when a cutting sensation suddenly tore through her.

'No! What's happening?' she mumbled, as yet another convulsion thrust her backwards in the chair.

Instinctively, she directed her eyes down. The bleeding from between her legs had increased.

She trembled all over for a few seconds, and then it went totally quiet inside her. Far too quiet. The throbbing beat of her pulse. The movements in her uterus. The impulses that could give her an idea about her general condition. All signals stopped at once.

Pirjo began to cry. Just like the time when with a child's naivete she'd asked her mother to love her as much as her sisters, she knew that the tears were shed in vain, that crying was of no use. Fate followed a path all of its own and you just had to follow along, no matter how terrible and sad it could seem. That was the realization she was left with now. From one moment to the next, everything became suddenly insignificant. The little being inside her had decided that they should part ways now. She'd gone into labour but her waters hadn't broken because the baby was dead inside her. She knew this with certainty.

She stared for a moment at the telephone, completely lost.

Why should she call for help? Why should she save herself when all was lost? She wouldn't get Atu to impregnate her again. She'd never have the child who should have carried things on, so what was there to live for? Atu's promise that they'd be united at the timber circle wouldn't be granted anyway, not as things were.

And then there were the men in the control room. She wouldn't be able to get rid of them for a long time if she allowed herself to be hospitalized. The electrician would find the bodies when he came back in a few days.

Now Pirjo was shaking all over. Even the severe Finnish winters hadn't made her feel so cold.

Broken, she let her shoulders fall. Not because of her own fate, but because of Atu's. When they found the bodies, they'd work out connections that she couldn't allow. At some point they'd find Shirley, and then both she and Atu would pay for their actions.

So there was only one way out: she had to sacrifice herself for Atu one more time, and this time with her life. She'd write it all down as she bled to death. Take the blame for everything. Everything. And the men in there wouldn't be around to prove otherwise. Their fate would have to follow hers. They'd made the choice to come so close.

For a long time, she looked tenderly at the little wooden figure the policeman had had with him.

Then she kissed it lovingly and began to write.

*   *   *

Carl told himself not to panic now. To remove himself from the pain and use the time he still had left.

He was somehow able to look around the room, despite the painful aftermath of the last wave of shocks, which had led to severe cramps in his arms and legs.

The biggest threat now was that Assad wouldn't be capable of keeping his finger pressed against the wall. If he couldn't, their bodies would be immediately thrown back in cramps, and Carl knew full well what that would lead to. Just now, it wasn't death itself he feared, but that it would be prolonged. That the current that would be sent through Assad's finger, through their bodies, and out through Carl's left leg, wouldn't kill them without incredible suffering. Terrifying pictures of executions in the electric chair, victims with blood coming out of their eyes and unbelievably contorted bodies, were all too clear in his mind. He'd already experienced how it felt, as if the brain was being cooked and the heart could fail at any moment.

But how to avoid that fate? Was there any possible way out, given that that evil woman had so thoroughly tied them together? The cables were extremely tight, the hooks on the wall behind them far too strong. The angle they were sitting at made it impossible for them to wriggle their bodies to a better position or one even totally free.

'When . . . when . . . when my finger is totally burned,' mumbled Assad beside him. 'The cable . . . the cable . . . will fall down . . . down on me if . . . I . . . can't push it . . . away and down on the floor.'

Carl tried to say something but the muscles in his neck were still so tense that not a sound came out. In desperation that even his voice had been taken from him, his eyes began to well up.

He knew he had to make sure not to cry. Moisture on his face wouldn't help in this situation.

He wanted to say to Assad that he'd help him when it happened. That they'd wriggle themselves as much as they could so that the cable fell to the floor. But all he could do was nod.

He wondered why a fuse didn't blow. Was there even a fuse? He stretched his head back and looked straight up at the bottom of the junction boxes and panels that controlled the whole system. It was up there that the woman had screwed the two cable ends. If only he had a free arm. Just a free hand. Then he'd . . .

He turned his head to his friend when he heard the awful sound. Now it was clear that Assad's finger had begun to sizzle. His face was whiter than an albino's.

But Assad held out.

* * *

Pirjo had sat for a moment with her hands on the keyboard, her mind elsewhere. She was really exhausted now. Things were happening so quickly.

Now there were hundreds of 'n's on the screen at the tail end of the words she'd written. Her finger must have been resting for a few seconds on the 'n' key.

She began to delete them.

Just as she was thinking to herself that it wouldn't be long before Atu arrived, and that she'd have to be quick, she heard the door open to his quarters.

She felt a stab in her heart when she caught his scent. If those two policemen hadn't come, this would've been the most blissful moment in her life. She could almost feel the embraces that wouldn't come to anything. The caresses that would never be between them. And worst of all, the smiles and giggles of the child they'd both wished for most would never come to be.

Pirjo was about to faint in despair at the thought as she turned around and saw how Atu radiated. He was dressed all in yellow with tight trousers and a polo shirt, looking like a young man out for a good time. She tried to smile back, but her face wouldn't obey.

She knew that he wouldn't be able to see the blood, thinking that it was fortunate that the front of the desk hid it.

'You look wonderful, Atu,' she said, trying to raise her arm towards him so she could give his hand a squeeze, but she just didn't have the energy.

'I'm just finishing something,' she said instead, succeeding now to smile a little. 'It'll just take five minutes, and then I'll be with you.'

He took a step closer, his head to one side.

'Is something wrong, Pirjo?' he asked. Of course he noticed that things weren't as they should be.

He scanned the desk instinctively, fixing his eyes on the little wooden figure that lay beside her hand.

It made him start, and his smile disappeared immediately. The reaction was noticeable, as if he'd been punched. Several times his eyes jumped from the figure to her eyes with a mixture of confusion and shock.

Then he grabbed the figure and looked at it close-up, his face contorted as if the sight of it brought on physical pain.

'I recognize this figure,' he said, his voice full of unanswered questions. 'Where did you get it?' he asked sharply.

Now she noticed only too clearly what the loss of blood was doing to her. How her energy was ebbing away and the cells in her body lacked oxygen. She told herself that she needed to concentrate on speaking clearly. That she had to talk slowly or she'd end up slurring.

She smiled with her eyes, which didn't come easily. 'You recognize it. That's wonderful, Atu. But let's talk about it in a little while. I'll just finish up here.'

'Has Bjarke been here?' he asked to her surprise.

She looked at him, confused. What did he mean?

'I don't know who Bjarke is,' she said.

It was obvious the answer irritated him.

'You must know, seeing as the figure's here.'

She shook her head slowly. Her heart began to beat faster in an attempt to oxygenate her blood.

He really didn't understand. That much was clear. 'I remember it. It was a young man on Bornholm who carved it.' He frowned. 'He said he wanted to give it to me because he was in love with me.'

Pirjo didn't understand. 'I don't know who you're talking about. You've never mentioned that.'

'Just tell me what that figure is doing here, Pirjo. It's a simple question. It hasn't come from me because I refused to accept it. He was a pest and I couldn't stand his advances, so do me a favour and don't deny that he's been here.'

'In five minutes, Atu,' she said, more insistently this time. If she was going to save the centre and Atu, she had to finish writing her confession.

'What is it that's so important?' He was about to go around the table to check the text on the screen when she stopped him.

'Fine, I'll tell you! I'm taking all the blame, Atu, and you can't stop me. Do you understand? I'm confessing to what you've done.'

Now Atu looked at her in a way she'd never seen before.

Displeasure was the first word that came to mind, but it could also be loathing.

Loathing? Didn't he understand that she was sacrificing herself for him?

'What is it I've done, Pirjo, and what's it got to do with the figure? Is it your way of telling me that you regret what you just promised me? I don't understand anything just now.'

She wanted to take his hand but didn't dare lean forward for fear of passing out. She couldn't let that happen.

'You killed Alberte,' she said quietly.

'*What* did I do? Alberte?'

'Yes, the girl you were with on Bornholm.'

She'd expected that he'd look at her with shock. That his face would express that his secret was out, but not that he'd fall backwards against the wall as if his legs couldn't carry him any more.

'Alberte! Is Alberte dead?' He swallowed a couple of times and groaned.

Why was he denying all knowledge of it? Was he really so coldhearted?

'I don't understand why you're acting as if it didn't happen. You know more than anyone else what happened. That's why you wanted to get away from Bornholm, so why don't you just say it like it is? What's wrong with you? You're as white as a sheet, Atu. What's going on?'

He remained where he was, as if they were each in their own world, each with their own language, and it made her angry. So many years of silence between them, and now when it was finally out in the open, he kept silent. She hadn't reckoned on this. That he was so cowardly.

'You disappoint me, Atu. I saved you back then. I covered up that you'd killed her. I worked it out on the same day we left the island. Did you maybe think that I could ignore how much you talked about her? You hadn't talked about anything else for a few weeks. Maybe you didn't think it hurt, but it did. And then I heard on the radio that they'd found her murdered, thrown up in a tree following a hit-and-run. That was just two mornings before we left the island. I knew straightaway that it was you, Atu, and that they'd find you if I didn't do something. They searched all over the island for the van. You do know that, right? And then I found the sign in the VW with blood on it.'

'I don't understand what you're talking about. This is totally insane. I had no idea about any of this. I didn't know Alberte was dead, and it makes me more than sad if it's true. And what's this sign you're talking about?'

'Do I need to explain that to you, too? The sign that hung over the house at Ølene, of course. The Celestial Sphere! You painted it yourself so don't try and say you don't remember it.'

'Yes, of course I remember it. I caught myself on the screws when Søren Mølgård and I took it down, and I bled quite a bit. So what is it about that sign and what's it got to do with Alberte?'

Atu was a master at manipulating others, but did he really believe that he could now manipulate her, too?

'Is it true? Is she dead?' he asked again. It was pathetic.

Pirjo clenched her teeth. She'd met resistance often enough in her life. The least he could do for her under the circumstances was to be honest. 'You secured the sign on the front of the VW and used it to fling her up in the tree when you ran her down. But relax. I got rid of it for us. I burned it, Atu, so you can thank me for that.'

At that moment his eyes changed from desperation and anger to icy cold. 'I'm very shocked by everything you're saying, Pirjo. Really horrified!'

Then his face changed expressions again. He suddenly smiled with a serene expression.

He turned toward her.

'Aha, this is a test. You're testing me. It's a game. But then where did you get the figure, Pirjo? Is this something you've been planning for a long time?' He slammed it on the table in front of her.

Didn't he get just how vulnerable he was right now?

'Get away from here, Atu! Go, they're after you,' she said, her voice weak. She owed him that much at least.

'Who's after me?' He remained standing in front of her, smiling as if nothing was wrong. Didn't he believe her?

She took a deep breath. 'The officers who came with the figure, that's who. The police have been looking for you all these years. They know it was you. But I'm taking the blame for you, so just get out of here. It's all lost anyway.'

'I don't understand anything. What officers?' He wasn't smiling any more.

'I remember that time well, when you began to talk about wanting to stay on the island because of Alberte. You were totally obsessed with her, and she consumed you. You weren't yourself when you came home. It wasn't anything like with the other women, and that worried me. But you realized, thank God, that it went against what you wanted for your own future, against what we'd agreed. Against everything.'

'Yes, I remember that discussion, and I also recall your jealousy, Pirjo. It's always been your biggest weakness. But I promised you to rid myself of her, and I did, but not in the way you're suggesting now. I don't know what you take me for or think of me any more, Pirjo. I don't recognize you at all. I could never take another person's life. I'd sooner take my own.'

He put his hand to his forehead, hovering momentarily between the totally incomprehensible and reality.

'When did this happen with Alberte?'

'I've told you. Two days before we left.'

'That's crazy.' He hit his forehead with a clenched fist, as if to knock everything in place. 'Then it happened the day after I broke up with her. She cried about it, and I cried, too, but that was all, I assure you. I regretted it later, but too late.'

Pirjo was getting cold now. Her legs were trembling beneath her, her lips quivering. It was difficult to concentrate. What was he saying? He regretted? Regretted what?

'Well, where were you then that morning, two days before we disappeared from Bornholm?' she asked.

'Disappeared? We didn't disappear. There was never any intention that we should stay there any longer. I was finished with what I'd come for, you know that.'

'Where were you?'

'How should I be able to remember that now? I was feeling down, so I was probably out somewhere meditating with the sunstone, like I normally do.'

'There was also blood on the side of the fender. A lot of blood.'

'But that was from the fox Mølgård hit. You know that, too. I told you.'

Yes, that's what he'd asserted. What else should he have said?

'You say that two officers came here with the figure. What did they want with it? And where are they now?'

Pirjo half closed her eyes. She was so tired now.

Atu nodded and shook his head in turn. He was in a state of inner turmoil. Did he imagine that he could think everything away? Why didn't he just make his escape?

Pirjo looked at the screen and began again to delete the 'n's. Time was running out, she could feel it.

Now the room changed colour. Was this what death was like? Did the world become suddenly light and warm? She slowly turned her eyes towards the window. A flickering light caused her to blink. The sun was breaking through. How beautiful it was.

Then she saw out of the corner of her eye how his hand took hold of the figure again.

'It was him,' he whispered. 'Of course it was him who did it.'

He almost looked frightened. It seemed real, but was it?

'Bjarke was just a big Boy Scout. He was obsessed with everything I did, so I let him help with the excavations. Up on Knarhøj. And then he wanted to give me this, declaring his love for me. Naturally, I didn't want it. I told him that we were leaving, and he said that it was all Alberte's fault. I remember it now. Oh God, it didn't make any sense.'

Pirjo was shocked. She didn't know what to believe.

'I broke up with her and never saw her again.'

For a moment, Pirjo felt relieving warmth on her face. Now the sun was out at full force, and it was like her office was lit up by floodlights. Pirjo opened her mouth, trying to breathe in gasps. She thought how the strength of the sun would be sure to kill the men now. Then the muscles in her neck slackened, her chin fell towards her chest and the shaking stopped. Her body didn't even have enough energy for that.

But if it was true what Atu was saying, what then?

If it was really true, and if she'd known, none of these terrible things would've happened.

In the next few seconds, the possible consequences became apparent to her. It *could* be true.

If Atu hadn't killed anyone, how could she do it? In that case, she'd lived a lie, reacted to a lie and allowed others to pay for that lie. She'd killed three women, nearly four, including Shirley. Jealousy and misunderstandings had consumed her, eaten her up.

There was a roar. Had it come from her? She didn't know.

Atu disappeared from the table and there were noises. He was shouting something or other.

Pirjo opened her eyes. There were still 'n's that hadn't been deleted. Still a few sentences that hadn't been written.

'*What have you done?*' came a shout from the control room. It was Atu's voice.

The screen flashed a couple of times.

She fell back in her seat. She could no longer feel her arms and legs.

'You lunatic!' Suddenly, Atu was standing in front of her, snarling in her face.

'They're unconscious but they're alive. You can be grateful for that,' she thought he said.

Then he grabbed the telephone on the table and started dialling like crazy. She heard words like 'police' and 'ambulance'.

'Now you've seriously thrown suspicion on me for something Bjarke did. Do you realize that?'

She tried to nod as he pulled open a drawer and took all the money that was inside. 'You've ruined my life. Do you know that, Pirjo? My life's work will be ruined if I don't get Bjarke to confess.'

Just now, she really wanted him to embrace her. To say goodbye and hold her hand until it was over. But he didn't even look at her.

'You'll have to take your punishment for this, Pirjo,' he said, turning his back on her. 'I demand it of you. In the meantime, there's something I have to do.'

It was the last thing he said to her before he disappeared.

And the last things she heard before she finally gave up were desperate voices from down in the courtyard.

'*Fire!*' they shouted. '*Fire! Fire!* . . .'

51

Carl woke with his face pressed against the cement floor. His entire body was throbbing and buzzing. His heart was pumping so much that he felt sick and had to regurgitate.

'What happened?' he said, and threw up, but no one answered.

He looked down at his body. His arms were still shaking, but they were free. Now he noticed that there were bits of cable spread all over the floor. There was also a wire cutter a little further away, and the door to the corridor stood wide open.

'Assad, are you there?' he asked with a shaky voice.

'*Pirjo*, why aren't you doing anything? The place is on fire!!' he heard someone shouting out in Swedish.

Then someone screamed. From inside the office came the sound of more and more hectic footsteps.

'Don't touch anything!' someone shouted. 'She's dead!'

After that, the screams became deeper and more intense.

'Help,' Carl tried to shout, but he couldn't make himself heard above the commotion.

He tried to roll out of his position, but he couldn't.

A dark shadow covered the light from the office, and then he heard footsteps approaching.

'*Help!*' he shouted again, feeling muscle group after muscle group beginning to relax. He became extremely hot as the blood began to rush, and it bloody well hurt. It was almost as if all his veins and arteries had hardened and couldn't let the blood pass.

The outline of a body stood in the room. 'There are two men lying on the floor here in the control room. Something's definitely not right, their feet are tied together,' screamed the voice suddenly.

For some time, Carl anxiously watched his unconscious friend being given mouth-to-mouth in the room they'd been moved to.

Outside, people shouted for more water and makeshift firefighting equipment. Some people were trying to get hold of Atu, but without any success it would seem.

They said that the body by the desk was Pirjo, and that she was dead. Someone had covered her with a cloth that'd been lying on the table in the reception. Probably Nisiqtu because she was standing totally paralysed at her side, white as a ghost, crying.

There were quite a few people in there, standing passively and watching. Men and women dressed in white who no doubt realized that the dream was over. They were probably dumbstruck, unable to take it all in.

'Look at his hand,' one of them whispered, pointing at Assad's severely burnt hand and black thumb.

Carl observed the men who were working on Assad with gratitude. They knew what they were doing, that was for sure, so God bless them for that.

'He'll make it,' one of them said. 'The heart's beating fast and hard, but it's beating.'

Carl took a deep breath. As long as they helped Assad, he'd be all right himself.

He sipped from the glass of water that a compassionate soul gave him, but found it very difficult to swallow. For a moment, he had to hold his head steady to stop it from moving from side to side like a pendulum in a clock. His left ankle ached as if it had been cut, and his lungs produced mucus as if they were inflamed. But despite the discomfort and pain, and the after-effects that might come, he was alive and knew that everything would be OK. And only ten minutes later, he was already feeling better.

Assad had saved him.

If only they could save Assad now.

The sirens had been going for some time before they were turned off right outside the windows. Ambulances, police, fire engines – a whole regiment of rescue workers had mobilized to action.

Carl was on his feet now, giving his version of events as much as his voice would allow. In the meantime, a pair of their Swedish colleagues routinely checked his and Assad's ID on the telephone. Hopefully, they'd get hold of Lars Bjørn, and hopefully he'd get a shock.

Over on the sofa, Assad had exclaimed a couple of inarticulate sounds, but when the doctor gave him an injection, he woke suddenly, looking confused at the horde of people around him.

When he saw Carl, he smiled gently. Carl could easily have cried.

Fifteen minutes later, when the doctor had treated Assad's hand with a provisional dressing, and put a bandage around Carl's ankle, they listened to the preliminary report from the police.

They'd been discovered in the control room, lying on the floor with multiple injuries, tied by their feet with cables. Who'd cut them free, nobody knew, but it could hardly have been that woman who'd bled to death.

The doctor deemed it necessary to admit them for observation at Kalmar Hospital, even though they'd seemingly escaped any life-threatening injuries. Apart from Assad's thumb, which would in all probability have to be amputated, and which he seemingly didn't react to.

Carl assumed he must be in shock, putting his hand on Assad's shoulder and giving it a squeeze. He couldn't express in words how he felt about Assad sacrificing himself. All the pain he'd endured.

'Thanks, Assad,' he said. It didn't seem enough.

He nodded. 'I wanted to save myself, too, Carl, don't read too much into it,' he gasped.

They were asked to identify the dead woman as the person who'd knocked them out and tied them up. Afterwards, the technicians came and took pictures. The forensic pathologist wrote a temporary death certificate, but was convinced the cause of death was extreme blood loss caused during premature labour. He put a stethoscope to her stomach and shook his head after a few seconds. The child was no longer alive either.

Then the paramedics put the body on a stretcher and carried it out.

The amount of blood around the area she'd been sitting in and under the table was awful. So much blood from such a small woman was hard to fathom.

'She's confessed to attacking you. Look here,' said one of the officers, pointing at the computer screen on the desk.

Carl read. It was in Swedish, and made for horrifying reading.

'What does it say exactly, Carl?' asked Assad looking concerned. 'I don't read Swedish too well.'

Carl nodded. Of course he didn't. How much could you expect from someone who allegedly didn't understand a word of Danish sixteen years ago.

'It reads: I confess my deeds. I've killed two officers in the solar-power control room. I killed Wanda Phinn. She's buried down in Gynge Alvar, about eight hundred metres from where the path stops, and then a hundred metres to the right. I pushed a German woman in front of a car down at the ferry terminal in Karlskrona. Her name was Iben. I drowned Claudia, who was found in Poland. I don't remember their surnames at present. It all started with Alberte on Bornholm, where Atu, called Frank at the time, began . . .'

And there her confession ends with a mass of 'n's and some spaces. Her finger must've fallen there when she lost consciousness. Carl pointed to the 'n' key on her keyboard. Exactly one key above the space bar.

'Where's Atu?' Carl asked around the room.

People shrugged. Everything pointed to the rat having abandoned the sinking ship.

'His car's not there,' someone said.

So he'd slipped away before everything came burning down around him.

'I think he's directing a massive accusation at himself, running away while his chosen one, Pirjo, was sitting here dying and the buildings were on fire,' said Carl.

'Yes, but what she wrote . . . can be understood in several ways,' said Assad.

Carl nodded. 'It can. It can also mean that she's trying to make him responsible for Alberte's death. We can't know from what's here. We don't know anything about what her motivation was. Maybe she was insane. But, the fact that he ran away, leaving his fiancée and lifework in flames, speaks volumes.'

'Then we need to find him, right?'

Carl nodded. But where? And how? Now they were being taken to the hospital. Assad's injuries weren't the sort you could ignore. Just taking a couple of steps, he looked like a zombie. His limbs were obviously stiff and were with all probability damn painful, just like his own. And then there was his hand. It was almost unbearable to think about.

'We'll put a call out for Atu Abanshamash Dumuzi and his car,' said one of the Swedish plainclothes officers.

'Good. Listen, we need to find our car keys and mobiles,' said Carl. 'Otherwise—'

'You'll have to leave that for someone else, because you won't be doing it now,' interrupted the doctor. 'We've got some patients to transport and ambulances waiting outside.'

Out in the courtyard, there was a multitude of flashing blue lights and people in uniform, lost in a fog of smoke and damp. Not far from there, it was still possible to see black clouds rising up, but the fire had already been brought under control, according to the on-site commander.

Carl looked over the body that only an hour and a half ago had been a smiling and happy woman with Atu's cape over her shoulders and sunstones in her hands. Her deathly white face hadn't yet been covered, and many white-clad men and women stood around her, totally lost and crying.

Then a team of stretcher-bearers approached from the area of the fire. People whispered, put their hands to their faces and followed the unravelling events in disbelief.

'Shirley!' some of them said.

The woman they were carrying was still alive. A man walked

alongside them, holding a drip, while another held an oxygen mask over her mouth. She held out her hand a couple of times to the people they passed on their way, touching their hands. She didn't get much back, but there were a few who stroked her fingers as she was hurried past them.

'She'll take one ambulance, and the dead woman the other. The Danish officers can be driven in one of the emergency cars,' said the on-site commander.

The battered woman on the stretcher was placed alongside the dead one. They took her mask off and spoke to her. She coughed, but was seemingly in a fit state to answer questions. Then a rescue worker came to rinse the area around her eyes of soot. Even her hair was black with soot, just like her skin. Everything was black. Amazing that she'd survived. They must have rescued her in the nick of time.

She looked extremely sad, lying there. Maybe she hadn't reckoned with getting out of that place alive. She was presumably still in shock.

Then she turned her head towards the other stretcher, trying to focus. She blinked a couple of times before she really understood what she saw.

And then something strangely grotesque happened that Carl knew he'd never be able to forget.

With her eyes on the corpse, she began to laugh. To laugh so uncontrollably and resoundingly loud that everyone in the courtyard stopped, frozen to the spot.

52

Friday, May 16th, and Saturday, May 17th, 2014

The information from Kalmar Hospital was completely unambig-
uous. Assad needed to have his left thumb amputated, and Assad
had said no. If it had to come off, then he'd be the one to do it, he
said.

Carl felt sick at the thought and stared at the unfortunate hand.
If a usable finger ever came from that thing, which on the surface
looked totally charred, he must have good connections with the
powers up above.

'Are you sure, Assad?' he asked, pointing at the marbling on the
skin some way up the heel of his hand.

He confirmed without hesitation. He claimed to have had similar
burns to this before. And he'd weathered the storm himself just
fine back then.

The doctor then delivered unveiled admonitions about what
would happen if gangrene set in, adding some instructions of vary-
ing character about what he shouldn't do under any circumstances
in this unpleasant situation.

Carl could tell that Assad was in pain, but he took it on the chin. The doctor wasn't going to have his way.

Then the staff checked their kidney and heart function, did a number of neurological tests, asked them to perform a series of muscle exercises and finally asked them at least a hundred questions before they were finished.

'We're keeping you here tonight because Carl's cardiogram is still showing some irregularities. When it isn't any worse than this, our experience tells us that it'll sort itself out within a few hours, but we'd like to do an ECG tomorrow morning to be on the safe side.'

Assad and Carl looked at each other. It wouldn't exactly make their hunt for Atu any easier.

The consultant, a stereotypical-looking smart Swedish man in his prime, pushed his rimless glasses back in place. 'I can sense that you're hesitant to accept the offer, but you shouldn't be. You've both been extremely lucky. Assad here, to the best of my knowledge, has sacrificed his finger, quite certainly saving your lives and definitely sparing you from any number of serious injuries. If it hadn't been direct current, and if you hadn't been so lucky with the bad weather, you wouldn't be here now. You would've been boiled alive. Your brain and nervous system would have suffered irreparable damage. And, best-case scenario, your muscle tissue would've been subjected to far more damage, resulting in far greater pain than what you're suffering now.'

They protested when they were asked to put on hospital robes. Grown men in bed gowns that were too long, all bare arses and hair, were a sight no one wanted to see.

'I'd ask you to be aware that in the coming twenty to thirty months, there can be delayed injuries following such a violent and traumatic case of physical stress. So if you notice any significant changes in memory, sensory irregularities, impaired vision or hearing, you must seek medical attention. Are we agreed?'

They nodded. Who would dare to disagree with a doctor wearing rimless glasses?

'One thing more,' said the white coat on his way out the door. 'Your Swedish colleagues have been here with your mobile phones and car keys, and they've parked your car down in the car park.'

Now *that* was information they could live with.

It was hard to get out of bed the next morning, their bodies protesting as they did. Carl looked over to Assad, who was asleep on his back in the hospital bed. He'd taken his dressing off, lying with his thumb in his mouth. Almost like a baby comforting itself.

And he was still sitting like that when three-quarters of an hour later they were in the car en route to Copenhagen. Despite an ardent search, the Swedish police had no news about Atu's whereabouts.

'Do you really think that will save your finger, Assad?' he said finally when they'd driven between forty and fifty kilometres.

Assad took his thumb out of his mouth carefully, rolled down the window, and spat.

Then he pulled a small brown bottle from the Body Shop from his pocket. *Tree Tree Oil* was written on the label.

'I always carry one of these with me. It's something Rose taught me. It disinfects. You just can't swallow it,' he said, pouring a few drops in his mouth followed by his thumb.

'It looks like a third-degree burn, which means the nerves are dead, Assad. So it won't help, no matter what you use.'

Assad repeated the procedure, spat again and turned towards him.

'I can feel life in it, Carl. It might be a bit black, but that's just the skin. If there's anything that isn't in full working order, it's only the top joint.' With which, he took some more drops and stuck his thumb back in his mouth.

'We've had some feedback from the police in Ystad,' informed one of his colleagues from Police Headquarters on the car radio. 'The man you're looking for was seen driving on board the night ferry from Ystad to Rønne.'

What did he say?

'Why are we only hearing about this now?'

'They tried yesterday but there was no response from your phones.'

'We didn't have them. They brought them to the hospital them-selves, damn it. Why didn't they call the hospital?'

'You were sleeping.'

'Then they could have called this morning.'

'Look at your watch, Mørck, it's only seven thirty. I doubt their office hours have even started.'

Carl said thanks and ended the call. Atu was on Bornholm, but what the hell was he doing there? Wasn't that the last place *he* would go if he were Atu?

Assad spat out of the window again.

'He's gone there to get rid of some clues we've overlooked, if you ask me. He knows we can't pin anything on him without evidence.'

Then they'd just have to stop him in his tracks.

Carl looked out the window. The decision he had to make wasn't easy. He looked at his partner, fighting to save his thumb, keeping it stuck in his mouth, and felt a momentary twinge of shame. What hadn't *he* sacrificed over the last twenty-four hours? So couldn't Carl sacrifice himself a little?

'I'll hire a private jet,' he decided.

Assad's eyes looked like they were about to pop out of his head.

'Yes, yes, I'll be fine. Maybe the hypnosis has worked, too, who knows?' He looked at the GPS. 'It isn't too far to Ronneby Airport, so we can be there in half an hour. I'll try to see if Copenhagen AirTaxi can help us.'

Ten minutes went by and an extremely polite man apologized that they couldn't find a free plane on such short notice. 'But ask one of our former Swedish pilots, Sixten Bergström,' he suggested. 'He has a private jet, an Eclipse 500, at Ronneby Airport. It's got six seats and does seven hundred kilometres an hour, so maybe it's just what you're looking for. With a distance between the two airports of approximately a hundred and twenty kilometres, the trip to Bornholm can be done in no time at all.'

Never in his life had Carl thought he'd do something like this voluntarily. With his legs shaking, he sat in an extremely comfortable beige leather window seat, staring paralysed at the older gentleman preparing for takeoff.

'Shall I hold your hand?' said his wingman, comfortingly, having rolled a huge dressing around his left thumb.

Carl took deep breaths.

'I've already said a prayer for you, Carl. It'll be OK.'

Carl pressed himself back in his seat, oceans of sweat on his forehead, instinctively lifting his arms with the jet.

'No, you don't really need to do that,' said the pilot with a glance backwards. 'We've got wings enough as it is. Just take it easy.'

Did Assad suppress a laugh just then? Was he sitting there with a burnt-up finger and beaten-up body, laughing?

Carl turned towards him and noticed, strangely enough, that it was infectious. When he thought about it, it was very comical.

He let his arms fall and relaxed his shoulders. Actually, he wasn't at all scared. It was just something he imagined.

And then he laughed so much and so unexpectedly that the pilot nearly had a heart attack. What a twist of fate that would've been if they'd crashed.

Just as quickly as they'd gone up, they were down again. Carl sent Kazambra a few gentle thanks, crossing over to Police Superintendent Birkedal, who was waiting for them.

'We haven't traced the man yet. None of the hotels have put him up, and none of the campsites think they've had anyone staying who fits the description.'

'So he's either stayed in a bed-and-breakfast, in his car or with someone we don't know. Do you have a car for us?'

Birkedal pointed over to a small red Peugeot 206. 'You can borrow the wife's. She's left everything anyway.'

He looked a little bitter, but then he should have known better than to accept Rose's strange advances.

They agreed to keep in contact all day, because the man they were looking for shouldn't have any chance to get off the island. They'd put the ferries and airport under observation, too.

'Can you manage, Assad?' he asked as they squeezed themselves into the car. He got a bandaged thumbs-up.

Tough guy, that Assad.

'The circle's complete for Atu and Frank, then,' said Assad. 'He's back on Bornholm, but where do you think he is?'

'There's certainly no reason to believe he's gone back to the scene of the crime. That wouldn't make any sense. And if he does, he won't find anything that the investigators didn't find. I'm more inclined to think he might contact someone or other on the island who knows more than is good for them.'

'Who could it be good for?'

He had a point. Definitely not for the person Atu was after. Carl credited Atu with a lot of determination, maybe a bit too much.

'Do you think he could kill someone, Carl?'

'Aren't we looking for someone we think has done it once before?' Hadn't they seen the man being worshipped by a white-clad mob, and wasn't that a position of power he'd do anything to maintain?

'Inge Dalby's in Copenhagen, so we don't need to worry about her. So I'm thinking mostly about June Habersaat just now. What do you say?'

Assad nodded. 'That's right. She wouldn't talk about him either. You were right about her knowing something.'

Carl reached for his phone, like a reflex, but instead stuck his finger in a stuffed animal with *Mummy is the best* written across the tummy.

He doubted Birkedal's wife felt like that just now.

'You need to call June Habersaat, Assad. Pass me the phone when you've got hold of her. Something tells me she won't want to talk to you.'

After half a minute he shook his head. No signal.

They called her workplace at Joboland and were told that she was currently on sick leave, which you could easily understand, given the way one disaster had followed another with the deaths of both her ex-husband and son. But it didn't matter, the friendly woman concluded, the high season didn't start for another five weeks yet.

The next stop was June Habersaat's house in Jernbanegade in Aakirkeby.

'That's the second time today someone has asked about her,' said a young guy in overalls and bare chest, in the process of moving things into the house next door.

'Who?' asked Carl, marvelling at his enormous, dishevelled beard that couldn't possibly be practical with that job. He looked more like a teacher from the sixties. He just needed the corduroy jacket, but that probably came when he was finished. Strange fashion at the moment.

'He was an older guy dressed totally in yellow.' He laughed. 'He looked like a bad TV ad for a travel agency. Tanned, dimpled, the whole nine yards.'

Assad and Carl looked at each other.

'How long ago was this?'

He wiped the sweat from his forehead while he was thinking. 'Maybe twenty, twenty-five minutes ago, I think.'

Damn it. Twenty minutes earlier and they would've had him.

'But I don't suppose you know where June Habersaat's gone?' asked Assad.

'I don't know anything. But she said she was on her way up to collect something that she could place on her son's grave. Very strange. I think she got the idea from something I carried in.' He looked at Assad's hand. 'You look like you got your hand caught in something. What was it, caught with your fingers in the jar?' He laughed. Hopefully Assad didn't get the insult.

'What was it you carried in that you think gave her the idea?' asked Assad, clenching his healthy right fist. So he did know that figure of speech.

Carl grabbed his arm so he didn't give in to the temptation to sock the guy one.

'Yeah, I don't really know. It was one of the first things I carried in. Normally we have quilts and clothes on the top of the load in black plastic bags, but I think it was a collection of magazines in a box. Still, I can't be sure.'

Carl pulled Assad over to the car.

'Where on earth can she find something that was Bjarke's? Shall we take a guess at their old house in Listed or at that woman's place in Sandflugtsvej, where he rented a room?'

Assad nodded. 'The landlady's name was Nelly Rasmussen,' he said. Well remembered.

Then Assad pulled himself free, turned on his heel, and aimed directly back to the removal man. Were they going to fight now?

'What did she say exactly?' he shouted already from a distance of ten metres.

The guy stared at him, uncomprehending, with a removal box on his shoulder.

'About what?'

'She was on her way *up* to collect something. Wasn't that what she said? Are you completely sure that was it?'

'Yes, what the heck does it matter if she said it one way or another?'

'She didn't say that she had to go up to town, did she?'

'Then I must have been deaf.'

Carl came up behind him. 'That's right. It's important for us to know if she was driving to Listed or Rønne to collect the thing she thought of. Do you know anything about that?'

'Well, then it was probably Rønne. At least she pointed that way when she said it. Women do that all the time without thinking about it.'

'You didn't say that to the guy in the yellow clothes, too, did you?'

He looked unsure of what to say. So he had, then.

'Did he look as if he knew where to go?' asked Carl. Bjarke had moved after Frank left the island, so he wouldn't know that address.

'Maybe,' he said. 'At least he had a page from a local telephone book in his hand. Maybe he found the address there.'

'We've got to rush,' said Carl, beginning to run to the car. Assad beat him to it.

'Damn it, there's no GPS,' grumbled Carl, looking at the dashboard. Which way was the quickest?

'Relax, Carl, I'll find it on my smartphone.' Assad typed away for a moment. 'It'll take fifteen minutes if we drive south towards Lobbæk and Nylars.'

Carl put his foot on it. 'Call Birkedal. They need to send a car up there.'

Assad typed, obviously finding it difficult with the pain in his left hand. Then he sat for a minute, nodding, while he listened to the answer.

'Did you say that they should be discreet up there? I didn't hear,' said Carl.

Assad wrinkled his nose. 'They aren't coming, Carl, and you don't want to hear why. But all their cars were unavailable at the moment. Something to do with ferry and airport surveillance.'

'What?'

'He also said that we'd be there before them anyway. The Peugeot can drive pretty quickly, he claimed.'

'Then he can bloody well take the consequences if anything stops us,' said Carl, ignoring the speedometer quickly exceeding a hundred on a road with a limit of eighty.

'Take your shirt off, hold it out the window and let it flutter,' he continued, while pressing down on the horn. 'Come on, Assad. We've converted this tin can here to an emergency car at full throttle.'

Ten minutes later, through scattered built-up areas and dozens of gaping mouths, in the little red lightning bolt with flapping green shirt, Carl and Assad reached the house in Sandflugtsvej. If they'd expected cars in front of the house, they were disappointed. There was apparently nothing here that could justify their hazardous journey.

'Call the police station and report the emergency driving, Assad, and I'll go in and see if there's anyone home. And take a pill or two. I can see how much that thumb hurts.'

Nelly Rasmussen opened the door reluctantly. Wearing a hat, she breathed a sigh of relief when she saw who it was, and a sight for sore eyes she was when the door was finally fully opened. Not even an Italian or Greek mama in mourning could be as decked out in black as she was. A veil on her hat, ready to be pulled down. Tights, shoes, jacket, blouse, skirt, gloves, necklace, eyelids, eyelashes and hair, everything was pitch black. Rose would have loved her unconditionally.

'I thought you were the taxi driver,' she said, pulling a black handkerchief from her black handbag, ready to dab at her totally dry eyes. Truly a theatrical talent.

'Has June Habersaat been here?'

She nodded somewhat sullenly.

'What did she want?'

'Well might you ask. Do you really think she wanted to tell me? To collect a magazine from Bjarke's room, I think. She didn't show me, but that's what it looked like when she left.'

'Have you had a visit from a man in yellow clothes?'

She nodded, this time seeming a little scared.

'That's why I didn't just open. I didn't want him in again.'

'When?'

'Just before you came. Five minutes ago. I thought it was my taxi then, too.'

'What did he want?'

'He wanted to get hold of Bjarke. He was crazy and pushed his way in. He started shouting: *Where's Bjarke? Is he upstairs? He's bound to be home on a Saturday!* It was terribly unpleasant, especially on a day like today.' She dabbed at her eyes one more time.

She stood for a moment, impatiently shuffling her feet. 'Where has that taxi got to? I'll be late.'

'For what?'

She looked totally indignant. 'For Bjarke's funeral, of course.'

'Right. Is he only being buried *now*?'

'Yes, they kept him in Copenhagen. They had to do the . . . post-mortem first.' This time she shed a real tear.

'And the man in yellow, what happened to him? We're looking for him.'

'Why doesn't that surprise me? He was really unpleasant. When I told him he couldn't see Bjarke because he was dead and was being buried today, he turned as white as a ghost. His eyes became totally bright, looking completely crazy, and then he said it couldn't be true. That Bjarke had murdered a girl and that he needed to confess. It was really shocking to hear such an ugly lie about someone you've held so dear.'

Carl looked confused. 'Bjarke! Is that what he said?' He rubbed his forehead. There were more than a few things he needed to sort out in his head.

'Yes, he very well did. And then he mumbled something about Bjarke's mum having to help him. Then he suddenly looked ex-tremely worried, asking me if she was still alive. I was just about to tell him that she wasn't, but I didn't dare.'

'She's bound to be at the funeral. Did you tell him where it was being held?'

She nodded.

'Carl,' shouted Assad from the car, 'the police now know he spent the night at a bed-and-breakfast in Svaneke. Our woman in Listed, Bolette, called them to say that she'd seen him this morning outside Habersaat's house. She called you, too.'

Carl looked at his phone. Of course, the battery had died.

'Come on,' said Carl to the woman in her mourning attire. 'You can direct.' It would save her that taxi fare.

Assad had to take his shirt off again to signal their emergency status. Nelly Rasmussen gasped. He did have a good deal of hair on his chest for such a short man.

'What church?' asked Carl, pressing down on the horn.

Carl repeated what Nelly Rasmussen had said about Atu and Bjarke, while she sat nodding in the back.

'I think he's lying,' Assad added drily.

Carl nodded. It was a definite possibility. Atu was doing the rounds of the people who'd known him on the island back then, and he was probably very satisfied that Bjarke was now out of the way. They'd seen what he could do with words.

'Then we need to warn June,' continued Assad.

Nelly Rasmussen was silent.

There were very few cars parked beside the stone wall in front of Østerlars Round Church, and a few of those were pickup trucks belonging to local builders carrying in extra-large scaffolding.

'Maybe they're parked over at Kirkebogård. It can't be right that there are so few cars. And where's the hearse?' said Nelly Rasmussen in shock as they drove in the car park and Assad put on his shirt.

'Why aren't they ringing the bells?' she continued, looking at her watch. She tapped at it again and again. 'Oh God, it's stopped. We've come too late for the funeral.' Now she was *really* shaken.

'Look, Carl!' Assad pointed to a blue Volvo. Right enough, it had Swedish licence plates.

They leaped from the car, leaving Nelly Rasmussen to be Nelly Rasmussen.

She had been right. Down at the bottom of the churchyard, the internment was already coming to an end, and roughly a hundred metres in front of them a man in yellow was heading directly down to the group of mourners standing around the graveside. It was Atu. Carl and Assad picked up speed. If they ran, they risked Atu turning around. They couldn't risk him fleeing again, but on the other hand they had to protect June Habersaat. Who knew what the man was up to?

The vicar had already stood aside, carrying the small shovel in his hand, so they'd already thrown the earth on the coffin. Now they watched as June Habersaat went to the edge of the grave and threw something in.

There was an audible reaction from those who saw what it was.

Then she put her hand in her bag and took something out.

At the same moment, they heard Atu, aka Frank, shout June's name. He sounded desperate. The group by the graveside hesitated in surprise and then pulled back in one sudden movement.

Frank had almost reached the grave now. He stretched his arms out to the side and said something to June that they couldn't hear, while they quickened their pace to approach him.

Now they saw what it was that June Habersaat had pulled out. It was a pistol of the type of calibre you don't easily overlook.

Suddenly, what sounded like four to five shots rang out. The echo sounded against the walls as Atu doubled up and collapsed at the side of the grave. It was a clear-cut execution. Premeditated murder.

Carl and Assad stopped on the spot. It was a long time now since Carl had been armed.

At the same time, she noticed them. It was clear that the events of the last few seconds had happened too quickly for her, leaving her staring alternately between the lifeless man, the bottom of the grave, the mourners and the vicar, who was bravely approaching her with calming words.

'She'll shoot herself now, just like her husband did,' whispered Assad, as she put the trigger up to her head. But it wasn't just Assad who'd seen this coming, because the vicar sprang forward swinging his shovel directly at the pistol, as if he were an elite player in Major League Baseball.

She screamed when it hit her hand, and the pistol was flung to the side. Without looking back, she ran towards a bench up against the graveyard wall. She jumped onto it, over the stone wall that surrounded the churchyard and down towards the road beside the field boundary.

'You run after her, Assad, and I'll take the car,' screamed Carl, turning toward the paralysed onlookers. 'One of you, call the police, OK?'

He looked at Atu for a moment, who was lying with one foot over the grave with eyes wide open. The priest checked the pulse on his neck. His fancy yellow shirt had two deep holes in the stomach and one in the shoulder. You could just make out a piece of skin where the bullet had gone through. Right where he had a tattoo saying *RIVER*, Carl remembered.

The priest shook his head. Atu was dead. Not that Carl had been in any doubt.

How symbolic that the man lying there had wanted to be the guardian of enigma and the son of the sun, and here he was having ended his days at this most fabled location on the island, in the shadow of the round church that hid the mystical secrets of the Knights Templar.

He picked up the pistol. Just like the one Habersaat had shot himself with. It must have been the second of the two pistols that had belonged to the deceased teacher from the folk high school and which had never been found. So Habersaat had taken them both, and his wife must have somehow managed to take one of them without his knowledge. Not exactly something the ex-husband could've taken further.

Carl stood up and was about to rush off when Nelly Rasmussen pointed down in the grave, sobbing like never before.

There, amid red roses and three shovelfuls of consecrated soil, lay a glossy magazine with stark-naked men on the cover. Was it June Habersaat's manner of saying that she finally accepted the way her son had lived his life?

But why?

And then he ran.

53

Carl picked up Assad at the end of the road.

'June had her car parked at the farm down there,' he panted, pointing back. 'It was so close that I had my hand on the door handle, but I didn't manage. I'm still having muscle and breathing problems, Carl. I'm sorry.'

Carl understood. He had nothing to apologize for. Just the hundred metres he'd run himself had nearly knocked it out of him.

'Did you get the registration?' he asked.

He shook his head. Damn it.

'Look, I can see it driving down there,' shouted Assad, pointing forward.

Even though the car was at least five hundred metres in front of them, they could clearly hear June Habersaat putting the gears through their paces.

'That old rust bucket is being pushed right to its limit. She's driving like a lunatic, Carl. You'll never catch her.'

'Call Birkedal. I assume they can find a couple of cars that can help us go after her now.'

Carl put his foot down on the Peugeot as if he were trying to push the pedal out of the bottom, while trying to understand why June Habersaat would try to take her life at her son's graveside. Was it depression due to his death or something more fundamental? Was it something lying in the back of her psyche? She'd been hiding that pistol all these years, after all. And why had she shot Atu? Was it self-defence? But if it was self-defence, why had she run? Was it rea—

'Watch out!' screamed Assad, phone in hand. Smashed bottles littered the road in front of them. Treacherous needle-sharp shards that could stop anything with rubber tyres.

Carl slowed down, crawling along for the next hundred metres. If Assad hadn't seen it, the tyres would've exploded with a bang.

'Tell Birkedal, too. They'll need to send someone out to clean up.'

Another straight stretch of road lay before them so Carl put his foot on the gas.

When they reached the buildings in Gildesbo, the road was black with skid marks where it swung south. The sign pointed to Åsedamsvej.

'What do you reckon, Assad? Are they her tracks?'

He nodded to confirm. Now he'd managed to get hold of the duty officer in Rønne. It only took him a few seconds to relay the message, while Carl sped up to 125 kmh down a road where the visibility on either side was optimal.

'*There!*' shouted Assad.

Carl had seen it. Down at the end of the road the black car took a sharp right turn.

They reached the T-junction, followed her right turn and then found themselves unsure.

About a hundred metres further on, there were two options: take the left onto Almindingensvej or straight on.

'No skid marks this time, Assad. Straight on, do you think?'

He didn't answer straightaway, so Carl turned to face him. His head had fallen slightly down on his chest and his jaw muscles were working away. It was obvious that he was concentrating like crazy to avoid moaning.

'Shall we drive to the hospital, Assad?' asked Carl. At this moment, June Habersaat could go to blazes.

Assad screwed his eyes shut, opening them again after filling his lungs to bursting point.

'It's over now, Carl. Just drive,' he said. But it wasn't true, it wasn't over.

'*Drive!*' he shouted, and Carl sped off.

The forest cover was significant and dense now. Several small roads looked tempting but they drove straight on. No matter what, it was the right direction if you wanted to go to Rønne, and that was where they needed to go if this pursuit failed. Then Assad could get some painkillers that actually did something.

Now they heard the noise of screeching brakes up above the forest, followed by a faint muffled bang. If it was June Habersaat's car, not only had they gone in the right direction but they were close.

They discovered the car four hundred metres further down the road. It lay on its side, as if it had just gently toppled over, but two stripes of burnt rubber in a small parking space, really no more than an appendix to the road, and a mass of churned-up grass, told a different story.

'She was driving too fast and the brakes locked when she wanted to stop in here?' suggested Assad while Carl looked around.

'Maybe she thought she could drive it out into the high grass and let it disappear.'

JUSSI ADLER-OLSEN • 570

They stood still for a moment, looking around. She was gone.

It was a beautiful but also strange sight so close to the road. A hill in the middle of the forest in an otherwise flat and wet meadow.

Carl glanced over to some information posters showing a castle formation located on top of the hill.

Lilleborg it said on a sign with an arrow hanging between two red posts five metres further ahead.

Carl looked out in the direction of the arrow. As far as he could tell, you had to go up and round the hill.

'Do you think she fled over to the other side of the road and into the forest?' asked Assad.

'She certainly hasn't run around the hill down here, or she'd have trampled the grass down.'

Carl looked out over the meadow. It was a big open space. If she'd had a half-minute head start before they arrived, and it couldn't have been much more than that, it was enough time to have disappeared into the forest and also enough to disappear up the path and around the hill, but definitely not enough to have crossed the meadow.

'If she was injured in the crash, which seems quite likely, I wouldn't choose the forest if I was her,' he concluded. 'You'd get knocked all the time in there.'

Assad nodded in agreement, and so they turned towards the hill.

It was less than twenty-four hours since their bodies had been subjected to extremely harsh treatment, making their climb up the slight incline to the hill a steady challenge. Already after the first turn and a short distance over some bare rock, they were both breathing heavily and totally worn out.

'We're crazy, Assad. We should still be in bed at Kalmar Hospital,' said Carl after reaching the top of a second incline that gave them a clear view over the car park twenty-five metres below.

Assad raised his bandaged hand in the air and stopped. Carl had heard it, too. In westerns, twigs snapped. Here, it was a very big one.

'I think she's waiting for us, Carl,' he whispered.

They looked up at a granite boulder wall, which the grass and shrubs hadn't been able to cover. It was Lilleborg, a fortress whose layout they knew nothing about.

Carl regretted that they hadn't paid more attention to the information below, as he approached a slope going down to the lake behind the meadow area. To his left, along the edge, a path wound down, but the noise hadn't come from that direction. To the right, the path went over huge boulders and cliffs, enclosed by a metal railing stopping people from falling down into the gorge.

Behind him, Assad was trying to suppress the effect the slope had on him, so it was good that he took the lead.

Then they suddenly found themselves at the top. Long grass, cliffs, a picnic table for those who'd brought a picnic with them, and several walls, among them one with an opening out towards a spectacular view over the lake. But no June Habersaat.

'What was that noise we heard just before, then?' asked Carl.

Assad shrugged. Right now, he was utterly indifferent, that much was clear. His hand was all he could think about.

Carl recovered himself for a moment, his hands resting on his knees. This was simply pathetic. Understandable, yes, but pathetic. He hoped the situation wasn't one they'd have to endure for much longer.

Carl was pissed off with the whole thing because there'd been significant costs to this case. Assad's thumb, first and foremost, but also time and money. They'd worked flat out for weeks, trying to find a man who only a short while ago had been murdered right under their noses. Flat out to get answers from a woman who'd then tried to kill them and who was dead now herself. And flat out to untie the knots Habersaat had tied himself up in over the course of decades, and tried to give closure to a couple about what happened to their daughter. And where were they now? Nowhere. Just adding fuel to Lars Bjørn's fire.

Someone would maybe find June Habersaat in time, and hopefully still alive, but Carl doubted that now.

Then they heard Assad's phone.

'It's Rose,' he said, putting it on speakerphone.

Damn it. Now they'd have to explain everything. Carl almost couldn't be bothered.

'How are you?' was the first thing he said. 'Yes, it's Carl, but my phone's dead. Assad's listening in.'

'Hi, Assad,' she said. 'But we won't talk about me just now, OK? I'm not doing too well, but I'll be fine, so enough about that. What's all this I hear about you?'

'Yes, we've been through the mill, we don't mind admitting. Assad, well, he . . .'

He waved at him to stop. He didn't want any mention of his hand.

'Assad's standing next to me waving. We're on Bornholm, and June Habersaat has just shot and killed Atu.'

'*What* did you say?'

'Yes, so far so good, but we're no further forward.'

'Why did she do it?'

'We haven't spoken to her. She fled the scene.'

'Everything is complicated in this case, if you ask me. I've also got something that shakes things up a bit.'

'Shouldn't you be taking some time off, Rose? It is Saturday after all.'

'Very funny, Mr Mørck. Then what about you? Well, I've worked

through Bjarke's computer now, and it's been an interesting experience, I can tell you. Forty-five per cent of the memory is taken
up by PC games of different sorts. Some of them are extremely old,
so I don't think he's played them in years.'

'How old is the computer?'

'It's running Windows 95, which seemed to be an update of an
earlier version, so you can work it out yourself.'

Mamma mia! It was a wonder that the machine hadn't been
donated to an African village a long time ago.

'Fifty-two per cent are image files, and two per cent is made up
of spam mail, and then there's a single text file. A poem, actually.'

'A poem?'

'Yes, he's written a poem. The title is really quite transparent: *To
Frank*. The file was in among some exe. files in a Star Trek game
from 1995, so it wasn't easy to find.'

Goodness, she'd certainly been thorough.

Then she read the poem aloud, and regardless of how talentless
and inept it was, the meaning was inescapable. It was about rejected love and immense anger. Anger that Frank had brought their
world crashing down. Anger that Bjarke's family had been ruined
by Frank's decisions. Anger that Frank even existed.

'So Bjarke always knew about Frank and Alberte. He just didn't
want to tell his dad. Why?' Carl shook his head; it just didn't add
up. 'No, I'm totally confused now.'

'Hold your horses, Sherlock. If you'll allow me,' interrupted Rose.
'Firstly, I want to say that if there's ever another case where someone has to stare at naked men wearing nothing other than ugly
leather caps and studded belts in very compromising situations, it
will *not* be me next time. I dragged myself through more than five
thousand – *five thousand* – photos of that filth before finding the one

photo that makes sense in this case. You couldn't make it up! And I think we should tell the police on Bornholm that next time they get a computer in for examination, they should bloody well check *everything*, just like I've done.'

She was complaining, but weren't men in leather just up her street?

'Check out the MMS I'm sending to you – *now!*'

They waited a moment before a beep told them they had it.

A shiver went right through Carl.

It was a photo taken on a beautiful snowy day around Christmas time at a Boy Scout Christmas-tree sale. The price was reasonable, twenty kroner per metre, but that was the only reasonable thing about the photo.

Assad stood next to him, simply dumbfounded.

'Hello, are you there?'

'Yes, Rose, we're here,' he said on autopilot. 'And you're right. It's an amazing photo. Well done. You've damn well earned the right to take the rest of the day off.'

He looked at the photo again. He was really shocked. Here he was, forced to realize in a split second that all the leads they'd followed had been misleading: the arduous search for an imaginary wooden board because of a stupid little splint Habersaat had found; the hunt for the VW Kombi, not to mention all the resources they'd used to underpin their suspicions that pointed to Frank alias Atu; and days of investigations and often misleading interviews. It'd all been for nothing from the beginning, and here was the evidence.

Bjarke stood in the photo with a big grin on his face in his Boy Scout uniform. His cap was pulled well down over his forehead, wearing his shoulder cord, the knife in his belt decorated with various small shields. He was as proud as a peacock: proud of his troop assistant distinctions, proud of his small enterprise, which was probably for charity, and proud of the four-wheel drive he was leaning up against. And he seemed just as pleased with the idea that he'd probably come up with all by himself. Because onto the four-wheel drive he'd mounted a plough, and written on the plough in large white capitals:

BOY SCOUT GRAND CHRISTMAS TREE SALE – MERRY CHRISTMAS

It was shocking. They'd come to Bornholm to protect June Habersaat from Frank, and in reality it should have been the other way around.

'What are you thinking?' asked Rose.

'We're thinking that we could've done with this photo before. And Rose, it's the same old Toyota that June Habersaat escaped in twenty minutes ago, and which is now lying on its side in the meadow fifty metres further down. Damn it!'

'You said *we* could have used this photo before now?'

'Yes.'

'Don't you think Habersaat could've? Or, to put it another way, do you really think he didn't know his son had that plough?'

'He was a policeman, Rose. He sacrificed seventeen years of his life for this case. Of course he didn't know.'

'Listen to my theory. Habersaat had suspected his own son for years. That's what I think, and that's why he worked so insistently on the case. He had a suspicion, and he wanted to remove it no matter what. Wouldn't the most convenient thing be to place the finger of suspicion on the person he hated most? His wife's lover. What do you say to that?'

'Why did he put us on to the case, then? It would've been forgotten with his suicide.'

'He left the dirty work to us, hoping we'd bring it to its conclusion. Habersaat had hit a wall, but maybe we'd find Frank, and if we didn't, or if we discovered the real context of the case, then it would be *us* who'd have to do the heavy work of getting his son arrested. *That* was Habersaat's dilemma. He wanted to cover for the boy but realized in the end that it was wrong. Bjarke was guilty. That's why he chose to stand down.'

'That's one hypothesis, Rose. A well-grounded and reasonable one, but still a hypothesis. If you're right, I'll feel terrible. Several people have died in this course of events. Remember that, Rose.'

'That's life,' she said, correcting herself straightaway. 'That's death, I meant, of course.'

Assad threw his hand up in warning, looking over his shoulder.

'Brilliant work, Rose, thanks very much. We'll leave it there for now, OK? The battery is about to go.'

She just managed to say, 'Men! Can't they ever look after—' before Carl ended the call.

Assad raised both hands, pointing towards a couple of steps in the cliff, which many years ago had led to yet another level that had long since crumbled away.

Now Carl heard it, too.

'I'll just go over here and pee,' said Assad, tiptoeing to the right while he directed Carl to the left.

Then they jumped out at the same time.

There, up the stone wall, June Habersaat was lying in a bed of grass about a metre down. The second she saw them, she swung a thick branch at them, hitting Assad on his disfigured hand. His scream blended with hers and was so intense that it caused her to drop the branch, retreating to the corner of the wall.

Fuming, Carl lunged at her, dragging her up and pulling her arms behind her back to cuff her.

She screamed with pain straightaway, and Carl realized she was injured. Her left shoulder was hanging and several fingers on her left hand were sticking out, dislocated.

'Are you OK, Assad?'

He was holding his hand, but nodded.

'Then call an ambulance for her,' he said.

Carl led her carefully over to the picnic table, directing her with his hand to sit down.

She'd lost a lot of weight since the first time they'd met almost three weeks ago. Her eyes looked big in her hollow face, her arms like a child's.

'I heard everything that witch said on the phone,' she said after a few minutes' silence. 'And she's totally wrong.'

Carl nodded to Assad. He'd already activated the recorder on his smartphone.

'Now's your chance to tell us how it was, June. We won't interrupt if you don't want us to.'

She closed her eyes, presumably to block out the pain. 'I was glad you hunted Frank or Atu, or whatever you call him, back to the island. It was a gift for me to see him suddenly standing there. Don't you realize that?' She tried to laugh but her shoulder stopped her.

She opened her eyes and looked Carl straight in the eye. 'I wanted to shoot myself. Bjarke and I had drifted too far from each other over the years, and it was all my fault. After Bjarke's death, all I had left was guilt and it was too much to bear.'

'Guilt about what, June?'

'That I allowed Frank to have the influence he did over my family.

That he ruined my life and the lives of everyone in my family. Bjarke couldn't deal with it any more. Not after his dad had given up.'

'Your son committed suicide because he was jealous of Alberte and killed her. We've seen the car and the snowplough. What more is there to say?'

'That it wasn't Bjarke who killed Alberte. It was me.'

'I don't believe you. You're covering for your son,' said Assad.

'*No!*' She thumped the table despite the pain. Then she sat for a long time in silence, looking out over the hill and the forest on the other side of the lake.

When you get to the point where a suspect has opened up only to clam up, patience is the only thing that will help to get them going again. Carl had often sat that way for hours, and just now there was nothing else for it. Assad understood this, too.

After a few minutes, she turned her head towards him and caught his eye. Her eyes were seemingly begging him to ask her a question.

Carl thought for a moment. The question had to be exactly the right one, or she'd seize up forever.

'OK, June. I believe you, and I know Assad does, too. Tell us everything now from the beginning, and in your own way.'

She sighed, momentarily crying before looking down at the table and beginning to speak.

'I fell in love with Frank and thought we'd end up together. We used to meet up here, where you found me, and made love in the grass. My husband, Christian, couldn't do what Frank could, so I fell passionately in love.'

She pressed her lips together.

'We saw each other for a couple of months.'

Carl realized it must've been the same time Frank was seeing Inge Dalby.

'And then he broke up with me despite all the promises, which there were plenty of. Why would I cheat on my husband otherwise, who I had a son with and lived with? Why?'

They both shrugged. Yes, why?

'He promised that I'd have a new life, get away from the island, and that the age difference didn't matter. But he lied, the swine.'

She raised her head. The bitterness was visible.

'I knew full well that he'd found a younger woman. I could smell the cheap slutty perfume. He was stinking of it when he came to fire me, and when I thought about it, I'd noticed it several times before. I worked out that he'd been seeing her at the same time as me – *that* was the worst of it.' She snorted. 'So I followed him to keep an eye on what he was up to. My God, those two lovebirds thought they were so clever! I saw how they kept in touch with one another, how they left small notes for each other out by the boulder in front of the school. Frank and I did the same thing, only our notes were left where he made love.'

So that was where Alberte and Frank had left their messages. By the big rock they'd passed at least ten times. How ironic.

'Just the once, I went to find Frank out at the commune at Ølene, where he told me straight that he was in love with Alberte and was taking her back with him to Copenhagen. I hated him for that, but I hated her just as much.'

She sat for a moment, chewing her words. It was easy to see how she was recalling the hatred at full strength.

'I wanted Alberte out of his life before that happened. She needed to be mutilated, her perfect looks destroyed. She just had to be out of the picture. Maybe then Frank would take me back. I actually believed that for a long time afterwards. I waited for him to come back for years, which was crazy and naive. Since then, I just didn't want to hear about him. Not from my ex-husband, not from my sister, and not from you. Frank was just wiped out of my life.'

Carl thought to himself that he ended up paying for it anyway when he turned up again.

'I borrowed my son's car – the one lying down in the ditch – while he was at work at the workshop in Aakirkeby. He always left it in front of my sister's house because he got lunch there every day. It was really sweet actually.'

She smiled for a second.

'To make sure that the impact wouldn't leave a mark on the car, I took the snowplough he'd welded together himself, which was lying at home in the garage in Listed. I put it in the back of my own car and drove to Jernbanegade, where I attached it to the fender on the Toyota, just like it'd been constructed to fit.'

'Excuse me for saying something just now, June, but I *have* to know. How did you know that Alberte was going to meet Frank out there by the tree that morning?'

She smiled, as if she was about to present her test piece. Maybe she was.

'I left a note under the boulder very early in the morning before I drove to Aakirkeby. I could forge Frank's handwriting completely. It was very simple.'

'Yes, but how could you know that she'd see it so early in the morning?'

'She went out there every morning before everyone got up, even if there wasn't anything. She was just a stupid young girl. It was a game for her.'

'And Alberte was so stupid that she just allowed herself to be run down, is that what you're saying?'

There was that smile again. 'No, she was standing at the roadside

and I made it seem like I was going around her. She smiled at someone driving a snowplough with that inscription when there wasn't
even any snow, and it was over a month until Christmas. But she
soon stopped when I jerked the steering wheel and drove into her.
First her and then the bike.'

'And nobody saw you apart from her?'

'It was very early in the morning. We take things slowly over
here on Bornholm.'

'Then you drove back to Aakirkeby and parked Bjarke's car in
front of Karin's house where it'd been parked before? We spoke
with her at the nursing home but she couldn't help us.'

'Yes, that's right. But Karin saw me put the plough back in my trunk.
For years she threatened to report me, so it wasn't me who was angry
with her, like she always says. It was her who was angry with me.

'Afterwards, I drove back to Listed and put the plough back. The
day after, I found out that Karin had told Bjarke I'd borrowed the
car and that she'd seen me with the plough. By that time the search
for Alberte had already begun.

'All three of us were sitting around the dinner table that evening
when Christian told us that he'd found her in a tree, and that it had
left a terrible impression on him. I could tell that Bjarke had worked
it out. It was just awful. My Bjarke wasn't stupid, unfortunately, you
might say now. And he hated me for it, but he never let me down.
He never told his dad. So it was him he let down instead. That's why
he couldn't live under the same roof as his dad when I moved out
a few months later. He lived with Karin for a while and with me in
Aakirkeby, but then found his own place.'

'Did you ever talk about it?'

She shook her head and wiped away a tear from the tip of her
nose.

'No, we didn't talk so much. He also drifted away from me be-cause of his sexuality. It got too weird for me.'

'It was hard for you to accept?'

She nodded.

'And then you threw one of his magazines down in the grave for him, to show that you'd accepted it now after all this time?'

She nodded again. 'There was so much that had stood between Bjarke and me. It needed to stop there. Everything needed to stop there.'

'So you knew full well why he wrote sorry to his dad and not to you?'

She nodded, rubbing the back of her hand on the other with the poor fingers, pressing her lips together for a moment before answering.

'Well, how could he live with his dad committing suicide over a case he could've solved for him? I think his apology was his way of asking his forgiveness,' she said, while the tears slowly dripped from her eyes, leaving dark marks on the dried-out table.

'Do you think your ex-husband suspected Bjarke, like Rose sug-gested just now?'

She shook her head. 'No, he was too stupid for that. That Rose . . .'

All three of them heard the sound at the same time: loud whirling tones thrown above the treetops rising above them. First one and then another. Slowly but steadily they increased in strength, drop-ping in pitch before finally coming together. Help was on the way.

'There are two sirens,' she said, looking confused. 'Is there a police car, too?'

'Yes, I assume so. There tends to be when things like this happen.'

Her large eyes grew smaller. 'What'll I get?' she asked.

'I don't think you should worry about that now, June,' he tried.

'How many?' she asked Assad directly now.

'Probably ten to life, I imagine. Life is usually fourteen years,' he told her straight.

'Thanks. Now I know. I'll be seventy-six then, if I'm still alive. I don't think I'll have the will to be.'

'A lot of people have their sentence reduced for good behaviour,' said Carl to soften the news, while the sirens caused the birds to the west to fly away from the trees.

'I wish I had a river I could skate away on. But it don't snow here, it stays pretty green . . .

'Do you remember that? I quoted that song in Jernbanegade the first time you were there. It's from a Joni Mitchell song, did you know that?'

She smiled a little to herself. 'It was Frank who taught me that. He was the one who taught me to dream myself away to another place where I'd rather be. It means that you're no longer happy to be where you are. He taught me that, too. Do you know what I mean?'

They both nodded very slowly. The sirens were close to the car park now. In a moment she'd be in an ambulance under police escort. Of course she ended up thinking about that song.

She stood up so suddenly that they were caught off guard. Ran the four steps toward the opening in the wall, jumped four steps down and then took the big leap over the wall and out into eternity.

They lunged forward, reaching the outer wall at the same time.

Far below, they saw her mutilated body. She'd hit the cliff hard and had probably been killed on the spot before she slid out over the last edge, hanging now from a tree with her head facing down.

Exactly like Alberte seventeen years earlier.

Epilogue

They stood for a few minutes, following the flashing blue lights until they faded away in an ocean of green trees.

Carl inspected Assad's chalk-white bandage. It was tight and secure.

'What did the doctor say to you, Assad?'

'I showed him that I can bend my thumb, and then he gave me a shot of antibiotics.'

'And?'

'I could bend it, Carl. What more is there to say?'

Carl nodded. In a couple of hours Assad would be sitting on a scheduled flight to Kastrup Airport in Copenhagen, and the burns unit at Hvidovre Hospital was only a fifteen-minute drive from there. He'd talk Assad round in the end.

'Are we agreed about what to do now?'

'Yes, we drive to Listed.'

They'd hardly driven halfway before they heard Assad's phone, and he put it on speaker. The person on the other end introduced herself as Ella Persson, police secretary from Kalmar, saying that she was calling on behalf of Criminal Inspector Frans Sundström.

'We've found out who sent for the police and ambulance at the Nature Absorption Academy on Öland,' she said. 'By listening to the tape again from the emergency dispatch centre, it appears that it was the leader of the centre, Atu Abanshamash Dumuzi's voice. We also have reason to believe that it was the same person who cut you free. There's certainly nobody else willing to take credit for it. Criminal Inspector Sundström thought you'd be interested. He thought it would put Atu Abanshamash Dumuzi's actions in something of a different light. He just wanted you to know before you arrest him.'

Carl looked out over the landscape that the same Frank Brennan had trawled all over many years ago. And while he thought about that, Assad answered the police secretary that she could report that Atu Abanshamash Dumuzi had passed away and that they'd presumably receive a report from the local Bornholm Police.

They spent the remainder of the journey in silence. That information would take a while to sink in.

There was an aura around Christian Habersaat's house in Listed that hadn't been there before. The house was suddenly in the past. The estate of a deceased, a DIY offer, one man's monument of a failed life. There were still secrets in a way, of course, but the mystery was gone.

They looked in the windows and noticed how effective Rose's efforts had been. Apart from a few packing materials and furniture that had been used as shelf space, there was nothing left to remind anyone that there'd been a complete manifesto of a crime collected here.

They looked over at the double doors of the garage and noticed that the authorities had fitted it with a padlock.

'Shall we wait for a locksmith so we can come in via the house entrance to the garage, or shall I just open it?' asked Assad.

Carl was about to ask how he intended to do it without tools, but before he could, Assad put his good hand in between the doors and jerked them. The padlock was still hanging where it had always been, but the fitting wasn't, so the doors flung open to reveal a darkness that their eyes had to adjust to.

The sight was the same as before: tyre tracks, old inflatable water toys and tins of paint on the shelves, empty cardboard boxes here and there.

They leaned their heads back, looking up at the beams with the windsurfer sail, skis and ski poles.

They went back to the entrance, trying to get a better angle to see what might be lying on top of the other stuff. And when they still couldn't see anything new, they walked right out of the garage. And just there, standing at a very specific angle, it looked as if there might be something lying on top of the sailcloth, pushed right back towards the end wall.

'We won't get up there without a ladder, Carl,' said Assad.

'Come on, I'll give you a leg up.'

He put his hands around Assad's shoe and pushed him up. Amazing how Pirjo, slight as she was, had managed to shift him. He was heavy enough to do your back in.

'Yes,' was all he said from up there.

'Yes, what?'

'Here's the shovel blade. About one and a half metres long with white capital letters on it. I can't see what it says, but we already know that.'

Carl shook his head. How absurd could it be? If only there'd been a ladder back then, the search for Frank would've ended there.

'Take a photo of it. Put the flash on,' groaned Carl. It didn't feel very comfortable to stand like this any more.

There was a flash and Carl prepared to bend his knees to help his friend back to the ground again.

'Just a second, Carl,' he said. 'There's something hanging on the wall behind the shovel. Give me an extra push up.'

Carl struggled. It was the sort of manoeuvre that could go wrong, so he braced himself and pushed him up as well as he could.

'Yes!' Assad shouted from up there. 'You can let me down now.'

'What is it?' asked Carl, straightening his back.

Assad passed it to him. It was a crisp white envelope. No dirt or dust and no cobwebs. Just as untouched and unused as if it had come straight out of a drawer.

To the investigators was written on the front in Habersaat's unmistakable handwriting.

They looked at each other.

'Open it,' said Assad, and Carl did.

It was a compact, handwritten sheet of paper, which had been used before because there was something printed on the back.

To the investigators written again at the top, finishing with Habersaat's signature.

'Read it aloud, Carl. I can't read his crawl.'

'Scrawl, Assad, but never mind!'

He read:

You worked it out then, and the mission is complete.

    My suspicion of Bjarke was strengthened when some time after
Alberte's death I found this thing, which Bjarke had apparently used to sell
Christmas trees. I thought I remembered him working on something of the
sort and found it up here while the whole island was looking for it.

But even though a lot pointed to my son, my suspicion of my wife's ex-lover was also strong. Yes,

I knew full well about their relationship. My network on the island has many mouths, and through which I also received strong indications that the man with the VW Kombi was the same man who met up with Alberte.

Then I found the splint at the crime scene, and several other things gave me hope that I was wrong about Bjarke. The desire for revenge and the ingrained urge to protect go hand in hand too often, unfortunately. And I couldn't find a motive for Bjarke. Why should he kill a totally unknown girl? It didn't make any sense. I knew he wasn't interested in the opposite sex. That was a subject June and I argued a lot about. She found it really hard to accept. But I think that in the police we have a broader moral compass than so many others.

So my investigation pointed towards the man in the VW. And it continued that way until I found the crucial evidence that, despite everything, Bjarke did have a weighty motive.

I found it when one day, a month ago, I annexed Bjarke's old room for my investigation material, and found this in a box with old PC games.

That's what you can see if you turn the paper over.

Carl turned it over.

It was an old print of shortcuts to the Star Trek game, with notes in pencil, and at the bottom in very small capitals was written:

TO FRANK

It was the poem Bjarke had written about his fascination with him. They knew what it said.

'Read the rest of what Habersaat wrote, Carl,' said Assad.

It was only after finding this poem that I seriously understood it all. Bjarke was in love with the same man as my wife. And he killed Alberte because he'd been pushed aside to make way for the young girl. Bjarke must've written it sometime afterwards. Probably just before he moved out from here. It's now so clear and logical to me, and it's breaking my heart.

I apologize with all sincerity for being so insistent in my determination to pin a crime on an innocent man, when all along it was my son who'd committed the terrible deed.

Now I'm leaving his fate in your hands. I can't find it in me to go after my own son. So it stops here.

Christian Habersaat, April 29th, 2014.

They stood for a long time without saying a word.

They thought the same.

'He wrote this the day before he called you, Carl,' said Assad finally.

Carl nodded.

'He'd already made the decision to kill himself before that.'

'Yes. Of course it's a small comfort, what with everything else.' Carl shook his head. 'If only we'd seen that letter a bit earlier. Rose was right. Habersaat knew that his son was involved somehow or other.'

'Yes, but not that it was his wife who did it. We'd never have found that out if we hadn't investigated in the way we did, Carl. June Habersaat would've taken it to the grave.'

He nodded. 'We should call Rose and tell her she was right in connection with Habersaat, and that June Habersaat has confessed to everything.'

Assad gave him a thumbs-up with his healthy thumb, selected Rose's number and activated the speakerphone.

It was a while before someone answered. They were just about to hang up.

'This is Rose's phone, you're speaking with Yrsa,' said the voice. It certainly wasn't Rose.

'Err, is that you, Rose?' asked Carl. Had she fallen back into the role-play?

'No, I said it was Yrsa. I'm Rose's sister. Who am I speaking with?'

Carl was still unsure, but if she wanted to play, then she could play.

'Carl. Deputy Police Superintendent Carl Mørck, Rose's boss, if I can put it that way.'

'Oh,' she said, as if it was bad news. 'I've tried calling you, Carl Mørck, but your phone doesn't pick up.'

'I apologize, the battery has died. What—'

'Rose isn't good,' she interrupted, her voice sounding worried. 'I arrived here an hour ago. Rose and I meet once in a while on a Saturday for a cup of tea, you know, and I found her in the bedroom. She didn't recognize me at all. She kept saying that she'd done what she had to and now she just wanted out of it all.'

'Out of it all?'

'Yes, she'd cut one of her wrists with a pair of scissors. She also claimed to be Vicky, our other sister. She said she'd been hypnotized to believe she was Rose, but that she didn't want to be her because she was a bad girl. That the hypnosis had gone too deep. She said he told her that he couldn't help her because she was a cup that was already full.'

'That's awful.' Carl looked at Assad, who was shaking his head. This couldn't be true.

'She's been admitted to Nordvang Hospital, so you shouldn't expect her anytime soon, if she ever comes back.'

It was Assad's idea that they should drive down to Aakirkeby and order flowers for Rose and have them sent by Floragram. They could buy a bunch to put by Alberte's tree at the same time.

'You are aware that we can take the same route to the tree that June Habersaat took?' said Assad, when they were finished in town.

'Yes, I'm well aware of that,' answered Carl. 'But this time we won't drive quite like last time, OK? I don't think this car is up for it either.'

Assad sent him a grateful smile.

They stood for a long time watching the branches and the tree and the small bunch of flowers at the bottom of the trunk. The first time they'd stood in front of this tree, the leaves had barely come out. Now they were already dark green.

'I hope that her parents can finally find some peace,' said Carl.

Assad didn't comment. He probably doubted it.

They bowed their heads for a moment out of respect for the far too beautiful and naive young woman who never had the life she dreamed of. And then they drove off.

They were speaking about Rose and what they could do for her, when the folk high school suddenly appeared on their right-hand side.

'Stop the car, Carl,' said Assad when they reached it.

He jumped out, crossing the road towards the boulder with the school name engraved on it.

'Are you going to give me a hand?' he shouted after he'd pushed a couple of stones aside that surrounded the base of the boulder.

Carl only just reached him when Assad rolled a dark stone to one side, which was covering a small hole.

'Here it is!' he said triumphantly. 'This is where they exchanged messages, Carl. Where June Habersaat left the false note.'

Carl nodded and bent down. It was seventeen years ago, and yet the little hole was still there. He scratched down in the earth in the hole. It was strange to think.

Then the tip of his finger touched something smooth. Was it plastic or just a small stone? He took his pen from his breast pocket and poked it down in the earth, jostling the object free. It was a small clear plastic pocket of the type often used for stamps or recipes. The plastic was totally opaque after so many years in the ground. Strange that it hadn't been covered more.

'There's something inside,' said Assad.

He was right. Carl opened it carefully, pulling out a small piece of folded paper. It was in reasonable condition, although the paper had yellowed and become damp.

Carl unfolded the piece of paper and held it so they could both read it.

Dear Alberte, it began.

*Forget what I said yesterday. I really want to see you again when you get back to Zealand from the school. My number at the commune is 439032***

It was no longer possible to read the last two numbers. But the writing underneath was clear enough:

Until next time. I love you boundlessly.

Frank

Assad and Carl looked at each other. Frank must have left the message on the same morning Alberte had cycled out to meet her terrible fate.

Assad held his bad hand while Carl put his hand to his neck.

If only he'd left his declaration of love a few minutes before, none of this would ever have happened.

Carl sighed, but felt a little pat on his shoulder.

He looked into a pair of bright brown eyes, framed by smile lines.

At least they were together in sharing this awful knowledge.

Acknowledgements

Thanks to my wife and soulmate, Hanne, for endless encouragement during the long process of writing the Department Q project. Thanks to Henning Kure for pre-editing, research into sun cults and bright ideas. Thanks to Elisabeth Ahlefeldt-Laurvig for research and resourcefulness. Also thanks to Eddie Kiran, Hanne Petersen, Micha Shmalstieg and Karlo Andersen for alert and competent reading, and in particular to my editor Anne C. Andersen for our amazing partnership.

Thanks to Lene Juul and Charlotte Weiss at Politikens Forlag for great patience. Thanks to Helle Skov Wacher for informing readers with ongoing information. Thanks for lodging during the writing process to Gitte and Peter Q. Rannes, and to the Danish Centre for Writers and Translators at Hald. Thanks to Søren Pilmark for a great stay on Bornholm. Thanks to Elisabeth Ahlefeldt-Laurvig for my own and Henning Kure's think-tank stay at Tempelkrogen.

Thanks to Police Superintendent Leif Christensen for police-related corrections. Thanks to Carl Mørck's colleagues at the police station in Rønne for a wonderful welcome and briefing on the police work on Bornholm: Police Commissioner Peter Møller Nielsen,

District Attorney Martin Gravesen, Detective Jan Kragbæk, and Police Chief Inspector Morten Brandborg, as well as the competent people on duty.

Thanks to Svend Aage Knudsen in Østerlars Round Church. Thanks to the people at Bornholm Folk High School for the warm welcome, tour and excellent meatballs: Accountant Marianne Koefoed, Groundskeeper Jørgen Kofoed, Kitchen Manager Karen Prætorius, and the former rector couple, Bente and Karsten Thorborg, for a pleasant and productive afternoon.

Thanks to Karen Nørregaard and Anette Elleby from Listedhuset, for the inspiring talk and tour. Thanks to Poul Jörgensen, Kastlösa Glashytta in Mörbylånga, for heavy rock guitar playing and initiating me in the mysteries of Öland and Alvaret.

Thanks to Johan Daniel 'Dan' Schmidt for producing perfect clones of my old PC and making my IT life sweeter. Thanks to Nene Larsen for lightning-quick courier service to Barcelona. Thanks to my PR lady in Germany, Beatrice Habersaat, for letting me use her surname. Thanks to Peter Michael Poulsen, skipper on the guide ship Sam for 'swapping names'. Thanks to Kes Adler Olsen for the introduction to the Zeitgeist video. Thanks to Benny Thøgersen and Lina Pillora for making my writing environment in Sweden even more fantastic. Thanks to Arne and Annette Merrild and Olaf Slott-Pedersen for encouragement in Barcelona. Also thanks to Olaf Slott-Pedersen for sharing his experience with hypnosis.

Thanks to Cathrine Boysen for sharing her indomitable spirit with me. We can all learn a lot from her.